RETURN TO THE TOWER

THIRD IN THE
SCEPTER AND TOWER TRILOGY

MARK E. FISHER

Extraordinary Tales Publishing

RETURN TO THE TOWER BY MARK E. FISHER

Extraordinary Tales Publishing
P.O. Box 6196
Rochester, MN 55903

First Extraordinary Tales edition September 2019

Print ISBN: 978-1-950235-04-9
E-Book ISBN: 978-1-950235-05-6

Cover art by Nicole Cardiff
Cover fonts by Arpit Mehta
Interior Design by BookNook.biz

Available in print from your local bookstore or from Amazon.

For more information about this and the author's other books visit:
MarkFisherAuthor.com

Library of Congress Cataloging-in-Publication Data:
Fisher, Mark E.
Return To The Tower / Mark E. Fisher 1st ed.

Printed in the United States of America

Contents

MAPS OF ERDE

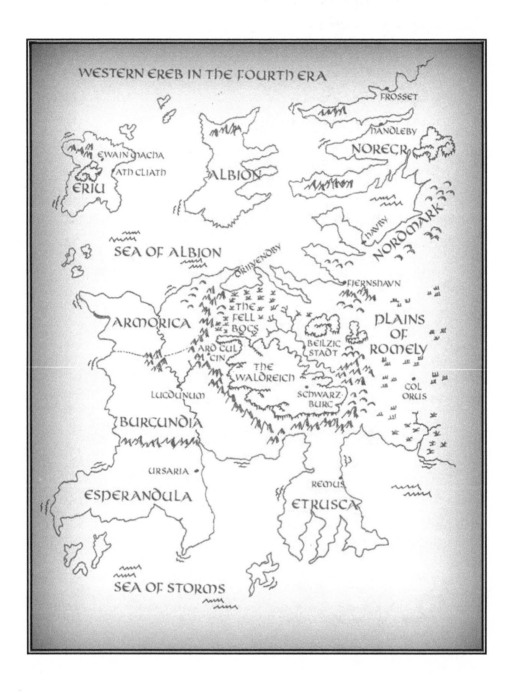

WESTERN EREB IN THE FOURTH ERA

FROSSET

HANDLEBY

NORECR

EWAIN MACHA

ATH CLIATH

ERIU

ALBION

HAVBY

NORDMARK

SEA OF ALBION

DRIINENDBY

FIERNSHAVN

ARMORICA

THE FELL BOGS

BEILZIC STADT

PLAINS OF ROMELY

ARD CUL CIN

THE WALDREICH

SCHWARZ BURC

COL ORUS

LUCDUNUM

BURGUNDIA

URSARIA

REMUS

ESPERANDULA

ETRUSCA

SEA OF STORMS

EASTERN EREB
IN THE FOURTH ERA

THE
FROZEN
SEA

FROSSET

HANDLEBY

NORECR

DAVBY

NORDMARK

FERACHTIR

TOLLAN
CAILLTE

FJERNSHAVN

CATHAIR
DUVH

AMRIDMOR

PLAINS
OF
ROMELY

ERDELSTAN

MAM
CIORAC

DROCHTAR

VALLEY
OF
FLOWERS

COL
ORAS

CONACHTIR

LOFOSPOLI

ETRUSCA

COPAL

SHUDERAH
BOSCH

SEA
OF
COPAL

KALIKKETRO

HEYERRAH
BOSCH

SARKENOS

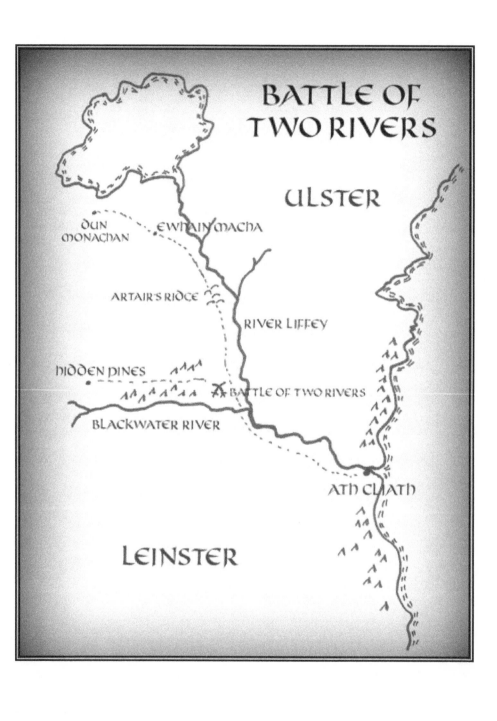

BATTLE OF
TWO RIVERS

ULSTER

ÒUN
MONACHAN

EWHAIN MACHA

ARTAIR'S RIÒGE

RIVER LIFFEY

HIÒÒEN PINES

BATTLE OF TWO RIVERS

BLACKWATER RIVER

ATH CLIATH

LEINSTER

Cast of Characters

- ❖ Angus mac Donaigh—King of Leinster.
- ❖ Brigid—Tristan's kindly aunt.
- ❖ Cairbre the Wise—Gray-bearded old scholar and head of the secret society of the Capulum. A renowned expert in ancient texts.
- ❖ Caitir nic Cathal—Tristan's childhood friend and stowaway member of the Company. Daughter of Cathal, the cooper.
- ❖ Camran mac Blàr—Short, voluble prince of Munster, and a former member of the Company who died in the Fell Bogs.
- ❖ Cé mac Colla—King of Munster.
- ❖ Connell mac Conn—The Ard Righ, or High King, ruler of Ulster and all Ériu, sitting in his palace at Ewhain Macha.
- ❖ Corc—High druid under the sway of Faolukan, advisor to King Connell in Ulster.
- ❖ Cowan mac Beisdan—Tristan's stern blacksmith uncle.
- ❖ Crom Mord—The dread idol inside which the Deamhan Lord now resides.
- ❖ Dermid mac Duff—Dark-bearded prince of Leinster, convener of the Council of Flaith, one-time leader of the Company who died at the mountain lake.
- ❖ Eacharn—A one-time captain of the guards at Ewhain Macha.
- ❖ Elyon—God.
- ❖ Ewan mac Ninian—Squire to Prince Neil mac Connell, he's now pledged in service to Tristan.
- ❖ Faolan the Traitor—[Fool-an] Faolan was once a siòg and their leader, but after he rebelled, Elyon banished him from Neavh and

forbade him to take physical form. Then he became the Deamhan Lord, a foul spirit living inside the idol Crom Mord.

- ❖ Faolukan the Grim—[Fool-oo-kan] The Deamhan Lord's arch druid. Once a monk of Ériu, he was turned to the Deamhan Lord's service and given immortality on Erde. Faolukan rules Drochtar in the Deamhan Lord's stead.
- ❖ Finnean mac Friseal—Red-haired archer, prince of Meath and member of the Company who died in the Fell Bogs.
- ❖ Fionn—A white-haired wolfhound.
- ❖ Glenmallen—Hidden valley of the eladrin in the southern Blue Mountains.
- ❖ Heiner—An annoying kobold who digs for gold and silver.
- ❖ Iùrnan mac Colla—King Cé's brother from Munster.
- ❖ Keenala né Hamor—Queen and high reginalia of the eladrin in Glenmallen.
- ❖ Luag mac Laise—Axe-wielding lehbrágan and member of the Company who died in the Waldreich.
- ❖ Machar mac Maon—Tall, silent, prince of Connacht and member of the Company. Sometimes called the Cloaked Rider.
- ❖ Maeve nic Connell—Princess of Ulster, sister to Neil mac Connell.
- ❖ Malavhìn—The siòg whom the Roamers captured and Tristan freed and the only source of the crimson oil.
- ❖ Milosh—A rogue bandit leader from Gol Oras, he's the bane of all who follow Drochtar on the Romely Plains. Now he's pledged to help Tristan find Elyon's second great gift.
- ❖ Searlie—[SHEER-lay] Tristan's cousin who ate a witch's cauldron mushroom and whom Tristan brought back from death with the crimson oil.
- ❖ Tomey mac Friseal—Along with his son, Artair, this Ériu expatriate captains *The Happy Lass*, a dilapidated ship stuck in Bredehaven port by Faolukan's ships.
- ❖ Torradan mac Rodachan—A regent of Ulster and Ériu.
- ❖ Vasil Catargiu—King of the Oasis of Lonely Sands, ruler of all who live under the red tent.

❖ Yuri—A Ferachtir youth conscripted for the armies of Drochtar.

❖ Zalán—A white wizard given immortality and living in the Valley of Flowers. After recognizing something in Tristan, he aligned himself with Elyon's cause.

PART I

MAM GIORAG

CHAPTER 1

TRISTAN MAC TORN

As Tristan's shaking fingers grasped the metal scroll, logs crackled in the campfire and threw wavering shadows across the clearing. Beneath their feet, Drochcarn, the mountain that never sleeps, rumbled. On the horizon, fire and lava spouted into the sky.

Beside him on the ground huddled Caitir, his betrothed; Ewan, his faithful squire; and Milosh, their rogue ally. Their eyes were fixed on the glowing golden artifact. They'd trekked across a continent, endured hardships and captivity, even lost three companions, all so they could behold what now lay in Tristan's trembling hands—

The second great gift of Elyon.

For thousands of years, until this moment, the scroll had been lost to the world. Flickering light now glittered on impossible words that, only moments before, had etched themselves onto its golden surface:

You, Tristan mac Torn, are the Toghaí.
No longer will you be Neil mac Connell, but Tristan mac Torn.
For you, Tristan, are the Augury.

He stared at the shimmering script and tried to comprehend their import. Against all logic, it said that *he* was the Augury.

But, then, why had the Company risked their lives to seek this artifact? Was the glowing golden object in his hands only a message for Elyon's true messenger? Gently, he laid the treasure on the ground. Still kneeling, he squeezed his eyes shut, and his hands found the top of his head, pressing against his temples.

"I don't understand anything anymore." Opening his eyes, he threw an impatient wave at the ground. "How can *I* be the Augury?" He cast a desperate glance at each of them.

"My lord," said Ewan, "you are he who . . . was chosen to save the world. For that's what Elyon has written here. And I believe in the one who created the worlds."

"'Tis difficult to wrap my mind around," said Caitir. "But it must be so."

"Before we came to this foul mountain"—Milosh nodded toward the black peak and its fiery summit—"did you not have visions of Caitir being led here?"

"Aye," said Ewan. "Were you not already seeing future events and happenings elsewhere on Erde—affairs no one should have been able to see?"

Caitir glanced askance at him. "Is this true?"

"I did." He dropped his hands to his lap, made a fist, and hit one thigh. "Someone help me understand this."

On the mountain beyond, molten rock shot up in a spray, sending flashes of light across the clearing.

"So if you were already developing such powers," she went on, "why do you question it?"

"Because I feel . . . unworthy."

"You are no longer just a blacksmith," she whispered. "That, at least, seems clear."

"More than once," he admitted, "I did see you being led as a prisoner toward Drochtar. But what does it all mean?" Exhaustion swept over him. His tunic became a cloak of granite, pressing down on his shoulders. "After everything that's happened today, I've no strength left. And now this burden . . ."

"My lord"—Ewan laid a hand on his shoulder—"you've already found both of Elyon's lost gifts. All that's left is to bring them home."

"And you will." A wide smile curved Caitir's moist lips. "I'm sure of it."

"I can't argue with them, my friend." Milosh grinned. "You've already done incredible things."

"'Twas Elyon who did them," said Tristan, "not me."

"Then you admit," said Caitir, "that Elyon was behind everything you did. So why question when he says you are the Toghaí?"

"Can you explain, my lord, how you freed us?" Ewan went to the small cask of ale Yuri had left them and filled his mug. "Maybe then we could judge—if you're willing—whether you are worthy or not?"

"Before I can judge anything"—Milosh held out an empty cup—"how about another draught?"

Tristan scanned his friends' faces, obviously eager to hear the story. And Ewan thought it would help resolve his quandary. He, too, passed his mug for a second draught, sipped the ale, took a deep breath, and began.

He told how, with his friends frozen in the field above, he crept through the corridors of Balor's Chasm of Doom and stole the golden scroll from the sleeping monster. But Balor woke, and as each layer of its leathery eyelids opened, its single giant eye burned with increasing heat, scorching everything in sight. After hiding in a crevice for a day, out of Balor's sight, Tristan enlisted the siòg's help and temporarily quenched the sleeping deamhan's eye with snow. That allowed him to escape the chasm and return to the field above.

"But the sacrifices were already in progress," he said, "and Crom Mord's presence was like poison pumping through my veins. I could barely walk or think."

He glanced at his hands, trembling even now. "The fear—I simply can't describe it. I was nearly paralyzed. But something urged me to take the wizard Zalán's ring up to the platform and throw it into Crom Mord's mouth. I know not how I found the strength, or the courage, but I did. That's when the spell broke."

"And that's when everyone in the field was freed." Caitir turned both her hands over, staring at them as if marveling that they moved. "I was a living statue, wasn't I? Frozen in position for days, maybe weeks." She shuddered.

"As were we all," said Ewan. "All except Tristan. Doesn't that tell you something?"

"Aye, my friend," added Milosh. "You, alone, escaped the druid's spell."

"And was it not Elyon," said Caitir, "who gave you the strength to face the lord of deamhans?"

Tristan gave her a weak grin. "Aye."

Steadily, she peered back at him. "Then do you not have your answer?"

He pulled his legs back and sat cross-legged. As if trying to find a different answer, his gaze swept the group, the shadowed scrub surrounding the clearing, and the rumbling mountain beyond. "I–I suppose I do."

"How did Balor escape?" Milosh drained his mug.

"Before I went through the chasm gates, I jimmied the lock so it wouldn't engage. From the outside, the doors appeared closed. But all Balor had to do was push to get out."

Milosh whistled. "And now the thing is loose."

"Balor is a powerful deamhan under no one's control," said Tristan. "Long ago, Faolukan locked him inside the chasm. Certainly, he'll be able to do so again."

"And then," said Ewan, "he'll be rounding up those as have escaped."

Caitir shot them a hopeful glance. "But maybe some will get away?"

"Maybe." Tristan threw a branch onto the fire. "I wonder where Yuri is. He was supposed to meet us here."

"You've mentioned him before." Caitir sat back and grabbed a clump of her filthy hair. "Who is he?"

"A conscripted Drochtar soldier we captured," said Ewan. "He joined our cause."

"'Twas he who led me to this campsite." Tristan waved up the slope.

"And he was supposed to be here?" She scowled at the greasy strands then flicked them over her shoulder.

"Aye." Ewan's worried glance searched the shadows. "But something must have happened to him."

Tristan shook his head. Too many companions had lost their lives on this quest. He hoped Yuri wouldn't be among them.

Bending down, he rolled the golden sheet back into its compact cylinder and stored it in his pack. For a moment, he held the rucksack and stared at it. How would he ever get this precious cargo safely back to Ériu? They were now at the farthest eastern end of the known world. What dangers and trials would they have to endure to return to the mountain lake where he'd buried the Scepter, the greatest of Elyon's gifts? How far away that lake seemed now! And then they'd have to traverse the rest of the continent and make a sea voyage before landing again on Ériu's fair shores.

Abruptly, he stood. Leaving his companions and the fire's warmth, he strode up the trail into the night.

Breathing deeply, he sucked in—not fresh night air, but a sulfurous, metallic, ash-tainted ether. He gagged. Looking up, he saw not stars, but the ever-present ceiling of roiling gray clouds, lit by occasional spoutings of lava from the restless mountain. Here was the belly of the Deamhan Lord's realm, as close to the Underworld as a mortal could get without descending the supernatural tunnel and the dread path to Ifreann.

His stomach churned. Tears ran down his cheeks. Was it the sulfurous air? Or the confusion, the fear, the wrenching change this night's revelation had brought?

Why was he entrusted with this task? Of all the people on Erde, why him? Before the sìog gave him the gift of fighting, he was no great warrior. He was a mere blacksmith's apprentice, by all accounts, a *bothach*, the lowest of the low, despised in his own village. His mother was a harlot, his father a wastrel, scorned by all. He didn't even fulfill all the ancient prophecies expected of the Toghaí. And yet, Elyon had said he *was* the Toghaí, in words plainly etched on the scroll.

Tonight, he was also declared to be the Augury.

It made no sense. He hadn't asked for this, hadn't even wanted it.

Now, somehow, he must carry the burden of this new identity and its great responsibility back to Ériu. And he must arrive back home before Faolukan, the arch druid. Only then could he keep the deamhan idol, Crom Mord, from spreading its darkness over the land.

It had been a long day.

He breathed out. He needed sleep. Whirling, he strode toward the fire and his waiting companions.

Stand firm, Tristan, son of Torn, chosen son of Ériu. Trust in me and press on to the end, for I am with you.

The words were fire-letters seared into his brain. Under their impact, he staggered into the circle before his companions.

Even as the fire-words faded, a surge of energy and tingling warmth spread out from his chest to his arms, out to his fingers, then down through his loins, legs, and feet. It rose up his neck, flushing his forehead and skull with unnatural warmth.

He fought for balance. Shaking his head, he tried, unsuccessfully, to clear the feeling. For several precious moments, he wavered, but avoided collapse.

Caitir's mouth hung open. Her eyes widened in more than astonishment. She slid away from him and put a hand to her mouth. Why had she done that? The startled, almost frightened expression contorting her face scared him.

"W–what's happened to you?" she whispered.

With something akin to awe, Ewan, too, stared at him. "My lord . . . you're . . . glowing."

"What?" Tristan lifted an arm. A shimmering warm light encased his forearm. A pulsing glow covered his legs and torso.

Milosh whistled softly. "Neil. Or Tristan. Or whoever you are—my lord, something powerful's come over you." Milosh rarely called him "my lord", and now, too much deference tainted that voice.

"Something wonderful." Caitir's shock seemed to subside as she sidled close and reached trembling fingers toward his cheek. She caressed it lightly, her fingers cool on his hot skin. They lingered on his head.

"And your hair." A gaping Milosh pointed. "Look at it."

Tristan pulled the locks hanging over his ears before his eyes—his mane had grown long on this journey. No longer was his hair the jet-black color it had always been. His hands now held strands so white and pure, they nearly gleamed. He gasped.

What is happening to me?

"Sure and certain." Ewan bowed. "The hand of Elyon is upon you."

"Aye," said Milosh. "Some powerful magic."

His eyes searched his companions. "What am I becoming?"

"Whatever it is"—Ewan's voice calmed and soothed—"it is he, the Creator of worlds, who's done it. I'd have no fear on that account."

Tristan stared at the squire, letting the words sink in. What Ewan said was true, wasn't it? Elyon was in charge of this night. It was he who had written the words on the scroll. It was *his* hand that had reached out and touched Tristan in ways Tristan couldn't yet understand. Yet it all must be for the good. For Elyon was nothing but good, and if Tristan had become his instrument, then this change, too, must be good.

Suddenly, he was a reed by the river's edge, soggy and trampled in the mud, his strength washed away by a current so swift, he couldn't fight it.

"I need to rest." He staggered to his bedroll. "I've not strength enough even to ponder what just happened."

Concern furrowed Caitir's brows. "I canna imagine what you've been through this day."

The others nodded as he dragged his furs close to the fire.

The air reeked of sulfur, the night was red with the glow from Drochcarn's eruptions, and the presence of Crom Mord's evil still hung heavy about them like a suffocating blanket.

But so exhausted was he that sleep pulled him down like a stone tumbling end over end into a dark well.

The last thought he had was—

What have I become?

CHAPTER 2

THE HIDDEN TRAIL

Tristan woke to shaking ground and rocks crashing through the scrawny trees beside the camp. Leaping from slumber, he peered around. Everyone else was standing by the fire, wary eyes focused on the unsettled slopes.

The last of the rocks and pebbles tumbled into the brush. Then quiet, broken only by the cawing of startled crows, returned.

The mountain spewed clouds of white steam. Overhead, gray clouds drifted, casting a dim light over the world.

"No damage done, I ken." Ewan scanned the clearing. "But that was close."

Caitir peered uneasily through the scrub at the bare slopes.

The rest resumed their seats by the fire, returning to a meal of sausage, goat cheese, and turnips from Yuri's cache.

"The sooner we leave here, the better." Tristan sat and accepted his share of breakfast.

"Worst sausage I ever ate." Ewan grimaced. "And since we arrived in this land, I havena had a wee bite of proper bread."

"I've eaten worse." Milosh grinned as he bit off half a turnip he'd been twirling between finger and thumb. He chewed but spit out half of it.

"Ewan, you do not ken how good it is to hear you talk about food," said Caitir. "I missed both of you so much." As her glance moved from Ewan to Tristan, a glint of moisture appeared at the corner of one eye.

Tristan grasped her hand and squeezed.

"We've missed you, too, lass." Ewan turned from her to Tristan. "You look much better, today, my lord."

"You shouldn't call me that anymore. I'm not a real lord."

"For me, you always will be."

"But I agree." Caitir rested a hand on his knee. "Today, you look more like yourself. Though it will take time to get used to that white hair."

With effort, Tristan swallowed the sausage he was chewing. "I don't feel any older." He ran a hand over his cheeks. "Do I look that much different?"

Sitting opposite the fire, Milosh swept his gaze up and down him as if examining a horse for sale. "Anyone who didn't know you well might miss you in a crowd. But you're still the same Neil—I mean, Tristan—you were before."

He nodded. But he didn't want to think any more about the change that had come over him or yesterday's revelations.

After they finished their meal and donned their packs, they hiked up the slope to the main trail.

"We must keep watch for anyone else using this route." Tristan scanned the path leading back to Cathair Duvh. "'Tis supposed to be hidden, but if Yuri knew about it, others might too."

"Aye," said Milosh. "Lead on."

Tristan veered left onto a narrow track that hugged the mountain. For leagues, they descended over a path so little used, brush often grew across the way.

"Look!"

Tristan knelt to where Ewan squatted in the dirt.

"A footprint." Ewan's finger traced its outline. "And I ken 'tis recent."

"So someone *is* using this trail." Tristan stood and glanced in both directions. "All the more reason to keep a close watch."

For the rest of that day, he led them, stopping once as his sword chopped the head from a six-foot viper curled across their way that seemed disinclined to move. At noon, they rested, ate, and then hiked until midafternoon when they topped a rise.

Below, the plains of Drochtar stretched—bleak, barren, and wind-swept—to the distant Sfarsit Mountains. Gray clouds shrouded the sky, swallowing the sun. Down on the plains, a fumarole spat a fountain of hot mud before settling below eye level.

Something rustled in the brush. He whirled, his sword flying out of its sheath. Beside him, Milosh's blade was also ready.

"Yuri, lad!" cried Ewan. "Whatever happened to you?"

Tristan resheathed his weapon. "'Tis good to see you, Yuri."

"Aye," said the thin pole of a youth pushing through the undergrowth. Pale blond hair fell over his eyes. His arms were sticks, and his thin, emaciated face and lifeless eyes bespoke a life of hardship and starvation. When he faced Tristan, his jaw dropped. "Your hair . . . what happened?"

"'Tis a long story. But why weren't you at the campsite?"

"I waited, but you never came. I thought you'd been killed, so I came to the plains to rejoin the army. But everyone in camp was talking about Balor's escape and how all the prisoners were freed from Faolukan's spell. Then I knew you'd succeeded. So I deserted them and came here to wait for you. What took you so long?"

"I'm sorry, Yuri." Tristan laid a hand on his shoulder. "Balor trapped me in the chasm for an entire day. Eventually, I escaped."

"Did you get what you were looking for?"

His heart warming, even as his insides quaked over what he'd discovered, he slid his hand from the youth's bony shoulder. "I did."

"You look . . . older, wiser. Did something happen to you?"

"Aye, lad." Ewan swung his rucksack back over his shoulders. "The hand of Elyon fell upon him. And Elyon revealed who Tristan really is."

"Tristan?"

"Aye," said Ewan. "Tristan has been masquerading as Prince Neil since we left Ériu. Elyon also told him he was to become merely Tristan again."

"So he's not a prince?" Yuri's brows pinched together, his face downcast.

"Something far greater." Caitir stepped forward. "He's the chosen one of Elyon. Elyon himself also said he's the Augury."

"You . . . you're the woman we found frozen in the field."

"And I canna tell you how good it is to be thawed out."

A smile flickered across Yuri's lips. "I'm glad to be among friends, again."

"Aye, lad. Aye, indeed." Tristan hugged him.

Yuri pulled back and bowed. "You will always be a lord to me. May I still call you that?"

Tristan smiled. "You may call me whatever you like you."

"Look there, my lord." Ewan pointed to the plain below. A patrol was climbing out of a gully.

"I don't think they've seen us." Yuri waved them toward a ravine in the brush below. "But we mustn't stand here. Do you still have those Drochtar uniforms?"

"We do."

"Then you should wear them. From a distance, at least, you won't attract attention. I'm not so sure about up close."

Heads nodded as the group rummaged in their packs for the disguises they'd used to bypass the troops on the road to Cathair Duvh many days ago. Tristan took out his Drochtar uniform with its blue and black interlocking swirls. He shook off the dust.

"What about me?" Cocking her head to one side, Caitir crossed her arms over her chest.

Yuri regarded her for a moment then opened his pack. He removed a spare Drochtar uniform, ragged and dirt-stained. "Will this fit you?"

She took it, scrunching her nose.

He winced. "I'm sorry it's in such bad condition. Everything they gave me needs replacing."

She picked it up between thumb and index finger then strolled toward the bushes. "Thank you," she muttered over her shoulder. "I think."

When all had become soldiers of Drochtar, Yuri lined them up and examined them. His glance stopped at Caitir. "Drochtar has no women soldiers. You will draw much attention. I'll try to get a helmet for you to hide your face and your hair."

Caitir's locks fell nearly to her breasts. She swept them from her face. "I haven't cut it since leaving Ériu."

"I can fix that." Ewan produced a scissors from his pack and, with Caitir's reluctant permission, cut until her hair was barely a few inches long.

"I also notice you have no *briocht*." Yuri handed her a small circle of brass encompassing a quarter-moon. "I took this off a dead man."

"What is it?"

"A charm made by the druids," said Tristan. "They keep the púcas from attacking. We all have one."

Grimacing, she hung it around her neck. Then her gaze swept along both arms to her feet. "These clothes are not quite wretched enough. Perhaps I should roll in the mud for a bit or slap on some dung?"

Tristan smiled and turned to Yuri. "As soon as possible, we need to return to the wilderness north of Drochcarn and the Pass of Tollan Caillté to—"

"You cannot go that way." Yuri's head shook back and forth.

"Why not?"

"They know you came from the north. They discovered the bodies of Sergei and Pavel, the two patrol members you killed. 'Tis common knowledge that two entire centuria went north to guard the tunnel entrance. They're looking for you. You'd never get past them now."

Tristan rubbed the back of his suddenly tense neck. "But that means . . ."

"The Pass of Mam Giorag." Milosh's face paled. "'Tis the only other way out of Drochtar."

Ewan was silent, his jaw set.

"But 'tis thick with soldiers," said Caitir. "And what's worse—púcas."

As he lowered his hand, Tristan's gaze wandered toward the south. He'd heard the tales, the warnings, and his heart quickened. "Is there any way to get through that pass unseen?"

"Nay. 'Tis a heavily guarded route, my lords, swarming with soldiers. They check everyone entering or leaving."

"But they're not expecting us there." Tristan stared off into the scrub. "And 'tis the only route left."

Milosh nodded.

Grim-faced, Ewan also agreed.

"Then let's do it." A smile lifted half of Caitir's mouth. "The sooner I get out of this wretched excuse for a uniform, the better."

"My lords, and my lady"—Yuri bowed to Caitir—"may I then suggest you follow the army? Any time now, it will head toward the pass. But do not think of joining them. Nay, far too risky."

"How can we get through the pass without joining them?" Milosh frowned. "If we approach the gate by ourselves, they'll surely suspect something."

Yuri shrugged.

"Perhaps you'd better tell us what else you've learned," said Tristan. "Start with what happened to Balor after I left."

"Faolukan recaptured him and confined him again in the chasm. But we heard the effort nearly exhausted the arch druid. He's recovering in what remains of his palace."

"What about all the people I freed from the spell?"

"Most ran down the mountain. All of Cathair Duvh and most of the units in the city fled in panic and evacuated to the plains. The soldiers have been searching, but they've only gathered half the prisoners. It will take weeks to round up the rest, and word is, Faolukan won't waste any more time on them. Tonight, on the Glebe of Sacrifice, they'll sacrifice to Crom Mord the few they've recaptured. But tomorrow"—a shudder rippled over Yuri's thin form—"tomorrow, Faolukan will bring Crom Mord down the mountain with the remaining units."

"Is most of the army already on the plains then?" Tristan waved to the north.

"Aye."

"We've got their uniforms." Milosh slid both hands down the arms of Ewan's uniform then patted his shoulders with a sly grin. "Why don't we just join them, pretend we're part of them?"

"You saw the difficulty we had back at the inn. That might work for a bit, but nay." Yuri shook his head. "You, Milosh, have the look of the Romely Plains about you. And this one"—he pointed to Ewan—"has an accent that would quickly give him away. And the lass is a real problem. No women serve in Faolukan's armies."

"So none of us could pass?" Milosh opened his hands in frustration.

"Master Tristan." Yuri faced him. "You could well pass for a Ferachtir. Especially now with your white hair. But only if you drove a wagon. All the Ferachtirs with the army of Drochtar tend the wagons and the aurochs. 'Tis a most lowly and despised profession—this aurochs tending. In keeping with the low quality of the Ferachtir units in general. But a wagon with an aurochs you do not have. And one look at these others"—he waved at them—"and they'll quickly be found out."

"I do not like this." Ewan's gaze settled on Tristan. "Has no one a plan to cross the pass of Mam Giorag?"

Tristan walked to the top of the ravine and gazed across the plains to the pall of smoke hovering over the enemy camp. He returned to his companions.

"What if we follow well in the rear of the army? Then, at the last moment, just before we arrive at the pass, we catch up and join them? Then we'll only be with them for a single day. Maybe less."

Milosh grinned. "What else have we got?"

"I ken naught else to do." But Ewan's face was downcast.

"Let's do it." Her eyes twinkling, Caitir arched her chin and slammed both hands on her hips. This was the Caitir Tristan knew. After all that had happened, she was still undaunted and hadn't lost her spunk.

"Then we wait until the army departs and follow in their wake."

"Do not follow this plan, my lords." Yuri's gaze found the dirt. "If you do, I fear they will catch you."

CHAPTER 3

IN THE ARMY'S WAKE

That evening, Yuri snuck down to the camp and returned with a helmet for Caitir. But as he passed it to her, Tristan noticed his eyes seemed vacant.

She tried on the helmet, and it covered some of her feminine features. From a distance, she might pass for a boy. Yuri had said many Drochtar youth had been conscripted to fight in the Deamhan Lord's cause. But up close, with her green, mesmerizing eyes and delicate cheeks, she was clearly a woman.

Then Yuri sat, lowered his head to his hands, and wept.

"What's wrong?" Tristan plopped down beside him.

"My village. Everyone in it. Every man, woman, and child. Last month, all were taken. All were given to Crom Mord. Then they burned everything. And I didn't even know it."

"How do you know this?"

"I met a man from my village. A soldier down on the plains. He saw my family taken up to the altar." His shoulders shaking, his hands trembling, Yuri curled into a ball.

Tristan laid a hand on his arm. "I'm sorry."

Caitir sat on the other side and hugged him.

Yuri looked up. Through teary eyes, he nodded his appreciation. Then he withdrew from them, hugging his knees as if that, alone, comforted.

Tristan watched him, wondering if Faolukan's armies would do the same across all of Erde? Would even Hidden Pines end up a smoldering, ruined heap by the trailside?

That night, as they bedded down in the ravine, the distant, chilling laughter of hyenas echoed across the plains.

"What's left for me here?" Yuri waved into the moonless, sulfurous dark. "My home is gone. And I'm alone."

"Why don't you come with us?" asked Tristan. "We can always use an extra sword."

The pack's insane cackling came closer then moved farther out. When they were gone, a wee, silent voice responded. "All right, Master Tristan. I'll go with you."

"Welcome to the Company," said Ewan.

"I'm glad you're with us," added Caitir.

Then she moved her sleeping furs closer to Tristan's and whispered in his ear, "And I'm glad to be back with you."

He groped for her face in the dark. Pulling her head close, he kissed her. "Aye, my betrothed. And you don't know how glad I am you are here with me."

She sighed, they hugged, and they fell asleep in each other's arms.

ALL THE NEXT DAY, THEY huddled in the ravine, waiting for the army of Drochtar to move. Then around noon, a great hubbub issued from the camp—Faolukan must have arrived.

But it wasn't until the following morning that the tents began to come down and the army broke camp. Slowly, a few units began moving southwest. From the rise where Tristan checked on its progress, it resembled a giant snake trailing south. By midmorning, the last stragglers—a collection of heavy-laden carts and wagons—followed in its wake.

"'Tis time," he said. "The camp is deserted."

Everyone gathered their packs, and they followed Tristan down the trail to the plains.

Once again, they trod between scrub bushes, barren scree, and bubbling fountains of mud. Occasional dust devils whirled past. His lungs were ever choked with a sulfurous, dusty haze. Leaden clouds clung to darkening skies.

When they reached the abandoned camp, legions of crows and vultures scattered before them. But the hyena packs just lifted smiling faces from their feasts before again burying their muzzles in corpses and garbage. Tristan and his Company veered far around them. Where the army had lived for weeks—months?—they'd left refuse, unfilled latrines, and an occasional corpse. The smell stole his breath away.

"In camp, there are many fights," said Yuri. "Many murders. And the commanders don't seem to care. They just drag the bodies to the edge of the tents and leave them for the scavengers."

"Beasts." Caitir spat the word. "Animals all."

Tristan wrinkled his nose. "Let's get through this quickly."

The remains of the base camp extended for nearly a mile. Where it ended, a fifty-foot-wide swath of trampled ground began. Keeping to level ground, the track meandered from ridge to ridge. They passed items fallen from soldiers' packs. A frying pan here. A dagger there. A single boot. A spare tunic. A trampled hat.

By noon, they caught up to the straggling wagons and carts at the rear of the main body. The rest of the day, they slowed their pace and hung back.

When the clouds of evening became a darkening blanket, they left the track, veered half a league north, and made camp.

Again that night, the hyenas' laughter broke the stillness.

The next morning, they had barely caught up to the army's track when Milosh called out. "What's that ahead?"

Tristan peered through the gloom. "A lone wagon. Broken down?"

"But look at the beast beside it." Ewan pointed. "'Tis huge."

One of the largest aurochs Tristan had ever seen was staked to the ground. It seemed none too happy, lowering its head and throwing clods of dust in all directions. The line of eight horses tethered to the wagon whinnied uneasily, shook their heads, and strained against their halters.

"And that wagon"—Tristan faced Yuri—"'tis enormous."

"They all are," said the youth. "The front's for hauling hay. The cage in back carries a single aurochs. Fresh meat for the army."

The two Ferachtir drivers were looking away from them. Standing above a broken wheel, they gestured wildly, apparently deep in an argument.

"Should we wait until they fix their wagon or go around?" Milosh waved an impatient hand.

"Let's wait." Tristan's gaze meandered over the scene.

"Why do they haul the animals themselves instead of salting and curing the meat?" asked Ewan.

"They do carry cured meat," said Yuri. "But fresh meat is highly prized. So they bring a few animals all the way from the Romely plains. But only for the officers. One aurochs can feed thirty officers for days."

For a time, they watched the two Ferachtirs argue. Then the men pulled out tools, a spare wheel, and struggled on a lever, trying unsuccessfully to lift one end of the wagon.

Tristan waved toward them. "How deep is that mow?" The front half, filled with hay and bounded by a slatted fence, was about twelve feet long by ten wide. "Big enough to hide my three companions?"

"Probably." The beginnings of a smile twitched across the youth's face. "Especially with a wagon that full."

"Let's see if we can convince those two to part with it."

Fingering his sword, Milosh grinned.

Tristan held up a hand. "If we can help it, we don't want a fight."

Milosh only shrugged.

Tristan walked behind a tall scrub tree, doffed his Drochtar uniform, and pulled on the Ferachtir clothing he still carried. Emerging, he asked, "Do I look like a Ferachtir?"

"You do, my lord," said Yuri.

"Caitir, you'd better hide in the brush and come out after we get the wagon."

19

She frowned but headed off to the side.

The four men hiked to the wagon. The Ferachtirs hadn't made any progress replacing the wheel.

"Ho, there." Tristan approached the two men, now struggling to lift the wagon with a lever. With the wheel broken, the bed leaned dangerously to the left. "Can we help?"

Startled, the two men dropped their rod and whirled to face the newcomers.

"W–who are you?" asked the first, a lean man with a thin, straight face, straggly white hair, and long, gangly limbs. "Why aren't you with your units?"

The second man, nearly as thin as the first, with red hair and a freckled face, put hands on hips and frowned.

"We were separated up at Cathair Duvh." Tristan pointed back the way they'd come. "By the time we came down, the army was gone. Trying to catch up."

"But you're Ferachtir," said the first man. "Why are you traveling with these men?"

"My wagon went ahead without me. I'm trying to find it."

The first man narrowed his eyes. "What is your unit?"

"Nicu Tăranu, fifteenth centuria, ninth legion, southern army. From Dealuri Ascunse." He might as well stick with his former ruse. It had worked before. "And these men are also trying to find their units."

"Dealuri Ascunse!" The man's head tipped back, his eyes alight. "My cousin's from there. Small village in the hills. Forests. Streams. So unlike the barren north. I'm Skender Ionescu. We're both from Pierdut Valea."

Tristan's heart leaped inside his chest. How was he to know he'd meet someone who knew the village belonging to the dead owner of his uniform? "I–I don't know it well."

Skender's companion frowned. "'Tis only three leagues away. How could you not know it?"

Sweat began forming on his brow. "They took me when I was young. Been traveling with the army ever since."

Skender stared at him a moment then offered a hand. Tristan shook it.

Nodding to his red-haired, freckle-faced companion, Skender said, "We've got big trouble with this wagon. Can you help us lift the bed?"

Milosh stepped forward, turned his back to the wagon, knelt, and grabbed the edge. Grunting, he budged it only a few inches. "Help me, Ewan."

Skender looked askance at him. "If you weren't wearing that Drochtar uniform, I'd swear you were from the Romely plains."

"Been nearly everywhere, lad. They conscripted me in Amridmor."

The man's lips pulled back in a question. He rubbed his chin and nodded.

With Ewan, Milosh, Yuri, and Tristan lifting on the wagon bed and the red-haired Ferachtir leaning on the lever, Skender removed the broken wheel and put on the new one.

Huffing from the effort, the red-haired man watched while his companion's hammer rammed a wooden pin through the hole at the end of the axle. "We'd have been at this all day without your help." Skender stood and regarded the result. "But we've yet to get that monster back on the bed."

With one Ferachtir pulling on a lead, and the others prodding the beast with goads from all sides, they coaxed the aurochs up the ramp and into the bed. Skender shut the gate, slid a metal pin into its hole, and locked it.

"Whew." Ewan wiped his brow. "'Twas a near thing, getting that monster to its home. No wee beastie, that."

As Yuri winced, both Ferachtirs whirled to face Ewan.

"Ewan? . . . Ewan?" The freckle-faced man tried out the word on his tongue. "That's a name I've never heard spoken for a man from Drochtar." He stared at the squire.

Skender shifted questioning eyes over the newcomers. "That accent . . . a man from the Romely plains . . . and someone from Dealuri Ascunse who doesn't know Pierdut Valea." He backed away from the four, his hand on his sword hilt.

Frowning, his red-haired companion sidled up beside him, fingering his own weapon. "Who, exactly, are you?" His voice rose. "Tell us the truth."

Milosh's blade left its sheath. Ewan, too, brought out his sword.

Tristan took a step closer to the men. "Four men and a woman trying to escape this country." Tristan's blade came out. "We don't want to fight you. We only want your wagon."

"Never!" shouted the red-haired man as his sword swung toward Milosh.

Grinning, Milosh easily knocked the weapon aside. With three quick strokes, he thrust his blade deep into the man's gut. The Ferachtir fell beside the wagon.

Skender rushed Tristan with wild, untrained strokes.

Tristan easily blocked them. "Stop this. I don't want to kill you."

But that only intensified the Ferachtir's attack. Blow after blow, he struck. Undisciplined, violent thrusts that Tristan easily repelled.

Finally, when it was apparent the man wouldn't quit, Tristan found an opening and thrust his blade deep.

Both Ferachtirs now lay dead on the plains.

"I–I didn't want to kill him."

"He left you no choice." Milosh knelt and examined their packs. He found a spare Ferachtir uniform for Yuri, who changed behind the wagon.

When Yuri returned, Tristan regarded the beast they would haul. "I hope you know something about tending this thing?"

"I do." A frown crossed Yuri's lips. "But, my lord, there's something I should have told you earlier. 'Tis about crossing the pass."

"What?" Tristan's heart beat faster. What new problem would they face now?

"If you're thinking that your friends will hide in the hay, you should know that often they search the wagons. And then they'll drive spears through every corner to roust out deserters."

Caitir exchanged a worried look with Ewan.

Milosh grinned. "But sometimes they don't, hey?"

Yuri nodded.

"I'm willing to take the gamble."

"W–what choice do we have?" A tremor shook Caitir's voice.

"None," said Ewan.

Tristan looked at the stack of hay in the mow and then at Caitir, Ewan, and Milosh. The pass of Mam Giorag was feared for a reason.

But that's where they now must now go.

CHAPTER 4

MAM GIORAG

For the next two days, while Yuri and Tristan sat on the bench in their Ferachtir uniforms and drove, the others lounged out of sight in the haystack. Theirs was the last wagon trailing the army of Drochtar, and once or twice a day, an officer would ride back and urge them to catch up with the others. Whenever that happened, Ewan, Caitir, and Milosh would dive under the mow until the lieutenants departed. Claiming problems with the axle, Tristan never increased the pace.

Sometimes, the aurochs would emit an ear-shattering bellow. Too often, it drove its mammoth horns into the fence separating it from the three passengers, ripping and shaking the wood. All day they lived with the acrid, stomach-souring stench of aurochs manure and urine mixed with hay.

At night, after feeding and watering the horses, Yuri showed them how to take hold of the rope permanently attached to the aurochs's collar, how to use the goads to prod it out, and how to clean the bed. The goads were long rods ending in a sharp point, with an even sharper hook curving down from that. With much poking, prodding, and jumping away from angry horns, they returned the beast to its pen. Then it snorted, pawed the boards, and shook its head until they forked enough hay over the rail to satisfy its hunger.

By the third day, the peaks of the Sfarsit Mountains loomed ever larger and higher. The summits trailed wind-whipped clouds of snow. On the afternoon of the fourth day, the army's track entered bleak foothills. A wide trail cut into the side of a valley rising toward the pass.

When Tristan first spied the Gates of Doom, it was from the end of a long line of soldiers, cavalry, and wagons backed up for a mile down the barren, treeless valley.

"Guards will inspect everyone and everything," warned Yuri.

Theirs was the last wagon to enter the gate. Perhaps it hadn't been wise to be last. But now, even if they wanted to change positions, the traffic ahead barred their way.

Beside the trail, they passed tent after tent of ragged, dirty men with large foreheads, squat noses, and hairy bodies—púcas!

The three passengers now hid constantly in the trough behind the fence and bench. For the rest of that day, as guards carefully inspected every soldier and cart going over the pass, the wagon rolled forward a few yards, stopped, then groaned ahead again.

But the closer they came to the Gates of Doom, the more Tristan's heart fluttered. And even though a chill wind blew off the slopes, sweat beaded on his forehead. What was taking so long? Why were the guards examining everything so closely?

As night approached, the cloud ceiling over Drochtar darkened, and torches appeared ahead. Only two wagons rumbled in front of them now—two wagons between them and the massive black wall rising stark and ominous into the night.

With the darkness, one of the púcas at trailside morphed into its half-bear form. Slavering, it lumbered toward the team of eight horses, opening its tooth-lined snout. The animals whinnied, shook their heads, and reared.

Tristan jumped down from the bench and waved his sword. "Nay. Get away. Not food."

The bear púca backed off, pawed at its face, and ran down the mountain.

Shaking, Tristan returned to the bench.

Guards finished their inspection of the first wagon's barrels of cured meat. They waved it on.

A black-clad guard bearing a long spike walked past the next wagon and headed their way.

"Stay quiet!" whispered Tristan. "Someone's coming."

The hay rustled as the three passengers dove deeper under the stalks.

"You'll be next," said the guard. "Prepare to be searched." He whirled and headed back toward the wagon ahead of them.

The next wagon also carried an aurochs. The guards stood in the mow, driving their spears into every inch of hay, all the way to the floorboards.

"This is not good." Yuri's worried glance caught Tristan's. "If their spears don't kill your friends first, they'll find them. Then they'll kill us all for sure."

As Tristan watched the thoroughness with which the guards stabbed every section of the next wagon's mow, he gripped the wagon bench on both sides of himself to steady an onslaught of light-headedness. No one could survive that. He shot a glance behind to where his friends hid.

"Take the reins." He passed them to Yuri. "Let me know if anyone's coming." He leaped over the bench and landed on Ewan who let out a muffled cry. "Sorry."

There wasn't time to unpack the goads from up front. "Caitir, Milosh, and Ewan," he said, "scrunch toward the front." Already sweating, he began pulling boards from the top of the divider separating the aurochs from the mow. He dropped them, one by one, onto the hay. The massive beast watched, hooves pawing the floorboards, eyes glowing red by distant torchlight. When he had removed all but two boards, leaving only a two-foot-high barrier, it charged.

He leaped up one side of the fence and barely avoided being gored. The beast backed up and charged again. With all the strength he could muster, Tristan clambered up the fence to the bench. He watched, his heart pounding wildly, as its hooves missed his three friends, now thoroughly covered with hay.

The aurochs backed up, air hissing from its nostrils, eyes red and enraged.

"Now let them try to poke a spear back there." Yuri smiled and patted Tristan's shoulder.

But Tristan shuddered at what he'd just done. A twelve-foot-high monster with horns nearly as wide as the wagon, the aurochs pawed the bed. It bellowed and shook its horns. If it entered one of its maddened, thrashing fits, it could easily gore or kill. Faint, he tried to steady his breathing. But what else could he do?

The guard approached. "Your turn." He smacked the side of the wagon with his spear. "Pull up and get out."

Tristan snapped the leather once, and the wagon lurched forward. He pulled the team to a stop and tied the reins. He and Yuri jumped to the ground. His heart pounded so hard, he feared it would burst. Once on the ground, he wiped his brow. Hopefully, the guard wouldn't notice.

"Why is this gate down?" A second guard, a tall, black-turbaned Sarkenian bearing a long pike with a hooked point, peered into the aurochs pen with a sour expression. He jumped up onto the bench, searched under the seat, then regarded the hay.

By now, the aurochs's muzzle was deep in the stalks, munching on the feed he'd been denied all day. The guard stared at the hay and, gingerly, slipped one foot over the fence, bracing it on the second rail inside the pen. Holding his spear in one hand, he struck the weapon deep into the hay nearest the bench.

Tristan held his breath, hoping there was no arm or leg beneath that pike.

The aurochs snorted, lifted its muzzle from its feast, and fixed red eyes on the intruder. It pawed the wagon bed, readying itself for a charge.

For a second time, the guard raised his weapon. Then he froze. Wary eyes watched the enraged beast. Then the guard scurried back up the fence onto the bench.

The aurochs shook its head and resumed feeding.

Waving at the huge animal, the guard said, "No one right in the head would hide in that mow. You can pass."

Tristan exhaled, tried not to show his relief.

"You need to light a torch." The guard motioned to Tristan. "Then catch up with the others."

Tristan nodded, and he and Yuri climbed onto the bench. While Yuri lit a torch, Tristan whipped the reins, and the cart rumbled toward the gates. A massive black wall of tarred timbers, studded with iron bolts, stretched fifty feet into the night. Torches lit a path through the open doors.

They almost passed through when another púca with the head and paws of a lion ran at them. A Sarkenian guard intercepted it and beat it away with his pike. He ambled back toward his post, muttering something about accursed shapeshifters.

Tristan lashed the team, and the wagon trundled faster over the rocky ground. When the gates were a mile behind the last bend, and after the other wagons had surged far ahead, Tristan brought them to a halt.

With goads from under the seat, he and Yuri dropped into the hay, being careful not to step on anyone. The two prodded the aurochs from the mow into the pen's far side.

While Milosh took Tristan's stick and helped Yuri keep the aurochs at bay, Caitir and Ewan helped Tristan replace the boards.

Then everyone left the wagon to stretch their legs.

"When you let that beast into the mow, it could have gored us." Milosh grinned and slapped Tristan on the shoulder. "But I admit, 'twas some trick. And it worked."

Ewan brushed hay from his tunic. "You do not ken how close that beastie was to munching on my leg."

"Do you realize we've left Drochtar?" Tristan smiled. "We're now in Ferachtir."

Caitir gave him a mock frown. "And I was just getting used to the darkness and breathing the sulfur air."

Far down the mountain, the line of torch-lit wagons was emerging from behind a bend.

"Maybe we should find a place to camp a bit farther ahead." Tristan pointed at the line of wagons. "We could follow the army tomorrow from a distance. Then we—"

The clomp of hooves stopped him in midsentence. Two riders bearing torches rounded the bend. Riding fast, they were already a hundred feet away.

Everyone was standing in plain sight—too late to hide. He waved frantically to Caitir, who slipped into the shadows behind Milosh and Ewan. But the torch in Yuri's hands revealed too much.

The first approaching rider bore the insignia of an Optio, the second-in-command of a century of one hundred men. "Are you the last wagon?" He nodded back up the trail.

"Aye," answered Yuri.

The man rose in his stirrups, scowled, and plopped back onto his saddle. "Then what, in the name of Ifreann, do you soldiers think you're doing back here?"

CHAPTER 5

THE BLOOD MIRROR

"Our wagon is slow, my lord. The axle—it's bent . . ." Tristan pointed beneath the wagon.

Frowning, the officer stared at Ewan, Milosh, and Caitir.

The light was so dim, Tristan could barely see the man's face. The others might pass in the dark. But if either had a good look at Caitir, they'd be found out.

As if bemoaning yet one more instance of incompetence, the officer shook his head, closed his eyes, and reopened them. "Unless you want a flogging, get that wagon moving. Get you and your boy down to the Whistling Vale. Faolukan's called an assembly tonight and wants everyone there. So get moving!" Nodding to his companion, he yanked on the reins. Both horses spun about, and they picked their way back down the darkening path.

"That was close," said Tristan. "Caitir, he thought you were a boy, not the beautiful woman you are."

"That just shows how impoverished were his perceptions."

"And my perceptions," said Milosh, "tell me he now knows there are five of us." He clambered up onto the bench. "Where's the Whistling Vale?"

"Not far," said Caitir, the only one to have passed through recently. "The slope flattens out into a wide valley before the final drop to the flats." She joined Milosh up on the wagon.

"Can we slip past them in the vale?"

"In a new camp, there's always much confusion," said Yuri. "Many soldiers milling about. And if the army has stopped for an assembly—"

"Maybe we can pass?" Tristan finished his thought.

"Aye."

"We must." Tristan stared at the receding horses. "If we're still in their camp come morning . . . we'll be caught."

WHEN THEY ROUNDED THE LAST bend, thousands of tiny lights dotted the valley below. As they descended and approached the milling crowd, Tristan felt the familiar sensation of something cold skittering across his skin.

Crom Mord.

He was here.

Thousands, nay tens of thousands, of men bearing torches clustered before a wide central area where rose a flat spherical object—a giant mirror. Was that a Blood Mirror? Aye, its vertical surface shimmered darkly as if smeared with blood. Before the mirror, a pedestal bore the unmistakable silhouette of Crom Mord, the idol the Deamhan Lord had chosen for his home.

As a heavy, suffocating blanket of gloom settled over them, Tristan tried to guide the wagon toward the edge of the crowd. Milosh, Ewan, and Yuri now shared the bench. Darkness hid their faces, lit occasionally by a nearby, flickering torch. Soldiers also lit cressets filled with pitch atop high poles.

Caitir stood behind the fence in the haymow. The bench was so high and the bed so deep, her head barely reached the seat. "What's happening?"

"It's an assembly." Yuri shuddered. "I've been to many of these. Crom Mord—"

"Is about to speak." A cold ripple raced across Tristan's shoulders and down his back. "I'll keep to the side, try to get around them. I don't want to hear him . . . again."

He pulled the reins far to the left, trying to circle the crowd. But so many soldiers now jostled close around them that soon the heaving throng made it impossible to move.

With so many soldiers so near, Caitir slipped back deeper into the haymow below the line of sight.

A sudden dark light flashed from the towering brass mirror, washing across Tristan's skin like a shivering, undulating wind. Blue fire tinged with red replaced the swirling blood, commanding him to look. He faced it, as did those beside him.

No escaping it now. The Deamhan Lord would speak. And he was forced to hear.

As if sensing the approach of evil, the aurochs bellowed, kicked the fence, and snorted.

The Blood Mirror rippled and swirled with blue, black, and red flames. Then the image of Crom Mord, multiplied ten times its size, flashed on the mirror. Staring over the crowd with gleaming red eyes was a black claw-footed statue with the head of a lizard. Razor-teeth filled an open mouth, revealing a forked, red tongue. A lion's mane ringed the lizard head. But instead of fur, snakes as black as night writhed in the mane, their tongues lapping in and out.

Tristan's heart pounded against his ribs. Sweat broke out on his forehead. Then the thing's words wriggled into his mind.

Listen now, soldiers of Drochtar. It is I, Crom Mord, Lord of Drochtar, inheritor of Erde, who speaks.

Tristan's hands flew to his ears to stop the chilling, penetrating dissonance invading his thoughts. But it wasn't sound accosting his ears. It was words, forming like icy daggers inside his head. And mere hands couldn't keep them out.

Erde is a worm-eaten apple, ready to fall. Tonight, we stand on the eve of victory. Soon, you here will possess all the riches Ereb can offer. Then, my legions, the foul armies of Elyon will drop beneath your boots like ants. Tonight, I promise you plunder, rapine, and bloodlust. As much as you can stand.

A hoarse cry issued from throats on all sides. Men eager for murder, theft, and ravage shouted their basest desires into the night. The sound deafened, chilled, and cut through him like a sword plunged deep into his soul.

Tristan stared at a man standing beside the wagon. Eyes alight, the man's face became twisted, enraptured with dark desire. His body bent toward the mirror, shivered under the words forming in his mind, in everyone's minds. At that moment, he appeared not so much a man, as a feral creature intent on evil.

Down on the Ferachtir flats, two-thirds of this force will depart for the south and board ships. Half of that fleet will take the Kingdom of Etrusca. The other half will sail around Sarkenos, up the Saone River in Burgundia, and disembark at Lugdunum. There, my emissaries have convinced King Gundovald and his army to ally with us. For those of you going with that band, I give you the spoils of Armorica and Esperandula. May you forage and despoil all that you touch. May every village rise in flames. May every city wall tumble into ruin. May you slake your every desire, no matter how base. Leave nothing behind but the dead.

Again, the soldiers' approval resounded off the slopes. Wild, eager eyes drank in the idol as if it were some intoxicating draught made of sweetest honey. Primal cries assailed the night, promising violence, the fulfillment of profane desires.

My plans for the final third of this army are these—we will join a growing force already gathering at Fjernshavn. In that harbor awaits a fleet, the size of which has never before been seen on Erde. Those ships will take us to the seat of Elyon's power—to the shores of loathsome Ériu. We must arrive before the Scepter—that foul device of Elyon—is returned to its nest. My soldiers, in that place, we will trample and pillage and plunder and rape and murder all who stand in our way. We will lay waste that foul country, despoiling every city, village, and hamlet. Not a child, woman, or man will be left alive who has not felt the terrible wrath and power of Drochtar and of Crom Mord!

On for Drochtar, my soldiers. On against the Ériu! On for victory! Victory for Drochtar!

The clamor that shook the air stunned and deafened. It echoed off the mountain slopes and thundered through the valley. The soldiers around him had become frenzied, their eyes eager, bulging, shining with bloodlust, war, and hate. Shaking fists rose into the sky, dropped, and, trembling with rage, rose again. Those with swords banged them on shields until such a throbbing, rumbling thunder banged on his ears, Tristan feared they would burst.

It was as if an evil incense permeated the air, so thick and heavy he could almost taste the metallic, bloody essence on his tongue.

To his right, Ewan was holding his head in his hands, shaking it, trying in vain to shed the evil that had slipped inside.

Milosh stared at the Crom Mord idol, his face grim and set, his jaw tense.

"'Tis horrible," whispered a trembling Caitir. "Awful!"

White-knuckled hands gripping the seat, Yuri grimaced.

"Look at them, my lord." Ewan gawked at the impassioned men to his right, his left, and in front. "What has become of them?"

"They're possessed of evil."

"But why? How? Were they not once men like us? Did they not have mothers and fathers? Did not some of them also father sons and daughters that they love dearly?"

Tristan studied the squire, marveling at the words issuing from him now.

"Aye, my friend," whispered Milosh. "They did. But some of them are now púcas."

"Still, even the púcas were once men. So how did they become like this? How can they so embrace such darkness, becoming the enemy of all that's human?"

"I don't know, Ewan." Tristan shut his eyes. "They are ensorcelled."

"But was it done to them? Or did they let themselves become so? And could it not be the same with you and me? I fear 'tis so, aye. At any moment, any of us could drop as low as they and become like them, bowing before deamhans, cheering a deamhan idol, and pulling to our breasts all that's evil and dark?"

"Aye." Behind them, Caitir's feet rustled the hay as though her whole body were shaking. "I, too, fear 'tis so. I see it in their eyes. And I feel it"—she pounded her breast—"even here."

Tristan turned to look at her. "Is it true? Even in you?"

"For a moment, just one moment, I felt the same bloodlust, the same desire for destruction and defilement as these wretched souls around us." Pained eyes fixed his. Tears streamed down her cheeks. "What's wrong with me, Tristan?"

He reached a hand back to where she stood in the haymow. Their hands grasped and tightened. He tried to pull her close, but the slats prevented it.

He released his grip, closed his eyes, and whispered, "O Elyon, protect us from this place."

"My friend, look ahead!" Milosh spat the words. "Let's get out of here."

A temporary gap had opened. Tristan spun in his seat and snapped the reins. The wagon jolted ahead. They rushed forward thirty yards before the crowd again closed around them. Soon another opening appeared. Again, he thrashed the reins. This time, the wagon rumbled out of the worst of the throng and kept going.

From behind, a rhythmic, reverberating cry thundered into the night—

"Drochtar!"

"Drochtar!"

"*Drochtar!*"

With each repetition, more and more voices joined the shout. A terrible furor had taken hold of the assembled throng. Tristan feared the crowd was so possessed, it could at any moment turn on anyone, for any reason, and do anything.

Following a heavily traveled track still visible by a few cressets burning even out here, the wagon bounced over ruts toward the field's edge, gaining distance from the assembly.

Finally, the echoing shouts of the maddening crowd dimmed behind them.

Then Ewan spoke. "He's going to destroy all of Erde. And his army is bewitched. I do not ken how we're ever going to get home."

Gloom seemed to hang so heavy over the carriage, Tristan could yet taste it.

"But maybe 'tis not so bad." Caitir wiped her eyes and fixed her friends with a sly grin. "Think on it. Thanks to Tristan, we possess the Augury. Now all we have to do is avoid a huge army of evil that wants us dead, then cross an endless wasteland, pick up the Scepter Tristan has hidden somewhere—assuming 'tis still there—and flee across a continent filled with unknown dangers, evil men, and monsters. Then—assuming Faolukan and his minions havena caught us and torn us limb from limb—all we have to do next, even though we do not have a ship, and the arch druid has a grand fleet—aye, all we have to do next is carry both those things back to Ériu and beat him home before he lands first and destroys the world. Sure"—she smiled at Ewan and Tristan, and even Milosh and Yuri now stared at her—"who couldna do *that*?"

Perhaps it was the length of the night, the hopelessness of her suggestion, or just the way she said it.

But at that moment, everyone burst out laughing.

PART II

THE RED TENT

CHAPTER 6

THE FERACHTIR FLATS

Tristan lashed the reins, and the wagon rolled ahead.

"We're beyond most of the camp." Milosh scanned the distant assembly and its thousands of torches.

"How far is it to the flats?" Tristan asked Caitir.

"Another half a night's travel. Maybe less."

"Will there be patrols on the way down?" he called to Yuri.

"This late? I doubt it. But there might be a guard between the camp and the trail."

Tristan nodded, and the wagon rumbled across the last stretch of valley. They left behind the camp, the soldiers, and the frenzied cries. But even this far out, the crowd's torches lit the cloud ceiling enough so he could see the track ahead. He quenched their torch.

Soon the wagon caught up to two lights in front of them.

"What is that?" Two chariots bearing three soldiers each were traveling about a hundred yards ahead, both going their way. He slowed the team.

The chariots were approaching a cluster of cressets and a small encampment—a dozen tents, a few campfires.

"A century's encamped here," said Yuri. "They're guarding the trail entrance."

Tristan brought the wagon to a halt.

"But where is everyone?" Milosh waved toward the tents. "I see only a handful of men at trailside. And no one in camp."

"They must be at the assembly." Tristan scanned the valley. But no one else moved.

"So now what?" Caitir frowned. "We can't fight a dozen men."

Behind them, the throng roared again, loud enough to hear.

"I know how to handle this." Milosh jumped down from the wagon and started crossing the field toward the tents. He whirled. "Bring the wagon a bit closer then wait. When 'tis time, I'll come running."

"How will we know when—" But Milosh had already sprinted out of earshot toward the camp.

"What's he doing?" Ewan sidled closer to Tristan.

"I don't know. He should have told us more."

They waited on the trail in the dark. Enough time passed for Tristan to have boiled two pots. Ahead, the chariot passengers lounged and talked with six men under the cresset light. They were passing around a flagon of something, laughing, taking long swigs.

Then, as one, they ceased their conversations. They faced the back of the camp. Then they began running.

At the camp's far end, two tents had become wavering walls of flame, lighting the dark.

Milosh burst in from the night. "Move!" he ordered, jumping onto the bench.

Tristan lashed the reins, and the wagon pitched forward. They bounced over ruts and stones, quickly crossing the distance to the now abandoned circle of cresset light.

"Put your gear in the chariots," Milosh commanded. "We'll leave them the wagon. And our friend, the beast."

Smiling, Tristan grabbed his pack and the torches. He left the wagon and leaped onto the first carriage's platform.

Caitir sprang up beside him, followed by Ewan.

Yuri was already standing in the second chariot's bed. Tristan threw him a torch then spun to look back at the wagon.

Milosh's knife was sawing on leather under the horses' flanks.

Tristan raised the whip and cracked it over the heads of his two-horse team. The chariot lunged forward.

Caitir clutched the rail to keep from falling off.

Tristan shot a glance back.

Milosh had jumped onto the second carriage bed. With whip in hand, he cracked it, and his chariot leaped forward.

"Stop!" came a distant command. "Come back."

Now half the guards had reversed direction. They returned to the cresset light only to find a wagon in place of their chariots. The six soldiers, armed with spears and swords, jumped aboard. The driver took the reins and snapped them.

Five horses burst away.

Pulling their reins from the driver's hands.

Galloping far ahead.

Leaving behind the wagon and the other three horses.

"I cut the traces," called a grinning Milosh. "By the time they get their team together again and coax that aurochs out of the wagon, we'll be far down the mountain."

Tristan smiled then glanced to the trail ahead. Ewan lit a torch and held it high.

Chariot wheels churned down the steepening slope.

Only a mile down the trail, they left behind the acrid cloud that made its eternal home over Drochtar. Then moonlight lit enough of the path that Tristan could douse the torch.

It was good to see again the moon and the stars.

Soon, deep pine forest blanketed the slopes beside them, filling the air with a piney scent, reminding him of home. After Drochtar's thick, gagging haze, the very air here refreshed and invigorated.

Several times, he glanced back but saw no sign of pursuit. Yet it would come. And tomorrow would bring with it the entire army.

Half the night later, the trail flattened out, and their carriage wheels ground to a halt on sand. He looked west across the Ferachtir flats. "I never thought I'd welcome this sight. But after Drochtar . . ."

All the way to the horizon stretched an endless flat sea of hardened sand, salt, and clay, broken only by occasional outcroppings of thorny scrub and cloven rock. But a short ways to the south, many lights clustered together at some kind of camp, with dark structures littering the sand as far as he could see. "What is *that?*"

Yuri squinted. "Probably the skimmer fleet they'll use to transport the army to the southern edge of the flats."

"What's a skimmer?" Caitir raised an eyebrow.

"How did you get here from the Conachtir forest?"

"We walked."

Tristan smiled. "Then we've got a surprise for you." He faced Milosh. "How far to the Valley of Flowers from here?"

"In truth, we're much closer now than if we'd gone to Tollan Caillté. 'Tis probably straight across and a few days less travel."

"Good. But where will we get a skimmer?" His gaze turned to the southern camp.

"My guess," said Milosh, "is that camp has commandeered every skimmer all up and down the tree line for ten leagues or more."

"Aye," agreed Yuri. "And they'll have built many more. The only skimmers we'll find will be among that fleet."

His chest constricting, Tristan exhaled a heavy breath. "Then we've got to steal one."

"Leave it to me." Milosh grinned. "I'll slip one out of their camp so quietly, they'll never know it's gone." He tipped a sly glance to his chariot passenger. "Join me, Yuri?"

Grinning, Yuri bobbed his head. "Aye."

Milosh tightened the reins. "Tristan, maybe you should get some distance from this trailhead?"

"Good idea. We'll go north until we're out of sight then stop at forest's edge. We'll leave our chariot so you can see it."

"We'll find you."

"May Elyon go with you." Tristan waved as the two raced off to the south.

⸻ ✦⋅⊰✦⊱⋅✦ ⸻

THE MOMENT THEY LEFT, TRISTAN wondered if it had been wise to split up. But who better to steal something than Milosh, the great rogue, the master thief himself?

He cracked the reins and took them a mile or so north, halting where a few stunted pines grew down to the sandblasted flats. "We can rest here until they get our transportation."

"And have a wee bite to eat." Ewan was already digging in his pack for Drochtar's version of sausage.

Caitir jumped from the carriage and headed straight for the pine needle bed under the nearest tree. "No one's yet told me what a skimmer is. But right now, I'm too tired to care."

Tristan lay beside where Caitir stretched out and closed her eyes. Soon, her quiet breathing told him she was asleep.

He shut his eyes. But sleep wouldn't come.

Without warning, words seemed to write themselves, in light, upon his thoughts.

Take up the scroll.

The words demanded immediate action, obedience. He jerked upright. Gripping his pack, he nearly ripped open the ties and, his hands shaking, pulled out the metal scroll.

Ewan's chunk of cheese stopped halfway to his mouth, and he gaped at what Tristan was doing.

The golden metal unrolled as easily as if it were parchment. Then its surface glowed, shedding an ethereal, heavenly light upon everything around him. Shapes began forming on the metal surface—not words, but pictures.

Moving pictures.

The scene presented in crystalline detail took Tristan from under the pines to a place far across the flats. And he knew he was looking with future eyes, feeling with future emotions, and glimpsing events that hadn't yet happened.

Fear enveloped him like a black shroud. Something was chasing them. Something dark and evil and vaguely familiar—not a man, but a creature nearly as old as Erde itself, nearly as evil as Faolukan. A being the arch druid had awakened, not by design but by accident. And Tristan feared it with every fiber of his being. He knew this being, but couldn't name it.

Beside him in the vision, Ewan, Caitir, and Milosh clung to the rails of a skimmer as it raced across the sands, their terrified gazes fixed on whatever followed.

He wanted to turn and look back. He felt the thing's presence as keenly as the Deamhan Lord's. And he knew what it wanted—human flesh. But something prevented him from turning around. In this vision, portrayed so crisply on the scroll's plate, the only place his glance could focus was forward.

A patch of green appeared on the horizon, grew in size. How quickly their skimmer sped over the sands!

The oasis held a grove of palms, a pool of clear water bubbling out of the rocks, and a red tent—huge, with a main top, smaller rooms off to the side.

He felt drawn to it.

But did it offer sanctuary? A place where the pursuing evil could not enter? He wasn't sure.

He just felt an overwhelming compulsion to go there.

Then another feeling crowded out the first—a warning. For if the tent suggested sanctuary, it also promised great danger.

Then the vision changed.

Now he was walking over a shelf of rock, looking out onto the flats again. But where? Was this the same oasis? He didn't know.

Before him opened a wide hole in the ground—a pit.

There, at the bottom, lay bodies. Skeletons tightly wrapped in desiccated flesh. Skulls with dark holes for eyes looked up at him. And one of these he recognized as his own.

The vision vanished. The scroll's glow dimmed. Again, he held in his hands a precious gold sheet that was already rolling itself back into a compact scroll.

He stared at the rolled metal in his hands, his heart pounding, his mouth open.

"My lord?" Ewan's mouth hung open. "W–what did you see?"

"A vision of the future. But of what, I know not."

At that moment, the noise of a skimmer's grinding wheels burst in from the flats.

"Get aboard, lads. And right quick!" Milosh's voice was tense. "Behind us—we've got trouble."

Tristan shot a glance to the south.

Milosh's theft apparently hadn't been as quiet and stealthy as promised.

Six large skimmers were racing across the flats toward them.

CHAPTER 7

THE BLACK CLOUD

Tristan threw the scroll into his pack, shook Caitir awake, and pulled her and her rucksack toward Milosh's approaching skimmer. Milosh let the sails luff, yanked on the brake, and slowed the wind ship.

Caitir barely had time to gawk at the strange vehicle before Tristan jerked her up onto its deck. Ewan jumped on behind, throwing their waterskins beside the packs.

Milosh yanked on the guy lines, tacking at an angle against the constant westerly winds. Slowly, the ship began picking up speed.

A half-dozen enemy skimmers were bearing down upon them.

Their ship hit a rock and bounced, jostling everyone off their feet. Tristan landed on all fours then crawled to where they'd thrown their packs. Two of their four waterskins were missing. He jumped to the rail and looked aft.

The skins lay in the sand behind them, receding fast. But they couldn't go back.

"We just lost half of our water." He gripped the railing as they hit another stretch of rocks.

"Drat!" Milosh glanced back. "Couldn't avoid those rocks and make distance between us and them. Now we'll just have to stop at an oasis somewhere."

Tristan rushed to secure their remaining packs, remembering Milosh's prior warning that they couldn't trust any of the oases. But now what choice did they have?

Standing up from his work, he examined their ship. Far bigger than what they'd used to cross to the Banshee Spires, this deck could hold perhaps a dozen men, twice their former craft. The mast, too, was taller, and the three spars heading out from the center, like some kind of demented landlocked starfish, were also longer. Unchanged was the spinning, crunching noise from the wheels, and the grit, sand, and pebbles thrown up from the front. Above, the sail was gray, not black like the one the Argyn had given them.

He went to the aft railing. Because Milosh had slowed almost to a stop to pick up his passengers, their adversary's crafts had nearly closed the gap. Now he could even make out those in the nearest vessel. Dark-eyed turbaned men from Sarkenos. Saber-wielding soldiers from Drochtar. And two snarling púcas, already changed into half-men, half-wolves standing at the railing, apart from their fellows.

Then he spied the archers.

Three bowmen were nocking arrows to strings, pulling back, aiming high. They released their projectiles.

"Look out!" he cried.

Heads rose to look, but what could they do? Who could see a falling arrow?

Two shafts bit into the sand just beyond the aft railing. A third dug into the deck beside him. If only they had a bow, they could return fire.

"Don't worry," Milosh called from the wheel. "We're not yet up to speed."

Even as he said this, the gap between them and the enemy ships widened.

The archers drew another round of arrows from their quivers, aimed again.

Tristan rushed to the front, as did Caitir, Yuri, and Ewan.

The arrows fell where he'd just been standing, biting into the deck.

"Faster," Ewan cried.

Milosh continued steering the spoked wheel—just like a real ship's—with ropes leading from the steering wheel along the front spar to the bow wheel.

The archers shot twice more, hitting sand, a spar, and the aft deck before the travelers' vessel pulled out of range. Gradually, the distance between them increased.

"Grabbed the biggest, fastest ship I saw." A grinning Milosh turned to watch the six wind ships behind them lose ground. "But this one lay in the middle of the mess. I guess driving that chariot past half the camp at top speed must have alarmed somebody."

"So much for slipping quietly out of their camp." Caitir gave him a half-smile.

"But look." Yuri pointed behind them. "They're giving up the chase."

Indeed, the skimmers were now turning with the wind and heading back to their camp.

"Strange that they'd give up so quickly." Milosh scratched his chin then attended to the way ahead.

"Maybe because we're so much faster?" Yuri offered.

"Nay." Ewan squinted off the port bow. "Do my eyes deceive me? Is that what I ken it is?"

Tristan stood beside him as did Yuri and Caitir, everyone peering east.

At first, all he could see was a dark smudge on the horizon. But was something churning the sand out there, throwing up debris? It was barely visible. He rubbed his eyes and squinted. Aye, something was out there, something dark and distant, like—

A Black Cloud.

On the horizon.

Heading their direction.

He grabbed the railing, his fingers tightening until they hurt. Now he knew the nature of the vision's nameless, vaguely familiar fear. Now he knew why the enemy skimmers had fled. Even *they* wouldn't sail with such a terror loose upon the sand sea.

He turned from the rail and closed his eyes.

"What is it?" Caitir's frightened voice rose in pitch. "Why are you all so white-faced?"

Tristan whirled to look behind at the distant black smudge. It hadn't come any closer. Had it seen them? He couldn't tell.

He faced Caitir. "Before you woke, the scroll gave me a vision. This thing behind us—'tis some kind of creature. Or spirit. 'Tis as old as Erde itself, something Faolukan awakened by accident. It chased us before." He glanced again at the Black Cloud, appearing slightly larger than a moment ago.

"And we have no idea how to defeat it."

As TRISTAN WATCHED THEIR PURSUER and fought to stay awake, Milosh guided their flight across the flats. Finally, at Milosh's urging, Tristan lay down on the bouncing, jiggling boards beside the others and slept a fitful sleep.

He woke to a bright Ferachtir dawn, already hot, becoming hotter. Immediately, he went aft.

The Black Cloud had grown larger, darker, but still lay perhaps a league or more behind.

While Milosh rested, Tristan took his turn at steering.

The sand churned under their wheels. The flotsam of this arid, barren sea flew up from the grinding front wheel—pebbles, grit, salt, and clay. Above, vultures circled on updrafts over some distant, hapless creature that had wandered too far from water. Ahead, the endless sand stretched to a murky horizon, wavering in the heat.

They sailed on without stopping.

Behind, the Black Cloud inched closer.

FOR FOUR DAYS, THEY FLED across the wasteland. And after four days, the Black Cloud had closed the gap to less than a mile.

On the morning of the fourth day, Ewan shook the remaining two waterskins they'd brought with them.

"We've plenty of food." He jostled the waterskins again. "But we're down to a few sips of water in both skins."

"So we need to stop at the next oasis," said Yuri.

Ewan scanned the horizon. "Since we started, we've seen only one."

"These oases serve up naught but trouble." Milosh scowled. "The Ferachtir are scum, at first welcoming you with smiles. Then they'll rob the tunics off your back and the toenails off'n your toes."

"But how can we stop"—Caitir swept her hand abaft—"with *that* thing behind us?"

"We'll just have to be quick." Milosh winked.

As he'd done a hundred times before, Tristan went aft, gripped the rail, and stared at the pursuing evil. It marred the eastern horizon, a massive, churning, formless storm of darkness. Within its black, roiling walls, lightning flashed, followed by rolling thunder. But worse was the feeling—growing ever stronger—of a deep, soul-numbing dread.

A sense that the Black Cloud wanted to kill.

He feared to stop. What had the vision tried to tell him? Did it identify sanctuary? Or peril?

If they stopped, and the Black Cloud overtook them . . .

He shivered. Nothing could defeat it. Of that, he was certain.

The sun burned hot in a cloudless sky, raising waves of heat off the flats. Without water, they wouldn't last another two days. If they saw an oasis—regardless whether it was the place of his vision or not—they'd have to stop.

The wind ship rolled on, churning up sand.

Behind them, the cloud edged closer.

AT DAWN OF THEIR FIFTH day out from the Sfarsit Mountains, Tristan ran to the aft railing, clutching it with white knuckles. Ewan, Caitir, and Milosh were already there, staring at the approaching menace.

A black, whirling wind, taller than a three-story building and just as wide, churned the sand only a hundred yards back. Another burst of lightning shot diagonally through its revolving murk, followed instantly by thunder. As this illuminated its dark interior, Tristan thought he caught a glimpse of something at its core, something solid and darker yet.

Last night, the feeling of evil had pressed so intense, so thick, upon him, he hadn't slept at all. To take his mind off the encroaching menace, he'd done more than his share at the wheel. If something didn't happen soon, it would catch up to them, engulf them, and then . . .

The closer it came, the more its presence weighed on him. He sensed its need—to kill, to devour the living. But not any living creature. Only human flesh would do. He closed his eyes and tried to shake the dread pressing closer upon him.

As he'd been doing all night, he said another silent prayer to Elyon.

Milosh called out from the bow, "Something on the horizon. Palm trees, I ken."

Tristan spun and faced forward. "An oasis?"

"Aye," said Milosh. "Only the second one since we started. We have to stop there. Someone get the waterskins. Make ready to fill them quickly."

"But 'tis too close," Yuri's high voice warbled from the stern. "If we stop, it will catch us."

"What keeps the oases protected?" Caitir asked. "How are they able to survive out here with that thing on the loose?"

Everyone stared at her. Why hadn't they asked that question before? "Of course," said Tristan, waving a hand across the sandscape. "Something in the oases keeps it at bay. Else no one could live anywhere out here."

Now his companions stared at him.

Milosh grinned. Ewan slapped his leg. Caitir smiled.

Then the front wheel began spinning up twice the usual amount of grit. A rain of sand flew over them, stinging their faces and arms. The skimmer slowed.

"Loose sand!" shouted Milosh. "We're in trouble."

Tristan ran to Milosh's side and scanned the way ahead. They'd entered one of the few spots where clay and salt gave way to loose sand. On the way east, they'd encountered only a handful of such places. By its lighter color, Tristan knew this stretch would end in another hundred yards. He whirled.

The Black Cloud was approaching fast. Only fifty feet away now. It filled the entire eastern view.

Tristan's whole body leaned to the west. Another two hundred feet to get free. They'd still be in the loose stuff when the thing hit them.

Behind, the cloud spun closer.

O Elyon, he prayed, *Help us out of this. Save us from this approaching evil.*

One hundred feet until harder ground.

But only twenty feet before the Black Cloud's whirling, spinning darkness engulfed them. Its noise became deafening—the sound of the whirlwind. Angry. Whistling. Punctuated by thunder.

"Everyone to the bow," Tristan shouted. At least that would give them a few more feet. Yuri and Ewan ran with him beside Caitir to the farthest section of deck.

"It wants one of us," screamed Yuri. "It won't be happy until one of us dies."

"How do you know that?" Tristan shot him a worried gaze.

"I just do."

Had Yuri felt the same thing as he?

Darkness engulfed the aft wheels. The ship lurched but continued on at the same rate. A dark storm crept toward them, a terrible wind of evil, spattering sand with such velocity, it seemed to eat away at the wood. The vessel began shuddering. The wood vibrated.

Everyone smashed themselves against the bow rails.

Caitir grasped Tristan's arm. She buried her face in his neck.

He gripped the rail and pulled them both as flat against it as he could.

Only five feet separated them from death.

"If it doesn't get one of us," yelled Yuri, "we'll all die."

Yuri was right. And at that moment, Tristan knew what he had to do. It was over.

All they had now was each other. And unless one of them gave up their life, they were as good as dead.

The Deamhan Lord had won. The Scepter, the Augury—none of it mattered now. Death had come for them all.

He shot a glance west. Fifty feet to hard ground. Too far. They weren't going to make it.

He pried Caitir's hands off his shoulder and held her at arm's length. He kissed her. Then he pushed her toward Ewan.

Caitir's horrified glance told him she knew what he was about to do. Her head began shaking back and forth. "Nay," said her lips, but the whirlwind stole the sound.

Pain scrunched Ewan's face, even as he grabbed and held both her arms. He, too, understood.

Milosh hadn't seen. His body was smashed up against the wheel, trying to steer.

Tristan took one step toward the darkness.

But Yuri yanked him back. Facing his new friends, he took three backward steps toward the whirlwind.

Yuri smiled once.

Then the maw of churning, roiling evil whisked him up. In an instant, he was gone.

The Black Cloud fell behind, contracted into a single, dense, spinning mass. The blackness seemed to whirl faster. For one moment, it turned red.

The wind ship hit the harder ground beyond. The vessel lurched forward. They began to pull away from the spinning evil.

Tristan ran to the aft rail and stood as the Black Cloud resumed its pursuit. But now it was two hundred yards distant.

In the west, only a half mile away—the oasis.

After slogging through the loose sand, the ship now seemed to fly. The oasis came into view.

Behind them, the cloud of evil suddenly halted its forward progress. Their vessel began opening a larger gap.

Milosh pulled on the sheets, shortening sail, slowing their speed.

Ahead and approaching rapidly—a grove of palms. A pool of bubbling water.

And an enormous red tent.

CHAPTER 8

THE OASIS

Tristan, Ewan, and Caitir remained at the aft railing, staring at the receding monster that had just taken Yuri.

Then the realization sank in. Yuri was gone. He'd given up his life for them.

Caitir threw her arms around Tristan and sobbed. He held her close, trying himself to fight off tears.

"He was a better friend than I'd thought," said Milosh, still guiding the ship. "Who else would have done such a thing?"

"He sacrificed his life for all of us." Ewan kept his voice low. "But Tristan, here, was about to do it first. You didna see because you were steering. Then Yuri stepped in and took his place."

Milosh gawked at Tristan. "Is that true, my friend?"

Tristan turned to face him. He wiped moisture from the corner of an eye but said nothing. He pulled a sobbing Caitir closer to his breast and faced east, where Yuri had been taken.

"Aye," answered Ewan. "'Tis true."

Milosh whistled then slowed the ship further. "You must be right about these oases, Tristan, my friend. Surely, they've got something that keeps the Black Cloud away. We've got to find out what it is."

Gently, Tristan held Caitir at arm's length. "We need to say words over Yuri. He cannot go to his death without words."

"Aye, my lord," added Ewan. "Say something. For all of us."

Still at the aft rail, Tristan closed his eyes. "O Elyon, creator of worlds, we thank you for the brief time we shared with our friend, Yuri. Faolukan destroyed his village and his life. Yet, at peril to himself, Yuri helped us escape Drochtar's evil. Now he's given his life so that we could go on. He did not know you, but please take him into Neavh. Please have mercy on him."

The wind ship ground to a halt. Milosh cleared his throat. "We're on the rock shelf surrounding every oasis. We'll have to anchor the ship and walk."

Tristan opened his eyes and wiped them again.

Ewan cast a disapproving glance at Milosh and again stared east. "Too many lost on this trek, my lord. Too many."

Tristan nodded.

Caitir laid a hand on his shoulder and smiled.

At Milosh's urging, they wrapped the sail against the mast, grabbed their packs, and jumped onto solid ground. Tristan tested his legs under him, savoring the feeling of standing on something other than a bouncing wooden deck.

Nearby rested another skimmer, its mast also naked of sail.

Unsteadily at first, they walked across flat rock toward a palm grove. Clear water gurgled from the center of a pool nearly fifty feet across. On its banks and in the field beyond, lambs and goats grazed on lush, green grass.

Tristan breathed deeply the scent of moist vegetation. After so long on the arid flats, it helped buoy spirits depressed from the loss of yet another friend.

They entered the grove and walked to the pool.

Ewan knelt and began filling their waterskins.

Before he'd finished, a man's voice, deep and sonorous, came from behind, "Turn around, my friends."

Tristan spun. Before him stood a tall, slim man, dark of hair and beard, with high cheekbones, eyes as black as night, and a face as gaunt as the flats itself. A gray robe dropped to his feet. Sandals clad his feet, and his hands held a bow, ready and nocked with an arrow. His thin face bore an expression of amused detachment. Around his neck—a silver torc.

Beside him, a younger man wore features similar to his companion—same dark beard and hair, same high cheeks, same gaunt frame. Tristan assumed he was the man's son. He stood with sword drawn. But his hand shook.

Behind both stood six men of varying ages. By their demeanor and the meanness of their dress, they must be servants or slaves. Four of these bore swords. Two carried bows nocked with arrows. All seemed thin and greatly malnourished.

"I am Vasil Catargiu, king of the oasis of Lonely Sands," said the tall leader. "Please announce yourselves."

The image from the vision flashed before Tristan's eyes—of a pit full of dried-up bodies. Biting his lip, he tried to rid himself of the memory. Then he smiled and bowed. "I am Tristan mac Torn of the distant land of Ériu. This is my betrothed, Caitir, my squire, Ewan." They bowed low.

"Ériu . . ." Vasil rubbed his beard. "Where is this country of which I've never heard?"

"From here, one must cross the Tatra Mountains, the Waldreich, and then go north through the Fell Bogs. Then one sails by ship for ten days across the Sea of Albion to our fair island."

"Of such great waters I have heard. Oh, to see such a sight! Water as far as one can see? What a wonder that must be."

"It is, my lord." Tristan smiled.

"And who is the one with you?" asked King Vasil. "For he carries not the look of your country, but of the Romely Plains."

"I am Milosh, my lord." And he, too, bowed low. "A trader who's joined his plight with my friends, here."

"Do you come as friends?" Vasil faced Tristan and raised his bow a notch. "Or as foes?"

"As friends, my lord," said Tristan. "Travelers seeking water, rest, and safe passage through your oasis."

"How"—Vasil pointed east—"did you escape the Fekete Felhö?"

"Do you mean the Black Cloud?"

"I do."

"One of our companions…" Tristan closed his eyes and shook his head. "He gave himself up to it. He died so that we might live."

Vasil's right eyebrow rose. Then he dropped his bow. He motioned to the others, and they, too, lowered their weapons. "Then I welcome you to Lonely Sands and our sanctuary. Our tradition requires us to extend hospitality to all who come in peace, as appears you do."

Tristan bowed again. "We come in peace. For the last five days, we've fled from the Black Cloud. This morning, we drank the last of our water. Now, we seek only to quench our thirst, fill our waterskins, and purchase a few more skins—if it does not presume on your hospitality to ask for such. Then we'll be off."

A fleeting smile crossed Vasil's face. "My friends, you are indeed welcome in my tent. But you must stay at least until tomorrow. You must feast and drink with us. Then we'll send you off with full skins, supplies, and our blessings. Too few sail the sand to my kingdom. And it's been months since we welcomed travelers, weary or otherwise."

"We'd like to, my lord, but our travel is most urgent." As a scowl began on the king's face, Tristan quickly added, "But we could certainly use a grand meal and a good night's rest. Perhaps we can delay our departure until tomorrow."

"Good." Vasil beamed. "Then you will come with me."

They followed the king's entourage across the grass toward the red tent.

At the entrance, the king stopped. "Before you enter, I must ask you to leave your weapons with my son, Grigore. None are allowed inside."

Milosh threw a suspicious glance at Vasil and grasped his sword hilt as if he wouldn't comply.

Ewan regarded the man, his own sword, and then started unbuckling his belt. Caitir nodded.

They handed their weapons to the shorter Grigore. Only then did Milosh give up his weapon.

❖

THE INSTANT HE ENTERED THE massive red tent, Tristan sensed its seductive opulence—like slipping under a cool spring after toiling all day in the hot sun. Multicolored carpets, thick and exquisitely patterned, covered every inch of floor where the stuffed pillows did not.

Two women in scantily clad shifts sat in one corner, playing a lyre and a flute, filling the air with a pleasing melody. More women lay on pillows beyond, smiling eagerly at the newcomers. But each appeared thin, on the verge of starvation.

"First, you must bathe." Vasil motioned to the right, toward a room in the next tent. "Then we'll dine. Please follow Madalina."

Fearing to offend their host, Tristan nodded. The thin, dark-haired woman with alluring dark eyes identified as Madalina wore only what appeared to be a flimsy undergarment. She led them under a bead-draped doorway into the next room. There waited three smiling women—all thin, all wearing little more than Madalina. They stood beside two pools of cool, clear water, fed by an underground spring.

"If you undress," offered Madalina, smiling, "we'll bathe you. If your custom demands it, your woman"—she gestured to Caitir—"can use the adjoining room." She pointed to a smaller pool peeking out from a curtain on the right.

Tristan took in the sparsely clad women. "I need no help bathing."

"After all that dust and grime," said Caitir, "a bath is welcome, indeed. But I, too, don't need any help." She made her way to the nearby pool.

"Me neither," said Ewan.

But Milosh eagerly began doffing his clothes and waved for Madalina to join him. She smiled, slipped into the pool, and gave her back to Ewan and Tristan. How thin she appeared!

Tristan motioned, and the rest of the women departed.

With some semblance of privacy, he and Ewan unclothed and dropped into the cool waters. Instantly, relief soaked into his bones, and the cares of the journey seemed to slip away. He sighed. Moments later, a blonde-haired woman appeared bearing a tray with goblets of some kind of spiced wine. They each took one.

Caitir's head was barely visible in her pool around the corner of the curtain. He nodded as she, too, accepted a glass.

The woman servant returned a moment later bearing a pile of cloth. "If it pleases my lords"—blinking seductively, she bowed—"I will clean your clothing and leave these for you to wear while dining. I'll have your garments cleaned and ready by this evening." She lifted robes of the most elegant silk.

After she'd taken their dirty tunics and breeches, Ewan turned to him. "This hospitality is unexpected, my lord." Only Ewan's head and a hand holding the brass goblet stuck up above the waters.

"Aye. It seems our hosts are eager for company."

"Who can blame them"—Ewan waved his goblet toward the east—"living out here in the middle of nowhere. But we must learn the secret of how they keep themselves safe from the Black Cloud."

"We will, Ewan. We will. Right now, I'm beginning to enjoy this respite."

"Methinks we should stay an extra day," called Milosh from the next pool. Madalina ran a cloth over his shoulders and forehead. Water dripped down his face. "Or even two."

"If only we could, Milosh." Tristan leaned back against the pool's edge. A sudden, irresistible urge to agree to Milosh's request welled up inside him. Why not stay an extra day? Or even two? What could it hurt? They were exhausted, worn out from constantly fleeing one danger after another. They had what they came for. Why couldn't they enjoy, a wee bit longer, such unexpected hospitality?

CHAPTER 9

UNDER THE RED TENT

After they'd bathed and dressed, Madalina led the travelers three tents away to a low table piled high with dates, figs, pomegranates, and oranges. Women brought in trays laden with lamb, dripping in a sauce so savory, Tristan couldn't stop eating it. Vasil offered them flatbread, with oil and honey, and something called rice imported from Gopal.

"We are overwhelmed by your hospitality, Vasil," said Tristan over a mouthful of spicy lamb. "'Twas most unexpected."

Vasil waved a dismissing hand and threw an olive into his mouth. "We enjoy visitors. Don't we, Grigore?"

His son sat beside him, only picking at his food. "For what they have to offer, aye."

"All guests have something to offer, Grigore. Company. News. Stories. Sometimes even a trinket or two. Is that not correct, Tristan mac Torn?"

Tristan swallowed and nodded. "But we have no gifts for you, my lord. Only news of the outside."

"Then let us hear it."

Then he told him what they knew of the army of Drochtar, how it was leaving the east but didn't reveal its destination or anything about the fleets assembling at Fjernshavn and in the south.

"Ah, how fortunate we are"—Vasil raised his goblet of sweet wine—"that they leave us alone. We send skimmers south only to trade. We are a threat to no one. All we want is to be left in peace. Isn't that right, Grigore?"

Grigore grunted and examined the food he'd hardly touched.

"But tell me, Tristan, what brings you to our fair oasis?"

Momentarily at a loss for words, he took another sip of wine. "Trade, my lord." He shot a glance at Milosh. "In Amridmor. We sought profit in trade with them. But . . . but—"

"Aye, my lord." Milosh stepped in. "We heard they were desperate for silk, wine, and gold. But our news was dated. Hard times have befallen that city, and they have little to offer in return." He shook his head dramatically. "Hard times."

Grigore narrowed his eyes at Milosh then at Tristan. "How did you cross the Tatras? If you came from the east, how did you get past Faolukan's stranglehold on the passes, past the Great Bridge and his army?"

"Why through the Valley of Flowers." Milosh flashed a sly grin. "We bribed the wizard Zalán."

Grigore's mouth dropped open, but Vasil only waved a hand and smiled. "Intrepid you are, my friends. I salute you." He raised his glass again.

Tristan drank to the toast then set down his goblet.

A man burst into the room, followed by one of the armed men they'd met at the pool. Emaciated, thin, and obviously starving, the man fell at Vasil's feet.

"Redeem me, lord. Save me from this affliction you've cursed me wi—"

A foot kicked his ribs so hard, the man grunted and slumped to the side. The soldier's heavy hand grabbed his arm, jerked him to his feet, and began to haul him away. The soldier shot a glance at Vasil. "Forgive me, my lord. We couldn't stop him."

Vasil's glance bored into the man. "See it never happens again."

The soldier bowed and dragged the still gasping wretch from the tent.

Vasil turned to his guests. "I'm sorry for that. We found him wandering on the flats. His mind"—he waved a hand—"'tis gone. He imagines many things. Once he's nourished, he'll recover, I expect."

Tristan nodded. But as he picked up a piece of bread, he wondered: With such food as this tent offered, why did all the men and women of Lonely Sands appear so thin, gaunt, and sickly?

Was it was just the physique of their race? He shook his head and returned to his meal.

Soon, the warm bath, the sumptuous food, the excellent wine—everything seemed to call for sleep. "My lord, this meal—'tis the best we've eaten in a month. And your wine, 'tis—"

"'Tis the best I've ever drunk," added Ewan.

"Aye to that. Here's to our host." Milosh lifted his goblet and drank what must have been his sixth glass. "And to his excellent table."

"I hope 'tis only the first of many such meals you'll share with us." Vasil waved off the compliment. "Perhaps now, having tasted what we have to offer, you'll stay an extra day?"

"If only we could, my lord." Tristan pushed back from the table, his belly full. "But we . . . we must—"

Ewan laid a hand on his shoulder. "One more day canna hurt, can it? Such food I've never tasted. I could sore use a longer rest."

"Aye, Tristan," Milosh agreed. "One more day?"

"What about you, Caitir?" Tristan faced her.

"Who could begrudge us another day to regain our strength? Let's stay."

He smiled at Vasil, now beaming. "One more day, my lord. Then we must surely depart."

THAT NIGHT THEY LAY UNDER soft furs. Tristan slept so soundly, he marveled at how late he slept the next day. Upon wakening, they found their traveling tunics folded and cleaned beside their packs. On a whim, he opened his pack, checked it, and was satisfied everything was still present.

When he went outside to stretch his legs, the afternoon sun was already low in the sky.

"It appears you've slept through the day, my lord." Vasil smiled and stood beside him. "Come join us for a midday meal."

A bit stunned by how long he'd slept, Tristan followed him back inside for a meal of dates, figs, flatbread slathered with oil and honey, some kind of goat's milk pudding, scrambled ostrich eggs, and more wine. Strangely, after the grand meal he'd eaten the night before, he was still as hungry as if he hadn't eaten in a week. He devoured everything put before him, even wanting more.

Then Vasil produced a tall pipe stuffed with some kind of aromatic weed. He gathered them in a circle, lit the pipe, and passed around the long tube that led to the base. The smoke swirled around Tristan's head with a lazy, comfortable feeling. Some kind of mild inebriate. That, combined with another glass of the spiced wine, made him nearly forget why they'd come here.

He shook his head to clear it and turned to his host. "Are you not troubled by the Black Cloud that prowls the flats?"

Vasil took another puff on the pipe and passed it to Tristan. "Nay. Every oasis on the flats holds the secret that keeps their people safe."

Tristan declined a second puff, as did Caitir beside him.

"And what secret might that be?" asked Caitir.

"If I told you, it would no longer be a secret, would it? But I will tell you this: 'tis magic as old as the flats itself."

Tristan bent forward, one elbow braced on an upraised knee. "Then the Black Cloud is truly ancient?"

"It is. And without the magic that the maker of worlds bestowed on us long ago, no one could live here. For the Fekete Felhö has stalked the flats since Faolukan awakened it by mistake from the belly of the Sfarsit Mountains in some forgotten past."

"You speak of Elyon?" Tristan's eyes widened.

"Elonin is the name our people once called him."

"Do you worship him now?" Ewan, too, declined the pipe and passed it to Milosh, who eagerly sucked in more smoke.

"We do not. We have our own gods. But we are grateful for his ancient gift. Occasionally, we offer Elonin a goat or two."

One brow rising, Caitir scooted closer. "Can we see this gift he gave you?"

"Nay!" Vasil's voice rose in anger. "As I've said, 'tis a secret. And you will speak of it no more."

"Forgive us." Tristan bowed his head. "We didn't mean to offend."

Vasil's smile slipped back onto his face. Receiving the pipe from Milosh, he sucked and blew a smoke ring. "Forgiven. Tonight, we will sup late. 'Tis a special dish of lamb in a red sauce so savory, you'll think the gods themselves provided the food."

"We believe only in Elyon, my lord." Tristan rose from the table. "But we do look forward to another of your feasts."

THAT EVENING THEY FEASTED ON a second offering of food so delicious, Tristan's taste buds seemed alive half the night later. His hunger knew no bounds. With everything they'd eaten already, he should have been stuffed. Yet he felt like a starving man. The wine was an ambrosia so sweet, it satisfied his innermost cravings and quenched desires he didn't even know he had. The more he drank, the more he wanted. But it didn't seem to make him drunk. And the food, though satisfying, never seemed to make him overfull.

Before he retired that night, Vasil offered the three men each a woman to bed with. Tristan had heard of such customs. The women stood before them in gossamer shifts, having freshly bathed, with smiling faces.

As Caitir scowled, Tristan declined, explaining his betrothal to her. He would never sleep with any woman but Caitir, and only after they were married.

Ewan, too, shook his head, nay. "I have a wife back in Ewhain Macha. She's not seen much of me these last years. But I'll stay true to her."

Vasil seemed disappointed as his glance settled on Milosh.

The Romely trader, of course, eagerly accepted. He followed Madalina to a separate room beyond the curtain where they'd slept the first night.

The man was incorrigible. He seemed to avail himself of every pleasure that came along, no matter how degenerate.

As Tristan fell asleep that night, dreaming of the meal they'd just eaten, the nectar of wine they'd drunk, a nagging feeling crept into his thoughts.

After everything he'd eaten and drunk, he could eat still more, drink still more.

And if his hosts ate and drank the same way he'd seen them do this night, why were they all so lean and gaunt?

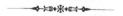

LATE THE NEXT DAY, HE woke, still marveling at the quality and quantity of food they'd eaten the previous night, for it still titillated his tongue. Even after yesterday's feast, today he was famished.

Again, the sun was low in the sky.

"You'll have to rise a bit earlier if you want to travel by day, my lord." Vasil came up beside him. "But let me offer you a late-afternoon repast. Then, perhaps, you'll be able to make a few leagues before sunset?"

Tristan stared over the pool, out through the gaps in the palms to the flats beyond. How could they leave without knowing the secret of avoiding the Black Cloud? He'd been in every room of the massive tent complex, seen everything, and still had not come across anything remotely resembling the magic Vasil had hinted at. Surely, that was a reason to stay. That and to partake of one more delicious feast.

"Or," Vasil continued, "you could stay an extra day?"

"Aye." Tristan turned back into the red tent, already anticipating another fantastic meal. "Perhaps one more day."

THE AFTERNOON BATH SOOTHED AND eased every pain. The evening meal surpassed even the previous two feasts. And last night's sleep was deeper, longer, and more restful than the previous two nights. Again, he dreamed of food, wine, and of luxuriating under Vasil's red tent.

But when Tristan woke to another late-afternoon sun, he asked Ewan, "Was it only two days ago we arrived? I've lost track. Last night's meal was so good, the wine so delicate and luscious, I feel like we've entered Neavh."

Ewan frowned, pulled on his mustache. "I believe you're right, my lord. We arrived only yesterday. Tomorrow, we should leave. But, my lord"—he pointed to Tristan's belt wrapping his tunic—"you could use a few pounds on you. Our trip from Drochtar must have taken its toll."

Tristan grabbed a section of skin around his waist and tugged. How much weight had he lost? "'Tis good, I think, that Vasil puts on such sumptuous feasts. I do believe we've all lost weight since our flight from Drochtar. I've also noticed I cannot keep my armband in place. I've stored it in my pack." He glanced at Ewan. "You, too, could use a few good meals."

Ewan nodded. "I feel like a starving man. And I'd never refuse a feast like the ones this Vasil puts on."

MORNING AFTER MORNING, TRISTAN WOKE to the same late-afternoon sun, thinking he had only just arrived two days before.

And whenever he asked Ewan and Caitir how long the Company had stayed with Vasil, they concurred. Only two days. Always, he ascribed it to the profound weakness their five-day flight across the flats had brought them.

Night after night, Milosh slept with every woman who came to him, Madalina most often, but no one remembered. Always did Milosh wake last. And whenever Tristan confronted him with the same question he'd put to the others, Milosh simply shrugged. He no longer seemed to care.

Every morning, Vasil came to him, appearing to have fleshed out a bit more since the day before. But Tristan didn't notice. Likewise, Grigore, and the soldiers and the women inside—all became healthier.

Each day was the second day, and Tristan would search for the secret of avoiding the Black Cloud. But though he wandered every corner of the red tent and the oasis environs, he saw nothing hinting of Elyon's magic.

And each afternoon when they woke, it was ever the same. Always, they'd arrived only two days hence. And each night before they slept, they marveled at how much weight each had lost on their five-day trip from Mam Giorag. Always, they vowed to stay just one more day, partaking of Vasil's feasts, for surely, they must regain their strength before starting out again.

◄ ►◄◊►◄※►◄◊►► ►

TRISTAN WOKE IN THE MIDDLE of the night, his heart pounding, sweat beading on his forehead. In his dream, he'd been standing at the edge of the pit, looking down at an emaciated version of himself, nothing but dried skin stretched tight over bone.

The pit. He'd almost forgotten it.

Sitting up on his furs, he shook his head to clear it. A single cresset burned in the corner. To his right, Caitir lay beside him. To his left, Ewan snored.

He pulled on the silken robe Vasil had given him and stood. Taking one step, he staggered and rubbed his eyes. He needed to use the latrine outside.

As quietly as he could, his bare feet walked the carpet, passed the curtains separating their sleeping quarters from the main room. Beside the main flap, one of Vasil's armed servants snored in a divan.

Tristan pushed through to the outside. He sucked in the cool night air washing across the flats, driven by the constant westerly wind, then made his way north to the latrine. After relieving himself, he stretched.

What was that dream, again? He couldn't remember. Was it all the rich food and wine he'd eaten and drunk last night and the night before that addled his brain? Aye, it must be that. He yawned, started walking back.

You dreamed about the pit.

The words seared themselves into his thoughts, and he stopped.

The pit. Elyon had called attention to it. It must be important. And he'd almost forgotten it.

Only yesterday, he'd circumnavigated the oasis and found nothing. Hadn't he? Perhaps tonight, he'd see something different. To stroll around the entire oasis would be about a mile. Walking southeast, he followed its perimeter. As before, flat rock fought with sand and clay.

Ahead was the skimmer they'd parked two days ago on the edge of the rock. He approached it.

Odd. Every flat surface was covered with a thick layer of sand as if it had lain here for weeks.

He passed the skimmer belonging to the oasis, a wee bit smaller than theirs. Its deck and rails were clean. It had recently been used.

Crossing more barren rock, he came to the westernmost point of the oasis. A short ways out on the flats, one of the frequent rock outcroppings rose above the plains. A jackal stood there now, pawing at the sand. On his walk yesterday, he wasn't certain, but he had a vague recollection of seeing this outcropping. Something now drew him toward it.

His bare feet crunched over sand, clay, and salt. Pebbles dug into his soles, bringing him even more awake. He stubbed a toe on the hidden stump of some dead bush. As he approached the rocky rise, the jackal lifted its head then loped across the sand into the night.

He walked to the dark place in the outcropping where the animal had been.

Flat rock surrounded an open pit about forty feet across. He peered into its depths. Covering the floor about ten feet down were hundreds—nay, thousands!—of skeletons. But no ordinary skeletons, these. The bones were dressed with skin drawn taut, skin dried and desiccated until it barely covered the skeletal forms. Staring up at him was a man he vaguely recognized. A man from a day or two ago. Or was it longer than that?

Suddenly, his mind cleared. The spell that had fogged his brain for the last—what? Four weeks?

Gone.

Aye, a spell had ensorcelled them all. He and his companions had been bewitched!

The man looking up at him was the same unfortunate who'd burst in on their second evening's meal. Now he was skin-wrapped bone.

Now he knew. That evening occurred four weeks ago.

He shuddered. How was this possible?

With new eyes, Tristan examined his own arms. They'd lost half their bulk. He felt his face. Skin barely covered his cheekbones. His legs, too, were nothing but sticks.

Oh, Elyon, what has happened to us?

He circled the pit, peering at the thousands of skeletons down there. This had been going on for a long, long time. At the far end, not six feet down, lay the Company's weapons. Close by, a rope was anchored to a stake. Perhaps allowing access to the pit? To rearrange bodies and get them to the center? He shuddered at the thought of such grisly work.

They must leave here at once. Tonight?

Perhaps he should wake his companions, bring them here, retrieve their weapons, and escape? He started to untie the rope but stopped. He realized how weak he was. As were his friends. Now that he remembered every detail of their stay, he knew how, day by day, they'd steadily lost weight, energy, and life.

And all this occurred while the occupants of this oasis gained weight, became stronger, and increased their vitality.

Were he and his friends losing their life force? Was that what Vasil was stealing from them?

He slammed a fist into a palm. How could they leave in their present condition? They needed to eat a few meals while not under Vasil's curse and regain their strength.

But tonight, the spell still lay upon Ewan, Caitir, and Milosh—a spell he had to break.

He left the pit, hurried across the flats to the tent. He passed the still-sleeping guard. With clear vision, he was now able to compare the man's condition with what he'd looked like when they first arrived. Weeks ago, this man was thin, gaunt, sickly. Today the guard appeared healthy, well fed, and strong.

Back in his sleeping quarters, he shook Caitir and Ewan awake. Then he roused Milosh. Milosh's nightly companion was still asleep as Tristan pulled him beside the others.

"W–why have you wakened us?" Milosh yawned. "Let me go back to sleep."

"Nay." He fixed his gaze on each. "You must come with me, quietly. Outside. Tonight. I've something you must see."

"Canna it wait until tomorrow?" Caitir's eyes drooped.

He shook her shoulders until she focused on him.

"Nay, my friends! If you don't look at what I have to show you tonight, we'll all die here."

Their eyes were open and awake now. Then they followed him outside, across the sand, to the open pit.

Just as with Tristan, when they saw what happened to Vasil's previous guests, the spell departed.

Milosh stared into the pit and spat to the side. Anger bulged his eyes. Then he saw their weapons at the far end. "We should take our blades, kill them all, and leave tonight."

"Nay." Tristan held up a hand. "Look at yourselves. You're as weak and thin as I am. Let us instead eat a few meals they won't steal from us and gain back a bit of strength. Let us then leave the day after tomorrow, when all are asleep."

In turn, each nodded agreement.

"Will they notice, if we eat without the spell on us?" Ewan faced Tristan. "And if they do not gain from it?"

"I hope not. But we're too weak to leave tonight. We'd not survive the trip to the Tatras. If we can get away with it, we should try to sneak as much food off the tables tomorrow as possible."

"Aye," agreed Milosh.

Then Caitir spoke for everyone. "What kind of curse has befallen these people, that they must steal the very flesh off our bodies to survive?"

70

Chapter **10**

A FINAL REPAST

Tristan woke early the next morning and left the tent.

Since they'd been waking regularly in midafternoon for weeks, Vasil appeared immediately suspicious. "For only your second day here, I thought you would have slept longer."

Now that his memory stretched back to the day they arrived, Tristan remembered how thin and sickly the man first appeared. As he now regarded the king of Lonely Sands, he was shocked to see how healthy, strong, and vibrant the man had become. "I guess . . . I feel more rested today." He bit his lip. "I must congratulate you on the wonderful dinner you provided last night. I've never enjoyed such a repast more."

Vasil raised an eyebrow. "Then you will surely revel in tonight's feast. We've planned something truly special."

Tristan stretched and yawned. "I'm looking forward to it."

Because the others woke shortly afterward, their hosts provided them not only with breakfast, but another midafternoon dinner of flatbread stuffed with lamb and spices, and, of course, the ever-present spiced wine. At each of these meals, the group slipped as much bread and meat as possible into their tunic pockets. After another bath and a walk around the oasis, they sat down to one of the largest feasts yet— horse, curried and slow-roasted with ginger; lamb steeped in a red spice; imported, fermented cabbage; figs and dates; and more spiced wine.

When he pushed back from the table, Tristan could feel the energy returning to his limbs.

But Vasil regarded him with one eye raised and a frown tightening his lips. "Did you enjoy your meal, my friends?"

"Truly, one of the best I've ever eaten," said Milosh over a mouthful of horse.

"How about you, Ewan?" Vasil turned his attention to the squire, still shoving fermented cabbage into his mouth.

"Most excellent, my lord." Ewan swallowed. "Most excellent."

Vasil's head swiveled slowly toward Tristan. "And have you been exploring the grounds, seeing what little we have to offer?"

Tristan gulped. Could Vasil feel the difference now that the spell was broken? Did he know? "I–I did walk the grounds. But as you say"—he glanced at Caitir, who had just finished eating—"'tis a small oasis."

"But perhaps you've ventured out onto the flats a bit? Maybe beyond the perimeter?"

"Oh nay, my lord." Tristan waved off the suggestion. "Nothing to see out there, is there?"

"No, I suppose not." He faced Grigore, now staring at each of the guests in turn.

Grigore leaned over, whispered something in his father's ear, then stood and left the table.

Vasil, too, rose and regarded each of them. "I trust you will sleep well tonight, my friends. We take pride in giving our guests the most interesting experience we can. We're always reluctant when it's time for them to . . . depart."

"You have treated us well, my lord." Tristan tried on a smile. "We could not have imagined such savory food, such a restful stopover. My compliments."

Vasil bowed slightly, but no smile passed his lips. Then he, too, stood and left. But in all the time they'd eaten with their hosts, Vasil had never left the table before his guests.

Now only a few servants remained.

Caitir leaned over and whispered in Tristan's ear, "Do you think he suspects?"

"I don't know," he whispered. "But we're leaving tonight."

THAT EVENING AS THEY LAY in their beds, none of them slept. Madalina did not go as usual to Milosh's bed—another indication that their hosts might suspect something. Indeed, the rest of the tent was unusually quiet. When they'd waited long after the time most should have been asleep, Tristan rose and whispered to the others. "'Tis time. Let's go."

Leaping to their feet, they dressed in their original tunics, not the loose robes their hosts had provided. Then they grabbed the packs they'd arrived with, now filled with as much bread and meat as they could pilfer.

Tristan stuck his head through the curtain separating their sleeping quarters from the main room. He looked back at the others. "No guard at the entrance."

"Vasil must suspect." Milosh's hand formed into a fist and hit his leg.

Being as quiet as they could, they walked the carpet to the main flap. Tristan held up a hand for them to wait then opened it a crack. Not twenty yards in front stood all the men of Lonely Sands, armed with sabers and bows. He pulled the flap closed.

"They're waiting for us. We can't go out this way."

"I'm familiar with these tents." Milosh whirled and began walking back through the main room. "Maybe we can get out the back."

They followed him beyond their sleeping quarters to the far wall. Milosh rolled back the thick carpet on the floor. Beneath it, sewn to the tent walls, was a three-foot section of tarp extending along the floor. He lifted this up and ducked under. It was so tight he could barely slip beneath.

"No one on this side," came his muffled voice. Then he wiggled through.

The others followed.

When they left the tent, they were on the northern side of the oasis. Tristan motioned for them to follow, and he took them the short distance through the palms to the edge of the flats. "We need our weapons from the pit. Let's approach it from the rear. Just in case there's a watchman."

Milosh nodded. The others agreed.

Tristan led them north, far out onto the sand before he turned west. They walked south for a ways then came up behind the pit's outcropping. As he suspected, three armed men faced the oasis, watching for any attempt to cross directly from the east. Tristan led them to the back of the pit where a rope still led down to the pile of discarded weapons.

He shimmied into the mound of bodies. Even though the sun had long ago dried the corpses, tightening skin over skulls and bones, the odor made him gag. Beside the weapon pile, the skull of a young girl, now a scarecrow, stared up at him with dark holes where her eyes should have been. Her once-blonde hair dropped haphazardly over a cadaverous face. When he had to step on her ribs to get at the weapons, he shuddered.

Concentrate on the task, he told himself. Picking through the cache, he passed swords, knives, and even two bows with full quivers up to Caitir and Ewan. How many unfortunate travelers had stopped here over the years to feed the Lonely Sands curse?

As he climbed back out, he turned away from the pit and breathed deeply. "The evil in this place is overpowering."

"Aye." Ewan stared at the bodies. "I canna wait to leave."

Tristan took them behind the outcropping until they could no longer make out the backs of the watchmen. "Let's go far around on the flats before we turn back and get our skimmer. No one will expect us to approach from the south."

"But if we take the skimmer back out again," said Ewan, "won't the Black Cloud follow us?"

"It may. But what else can we do?"

"How does their skimmer come and go without being chased?" asked Caitir.

Tristan cocked his head, taking in her flashing eyes, still so full of life despite being sunken in her face. "Good question. Perhaps we should take a look at theirs before we leave?"

They walked due west for perhaps a mile before turning south and east for the same distance. The oasis became only a smudge of distant palms on the northern horizon. They sat on the sand to rest and catch their breath.

Oh, but how tired that wee bit of walking made him! "When we arrive at the oasis, the rest of you make ready our skimmer. Let's hope they've not put a guard on it. I'll go straight to their sand ship and search it. Raise sail, and I'll jump on as you pass."

"Don't miss us, Tristan," Milosh warned. "Once we get going, it'll be difficult to slow down."

"I won't."

After everyone had rested, they began walking north.

Sand and clay crunched under their feet. The westerly wind swirled around them. The palms grew ever larger, as did two silhouettes just beyond the skimmer. They faced north toward the tent.

When they were within a hundred yards, Milosh whispered, "Guards on the skimmer. But they're facing north."

"Can you take them out without alerting everyone?" asked Tristan.

"Aye." Milosh grinned.

Tristan nodded then separated from the others and headed for the oasis's skimmer. He clambered aboard and searched the holds under the deck for anything resembling a charm. Nothing. He searched the mast, the spars, even the sail. Then his glance fell on the steering column. An oval disk of purest gold was embedded in the steering wheel's post. He examined it more closely. What looked like a scepter was engraved in the center, with a crown at each end. He slid his fingers over it.

An electric feeling ran through his hand and up his arm. It was—

An amulet!

The blast of a battle horn interrupted his discovery. Milosh and the others were in the skimmer, approaching rapidly. Behind them ran two soldiers of Lonely Sands. The guards waved swords, tried to nock arrows to strings while running.

"Get ready!" shouted Milosh.

Tristan bent to the steering column. Jerking his knife from its sheath, he rammed it into the wood beside the amulet. It dug in. He tried to pry loose the charm, but it wouldn't budge. Turning to the approaching skimmer, he shouted, "Slow down! I've found it."

"Can't," cried Milosh. "Get aboard or be left behind."

Tristan stuck the knife into a different spot, leaned into it with all his might. Nothing.

The skimmer was almost beside him.

He jabbed the blade into a slot at the bottom. Again, he pried. The amulet moved a fraction of an inch. He pushed, wiggled, and then slammed the hilt with a fist, driving it deep underneath the amulet. When he lifted up on the blade, the amulet popped free.

He grabbed it, sheathed his knife, and raced for the skimmer.

But it was already passing him. He sprinted, running as fast as his legs would carry him.

Milosh applied the brake. But the skimmer sailed on.

He was only feet away.

Ewan held out a hand.

Only inches away, Tristan reached for the squire. He gave one last lunge.

Ewan's firm grip slapped onto Tristan's wrist and yanked him on board.

Tristan fell in a heap on the deck, panting, still holding the amulet. "I . . . I've got it."

"That's good." Caitir was staring aft. "'Cause they're right behind us."

PART III

THE VALLEY OF FLOWERS

CHAPTER 11

IN THE CTHYLLIN'S DEN

The king of Lonely Sands had managed to board five men onto his skimmer, and now it ground over the clay and sand only two hundred yards behind the fleeing travelers.

A cry of anguish rose from the pursuing vessel.

"He must have discovered we have the amulet." Tristan tightened his grip over the treasure.

"You will not escape me!" came Vasil's distant shout. "You'll condemn us all."

"Better they all perish," said a grim-faced Ewan, "than steal the life from one more unsuspecting wayfarer."

"Aye." Caitir stood at the aft rail.

As the moon rose and the traveler's sail cast a dark shadow behind them, the pursuing vessel came no closer. With the wind driving them ever on, they pulled steadily away.

"To the north!" cried Ewan. "What's that?"

Tristan grasped the rail and peered across the flats.

The Black Cloud. It had returned.

"Nay, nay." Caitir raised a fist to her teeth and bit. "What if that thing you took is not really the amulet?"

"It is." Still holding it, Tristan felt its tingling energy. "Aye, it is."

The dark, churning wind was traveling directly for the two vessels.

For one moment, the pursuing sand ship appeared not to have seen it. Then it veered off and headed back for the oasis.

The Black Cloud followed.

Both were soon out of sight.

Caitir breathed out and closed her eyes. She grabbed a railing for support and slid to the planks. "I've nothing left in me."

"Aye." Tristan also slumped to the deck. "This chase, that wee bit of walking, has exhausted me." He looked at each in turn, appalled by his friends' appearances. "Do you realize—we're all scarecrows."

She slipped in place beside him. "We need rest."

Ewan found a spot at the opposite rail. "Eat and rest. For about two weeks."

Milosh turned to look back. His cheekbones were sharp beneath a face become gaunt and thin. "Never have I felt this weak. But I think we're only about a day and a half out from the Tatras."

"That's good news." Tristan's eyelids were already closing. "Can you steer for a bit?"

"Aye. I'll wake someone when I can manage no longer."

Before the last word left Milosh's mouth, Tristan was curled up beside Caitir, asleep.

THROUGH THE NIGHT, THEY TOOK turns manning the wheel for short intervals. On through a second day they traveled, and as night fell again, the low, moon-shadowed outline of the Tatra chain rose in the west. When dawn broke, the mountains climbed, high and majestic, from the flats. Pine forests and green meadows graced the slopes. Streams glinted white and tumbled down high valleys, trickling precious water onto grasses, pines, and sparse meadows along the edge of the flats.

The Pass of Arr, a deep gap in the forbidding chain of peaks, beckoned.

"There's the pass." Milosh waved to the mountains. "But if we head north a ways, we should find the Argyn's camp and some needed rest."

"Aye." Ewan's loose cheeks crinkled with his grin. "That wee bit of food from Vasil's table is about gone. Some rest and proper vittles would be grand, indeed."

They traversed north until Milosh called out. "See that plume of smoke? Must be their camp." He guided the ship due west.

"I would even go for a cup of *kusik* right now," said Tristan. "And that *shaslik* wasn't so bad."

"What's kusik?" Caitir raised an eyebrow.

"Fermented aurochs milk," answered Milosh.

Her mouth scrunched. "A—and shaslik?"

"Fermented goat meat on a stick." Ewan licked his lips. "They put slabs of goat cheese between the meat. I wouldna mind sinking my teeth into that again."

"*That* I could eat."

The trees approached, and the sand ship hit tufts of grass, weeds, and healthier scrub watered by mountain streams. Finally, the vessel scraped to a halt in the underbrush. "From here, we walk." Milosh jumped down on wobbly legs.

Tristan grabbed his two rucksacks, including one empty food bag. Before leaving the skimmer, he took the Ferachtir uniform from Yuri's pack and gave it to Milosh. No telling when they might use it again.

On foot now, they entered the pines. Tristan breathed the welcome scent of fir and yew. But as the slope steepened, his legs wobbled and his knees buckled. He stopped, grasped a trunk for support, and took deep breaths.

"I hope"—Ewan rubbed his stomach—"that the Argyn have a grand meal in store for us."

They trudged on, stopping often. After one long rest, Caitir even needed help standing again.

A crash reverberated through the air, as of someone chopping a tree with superhuman force.

"That's odd." Milosh stopped a moment to listen. "I've never heard the like."

The thunderous sound trembled the mountainside.

ropping the sloth's limp form onto the rocks, it produced a crude knife and began skinning. After gutting the body cavity, it threw emained into the boiling cauldron. Then it stood above the pot to it cook.

No good meat. Only little meat. Luka miss big meat."

s bony forehead jutted out above a wide bulbous nose and thick ale yellow tinted its skin. Shaggy brown hair covered an impossi-ersized head. Around its waist clung a ragged loincloth, stitched er with the random hides of different animals. More ropy hairs oned from a massive chest. Small, dull eyes, too close together, down into the pot.

3ad land." As its words echoed up the slope, the ice giant shook its "Luka lost in bad land. No big meat here."

—I do not believe what I'm seeing." Caitir whirled to face Milosh. t is that thing down the—" But as she turned, the rock upon which ind rested moved. It began rolling downhill. It hit a pile of scree. tarted a small tumbling landslide rolling down the valley.

he cthyllin turned dull eyes up the slope toward the travelers. t there?"

Run!" Milosh sprinted downhill. "Back to the skimmer. Run!"

ristan began racing back the way they'd come.

he others were already running.

rom the valley beyond came the crash of pines parting, branches swept aside. The cthyllin was climbing the hill at thrice the speed tortal man.

ristan and his three companions raced downslope, following the they'd just climbed.

Stop, little meats!" The thunderous voice was much closer now. "

Help!" cried Ewan's voice from behind. Tristan shot a glance back. quire was in the monster's grip. Then its hand swept down and ed up Caitir. Tristan watched, stunned and helpless, as the giant back up the slope, trees snapping, boulders rolling aside as if they ebbles. It topped the rise, disappeared over the crest.

"Come on," said Ewan. "My belly is eating i

They collapsed at the top of a rise and looke‹ a tree-lined slope into a valley. Instead of the yu what greeted them was a single dark hole in the l rounded by bone piles. In the center lay an enor runners. On top of this sat a cage constructed of ‹ Off to the side raged an oversized fire. Suspend it—a cauldron big enough for a man to bathe in.

"A c–cthyllin ice giant," breathed Milosh. "Ar never to see one again. Ever."

The Erde-shaking pounding came again, to t

"I absolutely hate . . . cthyllin . . . ice . . . gia side. "I swore never to go near one again."

His heart pounding, Tristan peered throug sound. The silhouette of a monstrous figure sta branches of a fir. It carried a hammer with a he‹ tree trunk itself. The creature swung its maul, l bone-shaking thwack. The tree shuddered. Branc down.

"Come down, little meat." Its voice boom‹ "Come down. Come down. Come down."

A large brown animal moved higher up the b.

The hammer swung again, this time with m‹ Three times. Limbs, needles, and twigs fell. Son from the highest branches. An enormous hand sh ing creature—a tree sloth?—around the waist. A grip squeezed the air from the sloth's lungs.

"All mine." The giant's voice echoed like thun "Little meat."

Tristan gawked. Nearly twenty-five feet high, i being he'd ever beheld. Still clutching the sloth, i the giant crossed the distance to the clearing just picked up the sloth by its feet. Three times, it slamr on a boulder. The cracking skull sounded like a sm

His heart pounded, and sweat poured off his brow. What could he do? It had Caitir. It had Ewan. Downslope, Milosh was racing between trees and boulders toward the skimmer.

But the giant would return. And go straight down the mountain. None of them could hope to outrun it.

As fast as his weakened legs could carry him, Tristan veered off to the side.

Moments later, as expected, the cthyllin returned, raced downhill at superhuman speed after the fleeing Milosh. As Tristan cowered beneath the low branches of a spruce on a side slope, the giant bore Milosh back up the hill.

But the moment it reached the spot where Tristan had veered away, the thing stopped. It raised its bulbous nose to the air and sniffed. Its head turned in Tristan's direction. "Can't hide, little meat."

Tristan burst from the pine and raced away across the slope. He slipped twice, sending pebbles and rocks scattering. Behind him, boulders rolled downhill and branches snapped as the cthyllin charged on. He ducked under a yew, hoping the low branches would protect him.

But a massive hand snapped a thick tree limb away from the trunk, reached in, and gripped his waist. Fingers as wide as his torso squeezed the air from his lungs. He was lifted off the ground.

Dizzy, Tristan tried to catch his breath, but the massive fingers clutched him tightly.

"I lets you breathe, little meat." The cthyllin loosened its grip, and Tristan gasped. The stench of the creature was overwhelming, like a hundred unwashed sheepherders.

It looked more closely at Tristan. "Ach!—only bones. Bad meat. Bad."

The cthyllin turned back up the slope, swinging its arms as it climbed. The world whizzed up and down as Tristan was thrown from front to back. The creature topped the rise, and in more dizzying strides, it crossed to the glen's bottom. With one enormous hand, it flipped open the door at the cage's top, held down by a boulder crudely tied to the bars.

It lay Milosh on the ground then pried the rogue's sword from his sheath. With great difficulty, it also wiggled Milosh's knife loose. Gently, it lowered him to the cage bottom, where Milosh stood and rubbed his waist where the giant had pawed him.

Turning its attention to Tristan, it fumbled with Tristan's sword, nearly crushing his pelvis before throwing the weapon onto a nearby pile. To avoid being mauled again, Tristan pulled out his knife and offered it up. What use was fighting such a creature? Taking the blade, it flung the weapon onto the pile. It set Tristan, too, inside the cage. A finger slammed shut the barred top, held down by its boulder.

The cthyllin's face smashed up against the side, looking through the bars. Its rancid breath washed through the cage. Eyes too tiny for an impossibly large head peered in. "Bad meats. Too much bone." It strode across the clearing, kicked a boulder, then cried out in self-inflicted pain. "Bad land. No big meat here. Bad land."

It crossed to a pile of knapsacks it must have collected from past victims. Scooping up half the pile, it returned to the cage, opened the top, and showered rucksacks onto the prisoners. One smacked Tristan on the head. "Eat, little meats. Can't eat bones."

Then it swiveled to the cauldron, pried the sloth's body out with a stick, and yellowed teeth greedily tore the barely cooked muscle from the bone. After sucking meat off the bones, it threw them onto the pile.

"Bad land. No big meat here." It crossed the slope, kicked a pine, and stomped up the mountain.

Caitir looked at the rucksacks, the cage, her companions, and the retreating monster. She faced Milosh with hands on hips. "You, who have been everywhere and done everything, tell us this—how one does escape a cthyllin ice giant?"

"Aye, Milosh," said Tristan. "Do tell us."

CHAPTER 12

LITTLE MEAT, BIG MEAT

"Cthyllin ice giants . . . aye." Milosh cleared his throat. "They used to live in ice caves north of Frosset and on the shores of the Frozen Sea, living on mammoth, aurochs, and an occasional polar bear. Something's made them migrate south. Maybe 'tis all the animals Faolukan's killed—all the meat for his armies. I've never seen them this far south. For years, the northerners have tried to exterminate them, but they're hard to kill. They're stupid. But once in a while, they'll surprise you with a bit of cleverness."

"So you've run across them before?" Tristan cocked his head.

"Many years ago, a clutch of ice giants trapped me for a week in a crevice south of Handelby." He shuddered. "Wanted to eat me in the worst way. I near starved and froze to death. Because of it, I swore I'd never go near that country again."

Ewan began rummaging through the backpacks piled on the floor. "This bread is full of mold." He tossed it through the bars. Then his voice rose. "But here's a wheel of cheese." He bit off a piece. "Ah, now here's something to sink one's teeth into."

He tore off chunks and passed one to each. As he chewed, his hands were busy opening other old packs, fishing around, discarding most. "Aha!" He pulled out a wineskin, opened the stopper, and drank. "Still good." This, too, he passed to the others.

"What did it mean by 'big meat'?" Tristan glanced up the slope in the direction the creature departed.

"Must be the mammoths." Milosh chewed around his words. "They require a lot of meat to survive. This one surely is starving. It's wandered far from home."

"Will it . . . eat us?" Caitir's voice trembled.

"It's not happy we're so thin. Maybe it'll try to fatten us up? Let's hope."

"And if it canna wait?"

Milosh only grinned.

By the time Tristan ate his fill of cheese, Ewan had searched all the packs. They discovered more cheese, a bit of edible, unspoiled sausage, and some dried dates. Then Ewan discovered the best find of all.

"Look, my lords." He held up a knife about four inches long. "Can we cut our way out?"

Tristan examined their cage. Heavy vines wrapped thick logs, each spaced a foot apart. "If we cut the vines on one of these vertical logs, we might be able to squeeze through. But we'd have to cut the entire log free."

Ewan nodded and began sawing. But the vines had been soaked in something and dried, hardening them. After slicing for a while, he'd made hardly a dent. "This'll take all day."

Heavy footfalls, sliding rocks, and snapping branches announced the return of their captor.

Ewan hid the knife in his pack and sat with the others.

The ice giant stomped to the cage and peered inside. "Poor meat. All bone. Bad land. Poor Luka." It shook its head then tramped to a nearby spot and sat down heavily.

Tristan watched it for a time then said in a voice loud enough for the creature to hear, "We shouldn't tell it where the big meat is, Caitir. 'Tis our secret." He nudged her.

Her eyes widened, and she smiled. "Nay, Tristan. Why should we?"

"Aye, if it's going to eat us anyway, let it starve." He was almost shouting. "We'll go to our deaths with the secret of how to find the big meat."

Milosh leaned next to him and whispered, "Where's the big meat?"

"In Zalán's valley, of course," came Tristan's quiet reply.

"Only *we* know where the big meat lives." Milosh's loud voice held too much glee. "Aye, let it starve."

That, apparently, was more than the creature could bear. The giant rose. Heavy footfalls shook the ground as it approached. Dull yellow eyes peered in. "Where big meat?" Its hands grabbed the cage and shook it violently. Tristan clung to the bars for support. "Tell Luka now—where big meat? Or die." Again, it shook the cage.

"If you kill us," said Tristan, "you'll never learn the secret."

Something like puzzlement twisted the cthyllin's face. "Tell. Tell where big meat. Tell now."

Tristan crossed his arms and turned away from it.

"Tell Luka! Tell Luka, now!"

The cage lifted off the sledge, throwing him and everyone else off their feet. When Tristan could stand again, he faced the ice giant. "I can't tell you. The way is too complicated. I must show you."

"Show?" Again, the cage rattled. "Then show. Show, now."

"I will. But I have conditions."

"Conditions?" Again, the face contorted in what appeared to be deep thinking. It sat down, its face towering above them. "What are ... conditions?"

"You must promise. Don't harm us. Promise on your life. Then I'll show you how to find the big meat."

Its brows scrunched together. "What is . . . promise?"

"Say you promise. Say you won't harm us. Then I'll show you big meat."

"Do promise."

Tristan suppressed a smile. "Then you must first go south."

"South?" With those brows pinched so close together, its confusion appeared painful. It raised a hand to its head and scratched. "Where south?"

Tristan pointed.

Something like a smile lifted the corners of its heavy lips. "Big meat south. Must save treasure. Good treasure." It emptied the cauldron onto the ground, hot water sloshing everywhere. Then it slammed the container into the sledge's hold. Gathering the weapons strewn about the camp, it threw them inside the pot with a clanking.

But all the weapons were beyond the reach of the cage.

Once more, it looked around then tromped to the front of the sledge. Wrapping a thick leather harness about its shoulders, it looked back. "Show way."

Tristan pointed toward the flats. It would be easier to travel there than through the pines.

The cthyllin spun the sledge and took great leaping steps downhill, knocking Tristan and the others off their feet. The crude vehicle bounced and rumbled over rocks and bumps. The cthyllin ran straight over saplings that bent and sometimes broke under his feet then scraped the sledge's underside. While the ice giant lunged forward, Ewan worked at the vines with his knife, making scant progress. But he could only cut when the going was smooth.

In moments, they were on the flats again, and Tristan directed it south. Here, they made even faster time, covering the ground quickly. When they were level with the Pass of Arr, he commanded the ice giant toward the top. Again, the sledge was yanked so quickly, Tristan lost his footing.

On the ascent, the sledge jostled and jumped over the uneven ground. Every so often, they were lifted off their feet as the cthyllin bore them over ledges or the sledge tipped dangerously on a side slope. Ewan cut through one vine, discarded it, and started on another. But he had five to go.

Tristan marveled that the cthyllin reached the pass before noon. At the summit, the snowfields had mostly melted, though streams of meltwater still trickled down the side slopes. A cool breeze whistled past.

The cthyllin looked around, puzzled. "Where big meat?"

"In the valley. On the other side."

"Huh?"

"Go down." Tristan pointed. "There."

The sledge lurched, but now Tristan was prepared. He grabbed a bar and held on.

The trip down the other side was even worse than the trip up. He couldn't count the number of bruises, bumps, and scrapes the jostling inflicted on him before they reached the valley. When the cthyllin pulled the sledge onto the flower field's perimeter, the sun was setting over the western hills.

Tristan's plan was to get to the black flowers first. Only by smelling the black flowers could they keep from falling under Zalán's sleeping spell.

On the trip up, Ewan had cut through three more vines, and now only one remained. But that vine held the log so firmly in place, it was as if he hadn't cut through any at all.

The cthyllin flapped an arm toward the field, sending a breeze Tristan's way. "Where big meat? You promised. Where big meat?" A scowl crossed its features.

"Close, very close. You have to let me out so I can show you."

"Let out?" Again, puzzlement twisted its face. "Trick Luka?"

"Nay, nay. 'Tis in a glen, not far from here. Hidden. Big meat in glen. Very big meat."

The monster scratched its forehead, looked across the valley.

Violets and buttercups, lungworts and stichtworts, vetchling and larkspur spread a patchwork of color over the land, filling the air with a thousand scents.

In the distance, Zalán's house occupied its grove. But no smoke issued from its chimney. Was he still here?

Tristan rattled the bars. "Let me out. I show you."

It dropped the harness and walked to the sledge. The cthyllin grabbed the boulder roped to the top grate and yanked the lid open. Roughly, the cthyllin reached in and grabbed him. Tristan's lungs expelled air. The lid, with its heavy stone weight, slammed shut.

When it had placed Tristan upright on the ground, he tried to catch his breath. "I show you. I walk." Now he was talking like the thing. "I show. You follow."

"Follow. No tricks. Show Luka big meat." Its eyes tried to focus on him, seemed to cross. Then its lips frowned. "Or Luka kill. Little meat better than no meat."

Tristan swallowed.

Then it pulled on the harness and jerked the sledge forward.

Tristan raced to catch up. "Slower." He pointed to his feet. "Little feet."

"Slower," the giant repeated then started out almost as fast as before.

Tristan found himself running beside it. He searched the way for the patch of black flowers. They were supposed to be at the entrance. But where were they? The giant was going too fast. Already, they'd entered the flower field.

A powerful fragrance welled up around them. Nay, nay. If they entered much farther, it would be too late. He stepped to the side, yawning.

The giant stopped walking and gawked stupidly at him. "Where big meat?"

Tristan's glance swept from side to side.

The cthyllin's feet nudged the flowers. "Pretty." It knelt, ripped a handful out of the ground—roots and all—and held them to its nose. "Pretty." It breathed deeply then dropped the flowers and bent down to Tristan, his putrid breath fogging over him. "Where . . . big . . . meat?" Its speech slurring, it teetered.

Tristan backed up, woozy.

The giant staggered forward then backward. Then it fell facedown in the field, shaking the ground. A whoosh of petals swirled up around Tristan.

Slowly, he spun toward the entrance, took a step. Weights tugged on his shoulders. His arms were anchors of lead. His feet, anvils. A heaviness dragged on his eyelids.

He mustn't give in to it. If Zalán wasn't here to wake them . . .

In the cage, his friends were already slumping down, falling asleep inside. They might all slumber here forever.

He put one foot before the other, tottering forward.

On wooden legs, leading down to anvils, he walked.

There, just ahead. Black flowers.

The cthyllin had simply raced past them.

But the world was spinning. And sleep was calling.

Chapter 13

THE VALLEY OF FLOWERS

When Tristan's knees gave way, he was only feet from the black flowers. He dropped onto all fours and stared at the black blossoms. Green stems held a fan of petals surrounding a yellow style. How pretty they were.

Then he fell face forward.

Sleep, blessed sleep, was calling. Nothing else mattered.

He breathed deeply, letting slumber take him. But no sooner had his eyes closed, than a surge of energy rushed through him, and he awoke.

He sat up. A few yards away, the ice giant lay prone, snoring heavily.

In the cage, the others also slept.

Grabbing a handful of black petals, he climbed the sledge. Caitir lay closest to the bars. He waved a flower before her nose.

She stretched and opened her eyes.

"Here." He shoved the rest of the bouquet into her hands. "Wake the others."

At the front of the mammoth sledge, he retrieved their weapons. With his sword in hand, he hacked at the remaining vine holding the last vertical log in place. The timber crashed to the ground.

When Milosh, Ewan, and Caitir were awake and had gathered their packs and weapons, Tristan pointed across the field. "'Tis almost dark. Let's go to Zalán's." Just in case, he stuffed some black flowers into his pocket.

Tristan led them on the short walk over the field of blooms. They passed the grave they'd dug where they'd found the map to Tollan Caillté.

How long ago that seemed now.

By the time they reached the wizard's log hut, only a sliver of setting sun peeked over the western mountains. But inside, the house was dark.

Tristan knocked and called Zalán's name but received no answer. "Odd." He stepped over the threshold. "I thought he never left his valley."

"He doesn't." Milosh stepped in behind Tristan, squeaking the floorboards.

By the failing light, Ewan started a fire in the brazier and lit some candles.

Tristan examined the room. Most of the herbs and dried flowers still hung upside down from the ceiling. But some of the clay jars lining the long shelves were missing, as was the wizard's harp. Dust lay over most surfaces.

"The place has the air of abandonment." Caitir stood in the center, wrapping her arms about her chest.

"Aye." Ewan poked in some bins and baskets by the wall. "But there's flour here. And—oh!" He faced them with eyes alight. "Jars of honey. Bins of nuts. Dried fruit. Even a vat of wine."

"Glad will I be for a full belly and a mug or two of wine." Milosh grinned.

As Tristan examined the jars on the shelves, Caitir called out from the table, "What's this—a note? And bottles?"

Tristan and the others hurried to the table where lay a scroll, held open with pebbles. Near it stood six clay jars, a symbol painted on each. Bringing a candle close, Tristan began to read. At the top was a single sentence, in Gaelic: "For the traveler with whom I spoke privately—if ye pass this way again, rub the parchment with that which wakened ye, and the rest will be revealed."

"What's he talking about?" Milosh yawned.

"The black flowers," answered Tristan.

"But we left those back at the entrance." Ewan spoke around a mouthful of nuts and fruit.

"Nay. Fortunately, I brought a few with me, and over here . . ." Tristan walked to the rows of shelves. He searched the jars until he came to a clay crock he'd seen earlier, inscribed with the words *Flori Negru*. Taking the vessel to the table, he dumped a few petals onto the page and rubbed. Parts of letters appeared. He spread the crumbled remains over the parchment and worked them in. Now the entire message revealed itself. He bent over and read:

For the eyes of Tristan mac Torn, a true son of Ériu,

If ye, Tristan, are reading this, then ye know I have abandoned my beloved valley. For millennia have I lived here, watching over my animals, flowers, trees, and herbs, keeping them safe, I thought, from danger. How content was I in my isolation, keeping out the evil from the east! But contentment can lead to a smug satisfaction and a false sense of security.

For after ye passed through, ye left in me serious doubts.

As mentioned when we talked, I often pondered a certain question: Why, through all the centuries, was I allowed to keep this valley safe? Was my magic as powerful as that? Or was my being here meant for some grander purpose? After ye left, I wondered—were ye and yer mission the reason for it all?

Then something else began calling me, eating at me, telling me to act. Go west, said this feeling. Go west, and I will show ye a new task, said a voice within myself, a small voice growing louder with each rising sun. Or was it not me, but a voice from without that spoke?

And if so, then who?

I think ye and I both know the answer.

For weeks, I resisted. But the feeling grew so strong I could no longer fight it. So now, I am leaving.

Some of the trees here will die. Some will live on. Within a few months, the flowers will wilt and lose their potency. When winter comes, the magic will finally be gone. With the falling snow, for the first time in millennia, the Pass of Arr will be open to all. I trust that long before then, ye will have passed through.

So now, here ye are, in my abandoned hut, reading this. And I fear yer travels will have taken their toll upon ye. I can only guess what travails, injuries, and illnesses have been inflicted upon ye. For this reason alone, I almost stayed—to minister to yer ailments. Instead, I will guess and leave six jars of powerful herbs and remedies, each labeled for appropriate use.

The first contains crushed leaves of colliphor, an herbal remedy for regaining lost strength. Mix sparingly in morning tea for three days.

The second is tincture of punt weed. Use for burns. Make a paste with butter and spread liberally.

The third is ratsnip. It lifts broken spirits. Again, mix in tea. Drink once only.

The fourth is bark of aspringula, good for regaining weight after imprisonment, illness, or times of famine. Chew as small a piece as ye can snip off, once a day for three days. And eat heartily. Help yerselves to what's left.

The fifth contains sprigs of bitter koltia to heal wounds. Lay a few leaves on the wound. Wrap tightly for three days. Never eat it.

In the sixth jar at the bottom, ye will find a single flask. I trust ye know this potion. Of all the gifts I leave ye, this is the most precious. It is oil of crimson. Three drops, three times a day, for three days. There's only enough to restore one soul on the verge of death.

Ye have greatly upset my world, Tristan mac Torn. Ye have shown me I dare not sit here, content to hide in my garden while just outside my gates, evil destroys all that is good and right and just. To do nothing in the face of evil must surely be evil itself. Ye have dedicated yerself to a grand task. And yer bravery and calling and fealty to yer cause—to Elyon's cause—have truly shamed me. Thus do I choose now to fight against the Deamhan Lord and all that he is, with whatever weapons I possess.

I do bless ye, Tristan mac Torn. May honesty, truth, and light shine ever before ye. May the goodness, mercy, and love of he who created the worlds live forever in yer heart. And may the guiding hand of Elyon be ever upon ye.

Zalán, A Wizard of Erde, in service to Elyon

When he had finished reading, tears ran down his cheeks. Zalán had reminded him of the importance and gravity of his task. And to think that Zalán saw in Tristan such a great example of honor, duty, and trust in Elyon. He steadied his shallow breathing. Zalán's trust in him was . . . humbling.

How could Tristan ever be worthy of such faith? How could he ever have appeared to the wizard as so shining an example worthy of such fine words? How could Tristan have so moved this powerful wizard that he abandoned what he'd so diligently protected over the millennia? He closed his eyes and shook his head.

"What does it say?" Caitir came up behind him, wrapping her arms around his waist.

He broke free, turned his back to her, and waved at the parchment.

She read, as did Ewan and Milosh.

"Seems the wizard has gone west, my lord." Ewan faced him and must have seen the tears in his eyes, for his brows furrowed. "And seems you've awakened his conscience in a mighty way."

"A grand ally he'll become." Milosh whistled. "I wouldn't want to stand against him."

"I didna ken the man," said Caitir. "But I ken you've made a powerful impression on him."

Tristan wiped his eyes and nodded. "I do not deserve such fine words."

"Ah, but you do, my lord." Ewan smiled. "You do, indeed."

"I agree." Caitir hugged his neck and planted a kiss on his cheeks.

Then he couldn't help but smile.

"And he's left us potions," she said, slipping away.

"Aye." He wiped his eyes. "Let us take what remedies we can tonight before we sleep."

Caitir then filled a pot with water from their skins and put it over the fire to boil. "I'll make the tea for the potions."

FOR THE NEXT WEEK, THEY rested, ate, and recovered. Milosh rounded up stray goats and lambs, slaughtered them, and roasted them over a spit. Some goats they kept for milk. Ewan made loaf after loaf of honey bread, sometimes mixed with nuts and berries. Caitir churned butter to slather atop the bread. She also mixed the potions they needed. Tristan slept, rested, and they quickly regained the weight they'd lost.

One morning, barely six days later, he stood smiling before his companions. "Everyone's filled out considerably these last few days. I can even wear the armband Caitir made for me again." He patted Ewan's belly. "You've even got your figure back."

Ewan smiled. "Glad I am for it. A thin man I'll never be."

"'Tis time, my friends." Milosh grinned.

"Aye." Tristan stretched out his arms, feeling his energy, strength, and weight restored. "We leave today."

They gathered their packs, some now bulging with food, and trekked across the valley to the forest's edge and the remains of an old fire.

"Here's the place where we camped on the night before we first entered Zalán's valley. This is where we saw the stag. Now we hunt."

Caitir and Ewan pulled out their bows.

"Hunt?" said Milosh.

"The giant white stag," answered Tristan. "Remember the beast we saw the night we camped here? We must hunt it."

Milosh stared at him as if he'd lost his mind.

CHAPTER 14

AN OTHERWORLD PASSAGE

As Ewan and Caitir strung their bows, Tristan faced Milosh. "Only when the white stag senses we are hunting will it take refuge in the Otherworld tunnel."

"I vaguely remember you said something about this." Milosh scratched his head. "Lead on."

Tristan nodded to Ewan and Caitir, and they began the hunt. But as before, the day passed without sighting the white hart. As dusk approached, all were worn out from tromping through the brush and thick woods at the edge of Zalán's valley.

They made camp at the base of a large hill. After eating, Tristan and Ewan climbed a hill, the tallest for leagues around. Far to the north, many campfires burned.

"Faolukan's army?" asked Ewan.

"Aye. On the border with Erdelstan. I'm surprised it hasn't moved."

"Let's hope our hunt doesna take us in that direction."

"Let's hope."

The next morning they'd barely begun hunting when the white stag appeared on the trail, not fifty yards ahead.

A huge, regal animal, its rack bore so many points, Tristan couldn't count them. Standing four feet higher at the shoulder than any buck he'd ever seen, it shimmered and glowed, even in the morning light.

For several frozen moments, the group stared at it and it at them. Then Tristan broke the awed silence with a call to the hunt.

Ewan and Caitir raised their bows, aimed, and shot.

The buck stepped a few feet to the side. The arrows bit into the dirt. Then it turned and bounded through the trees at a leisurely pace.

Ever north it went, and the Company followed. Whenever it appeared they might lose the beast, it slowed and looked back, almost as if taunting them to keep up. Several more times did Caitir and Ewan fire useless arrows in its direction. But it seemed to know where they'd land, and the missiles always missed. They stopped to retrieve them before racing on.

For half the day, the chase continued. Now they came dangerously close to the enemy camp.

"'Tis leading us toward Faolukan's forces," said Milosh as he jogged.

"But we can't . . . stop the hunt." Tristan was breathing heavily. "We don't know if we'll ever get another chance."

When the tents of the main encampment were in sight, the stag changed direction and headed east, into the hills. They followed. But at that moment, a Drochtar patrol spotted them.

"Halt!" came the cry. Then a full decanus of ten men, bearing long lances, jogged in pursuit about seventy yards behind.

"Now what do we do?" Caitir peered behind them. "We're caught between a needle and a thimble."

"We follow the stag." Tristan huffed. "We've no other choice. If we enter the tunnel, perhaps they won't follow."

But the Company was exhausted from chasing the hart all day, and the soldiers steadily gained on them.

When they entered deep woods, the pursuing soldiers were only a hundred feet behind.

"Halt, intruders!" came a shout.

Tristan jogged on. The trees here grew tall, spreading dark shadows over everything below.

Ahead, a clearing. The white stag bounded toward the center, turned to look back. A halo of ethereal white clung to it. Then it raced to the center and loped into—

The open maw of a mound tomb.

Vines and ferns clung to the top and sides, but where the great buck had gone in opened a dark, gaping hole.

"The entrance!" Ewan shouted. "Follow it!" He jumped across the portal. Instantly, he appeared on the other side as a dim shadow.

Milosh slowed and gawked at the shadowy entrance.

Tristan, though he knew he must enter, also stopped. He'd been sweating from the chase, and now a cold shiver ran along his back and shoulders. He stared.

A dark hole in the ground. The old, nameless fear was always there, creeping back. He'd defeated it before, but—

Caitir grabbed one hand and yanked him across the threshold.

He was inside, and the panic he always felt in dark, underground spaces, rose up like a shade from its grave.

Then Milosh jumped across, nearly knocking Tristan off his feet.

On the floor were a number of half-burnt torches. Ewan struck flint to stone and raised a flame, dispelling the darkness and Tristan's fear.

"Look." Caitir pointed back at the racing soldiers. "They're almost upon us."

Ewan took his light and led them deeper into the tunnel.

Behind, Tristan saw three—nay, four—soldiers cross over. But the rest pulled back and only stared, perhaps afraid to enter. He called to the others, "Four of them have followed."

Milosh fingered his sword. "Should we take them here?"

The black walls close around him, Tristan shuddered. "Nay, let's go down. Perhaps they'll turn back?"

Milosh nodded, and they ran down the dark chute.

As before, the walls soon shimmered with a faint greenish-yellow. Soon, it was light enough so Ewan could douse his torch.

A bit farther, the tunnel's sides burst with eddies of brilliant color—blood red, sky blue, emerald green, sunflower yellow. The colors joined and separated, twisted together in circles, then ran in wavy, parallel rivers before mixing again. Luminescent leaves covered the floor. Though solid, they didn't crunch underfoot. Small trees with glowing orange trunks and phosphorescent leaves waved their trunks aside as they passed.

Behind the shimmering walls, glowing beings of light swam up from the other side, stuck oblong, surprised faces with wide, dark eyes to the wall, then swam away.

"The soldiers are still behind us," said Ewan, looking back. "But they're mightily distracted."

Tristan glanced back. Their pursuers had stopped and were staring at the trees, the walls, and the floor of the strange world they'd entered. "Let's not fight them. Let's try to lose them."

"Aye." Caitir faced the way ahead. "The less time we spend down here, the better."

Though he was as tired as he'd ever been, Tristan led them in a slow jog as they descended the Otherworld tunnel.

They passed the first exit leading up. As before, a circular window at the end of a dark tunnel showed where it led. The moon shed a dim light on the smoking remains of a village. Dark shadows of corpses littered the lanes. Spears jutted from lifeless torsos, and jackals fed on the fallen.

Another village sacked by Faolukan's forces.

Already, he sensed that much time and distance had passed in the world above.

Tristan shot a glance back. The soldiers were far in the rear, their enthusiasm and resolve apparently ebbing. Or were they simply distracted?

Beside him, Milosh was also staring, openmouthed, at the strange world they'd entered.

Tristan grabbed his arm and tugged. They jogged on.

More exits appeared and were passed. Some opened on locations within Erde. Others led to worlds, distant and bizarre.

One exit led to a sandy beach at twilight, where the waves lapped, palm trees hung over white sands, and slow, soothing music drifted from a circle of young men and women with pointed ears, huddling around a fire of driftwood.

Another exit led to a night world where snow pelted the slopes of tall mountains. A thin, blue-black sky held stars that blazed with too much light.

Across the ice-covered grade, a caravan of hairy, dog-like creatures with fluffy ears lumbered in single file. They were ten times larger than any dog he'd ever seen. Atop these beasts of burden sat bearded men bundled in heavy robes coated with snow. Behind them, tarps carried mountainous cargos.

Still another exit led to somewhere on the Romely plains—a view to a village where Drochtar's troops were gathering at midday, ready to depart on some journey. Women from the village beyond stood in a circle, watching their men leave.

For a great distance, no exits broke off.

Then Tristan heard shouting from behind, and he whirled. One of the creatures from the Underworld had come through the tunnel walls. Tristan shuddered at its long razor fangs, its sickly yellow eyes, and its six, black, grasshopper legs. The soldiers were barely holding it at bay with their lances. One of them already lay dead under its pincers.

Tristan spun and began jogging. "Let's get out of here. Fast."

The others followed.

Exit after exit they passed until they came to their goal—the tunnel leading to the mountain lake.

In the world above, the sun was setting, glinting off the lake and the snowcapped peaks beyond.

"This is it. Let's go." He began the ascent with the others following close behind. As before, the tunnel's walls lost their color, and darkness swallowed them. But Ewan had kept the torch they'd found at the far entrance. Lighting it, he led them on.

With each upward step, the fatigue Tristan was dreading returned.

"Why am I so tired?" asked Milosh.

"'Tis what always happens when you leave the Otherworld tunnel." Caitir's voice betrayed her own exhaustion. "The minute we're out, we'll have to find a place to sleep."

He grunted, and they trudged on.

They burst through the entrance, stopping at the foot of another mound tomb. Behind them, grasses and weeds appeared as if out of nowhere, completely covering the entrance. The mound faced the lakeshore, with a slope leading up to a grove.

It was early spring. They'd left winter behind.

"Let's find shelter in the trees," said Tristan. "Before we all collapse."

"Aye." Ewan started up the slope. "This lake is a meeting place for soldiers. 'Tis not safe."

Each step up the slope was agony. Every fiber of Tristan's muscles complained. They'd chased the stag for nearly a day, and then they'd jogged and walked through a tunnel that was storing up weakness for every league traveled. At least this time, they hadn't spent as long in the passage.

When everyone had climbed the slope and they were well inside the shadows of the pines, Caitir dropped onto a bed of needles. "I canna walk another step." She closed her eyes.

The others fell beside her. Before Tristan could even take off his pack, he heard Ewan's snoring. Milosh curled up nearby.

But before he joined them in sleep, his thoughts drifted to the reason they'd stopped at the mountain lake, the place where so much trouble had earlier befallen them.

Somewhere nearby was a rock mound. And there, he'd hidden the object of his first quest, the greatest gift Elyon had ever bestowed upon the world—

The Scepter.

Tomorrow, they would retrieve it.

He'd buried it under a rock pile.

He hoped it was still there.

PART IV

THE WAY WEST

CHAPTER 15

THE SHAFT

When Tristan next woke, it was midday, and the others still slept. He rose and walked out of the forest to the lake's edge. No troops. Good. But they mustn't stay here long. The lake might still be a way station for troops.

Looking across the slope of the near shore, he saw what was hidden in yesterday's twilight—hundreds of skeletons, bones of the fallen that he, Tristan, had killed so many months ago when he took up the Scepter in anger. Anguish, bitter as a mouthful of horehound herbs, choked in his throat. It was here where enemy troops had captured Caitir, Ewan, and Machar. Then Tristan had used the Scepter to slaughter the soldiers of Drochtar, Ferachtir, and Sarkenos. So many dead by his hand. Elyon had told him to walk away. But he'd disobeyed. And because of it, Dermid had died. He whirled from the sight.

How long ago that seemed now. At the same time, it was only yesterday.

He returned to where the others still slept. Only Caitir was awake, eating the bread Ewan had baked in Zalán's hut. Ewan's concoction, with honey, nuts, and berries, satisfied and filled.

"Where were you?" asked Caitir.

"Checking the lake for signs of soldiers."

"See any?"

"Nay. Only the skeletons of the men I killed." He took some bread from her. But she cocked her head, her brow creasing, and he realized he'd never told her what happened at the lake or how Dermid died. So he told her the story.

When he'd finished, she laid a hand on his shoulder. "You did what you thought best. Do not blame yourself for taking up the Scepter. You were only trying to save me. And Ewan and Machar."

"I know." He closed his eyes. "But I disobeyed Elyon. Dermid's death—it will never leave my conscience."

For a time, she watched him with narrowed eyes. Then she sidled up close and planted a kiss on his cheek.

He looked sideways at her and couldn't help but smile.

Now Ewan and Milosh rose. They, too, ate.

"That trek through the tunnel . . ." Milosh whistled. "It took much out of us, did it not?"

"Aye," said Tristan. "We walked less than a day and traveled hundreds of leagues. And now 'tis spring, and many weeks have passed."

Milosh gaped. "Weeks?"

"Aye, travel through the tunnel extracts a heavy price."

"And we have to go back in again?"

"Once more."

Shaking his head, Milosh continued eating.

Soon, the group was standing, ready to depart, wearing their packs.

"I hid the Scepter in the same place we buried Gamil."

"Can you find it again?" asked Caitir.

"'Twas a rather large rock mound. Easy to find." He led them through the trees. But soon they were following wheel tracks heading in the same direction. Odd. "What are these?"

"Some kind of small cart." Ewan waved. "And they're heading from the lake toward that rock mound."

With greater speed, Tristan led them through the forest until the rocks fought with the pines. They lost the tracks on the rocks, and now he worried about any unfamiliar activity in the Scepter's vicinity. The rock pile was just ahead, just around the next cluster of yew. He stepped into the open. And there he found—

A hole in the ground.

Where he'd hidden the Scepter, where once sat great slabs of stone, was now—a hole in the rocks.

He raced to the edge and stared down into a shaft dug through solid rock. About six feet wide, it dropped for twenty feet. Hovering over the pit was a winch leading to a pulley dangling from a mast suspended by ropes. A rope from the pulley led to the bottom. He peered down. At the bottom was another shaft, cut horizontally.

"Where's the Scepter?" Caitir glanced at him, her brow scrunching. "Down there?"

"Nay." His hands flew to the top of his head. He staggered back from the edge and spun in a circle. "It was here. Right here. This was a rock pile. Now 'tis a shaft in the ground. A mine?"

"Are you sure this is the right place, my lord?" asked Ewan.

"Aye. I'm sure."

What happened here?

What dug up the rocks?

Who took the Scepter, the greatest gift of Elyon to mankind?

These questions and more pressed in upon him. He stared at his companions. They gawked back at him with blank expressions.

He took a deep breath. Then he returned to the shaft. Dropping to his hands and knees, he examined the sides where picks and chisels had worked their way down. Just below, were handholds cut into the shaft.

"Look, my lord," came Ewan's cry from behind. "Footprints between the cart tracks."

Tristan ran to a spot a few yards away and knelt. Small feet. Three toes in front. One slim claw behind. "What is it? Has anyone ever seen anything like this?" He faced the others.

Milosh knelt to examine the prints but shook his head. Even he—the traveler who'd been everywhere, seen everything—couldn't explain it.

"Let's follow the track." Tristan left the shaft, walking beside the trail. The tracks disappeared on rocky ground, reappeared where pines fought with shelves of rock, occasional boulders, and piles of loose stone. Then the footprints entered solid rock and disappeared for good.

While the others remained behind, Tristan walked on, searched to the far edge of the stony ground, but found nothing. Returning to his friends, he slumped down on a boulder. "I don't know what to do." His hands again found the top of his head. "The Scepter is gone. Something's been digging—mining?—exactly where I hid it. And I don't know what to do."

"Someone needs to go down in that shaft and see where it leads," said Caitir, frowning. "It was dug for a purpose."

She was right. "Aye. Do you still have that torch, Ewan?"

"I do." Ewan untied it from his pack and handed it to him.

Tristan took it, and they returned to the place where the Scepter should have been. Striking flint to steel, he lit the torch. About half remained to be burned. He dropped his rucksack.

"I'll go with you," said Milosh, slipping off his pack.

Tristan lowered his body over the edge, his feet finding the slots cut in the rock, and he descended. The farther he went, the colder it became. The old, familiar fear of underground places welled up, and his heart beat faster. But he had the torch, didn't he?

At the bottom, the rope from the hoist ended in a metal hook. He waited for Milosh to join him. Then he ducked and shone the torch into the second, horizontal shaft. Only four feet wide and as many high, it bored straight through. Cart tracks led into darkness.

Swallowing his fear, he got down on all fours and began to crawl. Milosh followed, but had the larger man been the best choice for this? His shoulders were wider than the others.

Tristan hadn't gone twenty yards when he thought he heard singing. The voice was faint, echoing occasionally down the shaft, followed by periods of silence.

"Do you hear that?" he whispered to Milosh.

"Aye," came the muffled reply. "Far off, I'd say."

"Let's follow it."

"Aye."

Tristan continued to crawl until the way dropped into an enormous underground room. They both gaped. Wet, dripping rock teeth knifed down from above. Tristan's torch shone red and yellow over multicolored surfaces. Round, glistening rock incisors jutted up from the bottom, trying in vain to reach the teeth above. Across the floor, the miner had made gravel paths to four holes in the far wall. Outside the paths, bulbous mounds of slippery rock made for a treacherous crossing. The sounds of singing came louder here, but from which of the four passages, he couldn't determine.

He had visions of the maze beneath Castle Schwarzburg. The room swam before him. For a moment, instead of the cave, his eyes beheld swirling blackness. He grabbed Milosh's shoulder for support.

"Are you all right?" Worry tightened Milosh's voice.

The vision passed. But Tristan's heart was pounding. "Aye. Just . . . just a bit of queasiness. Underground places . . . don't agree with me." He moved to the exit that had led them here. He knelt and, using a rock from the floor, made a single long slash beside it. "So we don't get lost."

"Look." Milosh pointed to a natural alcove on the room's opposite side. Something—a figure?—sat within.

Tristan crossed the twenty yards on the cart track and approached. He raised the torch and shed light on a figurine atop a pedestal. Carved from solid rock, it was the image of—

Crom Mord.

Claw-footed. Lizard-headed. Open-jawed. Forked-tongued. Razor-teethed. With a mane of snakes.

Tristan reeled back. The shock of seeing this abomination down here made him gasp.

"The Deamhan Lord." Milosh turned his face in disgust and spat. "Whatever dug this tunnel must worship it."

"Aye." Tristan pulled his sword from its sheath, intending to strike the idol in two but stopped. The sword would only break. He hadn't the right tools. Resheathing his weapon, he turned his back on it. "Listen," he whispered. The singing had stopped. "Do you think it heard us?"

"Maybe. For a moment there, we were not whispering."

Tristan nodded then led them to the nearest tunnel. Before entering, he made two slashes with another rock beside the entrance. Then they followed cart wheels down a narrow passage with many twists and turns.

On the floor, he found an occasional nugget of rock—fallen off the cart? Each nugget contained wide threads of silver. So the shaft followed a vein?

They continued until the way dead-ended.

Retreating to the main room, he examined his torch. They had only a short while before it burned itself out. "We must return or lose our light." Even saying the words brought a pounding terror to his heart, sweat to his brows.

But Milosh was examining something behind the idol. "What are these leather bags?" Milosh dragged one from its hiding place. He untied it and stuck a hand inside. When his hand reappeared, it sparkled with silver. "I'm taking one."

"What are you going to do with it?"

"Take it with me. Wealth, my friend."

"You can't carry it where we're going."

"I'm going to try."

With an impatient huff, Tristan searched the other bags to make sure they didn't hold the Scepter.

The singing resumed, but from which way, he couldn't tell. He tightened his grip on the torch. Only an inch of material left to burn. "We must hurry. Or we'll be left in the dark."

They clambered back the way they'd come.

BACK ON TOP, TRISTAN DROPPED onto the rock shelf and exhaled in relief. Throwing the torch aside, he told the others what they'd found.

"So it digs for silver," said Caitir. "And its cart wheels came from the lake, where Ferachtir and Drochtar troops congregate."

Smiling, Milosh plunked his bag beside his pack.

"Aye," continued Tristan. "And the rocks where I buried the Scepter were laced with it. So when it started digging, it surely found and took the Scepter."

"May I suggest, my lord." Ewan held up a hand. "That you not return to the tunnels. Who knows how far they go? That is its territory. Up here, we have the upper hand. Why not wait for it to emerge, and we'll capture it?"

Any plan that didn't require him to go down there again was a good plan. "Aye, sounds good to—"

Something clattered onto the stone near the shaft.

Tristan whirled.

Standing beside the steps was a three-foot-high blue-skinned creature, with saucer-wide yellow eyes, a wiry mop of black hair, and a deer-skin tunic crisscrossed with leather straps. Three bony fingers on one hand wrapped a two-sided pick.

A gravelly, low voice spoke, "Who trespasses here on mein dig?"

CHAPTER **16**

THE KOBOLD

"Ach!" The blue-skinned creature waved its pick and took a menacing step forward. "Begone, intruders. Leave at once! Go away!"

But the Company just stood and gaped.

Then Milosh raced for it.

But the creature jumped out of the way so fast, Milosh's hands grasped empty air. It ran to a spot a few yards away and, still holding its pick, placed hands on hips. "Leave mein shaft. It ist mein!" It stomped its foot for emphasis. "Sie ist not welcome here."

"What are you?" Tristan stepped toward it.

The creature hopped back. "A miner. Ist sie dumb?"

"Nay, what kind of creature?"

"Ach! Hast sie nein sense, empty skull? A kobold, I am! Heiner ist mein name."

"When you started digging . . . Heiner"—how odd it felt calling this creature by a man's name!—"did you find a rod about this long?" Tristan held his hands apart. "With gems on it?"

Its saucer eyes, with yellow irises and jet-black pupils, narrowed. "Why dost sie want to know?"

"I buried it here. 'Tis mine."

"And now it ist mine. I found it. I keep it. Too bad." Then its glance fell on the bag of silver beside Milosh's pack. "Ach, thieves! Sie hast stolen mein treasure. Give it back! Or be sorry."

"Let's trade."

"Nein. Never."

"What do you want for it?"

"Nothing. The wand ist mein. Und the silver ist mein also. Give it back!"

Faster than Tristan thought possible, the kobold darted between him and Ewan. Still carrying its pick, its fingers touched the bag.

Milosh's hand snapped out and grabbed a leg.

With lightning speed, the kobold twisted and writhed free. Milosh chased it a dozen yards, but it moved so fast, it was soon standing out of reach, staring at them, while Milosh tried to catch his breath.

"Give us back what you stole," said Tristan, tightening both fists. "Then, and only then, will you get your silver."

"Nein. The wand ist worth more. I vill keep both. Sie vill never have it." The kobold began circling them. Then it darted in again, heading for the bag of silver. Ewan rushed forward, laid hands on its arm.

But again, it twisted out of reach.

Caitir then strung her bow, nocked an arrow to the string. "Give us the wand, little kobold, or I'll shoot you."

"Little kobold?" It scowled and stomped a foot. "Little kobold, it says. I am the biggest kobold in mein family. Insulters! Trespassers! Thieves!"

"I mean it. I'll shoot."

"I dare sie! Shoot, little woman! Little, empty-skulled woman." It shook its pick at her.

She released her arrow, but it jumped aside so quickly, the missile simply clattered over the rocks. She walked over to retrieve it.

As soon as she approached, it backed off. Again, it stood out of range. Then it began circling them.

"What an annoying creature." Caitir returned to the group with her arrow.

"I'm beginning to greatly dislike this kobold," agreed Milosh. "I wished you'd brought it down."

"Not before we get the Scepter back." Tristan paced slowly as it kept circling. Then he faced the others. "Stay here while I talk to it alone." He approached it with his hands up.

The kobold stood still, head cocked sideways.

"Heiner, what do you do with your silver?"

"Ach! It wants to know mein business. I trade it, empty skull!"

"For what?"

"For presents." Its hand shot to something around its neck and gripped it. "And cheese. I love cheese. And aurochs meat. And wine."

"Will you take cheese in exchange for the wand?"

"Nein. Never. Dost sie think I am as stupid as sie, empty skull?"

Tristan closed his eyes and breathed out, trying to control his impatience. He opened his eyes. "What's that around your neck?"

"Mine. Ist mine. You can't have it." The kobold backed up a step, its hand gripping something on a chain.

"We're not leaving until you give us the wand. We'll guard your shaft and not let you down again until you return what I left there."

"I vill never give sie the wand. Never! It ist mein second . . . favorite . . . treasure." Its hand dropped to its side, revealing what it had gripped so tightly moments ago.

Tristan stared.

A quarter-moon amulet. A gift from the druids of Drochtar, laced with evil. The kobold was indeed working for the enemy.

"Sie vill be sorry you came here, empty skulls. I vill make sie very sorry. Very, very sorry." Then it turned and scampered over the rocks to a nearby stand of pines.

Exasperated beyond measure, Tristan returned to the group and shrugged. "I don't know how to get it back. But let's stand guard over its mine shaft. It's put a lot of work into this pit. If we prevent it from mining its silver, maybe it will relent."

"Good idea." Milosh picked up his pack and bag of silver and plopped both down at the edge of the pit.

Tristan walked over and looked down. A row of small carts bearing ore now waited at the bottom for the hoist to raise them up.

They grouped themselves in a circle near the pit access and waited. Noon came and went, but no kobold appeared. When the sun set, they made a fire, ate, talked, and set a guard for the night.

Ewan had the first watch.

Milosh unrolled his furs and put the bag of silver under his head. He slept with a knife in his hands.

When it was Tristan's turn, he took over from Ewan. "Anything?" he whispered, so as not to wake the others.

"Nay, my lord. Quiet as a tomb."

He stood to take Ewan's place.

"It's stolen my bow!" Ewan shouted. "My bow and arrows."

Tristan ran to Ewan's bedroll. "How did this happen?"

"I do not ken. I've been watching the dark the whole time. I never nodded off."

"What's going on?" Milosh was now awake. Caitir, also, was rising.

"Do you have your bow, Caitir?" Tristan asked.

She checked and affirmed that she did.

"It's sneaky. And quiet." Tristan scanned the circle of darkness around their camp. "We'll have to keep a closer watch."

Then came gravelly, high-pitched laughter from far away. "Ist only the beginning," it shouted.

Then everyone returned to their beds beside the pit. Tristan threw more sticks onto the fire and peered into the blackness. Time passed, and he grew sleepy. But it wasn't yet time to give up the watch. He heard a noise and whirled.

The kobold was racing off into the night with Caitir's bow and quiver.

Tristan ran after it.

"Hah!" It laughed. "Sie vill be very sorry. Leave mein dig. Leave me alone, und I vill stop. But not until." Then it ran off into the dark.

Everyone was awake and standing again.

Tristan slapped a fist into a palm. "Sorry." He faced his friends. "It was so fast. It ran in here, grabbed Caitir's bow, and left before I could stop it."

"What I wouldn't give to get my hands around creature's neck and . . ." Milosh twisted his hands around themselves.

"Everyone secure their weapons." Tristan went to his pack, removed the precious scroll he'd struggled so hard to retrieve, and tied it with a leather cord inside his tunic.

As Milosh took the watch, they tried to sleep. He stood with his foot resting on his bag of silver.

But again, later that night, they woke to a frustrated Milosh running and shouting after the kobold as it ran off with Tristan's sword. And Tristan had even placed the weapon beneath his furs.

"I don't know how it snuck in here." Milosh's eyes were fierce with anger. "I watched every shadow. I was constantly circling the camp. If I get my hands on that thing . . ."

Caitir stood from her bedroll. "Oh nay, nay. It took my sword as well. And my knife."

"My sword, too." Ewan's hands closed into fists. "This canna continue."

"Or it will soon have all our weapons." Tristan paced, checked in his food pack, and closed his eyes. "And it's taken most of my food. How did it *do* this with everyone standing watch?"

They all looked to Milosh. He was now so angry, he couldn't speak. His eyes bulged so much, Tristan feared they'd pop out of his head. "I—I was watching the whole time. That . . . little . . . kobold!" Again, he slammed a fist into a palm.

"Wait." Caitir planted her hands on her hips, her chin rising with a sly smile. "It wants the silver, nay? Then let's give it what it wants."

"Nay, we've little to bargain with as it is," said Tristan.

"But it must live around here somewhere. Not down in the mine. Wherever it lives is probably where it keeps its treasure."

"So?"

"So we let it have the bag, but put a hole in it so the silver drains out the instant it's lifted."

"Creating a trail leading to its den." Tristan smiled. He nodded to the east. "'Tis almost dawn. We'll be able to see soon. Put the bag out where the kobold can get it, Milosh."

Reluctantly, Milosh agreed. With one of the remaining knives, Tristan cut a small hole in the bottom.

Caitir took the next watch, and they all settled down, once again, to rest.

It seemed to Tristan he'd barely closed his eyes when Caitir called out. "It was here again. And it took the bag."

He shot to his feet, as did the others.

"I didn't see it leave. I only noticed just now that the bag was missing. Who knows when it came?"

"How does it do that?" Ewan shook his head.

They wrapped some cloth around the torch they'd brought up from the pit, lit it. Then, taking what weapons were left, they followed the trail of silver dust.

When the first light of dawn reddened the eastern sky, Ewan doused their torch. Crouching to see the intermittent sparkly stream, they crept through a pine grove, a field of flowers, and crossed another stretch of rock shelf. At a hillock, they climbed until the track ended at a cave in the hillside.

From within, Tristan heard humming. But it was slow, lazy, distracted, not like the singing down in the shaft.

Tristan swallowed and whispered, "I'm going in."

"Me, too." Milosh wrung his hands. "I've a score to settle with that thing."

"But, Milosh, we must get the Scepter first."

"Aye."

Tristan faced Ewan and Caitir. "You two stay here. If it gets past us, don't let it escape."

Ewan stepped to the middle of the path, spread his legs, and put hands on hips. "Let it just try to get past me."

Tristan lit the torch again, and, with Milosh following, they entered the cave.

116

CHAPTER **17**

WhAT WAS LOST

So narrow was the passage, they were forced to crouch. The way led straight into the hillside and widened. To deaden their echoing footsteps, Tristan stepped slowly, lightly, as did Milosh. The humming grew louder, mixed with the sounds of dripping water. Ahead, the path opened into a lighted room. He leaned the torch, still burning, up against the passage wall.

He peeked around the corner into the cave room. Two columns of glistening stone, narrow in the middle, rose from the center. To the right, the kobold had carved a flat space in the rock where he'd built a log frame bed covered with furs, a low table, and a stool. Humming absently, the creature sat now on the stool, facing the wall.

In a far corner, another stone statue of Crom Mord hunkered on a pedestal. Under its cold lizard gaze, Tristan shivered.

"I don't see any exits," he whispered. "Right now, it appears to be under the pendant's spell. I'm going to take it from him—I mean, from it. Stay here in case it tries to escape."

Milosh's brows furrowed. "Why not just grab it? Why worry about the pendant?"

"Trust me. Just wait here."

With a shrug, Milosh backed into the shadows inside the passage.

Tristan took a step forward, but his feet crunched on the gravel pathway. He raised a foot, laid it down softly. Then he took another step. In this way, he inched forward, his progress excruciating. At least, he kept the sound to a minimum. The kobold still faced away, humming, his fingers rubbing the amulet.

Now he stood behind it. Another step and he was beside it. As he suspected, its eyes were closed. Its head swayed, lost in a pendant-induced ecstasy. One hand held the amulet while the other caressed it.

A third step brought Tristan face-to-face with the blue-skinned creature. It was completely enraptured by the quarter-moon amulet.

His hands shot out and wrapped the amulet. Instantly, he felt the familiar, tingling, the icy warmth.

The thing's eyes opened in shock.

Tristan yanked, but the leather tie around its neck held firm.

"Noooooooo!" it cried. Its mouth opened, revealing a row of sharp teeth. Its jaws lunged for Tristan's forearm.

He jerked his arm out of reach.

Its fingers clawed at the hand now holding the amulet.

Tristan's right hand, grown strong from working the forge, closed about the pendant like a vise. The creature's hands tore at his, but couldn't open his fingers. With Tristan's left hand, he ripped his knife from its sheath.

The kobold grabbed that arm, trying to take the knife.

But Tristan was stronger. He forced the blade against the leather and, with one powerful motion, cut loose the tie.

Holding the pendant, he tried to ignore the all-too-familiar tingling, the icicles of ecstasy, shooting both hot and cold up his arm. He yanked the pendant away and stepped back.

"Noooooo!" it screamed. "Give it back! Ist mine." It leaped at him, fingers reaching for Tristan's face, its mouth open, its teeth bared.

Tristan slammed a hand into its chest so hard, he knocked the air from its lungs and sent it flying over a stool and against a table. Both table and kobold crashed against the cave wall. The creature fell to the floor. The table upended onto the ground beside it.

"Do you want the pendant back?" he asked.

"Ja. Ist mein. Give it back."

"Return the Scepter and our weapons. Then you'll get it back. Not until."

It stood, breathing hard, staring at Tristan's fist gripping the pendant. Then it backed away and shook its head. "Nein. Never. The treasures are mine. All mine. I'll not give sie anything."

"Aye, you will."

Faster than Tristan thought possible, it clambered over the slippery mounds beside the path, veered back onto the trail, and broke for the cave's only exit. It rounded the passage corner. Then he heard its muffled voice, "Let go of me. Sie are . . . killing . . . me." But its words were choked, losing strength.

Tristan ran to where Milosh grinned, squeezing the life from its throat.

The kobold's hands and legs flailed wildly. Its eyes bulged. It gasped for air.

"Loosen your grip," Tristan warned. "Or you'll kill it."

A gleeful Milosh caught Tristan's glance. His hands seemed to tighten further.

"I mean it, Milosh! Let up."

His hands left its throat and tightened about an arm. The kobold, nearly unconscious, sucked in breath.

Tristan tied a rope around their prisoner's neck, looping it tightly under the thing's armpits, with a lead running to himself. "You'll not escape, Heiner. And if you don't tell us where you've hidden the Scepter and our weapons, I'll let Milosh, here, have at you again."

Still gasping, it clawed its hands at its throat and the rope circling its neck. It stared at each of them. "Empty skulls, why should I tell sie any—"

Milosh's hands shot out, wrapped its neck, and squeezed. "No more of that, now."

Fear in its eyes, it nodded.

Reluctantly, Milosh withdrew his fingers.

"Ach!" It spat at its feet. Then its hands clawed at the rope. "Can't breathe."

"Tell us, kobold!" Milosh's fingers reached for its throat again.

The creature backed up as far as the rope allowed. "Don't strangle me. Ist back in the cave. I vill show sie."

Tristan motioned, and as he gripped the lead, the kobold led them to the cave room's far corner. Piled against the wall were small boulders. The kobold began moving them aside, one by one, until it revealed an alcove carved into the mountain.

When the last rock was thrown aside, Tristan beheld a cache of swords, axes, knives, lances, maces, bows, quivers, jewelry, torcs, and, shining on top all of it—

The Scepter.

Tristan ran to it and grabbed it.

Instantly, Elyon's power swept through him. Daggers of brilliant light shot into the cave's every crevice, pulsing, radiating, blasting away every shadow and dark corner.

He still gripped the pendant with the other hand, and now it began burning his fingers. He let it clatter to the floor. The Scepter's light seemed to focus on the druidic amulet. The pendant's color darkened from silver to gray to charcoal-black. Smoke and fire obscured it. When the smoke cleared, all that remained was a molten, black mass.

"Ach!" The kobold stared and pushed forward as far as the rope would go. "Sie hast destroyed it."

"It was evil. Elyon's power destroyed it, not me."

Milosh stared with awe at Elyon's device. "So that's it?"

Tristan nodded. "Aye, the greatest gift of Elyon to the world." The Scepter's light dimmed and settled into a pleasant, soothing glow.

Then he and Milosh retrieved all their weapons. As Milosh held the chastened, downcast kobold, Tristan set everything far out of the creature's reach. He took an axe from the pile and approached Crom Mord's idol. Raising the weapon, he swung, shattering the figurine into a dozen pieces.

"Nooooo!" The kobold put its hand over its ears. "Not mein god."

Tristan began crushing the shards into smaller pieces. "It's not your god. You don't know the evil that thing represents."

"Sie lied." It looked at Milosh, took a step away, and added, "Empty skulls lied to me."

Milosh yanked on the rope, jerked the kobold off its feet. "Keep talking, and you'll get more of the same."

Tristan faced Milosh. "Let's get back to the others."

◆ ⊱✦⊰ ◆

WHEN THEY MET CAITIR AND Ewan, the others' surprise and joy at seeing the Scepter and captured kobold lifted everyone's spirits.

They returned to the pit. Tristan made one more trip into the shaft where he pulverized the first idol. He didn't know if such things held a bit of the Deamhan Lord's power or not, but he would take no chances.

But something odd happened when he brought the Scepter close to his pack. After destroying the quarter-moon pendant, the Scepter's light had settled into a steady glow. But now, as he brought it near the pack, the light pulsed and increased. A shaft of white shot from the Scepter toward his pack.

"What's happening?" Milosh stepped back, his mouth open.

"I don't know." Tristan set down the Scepter, opened his pack, and began taking everything out, one at a time. When he brought out the Augury, the shaft of light followed it. "There's a powerful connection between the two."

As though he held the thunder of a mighty falls in his hands, Tristan felt power coursing and flowing between them. Gripping the Augury in one hand, he picked up the Scepter in the other and moved them closer together. A brilliant beam of multihued light, bearing all the colors of the rainbow and more, shot between them, curled and joined in arches above and below the two.

Ewan walked forward and waved his hand through the beam. "The power I feel. Why—they magnify each other!"

Tristan moved them apart, and the beam dimmed.

"Aye." Tristan stared in wonder as he brought them together again. "Do you suppose Faolukan knows this?"

"I do not ken." Ewan shook his head. "But he kept them far apart, did he not?"

Tristan wrapped both Augury and Scepter in leather. When he brought them together again, their glow greatly diminished, finally ceased.

Tying the kobold loosely to a tree, Tristan stepped back.

"Sie hast ruined me."

"Nay. You'll get over it. You should never take another pendant from the druids again. They're evil."

The kobold stared at him then spat in his direction.

Tristan whirled. The group left him struggling with his ties.

"Do you ken, will it be able to free itself?" Caitir looked back.

"Aye. But hopefully not before we're back inside the tunnel."

"I wished you'd let me strangle the breath from it." Milosh spat to the side. "It doesn't deserve to live."

Tristan glanced at him. "We must not take a life unless 'tis necessary. That's not who we are."

"Speak for yourself."

Milosh was too eager to take a life. Tristan remembered the warning from György, the Argyn elder, on the night before they first crossed the Ferachtir flats. "Be wary of Milosh," he'd said. "His heart is true, but too often good sense flies from him like sand grit from a racing wheel."

Many times since joining them, Milosh had saved them. Yet at Amridmor he'd been so blinded by the prospect of winning a fortune, Ewan nearly lost his life in Milosh's desperate game of *primejdie*.

Perhaps, in the future, he should heed György's advice.

Milosh was a friend, aye. Still, at times like this, Tristan needed to be wary of him.

Chapter **18**

WOLVES, AGAIN

At the edge of the lake, they again hunted the white stag. This time they'd barely begun stalking when the magnificent, shining beast led them straight for the tunnel. As before, they followed it down.

As the dark, glistening burrow morphed into a passage alive with yellow-green translucent swirls, they descended. Trees of orange and yellow light parted their own branches as the supernatural buck with red ears raced ahead. Once again, their feet trod a carpet of silent, translucent leaves of light.

Time and distance sped by in the world above as they hurried along the ethereal corridor. They passed exit after exit leading up.

Again, they saw a world where great towers of stone and metal reached for the sky, where metal monsters filled with people raced along rivers of smooth black tar. Hordes of men and women in strange, unnatural dress—not a fur or hide among them—walked with unsmiling, driven faces beneath tall, glimmering towers. High above, giant metal birds left trails of white smoke like dragons.

Soon, they came to the tunnel leading to Neavh, and Tristan sighed with pleasure. Bright, heavenly light washed down around them, lifting his spirits high. Beings like the siòg swam inside the ascending walls of this passage, singing songs so pure, delicate, and exalting, he never wanted to leave.

"What is . . . this place?" Milosh gaped in awe, a grin splitting his face.

"One of the passages to Neavh," Ewan explained. "But 'tis forbidden to go there from here."

Lingering only long enough to be refreshed, Tristan hurried them on. The less time spent down here, the better, even in Neavh's heavenly light.

Much later, the dark maw to Ifreann opened below. The tunnel's oily sides swirled with black and yellow fire. A cacophony of screams issued from below, but as before, they quickly morphed into a captivating song of suggestive power, luring him down. He jerked himself back.

Beside him, Milosh's eyes were too bright, his face too intent, his feet too ready to go down.

"Look away, Milosh. Those who go that way never return."

Slowly, Milosh's glance turned to him, his eyes finally focusing.

Tristan grabbed his arm and pulled him away.

Ewan and Caitir followed.

A passage to the Waldreich opened—a dark clearing, barely lit by moonlight. Colossal oaks spread impossibly large branches over a world of shifting shadows.

More passages opened to other, alien worlds, some he'd never before seen.

Then he saw it.

A clearing in full sunlight. A tall, stone obelisk carved with the faces of ancient kings. Beside those likenesses, runes marched up and down the pillar.

"This is it." He started up. "The way back to Glenmallen."

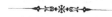

TRISTAN STEPPED OUT OF THE mound tomb following the others. As his feet touched dirt, the sounds of churning dirt and rustling vegetation filled the air. He whirled to see the passageway behind them close. Ferns, grass, and vines thick with age stretched and covered the barrow's dark hole.

He took two steps into the clearing and staggered. "We need a place to rest. I'm feeling the effects."

"Me, too." Milosh found a spot on the mound and sat.

"How about right here?" Ewan wobbled on his feet. "At least there's some sunlight."

"All right. But—"

A padding of feet came from Tristan's left. He turned his head, trying to focus through eyelids that each moment grew heavier. This was only the edge of the Waldreich, yet the trees here already grew tall, spreading their heavy, suffocating gloom on everything beyond this rarest of clearings.

Something big and dark moved in the shadows to his right.

With four legs. A hunched back. Bristling fur.

And yellow, gleaming eyes.

"A wolf," he cried. "Run!" He tried to sprint, but he was so tired, it was like running through waist-deep water. He stumbled toward the largest oak he could find.

Caitir was right behind, followed by Ewan. Milosh was just gaining his feet.

From the forest deep, no less than a dozen wolves loped toward them, their jaws open and slavering, their massive forepaws eating up ground, their eyes shining yellow.

He stopped at the first large oak with wide, spreading branches. As Caitir lurched to a stop, he cupped his hands for her foot and catapulted her up the trunk.

The wolves were gaining on the other two. Milosh had stood and was running. But he'd started late, and the pack was coming on fast.

Ewan arrived next. Tristan helped launch him up the trunk.

But Milosh wasn't going to reach the tree in time. Within moments, jaws with incisors as long as a man's finger would be upon him.

Images of Luag flashed through Tristan's mind. He remembered the sprite surrounded by Waldreich wolves, standing his ground, his axe swinging. Luag who'd gone down fighting beneath ripping, tearing jaws.

Tristan knew what he must do. He spun and clambered to the first branch.

When Milosh was twenty feet from the tree, he stopped, feet apart, sword in hand. But how could he fight against so many massive beasts?

Snarling, the wolves formed a circle that began closing. The beasts were so tall, their jaws came level with Milosh's head.

Nay, Elyon. Not another companion lost on this journey. Please, Elyon, nay.

Tristan's fingers fumbled to reach his tunic's inner pocket.

As the first wolf lunged, Milosh's blade swept in an arc, slicing a deep, red gash across its snout.

The thing whimpered and backed away. But another charged.

The bone flute was in Tristan's fingers now. He smashed the instrument to his lips. He tried to blow, but no breath issued from his lungs. The trek through the tunnel had sapped his strength.

Milosh leaped aside as the jaws of a second animal snapped shut on air. His sword thrust deep into the beast's throat and twisted. The creature's legs buckled, and it fell. Immediately, two of its fellows attacked the corpse, their jaws sinking deep.

The first two notes issued from Tristan's flute. But he was so weak, the sound fell flat, without force.

Milosh whirled to face a wolf at his rear. He staggered, nearly fell, and regained his balance. Again, his blade met an approaching lupine monster, neatly slicing off a paw.

The animal yelped and limped away, spouting blood. But two more took its place.

A wolf's jaws nearly clamped onto Milosh's leg.

He backed away, but not in time to avoid teeth ripping across his skin, spreading an ugly, red gash. Milosh's blade struck down, nearly slicing its throat. Blood spurted, and the creature dropped.

Taking a deep breath, Tristan blew on the flute. Finally, he found the notes. A soothing, calming melody burst from an ethereal well. The notes were not of this world.

As Milosh prepared to strike yet another animal, the pack halted their attack. They raised muzzles, cocked their heads, and sat on their haunches.

Though he'd barely begun playing, already Tristan felt light-headed, unable to continue much longer. His vision briefly blacked then returned. The music was like something he'd heard at the entrance to the tunnel to Neavh, but why he was able to recapture it now, he knew not. He just kept playing.

Milosh looked in wonder at beasts that, only moments before, were slavering for a kill. Sheathing his bloody sword, he staggered to the tree. Then he began climbing.

When he and the others had found branches high enough to be safe, Tristan stopped playing. Instantly, black spots popped before his eyes, and the world began spinning.

Just beneath the oak, he heard the wolves snarling, rustling the dead leaves.

Shoving the flute into his pocket, he felt at any moment like he would pass out. He began to climb.

A wolf leaped. Its jaws snapped shut just below his foot.

He clambered higher, but his fingers weren't working, weren't grasping as they should.

Another beast leaped high.

He jerked his leg out of range just before the creature's teeth closed on it. But his grip was failing. Only a few more feet to reach the next wide limb and Caitir's outstretched hand. But he was so winded . . . the world was spinning, swirling.

He reached for Caitir's hand. Missed.

Then he fell into blackness.

CHAPTER 19

A WALDREICH TREK

"Wake up," said Caitir, "and climb."

Tristan felt her slim hands grasping his. Other, stronger hands gripped an arm. Then he was lifted up, bark scraping his legs. He opened his eyes and gripped a branch for support. Ewan and Caitir straddled the limb beside him.

"You nearly fell, my lord." Concern drew Ewan's brows tight together.

"Thanks," said Tristan. "Playing so long took the wind from me."

"We're all exhausted." Ewan moved to a limb on the opposite side of them. "Now, again, we've got to sleep in the trees."

"Sleep in this tree?" Milosh frowned from a limb sticking out at right angles from theirs.

"Aye." Tristan sucked in breath. "Only way to be safe. They'll wait us out."

"Milosh, how's your wound?" asked Caitir.

"It hurts, but I'll be all right."

"Good, when we can climb down again, we'll make some tea and—"

"The wolves," interrupted Ewan's excited voice. "They're leaving!"

Tristan's glance searched the forest. Sure enough, the pack was loping with haste to the north. Had something frightened them?

"Look!" came Milosh's hoarse whisper. "To the south."

Here on the edge, the Waldreich was just thin enough so they could see a shaft of sunlight illuminating something Tristan had never before laid eyes upon. Moving ponderously through the forest was a line of animals

128

as large as houses, each covered with shaggy hair. Their legs were the size of tree trunks, their heads as wide as a man was tall, with long, curling snouts reaching nearly to the ground. Two tusks, each nearly fifteen feet long, curled up from their heads and swayed as they walked. Atop these gigantic beasts sat white-turbaned men in baskets carrying bows and spears. On the ground beside them, horses bore dozens of Drochtar cavaliers.

"Mammoths from the mountains of Gopal," whispered Milosh. "Never would I have thought to see such a sight before I died. So Faolukan has conscripted Gopalese mountain warriors for his cause. Not good."

They watched the procession tromping west. A dozen mammoths ridden by Gopalese riders, followed by possibly a hundred mounted horsemen. For long moments afterward, the woods were silent. When no further soldiers marched through, Tristan turned to the others. "We'll still have to sleep in this tree." He yawned. "The wolves might yet return."

"Aye," called Ewan. "But we'd better tie ourselves in."

With Caitir nestled against him and both tied to the limb beneath, Tristan leaned back against the trunk. Then, despite the uncomfortable position, he fell into a deep sleep.

WHEN HE WOKE, MORNING SUN washed the clearing. They'd slept through an entire day and a night. He removed his arms from around Caitir's waist and stretched.

Then she, too, woke. "'Twas good to sleep in your arms, husband-to-be." Her voice came soft and low.

"'Twas even better"—he whispered in her ear—"to hold you through the night."

She twisted so he could see her smile. "You make a fine pillow."

He leaned toward her but couldn't quite reach her lips. Instead, he kissed her on the cheek. "And you, a nice, warm blanket."

"If you two are done cooing at each other," came Ewan's voice, "perhaps we can get down and make a proper breakfast?"

Tristan felt his face getting hot. He began untying the ropes that held them safe.

"Are the wolves gone?" asked Caitir.

"Nary a sign." Ewan was already climbing down. "I've been awake for a while, listening to me empty belly."

"Good morning, my friends." A rustling erupted from the trunk's backside where Milosh had slept. "Breakfast sounds fine, indeed. And my wound needs tending."

They descended from their high refuge, made a fire, and ate. Caitir mixed a paste with Zalán's punt weed and spread it over the gash the wolf had scratched across Milosh's leg.

Then they began their trek west.

Moments later, Tristan said, "I fear the Drochtar soldiers and their mammoths follow the same track as we."

"Aye," said Ewan. "Headed for Glenmallen."

"Glenmallen?" asked Milosh.

Tristan explained about the eladrin's hidden valley and what the black-eyed folk had done for them on their way east.

"Aye, not good at all," said Milosh. "With most of the east in his grip or their leaders cowed, the Deamhan Lord is sure to send his forces west. I fear for your eladrin friends."

Silence fell on the group as they trekked on through the forest. This wasn't the deepest part of the Waldreich. Yet even here, the sound of their feet treading on ground was muffled. And the forest swallowed their words the instant they spoke. Above, the dark canopy of leaf held the world below in permanent twilight. They walked, not through a living forest, but a graveyard of ancient tombs, each masquerading as pillars of bark.

"This place"—Caitir waved at the dark trunks around them—"'tis suffocating. I canna wait to leave it behind. Forever."

"Aye, my friends." Milosh's glance warily scanned the giant trees. "This place—it fills me with disquiet."

All day they walked. And all day they saw no sign of either the wolves or the troops from the previous day. The trees thinned, and that night they camped in the open. To be safe, they set a watch.

The next morning, they continued on. By early afternoon, they left the forest. In the west rose the peaks of the Blue Mountains, extending from south to north as far as they could see. They followed a wide, low valley that gradually narrowed and climbed.

When a mountain stream bubbled across their path, Caitir stopped them. "Something's not right. I remember this place. Is this not where we saw the illusion of the raging river?"

Tristan looked ahead and behind. "You're right. And we should already have passed the great chasm. Where is it?"

When Milosh questioned what they were talking about, Ewan explained.

"If their illusions are gone . . ." Tristan shook his head.

"Aye." Worry scrunched Caitir's face. "Something's surely happened to the eladrin."

They walked farther until they entered a light forest of maples, beech, and white willows. Then Tristan knew for certain—something had happened to the eladrin magicians who kept the illusions intact.

The trail they followed opened into the familiar wide valley between mountain ranges that should have been Glenmallen. Yet before them, as far as he could see, stretched a field brimming with flowers—violets and vetchling, lungworts and stichworts, buttercups and larkspur.

"Is this their valley?" Ewan stood at the edge and scratched his head.

"Aye, see those mounds and the chimneys?" Tristan pointed to flower-covered heaps rising from the field. "Those were their roofs." A sense of familiarity mixed with a feeling that a place he once knew had become suddenly strange. "The flowers. This place."

"Aye." Milosh yawned. "Reminds me of Zalán's valley. Yet 'tis not."

Tristan felt suddenly sleepy. Then it struck him. "It reminds us because it *is* now his valley! We need to find the black flowers, fast."

Already, Caitir was stumbling along, nearly asleep on her feet.

CHAPTER 20

GLENMALLEN

With sleep threatening to fell him at any moment, Tristan hurried back to where they'd entered. He was already swaying when he found a patch of black flowers near the entrance. He dropped down on all fours and breathed deeply of their scent. Instantly, he was awake again. He brought a bouquet back to Caitir, already asleep. She, too, awoke.

They returned to the valley, walking farther than before.

Then Milosh called out. "Look, friends! The entire Drochtar caravan. With its mammoths!"

Ahead lay the sleeping forms of a dozen mammoths and a hundred horsemen. A few in the rear had tried to turn around and head back. But not one survived.

"So this is what called Zalán west?" Tristan smiled. "He started another valley. And look." He pointed farther ahead. "More soldiers caught in his trap."

Milosh whistled. "Perhaps an entire cohort of five hundred?"

"Aye, me friends," came a new voice, a familiar voice, from behind. "And I sees that this time, ye brings no more văduvă spiders to quench me desperate taste for the buggers."

Tristan whirled.

Standing before them, with hair and beard as white as snow and curling to his chest, was the wizard Zalán. Bushy eyebrows rose to the middle of his forehead. A smile lifted his lips and gleamed in smiling, pale-blue eyes.

"Zalán!" In the presence of this old man, warmth filled Tristan. He'd never known his father, and his uncle had never liked him. If he could have chosen a father, he'd gladly have taken this old wizard. "I'm sorry, but this time we have no spiders."

"I forgives ye, Tristan mac Torn. That I does. Because ye must have fulfilled yer mission. Or ye wouldn't be standing here in my valley with hair as white as mine. Ye must have passed through some kind of fire, I can see."

"I did. And I have both gifts of Elyon in my possession." But there was no more he wished to say about the past. He was eager for their adventures to be over.

Zalán's eyes lit up. "I would not terribly mind if ye would show such to me before I dies."

Tristan nodded. He reached for his knapsack, but the wizard put a hand on his. "Later. What think ye of me new glen?"

"A fine valley it is, my lord," said Ewan. "But what happened to the—?"

"I'm only a wizard, Ewan mac Ninian. A wizard who does what he can to slow the Evil One's westward march. But save yer questions." He began walking and waved them to follow. "For I'll answer all after ye've seen me new house and been properly feted."

"A feast, you say?" Ewan beamed. "Then lead on."

The four travelers followed Zalán past hundreds of skeletons and white bones picked clean by carrion. Some great battle had obviously occurred here, one the eladrin had lost. Mixed with the slimmer frames of the dark-eyed folk were only a few of the larger skeletons of the enemy and the deformed skulls of púcas.

"What happened to them?" asked Tristan.

"Gone when I arrived." The wizard pointed across the valley. "Not a one was left to tell the tale."

A shiver ran along Tristan's shoulders. One after one, the kingdoms of Ereb were falling to the Deamhan Lord.

A sense of urgency to complete his mission welled up in him. Too long had the Company been delayed under the red tent on the Ferachtir flats. Too long had they spent recovering in Zalán's former house. A necessary recovery, but now they must travel with haste. Or Faolukan's forces would beat them back to Ériu.

As they passed collapsing picket fences surrounding overgrown gardens and mound-houses, a weight grew in Tristan's chest. Somewhere here was Keenala, queen of Glenmallen, lying dead? She'd given them desperately needed help by sending them Gamil, he who led them to the Otherworld tunnel. And against her peoples' wishes, she had also sent the hiding stone that kept them safe at the mountain lake. But as he surveyed the devastation in this valley, now partially hidden by the wizard's flowers, he feared that she, too, was lost.

Caitir waved at a cluster of skeletons beside him. "I canna stand to see much more of this." She turned to face him, pain furrowing her brows. "The eladrin were so nice to us."

"Where does such evil come from?" he whispered.

"I fears, Tristan—and Caitir—that it comes from deep in the hearts of men." The wizard's face, normally on the verge of mirth, now became sullen, somber. "I sees into all who falls under me flowers—their innermost thoughts, their past, their desires. Often there's good in them, to be sure. But at the core of us, Tristan, lies a bent toward evil. We does not naturally do what's right, what's good, what's true. Somehow, we must change. We must learn to seek what's above and beyond. For when we doesn't"—he wiped a tear from the corner of one eye and spread a hand toward the ruins, the skeletons, the abandoned houses—"this is what we gets."

"I fear you're right, Zalán."

The wizard nodded then fell silent. He led them past the eladrin village, into a new grove of trees and an unfamiliar part of the glen.

Zalán's new abode looked much like his old one, a sturdy log house trailing smoke from its chimney, surrounded by herb and vegetable gardens.

Inside, the wizard's collie welcomed them with a wagging tail, paws on their chests, and a slurping tongue. Tristan ruffled its fur. He'd always wanted a dog, but his uncle Cowan would have none of it. Tristan had instead made friends with the neighbors' wolfhound.

"Sit, and I'll fix ye a feast the best I can. Though I've no tasty fried spiders to offer ye." Zalán showed them places on his bed, a single chair, and the floor. He was unused to receiving guests.

Outside, the wizard butchered four hares and cut them up. Inside, he chopped carrots, onions, cabbage, and turnips and dropped them into a boiling cauldron with the meat. While their stew simmered, he shoved loaf after loaf of bread into a stone oven in the yard.

As they waited for the bread to bake, Tristan showed the wizard the Scepter and Augury. Then he explained how, when he threw Zalán's ring into the mouth of the Crom Mord idol on the Glebe of Sacrifice, it broke the Deamhan Lord's spell of immobility and freed thousands.

The wizard narrowed his eyes. "Me magic is not that strong. Some other power—far grander than mine—was at work for ye."

"Elyon."

"Aye. And I now sees, Tristan mac Torn, that yer mission is even more important than I'd realized." The wizard scratched his beard. "I now sees what horrors the Deamhan Lord has wrought upon Erde, and I understands how great is the evil his magic weaves."

He walked to a locker, creaked open its lid, and fished around. Pulling out a package wrapped in leather, he brought it to Tristan. "I found this in one of the eladrin's secret caches. Do ye know of it?"

Tristan unwrapped the soft leather revealing a small, round stone beneath. He looked up at his host. "A hiding stone?"

"Aye. And I gives it to ye. 'Twill create an illusion big enough to hide yer group should the need arise."

"Thank you, Zalán."

"Take this as well." He handed over a pouch that clinked when Tristan received it.

Tristan opened it and found it filled with coins of all sizes and shapes from many regions over just as many eras.

"'Twill help ye on yer way."

Tristan thanked him again and closed the bag. Then he noticed Milosh's too-intense focus on the satchel and a lopsided grin shouting greed. Then Tristan wondered: Even now, after all they'd been through, would Milosh still crave a handful of gold so much that he'd put the rest of them at risk for it? He dropped the bag into his pack.

When the bread was ready, they ate their fill. Afterward, they found spots in the grass outside where they slept.

When dawn broke, they took leave of the wizard and left the valley by the route they'd entered so long ago.

◆ ▸◘◀✳▸◘◀ ◆

THE TRAIL NORTH FROM GLENMALLEN was now shorn of all illusion and magic. For five days, they traveled an ascending path between mountain ranges. On the second day out, their arrows brought down a deer that kept them in meat until they arrived three days later at the junction of trails and the shelter where they'd stayed so many months ago.

Tristan looked west toward the pass that broke the peaks of the towering Blue Mountains. "Tonight, we sleep in the shelter. Tomorrow, we head for Burgundia."

"Will the traveling be easier there?" Caitir stood beside him.

"It will. Ériu sometimes trades with Burgundia and Armorica. We're coming closer to home."

"Aye." Ewan beamed. "More civilized. More villages. Better roads and waterways. And inns with ale, biscuits, and bacon. My lords, from here on, our trek will surely be easier."

They bedded down beside a crackling fire inside the stone shelter built ages ago by the priests of Ard Cúl Dín, a fortress now lying in ruins and abandoned to history, another victim of the Deamhan Lord. Tristan slept soundly, secure in the knowledge that ahead lay a smoother, faster trek.

After they reached Lugdunum, home was only three weeks travel by horseback, river barge, and ship.

It seemed a lifetime since he'd left.

PART V

BURGUNDIA

Chapter 21

THE INN

The next morning, as eagles cried and soared above, they climbed the trail to the pass. Though it was already midsummer, snow still covered the slopes on either side. Icy meltwater burbled and trickled over the stones down the path's center, creating a muddy trek.

They arrived at the summit before noon. "There's been nary a soul along this way for months," said Ewan. "Not a single track have I seen."

"Aye." Tristan was thinking the same thing. "Which means Faolukan never breached the tunnel from Ard Cúl Dín up to the high mountain trail. His armies would have had to go north through the Fell Bogs or south to the coast."

"At least something delayed them." Caitir's glance followed the barren slopes to the high snowpack.

Descending from the pass, they reached the foothills at dusk. They camped in a pine forest that night and set out early the next morning.

Within a few leagues, the trail widened, became a well-traveled road, and entered a village. Men dressed in striped, worn breeches and floppy fur hats pushed barrows, led oxen, or gathered at shop entrances. All looked warily upon the travelers. Blonde-haired women in tunics, bearing armfuls of firewood or bread, cheese, and cabbages stepped to the opposite side of the lane. Children stopped their games and stared from alleyways.

Beyond the village, the road led through a country of low hills, past fields brimming with wheat and barley. Heading ever northwest, they passed through even more villages. Each hamlet seemed less prosperous than the last.

On the third night out from the mountains, they camped in a field by a slow-moving stream. The next day, the waterway joined a larger river. Beside its banks, they traveled north. They passed more hamlets and occasional barges heading upstream loaded with barrels, cattle, or sheep.

As the sun set, they stopped at an inn and stable on the outskirts of yet another village. Across the lane, a man was butchering a cow on a wooden table. The smell of blood and the buzzing of flies drifted over to them.

"This will be the first inn we've stopped at since leaving Cathair Duvh," said Caitir. "What I wouldn't do for a bath."

"And a hearty meal," added Ewan.

"And a flask of good wine." Milosh grinned.

A dozen wolfhounds were chained beside the stable. Kneeling before them was a man with a scruffy black beard, dirt-smeared tunic, and wild, unkempt hair. The dogs appeared thin. Some had sores on their sides and faces. Some whined. Others barked or growled.

"Back!" The man set down his bucket of water, raised a club, and brought it down on a hound that approached, snarling and growling, teeth bared. "I've got no food for you today. Keep it up, and you'll get none tomorrow, either." As the man tried to pick up his bucket, one of the largest dogs with a shaggy white coat, lunged forward, its jaws snapping. His truncheon came down, smacking it hard on the snout. It whined. He kicked the animal's flanks with a boot. It slunk away. Finally, he set down the bucket and stepped back. "Be glad to get rid of you brutes, I will."

Tristan winced. No one should treat dogs that way.

He spun away from the scene and ran to catch up to the others as they pushed through the door of the inn. They entered a cramped room warmed by logs sparking in a central fire. Woodsmoke and the smells of bread baking in the ovens, stew simmering in a kettle, and spilt wine and ale on the planks accosted his nostrils. Two narrow tables, each bearing a single customer, faced the fire.

On the fire's opposite side was a clean-shaven young man wearing a black, belted tunic with blue- and white-striped breeches. A baldric hung across his chest bearing a longsword. Though his outward appearance was ordinary, the way he sat straight on the bench and his crisp swigs of wine spoke of military training. Or was Tristan just imagining this?

A second man, sitting at the table opposite the fire, sipped from a flagon of wine and smiled at the newcomers. One hand wiped a scruffy red beard and waved in welcome to the bench opposite him. With rosy cheeks and sparkling brown eyes, he presented the very picture of joviality and friendliness.

"Sit, my friends." The red-bearded man waved again. "Abbo's the name, and this is my inn. Sit and tell me the news from afar."

What better source of news than an innkeeper? With a nod, Tristan sat next to Caitir facing the man while Ewan and Milosh sat beside the man.

After they introduced themselves, Abbo raised an eyebrow. "Foreign names, to be sure. Thought you had the look of foreigners about you. Are you in need of food? Wine? Our region produces the best wine this side of the Blue Mountains."

"Aye, indeed." Milosh slapped both forearms on the table. "Wine first."

Abbo's eyes twinkled. "Sigoald," he called to the man sitting half-asleep beside two wooden casks at the wall. "Bring these folk wine. And dinner."

A thin, wizened stick of a man rose and began filling mugs.

"You must forgive him. Sigoald hasn't been the same since a mare kicked his head. But I keep him on anyways. He's got a wife, but a sickly thing, she is. I let them have one of the smaller rooms in back. Otherwise, they'd be sleeping in the streets."

His shoulders loosening, Tristan settled more comfortably on the bench. An inn where charity ruled was a place he felt comfortable staying.

Abbo lowered his voice to a whisper. "But I'd be cautious what you say near that soldier over there."

"So he is a soldier?" Tristan glanced toward the other table.

"A scout for Gundovald on his way back from the Allobroges border."

"Allobroges?" asked Ewan.

"A region southeast of here. Hasn't yet fallen to the Butcher of Burgundia."

"The Butcher of Burgundia?" Caitir's brows furrowed.

Abbo shot her and Tristan a quizzical look. "Where are you folks from, if I may ask?"

Tristan's eyes focused on the table. They needed a good story to explain their presence and their ignorance of what everyone here would view as common knowledge. "We're on a trade mission from a wealthy merchant in Etrusca. We're on our way to Lugdunum to speak with anyone willing to do business."

Abbo sighed, as if in relief. "We never get Etruscans around here. So glad am I that you're not from someplace under Drochtar rule." He turned his head and spat on the floor. Then he ground the spittle in with his foot. "Can't trust anyone from such places. I'll have no truck with them. None."

Tristan breathed out. They might be able to trust this man. "Nor will we, Abbo."

The innkeeper nodded. "I had no idea trade was still possible with the eastern lands—what with all the rumors of war."

"Forgive us. We've traveled long and were delayed some months at sea . . . when . . . we were shipwrecked." Unfortunately, the lies were necessary. "But, innkeeper, if you would, tell us the state of your country."

Before Abbo could answer, Sigoald brought a tray laden with flasks of wine, wooden bowls of stew, and loaves of bread with butter and cheese. As Sigoald retreated to his place by the wall, Tristan paid Abbo for the meal and a room for the night. His friends attacked the repast.

"Hide that sack well, my friends. This country is full of thieves and pickpockets."

Thanking the man, Tristan put it away.

"To answer your question"—Abbo took a swig of his own ale—"Burgundia teeters on the edge of disaster. After Prince Gundovald killed his brother and made himself king, his armies surrounded the village of

Surenais a bit west of here. When the villagers resisted, he slaughtered every last man, woman, and child. That's when folks around here began calling him the Butcher of Burgundia. Since then, he's taken over another three provinces with similar ruthlessness. Rumor has it he plans to take them all. My advice is to stay well clear of Gundovald and his ilk."

Tristan remembered the news Dermid had brought them back in Ard Cúl Dín. With knife in hand, Burgundia's Prince Gundovald had gone to the bed of his brother, King Cyricus, at midnight. Then he'd cut open his brother's throat, dragged Cyricus's wife down to the river, fixed a millstone around her neck, and rolled her and the stone into the water. Then he made himself king.

But apparently, Gundovald's ambitions were far greater than the kingship of Burgundia.

"Have any *foreign* troops been through here?" Tristan's glance fell again on the soldier.

Abbo lowered his head. "A month ago, an entire cohort of five hundred Drochtar soldiers marched through our tiny berg on their way north." He squeezed his eyes shut, opened them, and eyed each of them sternly. "I fear they were only an advance party."

At that moment, the man who'd been beating his dogs entered the inn, strolled to the soldier's side, and sat. Loudly, he ordered Sigoald to bring him beer.

"There's a wretched excuse for a man if ever there was." Abbo turned to the side and spat again on the floor. "Chlodric's his name. Taking war dogs to the king, he says. But his poor creatures are near starved to death. A 'dog master' he calls himself. But he's undeserving of the name. He stayed here last night, too. Been spending the money he was given for the dogs on beer and, last night, on a whore." He turned to Caitir, Ewan, and Milosh. "I don't care for that kind of thing in my inn. But what can I do? A nasty piece of business, he is. Says he keeps his dogs under control with beatings. Makes them weak with hunger. Says they're easier to control that way—half-starved and near beaten to death."

Tristan saw the man talking with the soldier. "What connection do those two have?"

"Both are heading to Lugdunum. But I don't think the scout really wants Chlodric's company. I'm guessing he'll leave first thing tomorrow. Alone." Abbo faced Tristan. "But, my friends, what news have you of lands to the north and east? Of Romely? Or Conachtir? Or the Nordmark? How far have the Deamhan Lord's troops advanced? We get so little news from the east. Only rumors."

Tristan rubbed his temple. "The Deamhan Lord's troops are massing at Fjernshavn in Nordmark. The Plains of Romely are overrun. In Connachtir, they control the Great Bridge over the Pruwyn and all the lands around. And Ferachtir is firmly in the Deamhan Lord's grip."

"And Etrusca?"

"Safe for now. But we fear an invasion is not far off."

Abbo closed his eyes and spoke to his beer. "My friends, what's to become of us? What if the rumors are true and Gundovald does make common cause with the Deamhan Lord? They say he wants to make himself king not only of Burgundia, but also of Armorica and Esperandula."

Tristan frowned and stared at the table. Burgundia might soon become enemy territory, if it wasn't already.

Abbo raised his mug. "Here's to that little isle of Ériu. Some believe they're our only hope, the only ones who can fight against this darkness sweeping Erde. Here's to that little isle, hoping it's true."

All raised their mugs and drank.

"Thank you for your company," said Tristan. "You are indeed a friend of all that is right and true." For a moment, he wanted to tell Abbo the truth about their mission, who they really were. But nay, secrecy was best. Even here, with this friendly innkeeper, they must not reveal what they were about. He stood. "I'm going for a stroll outside. I won't be long."

Caitir gave him a questioning look. He knelt to her ear and whispered, "I'm going to do something about those dogs."

She smiled as he stepped over the bench and crossed to the door.

CHAPTER 22

THE SCOUT

Outside, the sun had just gone down. A reddish glow on the western clouds lit Tristan's way as he crossed the lane to the butcher's table. As Tristan approached, the man was nearly done carving up the cow's carcass. "Can you sell me a five-stone weight of meat, divided into twelve equal portions? And twelve bones?" Beside the man's table was parked a wheelbarrow with which he'd hauled the animal. "And I'd like to borrow your barrow for just a moment."

Still holding his knife, the man wiped his forehead with the back of his hand and cocked his head. "What coin have you to offer? I'll not give up even a handful of this here cow 'cept I get proper coin."

Tristan pulled out his bag and produced a gold sovereign from some eastern land.

The man took the coin, bit it to gauge its worth. Then his eyes grew large. "Aye, mister. For this piece, you can have the whole animal."

"Twelve pieces and the bones are all I need. Put everything in the barrow."

It didn't take long before the man's work was done.

Tristan pushed the barrow across the lane to where the dogs were chained. He took the first piece of beef and stepped toward the pack. At the scent of the bloody meat, they barked and slavered and strained against their chains. "Here you go, boys." He threw the first steak into their midst. They immediately began fighting over it.

He picked up another piece from the barrow. Instead of throwing it, he reached out and let each dog grab onto it before ripping the beef from his hands. When he'd fed the last animal, he dumped the bones out of reach, gave the barrow back to the butcher, and returned to watch.

As the dogs ate the last of their meal, he waited. Then they sat, contented. For a time, they watched each other in silence. He approached the shaggy white hound, now lazily stretched out with forepaws facing him. But as he neared, its lips parted in a snarl. "'Tis all right, boy," he said in a low, soothing voice. "I'm a friend. 'Tis all right."

He inched forward. The white dog, a bit bigger than the others, lay at the edge of the pack. The other animals deferred to it. Was it the pack leader?

As his hand reached closer, its lips curled. A low growl issued deep from its throat. But its nose twitched as it smelled him.

"'Tis all right, boy. You're a good dog. I know you are." His hand was within striking distance of its teeth.

Then it laid its muzzle onto its paws and just peered up at him.

He reached closer.

A low growl began again. But its teeth weren't bared.

His hand froze. "I'm not going to hurt you. You're a good dog." His palm was an inch from its head.

It fell quiet. Then it looked up at him with sad eyes.

His palm touched the top of its head. Slowly, he drew his fingers through its thick fur, clotted and matted with dirt. He began petting it.

The dog raised its head, looked at him, then laid it back down.

Tristan brought his other hand around, scratched it behind both ears, and it whined. He patted its head some more then stood and backed away.

The other dogs rose suddenly to their feet, looking at something behind him.

"Well, that's a sight you don't often see." It was the voice of the innkeeper. "You're a brave one. Those dogs stand as tall as my waist, with teeth as sharp as wolves'."

Tristan whirled. Ewan, Caitir, Milosh, and Abbo were all standing well out of reach, watching him. He smiled, reached down for the first bone, and began handing them out, one by one, to the dogs. They eagerly grabbed them from his hands and began chewing.

"Are you a dog master, my friend?" asked Abbo.

"Nay, just a lover of dogs."

At that moment, the black-bearded Chlodric stepped from behind Tristan's friends, a truncheon in his hands. He faced Tristan. "What are you doing with my animals?"

"Giving them the food they need and deserve."

"What business is it of yours?" He slapped his truncheon once, twice, into an open palm.

"When I see animals being mistreated for no reason"—Tristan narrowed his eyes at the club—"it becomes my business."

Chlodric stared at his dogs, each busily chewing on a bone. "You've stepped over your bounds, whoever you are. If I say the dogs are not to be fed, they're not to be fed."

"And I say that kind of treatment is unworthy of anyone calling himself human."

Air whistled through the man's teeth, and his eyes bulged. He raised his truncheon and lunged, aiming for Tristan's head.

With lightning speed, Tristan's sword flew from its sheath. The blade cut into the bludgeon with such force, it embedded itself halfway in the wood.

As hard as Chlodric yanked, he couldn't dislodge it.

With a twist of his sword, Tristan wrenched the stick from the other's hands.

The other backed away.

Tristan jerked the club free, resheathed his sword, and broke the stick over his knee. He let the pieces fall to the ground.

"Y–you!" Chlodric blubbered. "You've no right. You'll pay for this, you will." Then he spun and stalked back to the inn.

Abbo laid a hand on Tristan's shoulder. "Well done, my friend. But Chlodric's a nasty piece of business. My advice is to leave early tomorrow. Then you'll not cross paths with him. He tends to get up late."

When they returned to the inn, the scout had already gone to his room. They found their own quarters and said goodnight.

EARLY THE NEXT MORNING, ABBO greeted them in the central room with a breakfast of eggs, ham, and bread. The scout was eating at a nearby table.

The innkeeper said he was leaving on an errand. Then he winked and informed them that Chlodric was still abed.

The scout finished his meal, walked to their table, and sat. "Good morning, friends. My name is Fardulf."

Tristan swallowed a mouthful of bread. "Morning, Fardulf."

"Yesterday, the innkeeper told me you were from Etrusca?"

Focusing on the bread, he barely grunted. He didn't want to start a conversation with this man.

"But that's not true, is it?"

He stopped eating.

"I serve my lord Gundovald. I often travel to the farthest parts of our region, keeping my eyes open and bringing back news of interest to him."

Tristan braced both elbows beside his trencher. What did this man want?

"And I suspect you are the delegation we were expecting from Ferachtir. Isn't that true?"

Tristan remained silent. Were they found out? Would they have to fight this man here?

Caitir's eyes showed fear. Ewan stopped eating.

"I understand why you might not want to make your presence known. Too many in these hinterlands are not yet allied with my lord. Soon, they will be. But your hair"—he pointed to Tristan's white mop—"though I've never been there, it is a telltale mark of the Ferachtir." The man was smiling.

"Aye," agreed Tristan. "You guessed rightly. We are the Ferachtir delegation. But please don't let anyone know, especially the innkeeper. We'll change into our uniforms right before we arrive in Lugdunum."

Fardulf smiled a conspiratorial smile. "I would have done the same thing. Business such as yours should be kept secret. And we've caught spies here. Like the foreigner we caught a few months ago."

"A foreigner?"

"A tall man with a brown beard and eyes that seemed always to look beyond. Those are the kind of men I keep a watch for."

Tristan cocked his head and thought to ask his name. Fardulf's description could match Machar's. But that wasn't possible. Machar was too experienced. And he should have passed through earlier. "I commend you for your devotion to duty."

The young man smiled again and stood. "Perhaps I'll see you on the road then?"

"Perhaps." But he hoped not.

Then Fardulf picked up his pack and left the inn.

"That was close," said Milosh. "We had better *not* see him on the road or anywhere else."

"Aye," answered Tristan. "If we can, let's bypass Lugdunum altogether." But a nagging thought plagued him. Who was the man they'd caught in Lugdunum? If it *was* Machar, then Ériu would be unable to make any preparations for the coming invasion. He should have asked for more information about who they'd caught.

Not long after the scout left, they began their trek north. As before, the road followed the eastern bank of a great river the innkeeper called the Rhone. They ducked in and out of groves of ash, birch, and maples. A lone barge filled with hay shocks floated past them downstream, the man at the tiller singing a tune. When they caught sight of the scout a half mile ahead, they slowed their trek.

Tristan looked back. "I've no wish to encounter the scout or more Drochtar troops. But this road follows the river. We'll wait until we reach Lugdunum then try to find a way through the city."

Shortly after noon, they rounded a bend in the river. Not half a league ahead, the stone houses of Lugdunum began. But it was the metal sculpture that rose from the roadside that made Tristan catch his breath and step back—

A giant quarter-moon crescent, stained with rust.

Faolukan. He'd been here. Already, the city was allied with the Deamhan Lord.

"Nay, nay." Ewan groaned. "This is not good."

"Aye." Milosh glanced up the hillside. "And now we cannot climb or go around. We have no choice but to follow this road."

Caitir shuddered. "I thought we'd seen the last of that symbol."

Tristan tore his glance from the sculpture. Ahead, the river split in two. A bridge led west. Straight on, the trail followed a river veering east, toward dozens of tents and an encampment of troops. A flag bearing the quarter-moon crescent screamed "Drochtar."

Farther up the river, Tristan spied the camp of an even greater army. They flew a foreign flag that could only have been Burgundia's. The tents went on and on, proclaiming an army of thousands. Perhaps a legion. Maybe more than one. Tristan shuddered.

"We're not going east through those troops. Besides, our path lies west. That branch must be the Saone River. But unless we backtrack, I see no way to avoid the city."

"Then let's go on." Milosh waved ahead. "With so many people here, we should be able to blend in."

Tristan exhaled a low, resigned breath. If they turned back and climbed the slopes, they'd lose at least a full day.

He led them over the bridge into a maze of streets bordered by thatch huts and a poorer section of town. Gradually, two- and three-story stone houses and stores replaced them. A castle with five towers on each corner sat atop a hill to their left.

As they cleared a rise, not far ahead Tristan saw where the houses thinned and fields began—the city's end. Soon, they'd be out of the town and away from—

"Hello, my friends." The voice belonged to Fardulf.

Tristan spun. Beside the scout stood a ten-man unit of soldiers.

They were trapped.

Chapter 23

THE CASTLE

Tristan swallowed. How were they going to get out of this? The last thing he wanted to do was follow Fardulf up to that castle.

The soldiers wore black shirts over tan tunics. They carried swords, axes, and spears. To a man, their hardened faces bore the look of veterans.

"Glad am I to meet you now," said Fardulf, "before you go up to the castle. These men I know. They're returning from a patrol. But"—he frowned—"you haven't yet changed into your uniforms."

"We . . . we were surprised by how many houses cropped up by the roadside." Tristan waved behind him. "We couldn't find a proper place to—"

"This is not a problem. There's a guardhouse on the way ahead where you can change."

Tristan's glance scanned the soldiers. Too many to take on. He scoured the road in both directions. Neither could they run. He eyed Fardulf. "Thank you. But I have been wondering about the man you say you caught a while back. From what country did he come?"

Fardulf narrowed his eyes. "From Ériu, my friend. And because my lord now aligns himself with Drochtar, Ériu is now our enemy as well as yours."

"Aye, Ériu." Tristan's heart raced. He staggered and nearly lost his balance. The man they caught must be Machar. Who else could it be? Tristan didn't know how they'd do it, but somehow they must free Machar from his imprisonment.

But now, Fardulf was watching him with a frown. "Are you all right? You look pale."

"Fine. Just need something to eat. Lead us to the guardhouse, if you please."

He led them down a lane toward the hill. Barely a shack, the guardhouse stood at the bottom of a long trail leading up to the castle. Tristan, Ewan, and Milosh exchanged Ferachtir uniforms in an attempt to find one Milosh could wear without it bursting. As they dressed, Tristan whispered, "The man they have in prison is certainly Machar."

"It has to be." Ewan removed his travel tunic and packed it away. "So he never made it back home."

"We must free him. We have no choice."

"But we know nothing of this castle." Milosh frowned. "How deep are their dungeons? How many guards patrol their prisons? This is folly."

"We canna leave him here." Ewan finished dressing. "'Twould haunt me all my days."

"Aye." Tristan smoothed the blue-black swirls of the Ferachtir garb, differing from the Drochtar uniform only by a red band across the shoulders. "And it seems we have no choice but to play along for a while and be the Ferachtir delegation they want us to be."

"There is that, isn't there?" Milosh stood, and his shoulders nearly split the cloth. He loosened the brooch holding the top together. "Doesn't fit."

Tristan smiled, and the group left the guardhouse where Caitir waited outside. "You must be my slave, Caitir. They have no women soldiers in Ferachtir."

She arched her chin, her eyes flashing. "Aye, husband-to-be. Your slave I'll be. But only until we're away from here."

He nodded. Then they joined Fardulf and his escort waiting on the cobbled path leading up the hill.

"Ah!" Fardulf beamed and spread his arms wide. "Now you are a proper delegation. Follow me." The scout and his band forged ahead.

Tristan and his group followed.

The path ascended a steep, rugged hillside. Rocks and gnarled trees clung to the slopes on either side.

Suddenly, a warning wrote itself in light inside Tristan's head, and he stopped walking.

Hide the Scepter and the Augury. Do not take them up.

Reeling from the unexpected command, he dove into the thicket. Ten feet off the path, a tree grew from a cluster of rocks. At the back of the pile, he lifted a few stones and laid the Augury in the hole. Hesitating, he added to it the hiding stone Zalán had given him along with the bag of coins, and for good measure, his dagger. He left only a handful of coins in the pack.

But as he was about to add the Scepter, something stopped him. He covered up the cache. Then he moved to a spot at the front of the pile and shoved aside more stones. At the sound of footsteps from behind, he spun. Milosh was staring at him.

"What are you doing?" asked Milosh.

"Hiding the Scepter." Tristan turned back to his work and buried it under three flat rocks.

"Why?"

"Because I heard a voice warning me to do just that."

Milosh scratched his head. "That bodes ill for our visit here."

"Aye. Come on." Tristan rushed past him toward the road. "We must act like a Ferachtir delegation, not spies. The scout is full of suspicion."

When Tristan exited the thicket with Milosh behind him, Fardulf was waiting. "What keeps you, my friends?"

"Pardon me." Tristan brushed his tunic. "But before I met your master, I needed to relieve myself."

"Me, too." Milosh grinned.

"Understandable. Then let us go to the castle." Fardulf forged ahead.

As he followed, Tristan scanned the path for something to remember where he'd exited the trail. A short way up the slope—a cluster of boulders. That would have to do.

While climbing, Tristan mused on the sudden warning from Elyon. Why would he have to hide both the Scepter and the Augury unless something was going to happen to them? He shuddered. But he saw no way to back out of this, and they couldn't leave Machar behind.

Castle Lugdunum loomed ever larger as granite walls spread out to encompass the entire summit. High battlements topped by crenelated parapets looked down on their ascent. Beyond them rose a single, massive tower.

The thicket narrowed, and their path followed the edge of a cliff that dropped to a screed slope below. Behind them to the east, the Saone glistened in the afternoon sun.

At the drawbridge, now lowered, Fardulf talked with a guard who nodded and said to Tristan, "Do you have the letter with the seal of King Nicolae?"

Tristan swallowed. "Unfortunately, we lost a bag crossing a river. With it, we lost that letter."

The soldier frowned. "I'll inform the king. Wait here." The man disappeared into the castle.

"How unfortunate," said Fardulf. "Your travels must have been trying."

Tristan nodded. He hoped that excuse would work. As he waited, he examined the spike-lined moat under the drawbridge hugging the castle's western face. On the east, a sheer drop of seventy feet protected the fortress. He was about to turn away when a small wooden door slammed open about ten feet from the bottom. Out came a rush of refuse and sewage onto a mound of garbage below. From the cliffside under the castle, a stream of water trickled, circled the refuse, and washed down the center of a ravine.

Moments later, the guard reappeared on the bridge and talked with the scout.

"The king will overlook, for now, your lack of credentials," said Fardulf. "You have permission to enter." Fardulf and his soldiers began crossing.

As the group followed, Tristan's footsteps echoed over the bridge, under a massive iron portcullis, and into a cobblestone bailey. Ahead, a great tower rose on the perimeter. On one side of the yard waited a hangman's scaffold with six nooses dangling from a heavy crossbeam. But when Tristan saw the board on the opposite wall, he gasped.

A wooden wall, twelve feet high and fifty feet long, had been erected in the courtyard. White, painted lines divided the surface into five equal sections. Each section was further divided into squares with numbers. But in the center of the last section was the painted outline of a man with arms extended. Red stains marred the wood.

Primejdie! Gundovald played primejdie!

Tristan shot a glance at Milosh.

The rogue had spied the game board. The beginnings of a grin spread across his mouth.

"Don't even think it, Milosh," Tristan whispered. "If anyone asks you to play, you must decline."

Milosh grunted. But he kept watching the boards.

"I do not like this, my lord." Ewan's glance fixed on the scaffold. "Primejdie and executions—both!"

Tristan could only nod and follow Fardulf.

CHAPTER 24

CUNDOVALD

The scout led them across the bailey into a hallway ending at wide doors of blackened oak. He pushed through and ushered them into a high-ceilinged hall a hundred and fifty feet long and fifty feet wide. Landscapes, portraits of ancient kings, and depictions of battles lined the walls between silver candelabras.

At the far end, a crowd of nobles and petitioners clustered around the throne. Fardulf led them down a runner of blue carpet that deadened their footfalls. They joined the back of the throng.

A heavyset man filled the throne. His beard was black as tar, curly as inchworms, and his eyes yellow as gold, with jet-black centers. His hair curled to his shoulders, trying unsuccessfully to hide the shortness of his neck. Pudgy fingers gripped the sides of a massive mahogany throne. Covering a black tunic was a red velvet shirt, crossed with a band of leather, punctuated with gold buttons.

"My lord." A man in ragged peasant's garb, his feet bound with chain and his face contorted in fear, bowed so low his nose nearly touched the floor. "I says nary such a thing as the woman claims." The peasant glared up at a woman of high station, obviously *flaith*.

Her billowing blue satin waistcoat covered a white tunic, and it ruffled as she turned to leer at him. "When I tried to pay for his apples, the sot implied that I cheated him." A delicate hand lightly touched the back of a coiffured head. "But he was asking four pence for what was clearly a twopence apple. Then he threw insults at me. He claimed that's how the flaith got where they were—by cheating merchants and tradesmen of what they were owed. I said it was a lie. And then, my lord, he said this: He said that you, the king, got where you are by murder and foul play."

The man's eyes widened in fear. "I says nary such a thing, my lord. Nay, I'd nary say such a thing to a lady. Never. She only says that 'cause she tried to cheat me of what she rightfully owed."

Gundovald raised an eyebrow, breaking a face of stone. "I've heard enough." Eyes cold as ice focused on the apple merchant. "I'll give you a choice, merchant. The hangman's noose. Or the oubliette."

The peasant's face paled. His hands found the top of his head. "Nay, my lord. I didn't say what she said. I only questioned her honesty. She cheated me."

The king waved a bored hand in dismissal. "Vendor, your choice?"

"Not the oubliette." Shaking all over, he whispered, "The rope." Then his legs failed him, and he fell facedown, crying, "Mercy, my lord. Please, mercy."

Gundovald regarded him as a lizard might an insect crossing its path, his expression fixed, his eyes narrowing. Again, he lifted an eyebrow. Then he pointed a finger toward the door.

The guards dragged the man away.

The highborn lady smiled, tipped her head toward the king, lifted her tunic hem, and departed with her entourage.

A crisp, uniformed man with a thin frame and sporting a black mustache leaned down and whispered in the king's ear. Fardulf touched Tristan's arm. "That's Bertold, the king's secretary and chamberlain." Then Bertold announced, "Next is the case of Lord Evroul's son, Emmeran."

Guards brought forth a handsome young man with flowing blond hair and a young, shapely woman, about the man's age, with red curling locks. Soldiers' spears prodded them, and they fell to their knees. The woman was weeping.

Gundovald shifted on his massive throne. "What are the charges?"

"When the Third Storm Legion captured the town of Genève, the resistance in the city's upper quarter was fierce. Nearly seventy men we lost. Your orders were to round up everyone in that quarter and put them to death. The tenth centuria did as ordered. They gathered the entire quarter on the hillside. Emmeran, here, led the sixth centuria charged with executing the prisoners. But when he arrived at the site, he refused to carry out those orders. He was relieved of command and brought here."

"Why has this matter festered until now?" Gundovald's right eye began twitching.

"The campaign finished only days ago. A decurion only arrived with him and his wife this morning."

Gundovald's gaze bored into the young man. "Why did you not carry out your orders?"

Emmeran lifted his head and held Gundovald's stare. "It would have meant killing every man, woman, and child living in every house in fully one-quarter of the city."

"And did not that quarter resist our occupying legion?"

"A few did resist, yes."

"So then, is it not right and just that the source of that resistance—the entire city quarter—be put to death for their crime?"

"No, my lord, it is not."

Gundovald's head didn't move. Only his right eye twitched. He stared at the man before him. "Do you consider yourself a higher authority than your king?"

"No, my lord."

"Yet, disregarding orders, you placed yourself in judgment over your legate and your king. You refused to carry out my commands."

"I did, my lord."

"I see." As if he had all afternoon, Gundovald rose from his throne. He ambled toward a soldier in the crowd who carried a sword in both hands. Gundovald took the weapon, lifted it, then ran a finger over the metal surface. He twisted the blade to catch the light from the candelabras. "Is this your weapon, Emmeran?"

The young man looked up, saw the sword, and began to shake. He put a hand to his mouth.

"I asked you a question!" Gundovald's shout shattered the stillness.

The young woman began sobbing uncontrollably.

"Y–yes, my lord." Emmeran's voice shook. "It is."

"Then lower your heads!" The king's bellow seemed to rattle the very paintings on the wall. "To the floor. Now!"

Emmeran tried to keep his glance on the sword. But a soldier's boot came down on his back, pinning him to the marble.

Swiftly now, surprising everyone, Gundovald stepped to the woman, swung down with the blade and, with a single blow, severed her head from her body. Then, while a boot held Emmeran close to the marble, the sword came down upon the young man's neck. But the blade struck mostly marble and only cut through partway. Emmeran writhed beneath the boot. Gundovald's weapon rose and struck again. Then Emmeran's head rolled away to join his wife's. Two lifeless bodies lay before the throne.

His heart pounding rapidly, Tristan closed his eyes on the bloody mess. He feared he'd become sick.

"Clean it up." Gundovald's voice was quiet as he resumed his seat.

Trembling servants rushed forward and dragged the bodies away. Others appeared with buckets, mops, and rags. A long while later, the floor was as clean as Gundovald's slaves could make it. But the metallic taste of spilt blood still befouled the air.

Bertold, the thin, black-mustachioed man, cleared his throat and faced the court. "Next will be the delegation from Ferachtir. Please step forward."

Fardulf led Tristan and his companions to the front. Following Fardulf's example, Tristan knelt and bowed his head before standing.

Fardulf beamed. "I met them on the road, my lord."

Gundovald's head barely nodded. "Any ally of Drochtar is an ally of mine. But I hear you lost your note of introduction from Nicolae?"

Tristan swallowed and tried to keep the fear from his voice. "We did, my lord. Crossing a river."

"Well . . ." Gundovald focused on something across the room. "I welcome you to my lands anyways."

Tristan bowed. "Thank you, my lord. We are glad to have finally arrived. It was a difficult journey."

The king stood, cast a stony glance over his court, and whispered in Bertold's ear. Then he left the room.

Then the officer addressed Tristan and Fardulf. "This afternoon, you are invited to dine with the king in private chambers. Until then, quarters are prepared for you. When you come for dinner, you will leave your weapons in your room. Please follow me."

Bertold led them up two flights of stone steps to a third-floor hallway where he showed Tristan and Caitir to one room, Ewan and Milosh to another. "A small lunch will be brought to you," said Bertold. "You may bathe as you wish. A servant will come for you at sunset." He bowed then left.

Tristan pushed open the door to a room with a balcony overlooking the river and city beyond. A fire burned in a brazier, its smoke drifting toward the open window. Drapes enclosed three box beds hugging the wall. Tristan dropped his pack then sat at the table where Caitir had plopped heavily into a chair.

"I thought I was going to be ill." She lowered her head into her hands.

"Gundovald is a monster."

"And now we have to endure dinner with him," she said. "How am I going to get through it?"

"You will. We all will. As we must."

"And how are we ever going to find and free Machar?"

"Perhaps tonight, after we go to bed, I'll begin a search. There'll be fewer guards about then."

"Nay, Tristan. In this place, 'tis too risky—"

A knock on the door was followed by a girl bearing a tray with a flask of wine, two silver goblets, a bowl of apples, cheese, and bread. As she set it on the table, a second maid brought in two large pitchers of steaming water and towels. Both bowed then left.

Tristan grabbed an apple and bit into it. "Let's wait until after this dinner with Gundovald before we decide what to do. Perhaps we'll learn more."

She nodded. They ate a bit of the food then took turns washing themselves in the corner while the other faced away. When they had dressed again, they both lay atop the warm furs and snuggled together in the same bed.

"This is nice." Caitir faced him on the bed. "We are hardly ever alone, you and I."

His hands stroked her cheek. "Aye. On the trail, it is ever thus."

"Tell me, future husband, when we return to Ériu with this great treasure, what will we do—you and I? Tell me again."

"After the Scepter lies in the Tower of Dóchas and the Augury is tucked in its niche below, we'll return to some village—not Hidden Pines—and open a smithy."

"And you'll work outside while I sew and churn butter and wash clothes and have your supper ready at day's end?"

"Aye, lassie. And don't forget the little ones."

"Little ones?" Her lopsided grin told him she knew exactly what he meant.

"Babies."

"Of course." She raised her head and kissed him on the lips. "How many, do you ken?"

Caitir's green, enchanting eyes were smiling at him. She was so inviting, he had to remind himself what they'd promised—that they would not lie with each other until they married back home. "Twelve or thirteen, maybe."

A frown wiped the smile from her mouth, and her head bumped lightly against his. "Really?"

"Nay. Maybe three or four."

Her lips spread into a heartwarming smile. Then she seemed to grow somber. "Tristan?"

"Aye."

"We've seen so much evil and death. Even today. In this accursed castle. Is it really possible? Are we really going to get home and have a life together? Tell me the truth."

He lifted a lock of her hair, pulling it away from her eyes. "We are, Caitir. We are."

"And nothing is going to stop us?"

"Nay. Nothing."

"Because every time we get somewhere, something goes wrong. And the evil in this world around us only seems to grow stronger. And Faolukan always seems to be ahead of us. His troops are everywhere. He is so powerful . . . I sometimes do not ken how we can ever defeat him."

"Nay, Caitir. We *are* winning." He kissed her forehead. "Look how far we've come. Look what we've done already. We've acquired both of Elyon's great gifts. Now all we have to do is take them home."

She cupped his face in her hands. "'Twas you, my love. 'Twas you who have done this. But you're right. We have the Scepter and the Augury, and we're almost home. Once we leave this castle, what could possibly happen to prevent us from getting there?"

"Aye. What?"

"There is really a better world ahead of us, is there not?"

"There is."

She rolled over to face the ceiling. "I hope so. I canna wait to be part of it, to see the Scepter shining from the Tower. And to have our very own home. 'Twill be wonderful, nay?"

"It will be wonderful."

Then they fell asleep in each other's arms.

Much later, someone knocked on the door announcing it was time for dinner.

They rose from their nap, brushed their clothes smooth, and joined Ewan and Milosh in the hallway.

There, a tall man in a plain tunic bowed. "I am the manservant in charge of guests. I will take you downstairs. But a word of advice and a request: My master has a penchant for gambling for—what shall I say? High stakes? If the king asks any of you to join him in a game of chance, the chancellor has asked me to ask *you* to politely but firmly decline. This is for your own welfare, as well as the king's."

He bowed then led them toward the stairwell.

Both Tristan and Ewan shot a look of concern toward Milosh, whose grin seemed to split his face.

CHAPTER 25

A TROUBLED DINNER

At the dinner, the king occupied the seat at the table's head—more a throne than a chair. Tristan and Company were positioned on cushioned chairs on the king's left. As Tristan's slave, Caitir was required to stand against the wall with the servants. On the king's right sat Bertold, the chancellor; also a white-robed druid they called Fearghas; and a man in a military uniform with five epaulets named Baldger; and, of course, Fardulf, the scout.

As servants laid fresh bread trenchers before each, maids began pouring wine into wide silver goblets. Caitir helped.

"How many troops has Ferachtir pledged to send our way?" asked Baldger. "We could use them before the final push to the coast."

Bertold looked to Gundovald, received a nod, then faced Baldger. "Let us hold our discussions of such matters until after supper. The king finds it helps digestion."

"As you wish, chancellor." Thus chastened, Baldger fell silent.

The servants bore in trays of beef cooked with mushrooms, onions, carrots, and cabbage. A wine sauce was drizzled over all. The king received his portion first, then the right side of the table, then the left.

As Tristan ate, the king spoke for the first time. "Are any of you familiar with the game of primejdie? I'm told it is played in Amridmor. Even in the southern oases."

Tristan spoke quickly. "We are, of course, familiar with it, my lord. But none of us play anymore."

Gundovald narrowed his eyes at Tristan. "But surely, this is your country's claim to novelty, a game of chance unlike any other. Surely, one of you still plays?"

"I do, my lord," said Milosh. "I find it quite . . . enjoyable."

Tristan nearly choked on the meat he was chewing.

Bertold scowled at both of them.

A smile flickered over Gundovald's face then vanished. "And for what stakes have you played?"

Milosh waved a hand. "Oh, for never more than a bag of coins. A wealthy man I am not."

Gundovald stabbed a piece of meat with his knife like it was going to flee his trencher. "What is the most you ever won?"

Milosh shrugged. "I once had in my possession winnings equaling a four-mark weight in gold. But I lost it."

One of Gundovald's eyebrows rose. His knife froze on his trencher. "A significant sum for a man who says he's not wealthy."

"As I said, I lost it all."

"A shame, that." Gundovald put both elbows on the table and laced his fingers before his face, then spread his hands in a benevolent gesture. "What would you say if I gave you that very same sum right now? But on condition that you play primejdie with me for a bit?"

Bertold coughed and shook his head.

Tristan stopped eating and stared at Milosh.

Milosh's eyes grew bright. A grin spread across his mouth. "To that, I would say aye, my lord. Aye, indeed."

"Good, I'll—"

But at that moment, a courtier burst through the near door. He crossed to the king's side, bowed low, and whispered something in his ear.

Gundovald frowned. "Repeat to Bertold what you told me." He turned a stony face to Tristan. Not a flicker of expression told him what the man was thinking.

The courtier whispered for a time in Bertold's ear. As Bertold listened, a scowl formed on his face, again directed at Tristan. The chancellor nodded, pushed away from the table, and crossed to the king's side. The two conversed in whispers. Then Bertold stalked from the room.

"Something has come up"—Gundovald stabbed another piece of meat—"concerning our guests. Until we sort this out, do continue eating." He waved at the others.

But in the strained silence that followed, Tristan couldn't eat.

Neither could Caitir or Milosh. Even Ewan stopped lifting knife to lips.

Fardulf and Baldger exchanged glances, watched their dinner companions with newfound wariness, and merely picked at their food.

Moments later, Bertold returned leading in a troop of a dozen lancers. They marched into the dining room and took a position behind Tristan and Company. Bertold ordered Caitir to stand behind Tristan and wait.

Tristan's heart leaped against his ribs.

Gundovald lifted his knife and pointed it at the ceiling. "It appears, my friends, that another Ferachtir delegation waits at the drawbridge."

Feeling faint, Tristan braced both hands alongside his trencher, palms flattened to the wooden tabletop.

As if nothing had happened, Gundovald sliced a piece of beef. "They will be with us momentarily."

Milosh's grin seemed to freeze on his face.

Caitir stared at the floor.

Ewan looked to Tristan.

And Tristan felt the sweat beading up on his forehead.

When the doors opened again, five white-haired Ferachtirs crossed the long hall, their footsteps padding over the carpet. The tallest man stopped at the king's side and presented a parchment signed and sealed by King Nicolae of Amridmor. He glared with undisguised contempt at the interlopers sitting at the king's left.

The Ferachtir bowed before the monarch. "King Gundovald, I regret to inform you that our leader took ill on the journey. Your men put him straight abed. He bears instructions from Drochtar. He insists that he himself must bring them to you later."

Again, Gundovald put his elbows on the table. "What an unfortunate turn of events. Instead of a Ferachtir delegation, you turn out to be spies. Where are you from?"

"Etrusca, my lord." Tristan tried to keep his voice even, his face growing hot.

Gundovald's eyes narrowed. Then a fist came down onto the table so hard, the wine goblets near him danced, and Tristan jerked back. "Don't lie to me!" His voice, so quiet until now, took on such an increased volume that even the servants standing by the wall started. "You are *not* from Etrusca. Where are you from?"

"Where do you think?" Tristan kept his glance on Gundovald's.

The muscles on Gundovald's jaw tensed. "You are from Ériu, are you not?" He stared at the table. "We were warned to look out for more spies from your lands. Now it seems we have them." He motioned to the guards who roughly grabbed each of their arms and dragged them to their feet. "Instead of the meal we had prepared for you—and the dessert was something special—you will now experience our gallows." He pushed away from the table, stood, and faced the soldiers. "Bring the apple merchant, too. And that other fellow, the thief I condemned earlier today. We'll begin this dinner again—with the proper guests—but after the hanging."

As they led him away, Tristan's heart leaped. He could barely put one foot before the other. From the moment they'd sat down, everything had gone badly.

Beside him, Caitir's face had turned ashen.

Ewan now wore a mask of grim determination.

Even Milosh's grin had vanished.

The soldiers' steel-tipped lances guided them down stairs and onto the cobbled bailey, lit now by cressets standing at twelve-foot intervals. As the rest of the dinner party and the Ferachtirs followed, the guards marched them up the wooden steps to the row of gallows—six nooses expertly coiled, already hung from a supporting beam. Below each of the hangman's halters waited the dark outlines of six trapdoors.

The guards tied the prisoners' hands behind their backs. Starting at the third gallows, a black-hooded man slipped a noose first over Milosh's neck. Next, the hangman's knot wrapped the necks of Ewan, then Tristan, and lastly, Caitir.

When the executioner fitted the rope over Tristan's neck, its hairy bristles roughly scraped his skin. His heart was beating so fast, he began to see spots.

To his left, Caitir was staring at him with wide, frightened eyes. "I love you," she whispered.

All he could do was nod. His lips were so dry, he didn't think he could speak.

Guards marched two other prisoners across the cobbles. The black-hooded hangman placed the apple vendor on the first gallows and slipped the second noose on a thin, haggard man Tristan didn't recognize. Each of the six gallows' positions was now occupied.

Tristan looked up into a star-bright sky. Would this be the last day they'd see on Erde? Was everything going to end here? With his heart beating so wildly, he feared it would burst.

Meanwhile, Gundovald, his officials, and the Ferachtir delegation had gathered on the bailey facing the gallows. They had brought their wine goblets with them and now conversed quietly, laughing and gesturing as if they were attending some kind of party. Off to the side, servants held pitchers, waiting to refill any empty chalice.

When an aide whispered in Gundovald's ear, he finally noticed that the gallows were ready. He regarded the prisoners briefly. Then he lifted a finger in the hangman's direction.

Already waiting behind the apple vendor, the black-hooded man placed a gloved hand on a lever and yanked. The trapdoor dropped away, and the man fell. The rope jerked taut. A shock rippled through the supporting beam, vibrating even the platform where Tristan stood. The strands twisted, turned, as the man's feet kicked and writhed. From below the trapdoor, Tristan heard the man gasping for breath. Then the rope stilled.

The hangman moved to the next prisoner, the haggard thief. Again, he pulled a lever. The trapdoor slammed down on squeaking hinges, and the man fell. With a sickening jerk, the rope tightened. It must have broken his neck, because Tristan heard no death struggle.

The black-hooded man now moved behind Milosh. The rogue was staring straight ahead with a frozen half-grin. The hangman's hand reached for the handle of the mechanism that would drop the floor, when—

"Stop!" came a strangled cry from across the bailey. "Don't kill them."

Gundovald raised a hand. The hangman backed away.

Two Ferachtirs held between them an elderly white-haired man, his face pale and wan. He staggered across the yard and approached the king. "Forgive me, my lord. I am unwell." He bowed and almost collapsed. The younger Ferachtir at his side helped him stand. "I am our delegation's leader. And I bring orders that if you capture the spies"—he faltered, went down on a knee until his assistant lifted him upright again—"you must keep them alive for questioning. They carry a device of the greatest interest to the Deamhan Lord."

An eyebrow rising, Gundovald tilted his head. "What kind of device?"

"A Scepter, it is. A magical device of colossal power. And in the wrong hands, it could inflict great harm on our master's plans. You are requested to determine its whereabouts and, if possible, secure it. This request is of the highest importance."

"Search their bags!" Bertold ordered.

One of the servants stepped forward. "Before dinner, we already searched everything they brought. We found no such device."

Gundovald nodded. "For the moment, leave them on the scaffold." He gave the entourage his back, casually strolled across the yard, then sauntered back. He stopped before Milosh. "You say, my friend, you are a player of primejdie?"

Milosh's grin was frozen, his face pale. "I am, my lord."

"Do you know the whereabouts of this Scepter?"

He glanced to his left, toward the others, then back at Gundovald, but said nothing.

"Ah, so you do know." Gundovald rubbed his beard. "So I'm guessing you hid it nearby. Am I right?"

Milosh shook his head nay.

"You're lying. But let us make some sport of this, you and I." A hint of a smile lifted one corner of the butcher's mouth then fled. "If you bring this device to me from its hiding place, this is what I offer: I will play primejdie with you." He turned to Bertold standing beside him. "His name is Milosh?"

"It is," said Bertold.

"If you will play with me, Milosh, I promise to free all of you, no matter the result of our game. If you lose, you will allow me to keep the Scepter. But if you win, you may take the Scepter with you. To sweeten the contest, I will also give you, as a starting sum, the same amount you previously lost—a four-mark weight in gold. What say you?"

"Don't do it, Milosh!" Tristan nearly screamed. "He's only trying to find out where it is."

"Aye," Ewan added. "'Tis only a trick."

But Milosh's eyes seemed alight with an inner fire. "Aye, King Gund-ovald. For those stakes and for freeing all of us, I will certainly play."

"But, my lord"—the Ferachtir leader, his face now white as a druid's robe, spoke up—"if you lose, the Scepter will—"

Gundovald's whole body turned toward the man, and he began to shake. When he lifted a finger, it, too, shook. "My friend, I . . . will . . . not . . . lose." He whirled toward the soldiers. "Bring the prisoners down from the scaffold, watch them, and keep their hands bound. Also, pre-pare the primejdie boards for play. Four of you—release this Milosh, follow him to where he's hidden this Scepter, and bring him back here."

Gundovald gestured to the entourage milling about him. "As for the rest of us, let us retire upstairs and finish our repast. When all is in read-iness, we'll return for a game of high-stakes primejdie. That should liven up our evening, nay?"

PART VI

LUCDUNUM CASTLE

CHAPTER 26

PRIMEJDIE

Tristan waited with the others in the bailey for what seemed an eternity. The night brought cool air, welcome on his overheated forehead. With their hands still bound, he and Ewan stood beside each other. No one felt like speaking.

After a long wait, the guards led in Milosh. One of them carried an item wrapped in leather. But the guard held it in front of him, keeping a frightened glance on the package, not on the cobbles at his feet.

Milosh stopped ten feet away but avoided looking into Tristan's eyes. As one of the soldiers ran across the yard to a door, Milosh faced away from the Company.

"What are you doing, Milosh?" Tristan could barely keep the anger from his voice. "He'll not let us keep it. You know that, don't you?"

"I think he will." Milosh turned around and finally looked him in the eyes. "And he'll free all of you. That's what's important."

"Nay. What's important is what will happen after the Deamhan Lord gets his hands on the Scepter. This is treachery. Don't do it. Better we die on the scaffold than let the lord of evil win."

"I do not want to die here any more than you"—Ewan's voice was strained—"but I agree with Tristan. If Faolukan gets the Scepter, everything we've struggled for has been for naught."

"Everything is turning out . . . badly." Caitir's voice, too, was tight, strained, as though she was on the verge of tears. Her glance swept from one of her companions to the other, finally settling on Milosh. "Now you're giving them the Scepter we fought so hard to get."

"Don't worry, my friends." Milosh's grin faltered. "I know what I'm doing."

They waited in uncomfortable silence until Gundovald and his entourage once again entered the bailey. The king stalked straight to the nervous guard and took the leather-bound object from his hands. Leisurely, he unwrapped it. With his left hand, he grabbed it. The leather cloth fell to the cobbles.

Slowly at first, a cold, dark light began building. Then it burst out across the yard. Like a winter's blast racing over a snowfield, it chilled Tristan's face, arms, and legs. Dark shadows blocked out the stars and a sliver of moon that, only moments before, had filled the sky. Even the light from the cressets dimmed.

Gundovald's eyes widened. He stared at the Scepter in his hand, now shaking violently. Another rush of shadows swept out, nearly knocking Tristan off his feet. With that wave, Tristan could sense Gundovald's deep ambition, the coldness of his heart, the contempt he felt for everyone around him. In this man's hands, the power of the Scepter twisted into something ugly, cruel, and dangerous. Tristan staggered, took a step back.

Then Gundovald dropped the Scepter. It rolled, clattered over the stone, and came to rest.

The shadows vanished. The stars and moon reappeared.

"W–what?" Air whooshed from Gundovald's lungs. "*What* is that thing?"

The Ferachtir leader had gone back to bed, and the younger, taller man spoke in his place. "'Tis a foul device holding the power of Elyon. Its purpose we know not. The enemy plans to use it against us."

Gundovald's gaze couldn't leave the device lying on the ground. "The power it held! Never have I experienced such a thing. Never did I suspect such power even existed." He opened his hand. His palm was bright red, as if burnt. "Oh, to be able to wield that against my enemies! Oh, what countries I could conquer!" He gestured his injured hand toward a servant. Then the man brought him water, which he poured over the injury.

After a time, Gundovald motioned to a soldier who brought a bag of coins to Milosh. "Here is gold worth the four marks I promised you. We will play by Burgundia's rules. Minimum bet is one mark. Minimum number of plays is three. After that, we play until someone hits the square of jeopardy. We will use spears, and—"

"But, my lord." Milosh shook his head. "Primejdie is played with knives, not spears. That is what I agreed to."

Gundovald narrowed his eyes. "Then I will make an exception for you, and you alone, on that point. You may use knives. But I will use spears."

Both men moved to a spot some fifty feet from the primejdie wall. A soldier brought a knife and passed it into Milosh's hands. Black leather wrapped a long handle. Its one-foot blade gleamed by torchlight.

Another soldier bore to the king a spear tipped with a wide steel flange.

Caitir whispered in Tristan's ears. "How is this game played?"

"A player picks a square, and that is his target. The center square is always the square of jeopardy. Then they blindfold you. If a man's blade lands in his chosen square, he wins one-and-a-half-times the bet from his opponent. But if he hits the square of jeopardy, he loses everything he placed on the cloth. Both players must match what the other brings to the game. In Amridmor, Milosh started with nine pieces of silver and, within a few throws, ended up with one hundred and eight."

"Those are high stakes, indeed."

"It got worse. The game took a dangerous and unexpected turn. At one point, Milosh hit the square of jeopardy. He lost it all. Then they . . ." Tristan couldn't finish. He didn't want to talk about how Ewan stood against the wall as Milosh threw the knife at him.

"Because this is the game's ultimate prize, we'll place the Scepter at the head of the cloth." Gundovald motioned to the guard who used the leather to pick up the Scepter. He bore it to a large black cloth whose white grid lines matched the primejdie board.

"You may go first," said Gundovald. "What do you bring to the play, my friend?"

"All four marks." He placed them on the cloth at the lower right-hand corner.

Gundovald nodded, matching Milosh's four marks with his own in the lower left. "And your first bet?"

"Two marks in the upper right." Milosh placed two marks on that square.

"Good." A fleeting smile crossed Gundovald's mouth. "I see you are not a man for caution. As usual, the square of jeopardy is in the middle."

Milosh grabbed the knife by the blade, hefted it several times, threw it once in the air. It made a circle, fell, and he caught the blade in the same position from which he'd thrown it. "Good blade, this."

Then he eyed the board. The targets were two-foot squares in a nine-square grid. Big enough maybe with two eyes on the goal. But blindfolded?

"I'm ready," said Milosh.

A soldier wrapped a black bandana tightly around his eyes and stepped away.

Milosh took a deep breath, drew his arm back, and pitched the knife forward.

It struck the wall at the edge of his chosen square, the blade chattering.

Tristan breathed out. Milosh yanked the blindfold away and smiled at what he'd done.

"Nicely done." Gundovald moved three marks from his pile to Milosh's.

Milosh took back his two marks.

"I'll increase my pot to equal your seven." Gundovald plunked three more marks on his side of the cloth. "My bet will be four marks on the upper left." He placed his bet and picked up one of the spears. He hefted the lance several times before nodding to the soldier who blindfolded him.

Gundovald's upper body twisted, his arm reached back, and he thrust his spear.

173

It slammed into the wood in the center square.

He ripped the mask away, stared at the target, and scowled. "Well, you've won all seven marks." Gundovald pushed everything on the cloth onto Milosh's corner. "You've got fourteen marks already. Quite a tidy sum. I will add the same number to my pot." He dropped more heavy coins onto his circle. "What is your next bet?"

"Eight marks. Same target." Milosh moved eight pieces into the upper right square, picked up his knife, and hefted it. Grinning, he asked for the blindfold.

The soldier tightly wrapped his eyes, and Milosh hefted the blade.

He drew his arm back. Again, the blade flew from his hands.

And landed in the center.

In the square of jeopardy.

When Milosh saw what he'd done, he moaned.

"What does this mean?" whispered Caitir.

"He's lost it all." Tristan closed his eyes. "The game is over."

"And you were doing so well." A smirk lifted one corner of Gundovald's mouth. "That's the game, my friend. The Scepter is mine. And all your winnings."

Milosh stared at his still quivering knife as if it were all a mistake. "Is there . . . no . . . way to redeem this? Is there not a higher . . . level?"

"Ah." Gundovald's eyes gleamed. "I was hoping you'd ask. Yes, there is indeed another level. If you win there, you get to keep the pot you just lost and continue playing. But in the new game, you must play by Burgundian rules."

Tristan shook his head, waved his hands, trying to keep Milosh from making the same mistake he'd made back in Amridmor.

"I accept. Let's go to the next level. Give me another chance."

"You have it. But now we move to the target at the far right of the boards." Gundovald pointed to the outline of a man with two-foot squares surrounding the upper body. Everyone walked to that end of the boards.

Gundovald motioned to a soldier who brought forth a cluster of five spears. "By the new rules, it is *you* who will stand in the center as the target of jeopardy, and it is *I* who will choose which of your companions throws at you."

"W–what?"

"Aye, and now we switch to spears. They are much more effective at this level."

"Of . . . course." His eyes wide, Milosh walked slowly to the boards on the far right. To the outline of a man. He stared at the red stains marring the wood. Then he leaned back against it. Closing his legs together, he tried to keep them inside the squares on either side. He stretched out his arms, resting them on metal pegs placed to keep them within the target area.

"Good." Gundovald's gaze swept the three travelers, eyeing first Ewan, then Caitir. But at Tristan, he stopped. "You! I choose you."

Tristan looked at the man, unable to move. Then slowly, back and forth, he shook his head, the small motion alone a struggle.

"I've chosen you, and now you must throw the spear. You have no choice."

"The spear is not my weapon. I am no good at it." He raised his hands in appeal.

"That is not my concern. If you don't throw, I will order my men to shoot him full of arrows, and you will have forfeited a life you could have saved."

For a moment, Tristan froze. But it was no use. There was no getting out of this.

He walked to the position where the soldier held the javelins. Tristan accepted one. "Why are there five?"

"Because at this level, you must put three out of five throws into the squares around Milosh's upper body. If you do not put three out of the five into the targets—my men will finish the job with arrows."

"What if I miss or wound him?"

"If you haven't used up your five throws and if Milosh is still breathing, you may continue throwing."

Tristan swallowed. He closed his eyes and shook his head again. He tried to tell himself it was Milosh who had forced him into this. Now he had no choice but to play, however barbaric was this game. If he won, they would be free and keep the Scepter.

But could he trust this mad king to give them what was promised?

He examined the target area. Five squares nestled against Milosh's body—two under each arm beside his chest, two beside his head, and one on top of his head.

The right side square under the arm—that would be his target. He wiped wet hands on his tunic and hefted his weapon. He pitched it back and forth as if throwing it, aiming for his chosen target. "Blindfold," he called.

The soldier wrapped the black cloth around his eyes, shutting out the light.

He cocked his arm, held the position, and let the javelin fly. Then he ripped the blindfold away.

The spear had struck his chosen square, but only inches from Milosh's chest.

Milosh grinned.

While a soldier removed the first spear, Tristan breathed deeply and tried to calm his racing heart. Only two more throws to go.

He took a second weapon, hefted it as before, pitched it back and forth, aiming for the same spot. "I'm ready."

Once again, the soldier wrapped his eyes.

He drew his arm back, held the position, then pitched the weapon forward.

Before he could get the blindfold away, he heard a gasp of pain.

The spear had landed on the lower left square, not the right, and close up against Milosh's side. A dark red stain now spread along the side of his tunic. Milosh was breathing heavily, gritting his teeth. "I'm all right, my lord." But his words were strained.

Tristan had one more throw to save Milosh's life and give them a chance to keep the Scepter. But his last throw had gone so wide, it was a miracle it hadn't struck the chest.

As the soldier removed the second javelin, a sick grin lifted Gundovald's mouth. The king waved, urging Tristan to finish.

What barbarity was this? Throwing at his friend?

Tristan took the third spear, tested its weight as before and its balance. When he had the target square firmly in his sights, he called for the blindfold. But now he was breathing too fast, his hands were clammy, and his arm was shaking. As darkness closed off his view, his breathing quickened even more.

Jerking his arm back, he held the spear even longer. Then he hurled it forward.

The sound that met his ears was unmistakable. It was not the sound of metal quivering in wood. It was the liquid thud of punctured flesh, air exploding from lungs.

He ripped the blindfold away and stared at what he'd done.

Tristan's spear had struck just below the rib cage, piercing deep. Blood poured down his front.

Milosh stared at the weapon jutting out of his abdomen. His mouth was open, and blood foamed on his lips. He looked up at Tristan, his face contorted in pain. "Not. . . your . . . fault," came his last, barely audible, words.

Then he slumped, his body pulled away from the board, taking the spear with it, and his corpse crumpled in a heap to the ground.

"Nay!" Tristan screamed. "Nay!" He rushed forward. He knelt beside the rogue who had helped him find his friends when they had been taken captive in the salt works. This was the man who had led them across the Ferachtir flats. Many times had Milosh's skill and roguish nature saved their lives.

Now he was dead. By Tristan's own hands.

His fingers wrapped Milosh's right arm. "Friend, I'm sorry." His hands came back red. He turned to face the others.

Tears streamed down Caitir's face. Her fingers covered her mouth.

Shaking his head, Ewan walked toward him. "You did your best, my lord. He brought this on himself." His hand fell on Tristan's shoulder. "Nothing else you could do."

"Come, come, my friends." The king's voice held triumph and gloating. "Do not mourn over him. He knew the stakes, knew the game. This is how it is played."

Tristan stood and whirled to face him. "And now you will let us go free. That was the bargain."

With a smile, Gundovald opened both hands. "I made that bargain with Milosh, not with any of you. But he is no longer with us, is he? So I am under no obligation to continue that arrangement." He lifted a finger, waved it toward the castle. "Put them in the oubliette. But for now, keep them alive."

Guards stepped forward and grasped Tristan, Ewan, and Caitir roughly by the arms.

They marched up steps leading to a door in the tower.

Chapter 27

THE OUBLIETTE

The tower steps opened into a small foyer. A side door opened to the kitchens. But the soldiers herded them down a stairwell into an echoing darkness lit only by torches.

In a daze, Tristan somehow put one foot below the next. The lower they went, the colder it became. Ahead, Caitir stumbled and was stopped only by Ewan's outstretched arms. As Ewan turned to help her, his face was ashen.

With swords drawn, two guards led the group. Another two with spears followed. A fifth man carried their packs.

They passed a locked door where stood a lone guard. He grinned as the group continued lower.

Was it just earlier today that joy filled their hearts and they faced a trouble-free journey home? Then they had borne the precious gifts from Elyon that would end the evil spreading across the world.

Now, Milosh was dead. They faced imprisonment. And the Scepter was again back in enemy hands. Again, it threatened to give the Deamhan Lord and his allies powers they never before possessed. How had everything fallen apart so quickly?

The stone steps ended in a locked wooden door. A guard's key admitted entrance to an underground circular room lined with six cells on the outside wall. Two torches in sconces cast a dim, flickering light over damp stone. Metal bars enclosed apparently empty cells.

Behind Tristan, someone coughed. But whoever was inside that cell sat far back in darkness.

"You can't go down there dishonoring those uniforms," said the guard carrying their packs. "Put on your civilian clothes." He threw the packs onto the floor.

They each found their own knapsacks, pulled out their traveling tunics, and dressed. Only Caitir didn't have to change. But as Tristan fumbled in his sack for the tunic, he managed to slip his two lock-picking tools into the tunic pocket before bringing it out. He also slipped his bone whistle into the pocket.

When they had changed, the soldier threw their packs into a corner and left.

A lean guard with what appeared to be a permanent leer ushered them to the room's center, where a floor grill, six feet on a side, covered a pit. He took a key from a ring on the wall. Kneeling before the iron bars, he rammed the key in the lock, clicked it open. He slammed the heavy grate to one side with a deafening crash. He kicked a coil of rope beside the grate. When the rope, tied to a ring embedded in the floor, dropped into the hole, he waved toward the pit and grinned.

"Down you goes." His smirk widened.

The other soldiers pointed their weapons.

Tristan walked to the edge and peered down. He couldn't see the bottom. Blackness welled up around him, encircled and enveloped him. Once again, the old fear of dark underground places rose like a storm from a calm sea at midnight. He staggered back, breathing hard.

"I says down you goes." A spear jabbed his back.

Tristan took a deep breath, grabbed the rope, and closed his eyes. Then he lowered himself into the hole. Hand over hand, he climbed to the bottom of a dank, foul-smelling pit. His eyes soon adjusted to the dim light shed from the room above. The floor sloped a bit, leading to a cavern cutting a six-foot square hole in solid rock. In the lowest corner, stagnant water—or was that urine he smelled?—festered. He gagged.

Caitir climbed down next, followed by Ewan.

Then the three stood looking up at their captors in the dim light.

"Welcome to Castle Lugdunum's guest quarters." The leering man leaned over the hole above. "We serves dinner at sunset. Appropriate attire is requested."

Laughter burst from the other guards.

The grate clanged shut. The guard stuck the key in the lock and twisted until the mechanism clicked. The soldiers withdrew to a far corner of the room, exchanged a few inaudible commands, and the outside door slammed shut.

By the scuffling of a chair above, they'd obviously left only one guard above.

The three prisoners exchanged frightened glances.

Ewan slumped against the wall and faced the foul-smelling pool.

Caitir fell into Tristan's arms. "What's to become of us?" She was trembling. "How are we ever going to escape this place?"

He grasped her shoulders, gently holding her at arm's length and searching her eyes. "I don't know. But we must be strong."

"We're in deep trouble, my lord." Ewan's voice quavered. "That we are."

"Aye. And I killed Milosh." Tristan released Caitir and slid down the wall to sit beside Ewan. "Why did he say that he'd play? What could I have done differently?"

"Nary a thing, my lord. He was drawn to that game like a wolf to meat in a trap. Gambling was his downfall."

"Aye. You canna blame yourself for his death." Caitir sat beside him, nestling close. "I grew to like him—but what a knave!"

"He was a rogue, was he not?" Ewan slapped a hand on his knee.

"That he was," said Tristan. "And we'll sore miss him."

Then silence stole the words from their mouths. Only an occasional scuffling from the guard, the distant coughing of the lone occupant in his cell above broke a stillness like that of the grave.

Tristan stared at the dark niche opposite and shuddered. Again, the question nagged at him: What more could he have done to save Milosh?

Then the answer came to him. He could have prayed.

Gripping his head with both hands, he shook it. Once again, he'd failed to reach out to the one who'd helped him so many times before.

"I'm a fool," he whispered. "I should have prayed to Elyon."

At first, the other two remained silent. Then Caitir put an arm around his shoulders while Ewan said quietly, "We all should have prayed, my lord. You are not alone in that."

Time passed as the three huddled together in the cold and damp. Shoulder to shoulder, they completely filled the six-foot wall.

Finally, Ewan broke the stillness. "We've heard nary a word about Machar. We don't even know whether he's here."

"Aye." Tristan cupped Caitir's hands in his, trying to warm hers. "Maybe he never was here."

"Or maybe he was, and they killed him?" suggested Ewan.

"Look on the bright side," said Caitir. "Things canna possibly get any worse. Can they?"

"Nay." Tristan squeezed her hands, smiling. "From here, they can only get better."

AN ENTIRE DAY MUST HAVE passed while Tristan slept, huddled next to Caitir for warmth. When the grate slammed open again, he started, nearly jumped to his feet. Then came muffled plopping sounds and the noise of metal tinkling against metal.

"Guests of Castle Lugdunum." The leering guard's voice carried a hint of mirth. "Dinner is served." He lowered a bucket topped with a single wooden bowl. "Fill the bowl and keep it. Then I pulls the bucket back up."

Ewan rushed forward, grabbed the bowl, and set it aside. He peered into the bucket and winced. Then he poured what looked like a soupy gruel from the bottom of the bucket into the bowl. Shaking the pail, he tried to get out every bit of the porridge. Before he'd finished, the bucket jerked out of his hands, and the rope stole it back to the top.

"I'm sorry, friends." The guard snickered. "But I forgot the wine." He dropped a cracked waterskin, caught by Tristan, then broke into fits of laughter. "Maybe next time."

Ewan looked at the pile of mush in the bowl. He stuck in a finger, pulled it back, and smelled it. Then he tasted it. "Barley meal. Cold, but edible." He waved to the other two.

Famished, Tristan joined the others as they ate using their fingers. The meal was tasteless, without salt, honey, or butter, and it barely filled him. When he'd licked his fingers and sat back against the wall, he was still hungry.

"What I wouldn't give right now for a hunk of beef roasted over the fire." Ewan pushed the empty bowl to the side. "With onions, carrots, turnips, leeks, a wine sauce, and cabbage."

"Don't forget the bread, butter, and jam," said Tristan.

"Aye," added Caitir. "And honey cakes filled with apples and raisins."

"And a nice mug of mead to wash it all down." Ewan sighed. "How are we ever going to get out of here?"

Tristan peered up at the grate. He rose and tapped Ewan's shoulder. "Stand up, Ewan. Against the wall."

With a puzzled expression, Ewan did as commanded.

"Do you think you could support me if I stood on your shoulders?" he whispered.

A smile widened his mouth, and he nodded.

"Then stand under the lock. I have my lock-picking tools."

Caitir smiled, and Ewan grinned.

Ewan moved a few feet until the lock was directly above them. Then he cupped his hands.

Tristan placed his foot in Ewan's waiting foothold. Then, grabbing the folds of Ewan's tunic, he stepped and crawled onto the squire's shoulders.

"I'll steady both of you," said Caitir. Then her hands supported his legs.

He reached as high as he could, but the bars of the grate were just out of reach. Another inch and he could have touched it. Stretching once more, he lost his balance, felt himself tipping backward. He jumped off Ewan's shoulders and, as Caitir's arms helped break his fall, hit the floor feet first.

"Here now," came the guard's admonition from above. "What goes on down there?"

"Just doing some exercises." Tristan waved his arms. "Muscles getting stiff."

The guard huffed and returned to his seat by the wall.

"'Tis beyond my reach," whispered Tristan. Then he slumped back against the wall. "I'd need to be able to get my tools on top of the lock."

The others returned to their seats beside him.

"'Twas too good to be true," said Ewan.

"At least they're feeding us," said Caitir. "And there's some light. Not much, but some."

Tristan laid back against the wall. Soon, Ewan was snoring. The squire was curled up on the floor against one corner. Nestled beside him, Caitir also slept. Tristan stared again into the dark stone alcove.

What had Machar and Dermid always said? Press on to the end? But how was he to do that locked down here?

Suddenly, his vision changed. The room became lighter. The darkness receded, swirled, and out of the haze, images began forming.

He was having another vision—but without Elyon's golden scroll.

CHAPTER 28

A VISION OF ENEMIES

One moment Tristan was looking upon a putrid stone alcove. The next, he was transported into a large room decorated on one wall with the heads of boar, antlered deer, aurochs, and elch. Logs flared in a brazier in the room's center. Shields, crossed swords, and double-bladed axes covered the far wall. Facing the brazier was Gundovald, standing before an oval mirror of brass lying on the floor. Beside him waited two druids in black tunics, trying desperately to hold a squealing pig.

Beyond Gundovald, a window opened onto the eastern slope that led up to the castle—the same slope they'd climbed days ago.

The sun was low on the horizon. It must be early morning.

As Tristan watched, it was as if he hovered and moved to a position beside Gundovald. He now had all three men in his sight.

Gundovald whirled to the side and peered straight at him. But the king's gaze only found the wall. He frowned, shook his head, and, slowly, turned back to face his sorcerers.

The druids lifted the pig onto a brass basin in the corner. One of them pulled a long knife from his belt and drew it quickly across the beast's throat. As its life bled out into the basin, the animal collapsed. The men filled a brass pitcher with its blood, brought it to the mirror, and poured it. Bare hands smeared the blood over the mirror's surface.

Both druids now shifted the bloody mirror to a standing position, locking it in place by means of wooden supports. One man lit a torch from the brazier, hoisted it before the mirror, and spoke. "From the east and from the north, from the west and from the south, I call forth the wind."

He waved the torch before the mirror. From the open window, a slight breeze blew past Tristan into the room, flickering the torch's light. Then the druid spoke the same words Tristan had heard once before from another druid on the edge of the plains of Romely:

"By wind, by blood, and by fire, I command the Blood Mirror.

"By wind, I command it to hear.

"By blood, I command it to see.

"By fire, I command it to speak."

The bloodied mirror swirled, reddened still further, and presented a churning darkness.

Then the wavering image of a man appeared. It focused and sharpened.

There, standing by another open window in some far distant country, stood Faolukan. Tristan hadn't been this close to him since he'd approached the idol of Crom Mord with Zalán's ring on the Glebe of Sacrifice.

The black of night hovered about him, somehow darkening even the room from where Tristan watched. A coldness seemed to fall off the druid in waves, rippling down Tristan's back. A white scar ran down the druid's right cheek, under a gray beard that fell, long and thin, to his chest.

In the window behind the arch druid, for as far as Tristan could see, the masts of a great fleet so filled a glassy bay, it appeared now like a forest denuded of leaf. He gasped. Over a thousand vessels must be anchored in that harbor.

"Ah, 'tis you, my lord." Faolukan bowed. "Too long has it been since we last communicated. What tidings do you carry?"

"Good ones, my lord. We caught the spies you are looking for. They are in our dungeon now."

Faolukan tensed. He leaned forward. "And the Scepter?"

"I have it."

One corner of Faolukan's mouth lifted ever so slightly. His head barely nodded. "You've done well, my lord. I believe you and I are going to become great partners in the coming venture."

Gundovald slammed a fist against his chest in salute. "With you ruling the east, south, and north, and my rule encompassing the west, we will, indeed, make a partnership the world will not soon forget."

Faolukan returned the salute. "Without the Scepter, they will not be able to stand against us."

"I held it in my hands, my lord. I felt its power."

Faolukan's brows wrinkled, and he pursed his lips.

"If one could control that device"—Gundovald's eyes took on a far-away look—"one could accomplish almost anything."

"I know." Faolukan stared at his feet. "But at what cost?"

"I have been thinking about this. It greatly burned my hand when I touched it, but the wound is healing. So perhaps this Scepter could be used once, for one great battle, or against one great enemy? Not enough to harm the bearer permanently. But enough to deliver a crushing blow to our enemy?"

Faolukan cocked his head, looked to the side, and again faced Gundovald. "I've often wondered the same, my friend. But I fear Elyon's devices. They carry great risk for me. I am familiar only with the dark arts, for they, too, carry great power. And with our growing forces, we will surely overwhelm the meager defenses of Ériu. Perhaps without the risk of using the Scepter."

"Forgive me, my lord, but how can you be so sure?"

"My spies tell me they are unprepared. King Connell has surrendered himself to my charms. My druid, Corc, effectively rules in his stead. The provincial kingdoms of Ériu are divided, on the verge of war with ruling Ulster."

"Ah, that is good, very good." Gundovald bowed again. "But I would still consider using this device against them."

"Perhaps. What became of the spies who carried it?"

"One was killed. The others are now in the oubliette."

"Do you have the one called Neil mac Connell?"

"I'm sorry, my lord. He was not among them."

Faolukan frowned, crinkling his white scar. "A shame. Have the Gopalese centuria arrived?"

"They have. But the townspeople so feared the mammoths, I had to send them on ahead."

"What of their trackers?"

"They came with the mammoths. And what an odd lot they are. "

"Skilled assassins, every one. Send a courier to bring a few back with orders to find and kill the missing spy. As for the others, shut the grate on the oubliette, lock it, and forget about them."

"With pleasure." Gundovald's smile was as cold as Faolukan's face. "But, my lord, I was unable to contact you earlier. Have you just arrived at Fjernshavn?"

"I have. My admiral makes final preparations for the fleet's departure. Much remains to be done. But you did not mention the second item—what they call the Augury. Do you have it?"

"I do not. The prisoners made no mention of it."

Faolukan waved a hand. "It may be of little importance. 'Twas only a tarnished brass scroll, and I was unable even to open it. But 'tis best the device does not come near the Scepter." He narrowed his eyes, looked away from the mirror, and seemed to shiver. "What purpose it serves, I know not. I only know Elyon's devices must not be joined."

He looked back at Gundovald. "But now we must make ready for the final push against Ériu. The Scepter is what's important. And with that instrument in our hands, we will prevent them from mounting a defense."

Gundovald straightened. "What orders have you for me?"

"Take the Fifth Blood Legion and whatever army you can spare and march north against Armorica."

"The Armoricans' numbers are few. Still, they will resist."

"You have my Fifth legion and your own. Crush them. Leave an occupying force. Then proceed to Bredehaven on the coast. By now, a fleet should have docked at the river's mouth. One hundred and twenty ships await your arrival. 'Tis enough to carry a single legion. Pick the best of your troops and mine for the trip, including the Gopalese. You and I will meet offshore from Áth Cliath. Crom Mord will be aboard my ship. But"—Faolukan shook his head and winced—"his spirit within the idol grows increasingly restless."

"My lord, you look troubled."

"I am greatly concerned about him. I can confide this in no other but you. Ever since Neil mac Connell, that accursed prince of Ériu, threw Elyon's magic ring into Crom Mord's mouth at Cathair Duvh, he has not been the same."

"What do you mean?" Gundovald's face twisted.

"Increasingly, he rages for revenge. Almost to the point—dare I say it?—of insanity."

"But we all want revenge on Ériu."

"Not to the extent he now exhibits. He seems to forget our goal of bringing all of Erde under one rule. He desires only chaos, destruction, and mayhem."

"Has it not always been so?"

"Not like this. If he has his way, nothing will be left for us to rule. All of Erde will be in ruin and desolation. What use are slaves if they're all dead, land if it's stripped of life? For some time, I've worried about this tendency in him. It has made Drochtar the place it is. Increasingly, the land turns to iron, refusing to yield a crop, so hostile to life, the people's numbers dwindle almost daily. And after he sent his deamhan, Thrag, to join us at Schwarzburg, the country surrounding the castle became utterly desolate."

Gundovald looked down and scratched his beard. "Troubling, indeed. But what can be done?"

"Naught, I fear, that's in our power."

"I see."

"If you can suggest a plan for dealing with him, I will consider it. You and I are two of a kind—perhaps the only two in all Erde with the strength of will to control him. Only we two are capable of ruling, for he, being spirit, cannot."

"I appreciate your confidence in me," said Gundovald. "But how does one control a deamhan flirting with insanity?"

"That, my friend, is the question."

"I will think on it." Gundovald raised his glance to Faolukan's.

"Good. In a few days, you and I will be on the move and unable to contact each other."

"Then next we meet, the hills of Ériu will be on the horizon." Gundovald slammed a fist against his chest in salute. "Until then, my lord."

"Until then." Faolukan returned the salute.

When the mirror went dark, Tristan's heart was pounding.

Then he was staring, once again, at a wall of stone.

Chapter 29

The Fourth Prisoner

After the vision departed, Tristan realized he had been watching events not of the future, but of the present. So stunned was he, he sat for some time in silence, unable to move, trying to still his racing heart. If their captors were going to leave them locked down here and forget them, they must find a way out. And soon.

What he'd learned was of vital importance. He began shaking Caitir's shoulders. He must tell her and Ewan what he'd seen. But then—

The dungeon's outside door clanged open, and footsteps entered the room above. Voices held muted conversations with the lone guard.

Ewan and Caitir woke, and the three exchanged glances.

The door to one of the cells in the room above creaked open. Then came more inaudible speech, and footsteps led to their grate. A guard unlocked it. The metal door crashed open, echoing like thunder.

"Here now," came the familiar voice of the leering guard. "Down you goes."

A tall, bearded man stared down. Even from below, Tristan could see how thin he was. The man put one hand on the rope and swung over the side.

The guard stared down at them. "My friends, I regrets to inform you that the guest staff, including yours truly, has been called north with the legion. The proprietor apologizes in advance, he does, as the service from here on may not live up to expectations. I hopes your stay to this point has been enjoyable."

The other guards broke into boisterous laughter as the door clanged shut and the guard twisted the key and locked it. Footsteps led away from the grate toward the outside door. Then Tristan heard only silence. Had they all departed?

The newcomer was still staring up. But Tristan finally had a clear look at the man's face, and he gasped. His beard had grown long, and he'd lost much weight, but that tall muscular frame, those dark farseeing eyes, it could only be—

"Machar?" Tristan ran forward to hug him.

But Machar backed away. "Who . . . are you?" Slowly, he spun. Only then did he see the other two. "Caitir? Ewan?" Machar staggered, laid a hand on the wall for support. "Is that really you?"

"Aye, my lord." Ewan rushed forward, put him in a bear hug, and pounded a fist on his back. "All this time, were you in the cell above us?"

"I was. I heard only faint voices from down here. I couldn't make out who was speaking. And I must have been sleeping when you arrived."

Caitir came to him, and they, too, hugged. "Glad we are to see you, my lord."

"And I, you, but who"—he faced Tristan—"is this?" Then he narrowed his eyes and tried to focus. "Neil? Is that you?"

"Aye, my lord." Tristan grasped Machar's hands, pumped them.

Machar hugged him but soon backed away again, staring. "What happened to you? Your hair? Your face? You've changed. Aged."

"'Tis a long story, one that needs telling." Tristan took a deep breath. He knew this moment would one day come, but he'd been dreading it ever since their journey had begun. Now was not the ideal time, but what could he do? "I must tell you something, Machar— something Ewan and I have kept from you. There's a good reason behind what we've done. I just hope you will forgive me when I tell you."

"Forgive you?" Machar frowned, looked to Ewan, and back to Tristan. "Why?"

"My name is not Neil mac Connell. I am Tristan mac Torn, a blacksmith's apprentice from the village of Hidden Pines."

Machar's jaw dropped. His farseeing eyes narrowed on Ewan. "Is this true?"

"Aye, my lord. And 'twas my idea. Tristan is Neil's exact double."

"But you look, speak, and even . . . act . . . just like him."

"He does, that," said Ewan. "Which is why I convinced Tristan to take Neil's place. Otherwise, the entire quest would have been in jeopardy."

"What of Neil? Where is he?"

"He was killed by a púca as we traveled to Hidden Pines. My lord Neil—the real Prince Neil mac Connell, that is—insisted we go there. The creature fell upon us in the dark, took us by surprise. As usual, Prince Neil was a bit stocious that day. He couldn't properly fend the thing off."

Machar stared at Ewan, then at Tristan. "You, a commoner, took the place of the prince? You led us on this quest by deceiving everyone? That's an executable offense."

Tristan lowered his head. "I know."

"'Twas my idea, my lord," said Ewan. "But you do not understand. Tristan, here, he *is* the Toghaí. After we left you, he did retrieve the Augury. And we all saw Elyon's handwriting upon the golden scroll, telling us that he was such."

"Where's the Scepter now? And the Augury?" Machar's hands clenched at his sides.

Then Tristan told the story of how Milosh helped them cross the Ferachtir flats, how they entered Cathair Duvh, and how Tristan stole the Augury from Balor's chasm. He told how he freed his friends from Faolukan's spell. Next, he related how Elyon spoke to them using the golden scroll, how his hair turned white, and everything else that occurred up until they entered Lugdunum Castle, where Milosh betrayed them, giving up the Scepter, and the game that led to his death.

"So Gundovald now has the Scepter?"

"Aye." Tristan hung his head.

Machar shook his head. "All of it—'tis too much to believe."

"Believe it, my lord," said Ewan, "for 'tis all true."

Suddenly, the light from above flickered. A torch sputtered and went out. The light dimmed by half.

Tristan looked up. "We can talk later. The guards have left us here to rot—without food or water. Only one torch remains lit. We must use its light as best we can. And quickly."

"What do you suggest?" asked Ewan.

"Machar is the tallest among us. If I stand on his shoulders, maybe I can now reach the grate." Tristan raised his tools. "I was a blacksmith, Machar. I know how to pick a lock."

A flicker of a smile passed Machar's lips.

Tristan motioned toward the wall, and Machar stood as requested, making a foothold with his hands. Having clambered onto his shoulders, Tristan now could reach the grate and the lock. As his fingers fumbled for the opening, they grazed the rope beside the grill. After pulling his tools from his tunic, he jammed them into the mechanism. While the flat rod turned the bolt, the other moved the two pins into position, and—click! The lock was open. But his arms were rapidly tiring.

He slipped the tools into his pocket and pushed up on the grate. It wouldn't budge. Though his muscles burned, he pushed again. The grate moved an inch before crashing down. He dropped his arms. "I unlocked it, but I can barely move the grate. 'Tis a mighty weight."

After climbing back down, he breathed heavily from the exertion. Bent over, hands on his knees, he caught his breath, then straightened and eyed the squire. "Ewan, can you climb a rope?"

"Aye, my lord, I can."

"Then let me go up again."

Machar made another foothold, and Tristan climbed back up. With one hand, he was able to raise the grate a few inches. With the other hand, he pushed through enough rope to loop through a grommet used to secure the rope for the bucket. The grate fell back. Then he tied the rope and climbed down, sweating from the exertion.

When he'd recovered, he returned to Machar's shoulders while Ewan took his place and climbed. At the top, Ewan pushed up on the grate long enough so Tristan could wriggle through. Then Ewan let the heavy metal clang shut.

Now in the room above, Tristan stood, grabbed the grate, and was able to open it all the way. Machar and Ewan climbed out. They made a noose for Caitir's foot and hauled her up last.

Now everyone stood on the dungeon floor by the flickering torchlight. Lighting another torch from a pile beside the guard's empty chair, Tristan jabbed it in a wall sconce. He glanced around the room but saw only the bucket and the guard's chair.

He unlocked the outside door latch. When he pulled the door open, stone steps led to the tower's upper floors.

"Now all we have to do," said Caitir, "is sneak past about a hundred soldiers, cross a spike-lined moat, and hope no one shoots us full of arrows."

"Aye, lass." Ewan smiled. "That should be easy."

CHAPTER 30

ESCAPE

On the steps above, Tristan heard voices and pounding feet. For one moment, he feared the soldiers were heading back down. But the footsteps just seemed to pound to and fro across a room on the floor above. He pulled the door shut. Without the key, it didn't lock. "I know what's going on," he said. "And now I need to tell you about the vision I had right before the guards brought Machar."

"A vision, my lord?" Ewan cocked his head.

"You shouldn't call him 'lord', Ewan." Machar frowned. "He has no right to the title."

"You do not ken the things this lad has done." Bristling, Ewan put his hands on his hips. "He's got more right to the title than most of the flaith I've seen back home."

Seeming taken aback, Machar let it rest. "Go on . . . Tristan. What were you saying?"

"What you don't know is that I've been having visions of the future, with and without the golden scroll. Before today, I saw Caitir being led to Drochtar. But just before they put you into the pit, I had a vision of Gundovald talking with Faolukan through a Blood Mirror. It was as if I was in the same room with them."

Then he related everything that had passed between the arch druid and the king.

Ewan whistled, and Caitir frowned.

"And you saw and heard all this down in the pit?" Machar's eyes widened. "Just as if you'd been there?"

"Aye."

Machar turned away, ambled a few feet, and returned. "What you saw must be true. Once, I heard the guards talking, and I learned that the room above is the armory. They must be provisioning the legions for a march north."

"Before we do anything, we must wait until the army has left and the castle is quiet."

"Then we can go to the armory and arm ourselves," added Ewan.

"Aye," said Machar. "Your news adds even more urgency to our journey home. With a thousand or more ships sailing—why Faolukan must be bringing forty thousand soldiers against Ériu. Maybe more."

"How many can Ériu muster?" asked Tristan.

"At least two thousand from Ulster. From the other provinces—maybe an additional seven thousand. Far too few. But you say the Alliance of Kingdoms has fallen apart? And we are about to go to war against ourselves?" Machar paced a few steps, whirled, and again returned. "We feared this outcome. Connell and that accursed druid, Corc." He slammed a fist into a palm. "It seems they've finally driven the kingdoms to rebellion."

"We need to warn them, get them to come to their senses."

"If only it were that easy . . ." Machar continued to pace. "And without the Scepter"—as he spun toward them, pain glimmered in Machar's eyes—"what chance do we have?"

Ewan, meanwhile, was circling the room. He stopped at a bucket beside the guard's chair. "Here's our last meal. The guard made it up. But he wasn't going to give it to us."

"Cold, congealed barley meal." Caitir smiled, rubbed her hands together, and headed toward the bucket. "Just what I wanted for breakfast."

THE TRAFFIC TO AND FROM the armory continued for the rest of the morning. Much later—they guessed it was around noon—the footsteps ceased, and all became quiet. Tristan volunteered to scout the way.

He pushed open the door and walked quietly up the steps. He peered around the last corner. A lone guard sat in a chair beside the open armory door, a sword across his lap. Tristan ducked back, returned to the others, and reported what he'd found.

"Let's wait until evening," said Machar. "No one will be expecting trouble tonight. By then, he might be asleep."

They waited. Several times, Tristan tiptoed up the steps to check on the guard's condition until the man finally nodded off.

Then he and Machar returned to the armory. Machar pulled the guard's own sword from its sheath, and, with one quick stroke, knocked the guard out cold with the flat of the blade. They opened the armory door, dragged the man inside, then tied and gagged him.

Inside, they retrieved their own packs and sleeping furs from the quartermaster's stock. They also selected swords, knives, bows and arrows, and the only coil of rope they could find. Then they shoved into their packs the Ferachtir uniforms the guards had taken from them. With great caution, they mounted the stairs to the small foyer where they'd entered only days ago. A slit in the wall revealed stars and a quarter-moon.

"This is the kitchen." Machar pointed to an open door. "We should provision ourselves."

With Ewan's vigorous assent, they entered a circular room as wide as the tower itself. Against the outside wall nestled fireplaces, stone ovens, and a stone cleaning basin with a drain hole leading outside. Farther on, tall wooden storage bins held apples, beans, onions, turnips, wheat, and barley. Beyond these, barrels of wine and beer were stacked to the ceiling. A massive open tub held water. Tables in the center bore a few fresh cabbages, a two-foot round of cheese, and three loaves of brown bread. They crammed leather pouches with as much as they could carry, stuffing their packs full. Machar filled their water and wine skins.

Beside the cleaning tub on the floor lay a wooden door. Tristan lifted it. "Phew!" he said, backing away. The overpowering smell of garbage rose up around him. A vertical chute led down inside the wall. Slime, kitchen refuse, and garbage clung to the walls. He closed the lid and stepped away, breathing heavily.

As they worked, they ate as much cheese, bread, and apples as their mouths could swallow, followed by swigs of wine from cups Machar provided. It was their first real food in days. When they'd finished, Tristan led them from the kitchen to the outside door. Opening it, he peered into the yard from the top of the steps.

The bailey was empty. Beyond the execution scaffold, lantern light shone through open windows in the long wing devoted to the castle guard. Gundovald had left barely enough men to garrison the castle.

Stepping through the door, Tristan backed into the shadows. He peered up at the battlements. Two guards walked the western wall. Three more patrolled the southern parapet above the gate. Beside the gate, one set of steps hugged the wall and led from the yard up to the wall walk. Other steps accessed the parapet from the barracks. Above him, two more soldiers emerged from behind the tower on the north wall, stopped to talk, then moved on. But all the guards were looking outward. None appeared to send as much as a glance into the bailey.

He slipped back through the open door. "Guards are patrolling every rampart but the eastern route."

"Because that way leads to a sheer cliff," said Ewan.

Machar pointed south, across the yard. "The drawbridge is up, of course."

"The guards aren't paying any attention to the yard," said Tristan. "But if we alert them, there are soldiers in the barracks." He opened his hands in a question. "How are we going to get out of here?"

A sly smile lifted one side of Caitir's mouth. "We could go down the garbage chute."

Everyone stared at her.

"Lass," said Ewan, "you're glipe in the head."

"Even if the stench didn't kill us," said Machar, "we might not survive the drop."

"It must curve toward the outside," said Tristan. "Or the garbage wouldn't end up in the ravine. I saw it come out onto a great pile before we entered the castle."

Now everyone was looking at him as if *he* had lost his senses.

"But," he added, "even if we were facing twenty soldiers, I couldn't go down there."

"Nor I," said Machar. He scratched his black beard, grown long and unkempt during his imprisonment. "Better we take our chances at the main gate. Caitir and Ewan, if your arrows can quietly take out the three guards on the southern wall, Tristan and I will lower the drawbridge. One of the others might sound the alarm, but perhaps we'll get across and down the hill before enough are rousted out."

"Can we get horses from the stables first?" asked Caitir.

Machar glanced at the floor then back at her. "Nay. Hooves clopping over cobbles would certainly alert the guards. We'll have to flee on foot."

"Mighty risky, this plan." Ewan pulled on his mustache. "Could we not lower a rope from a window on the eastern wall and climb down?"

Machar shook his head. "Our rope is about sixty feet short. I ken going out the main gate is our only option."

Ewan nodded. "Then let's get out of here."

HUGGING THE SHADOWS BESIDE THE eastern wall, the four inched their way toward the gate. About a quarter of the way around the yard, they emerged from behind the primejdie board. Then Tristan slowed. "Where are the guards above the gate?"

The others stopped.

"There," said Caitir, pointing to the southwest corner.

While they had snuck behind the game board, three more guards had climbed the steps leading up. Six of them now congregated there, conversing.

"Nay, nay!" Tristan pointed to the western wall. "They're changing the guard on the parapets."

On the other two wall walks, more soldiers had joined their fellows. Twice as many watchers were now on the battlements.

"Quick!" breathed Machar. "Back behind the game boards before we're spotted."

Everyone hunched low and crept toward what little shelter the boards offered. But anyone looking down into the yard would be able to see them.

They'd just stopped behind the farthest edge of the primejdie board when someone called out from above, "You, down there. Stop!"

"Sound the alarm!" shouted a second voice.

Then came the clanging of a bell and more shouting from the wall walk. What followed was the heavy thud of something falling against stone.

"They've dropped the portcullis on the gatehouse entrance." Ewan gestured toward their intended destination. "Now we'll never escape that way."

"Back to the tower." Machar was already running toward the steps. "At least 'tis defensible."

Tristan brought up the rear. He glanced back in time to see guards rushing down the southwestern steps. Other men were pouring from the barracks, racing across the bailey. He sprinted up the steps to the tower behind the others.

Once in the small foyer, Machar peered out at the onrushing soldiers then ducked back into the kitchen. "Inside, quick. Let's lock the door."

Tristan followed, fearing what would come next.

Machar closed the bar over the kitchen's only door and ran to the trap door leading to the garbage chute. He opened it and stared down the hole.

When Ewan realized what was happening, he rolled his eyes to the ceiling and moaned.

Machar scrunched his face at the stench and peered over his shoulder at the others. "What choice do we have? It's either the chute. Or be captured."

Caitir's grin seemed out of place as she walked to the opening. "I'll go first. Just like the rock chute at the falls back home, hey, Tristan?"

"Not quite," he said.

"Hold your weapons and pack in front of you," came Machar's warning.

Caitir nodded, removed her knapsack, and gripped it and her bow. But as she peered into the black hole, her smile vanished. She sat on the edge, took a deep breath, gave Tristan a wobbly grin, and slipped over the side.

He listened for some sign she had arrived safely at the bottom. But he heard nothing.

Soldiers began chopping at the door with axes. Stroke after stroke fell against the wood. It would only be moments before they broke through.

PART VII

ARMORICA

CHAPTER 31

FLIGHT

As Tristan stared into the garbage hole, the only sounds came from the soldiers' axes on the door. Nothing from the chute. How would they know if Caitir made it down safely? He and Machar exchanged worried glances.

The Capulum warrior shrugged, sat on the edge, and pushed himself off. His sword scraped the tunnel's wall. Then he was gone.

Axes smashed against the door. It shuddered in its frame.

Ewan glanced at him, his face pale and wan.

"We have no choice," said Tristan, plopping to the edge with his feet over the side. He gripped his pack and sword tightly to his chest. The stench from the darkness below caught in his throat, making him gag. He took a deep breath of kitchen air and pushed himself off.

At first, he was in free fall, dropping straight down. Darkness rushed past him. Then his back brushed the wall, scraping slime and garbage debris onto his tunic. He put his feet out against the sides of the chute, hoping to slow his descent. A slurry of goo and slime scraped off the wall, slapping him in the face. Then the chute curved, and his back was sliding. Goop splattered up everywhere.

Suddenly, he was flying out into space, and the garbage pile raced up to meet him. He hit it feet first, lost his pack, and tumbled forward. He slid down the mound, his hands digging deep into mud.

He stood in time to see Ewan pitching face forward down the pile of muck and kitchen debris.

Tristan climbed back up to retrieve his and Ewan's packs that had been torn from their hands. At the bottom, he tried unsuccessfully to wipe the gunk off his clothes.

"What I wouldna give right now for a long, hot bath." Caitir examined her clothes as if they belonged to the poorest beggar. "And new clothes."

Ewan pulled garbage out of his hair, his face a mask of disgust.

"They must not have broken into the kitchen yet." Machar scraped slime off his pack and threw it over his shoulders. "Let's move."

Everyone followed as he led them beside the stream trickling down the center of the rock-lined ravine.

When they'd gone perhaps halfway down the hill toward the river, Tristan called out. "We have to climb the slope on the right somewhere here. That's where I hid the Augury."

Machar shot him a worried glance but waved him on.

Tristan began climbing. Here, the ravine was not as steep, but covered with scree. For every two steps up, the rocks slid them back one. Finally, he reached the top and entered the thicket. In the dark, branches slapped his face, brush snarled his feet, and sapling trunks seemed to pop up out of the night.

Eventually, he found his way back to the narrow road they'd taken days ago when they were forced to follow Fardulf. Breathing hard, he glanced uphill. At any moment, soldiers might be racing down the hill after them. But he snapped his gaze away. Now he needed to focus on finding the treasure. Without that, nothing else mattered. He scanned the trailside. "We're looking for a cluster of boulders. Below that is where I hid everything."

The others fanned out, searching for the landmark. Shortly afterward, Ewan called out from far down the trail.

Tristan raced down, passed the boulders, and found the place where he'd gone into the brush. He forged back into the thicket, brushing aside saplings, branches, and leaf clusters, and arrived at the clearing. He stumbled, fell to his knees, and received a whiff of the scum now drying on his tunic. They must smell horrible and look even worse. Before going much further, they'd need to wash. One look at them, and every townsman and villager would sound the alarm.

He began removing rocks, looking for what he'd buried.

From the top of the hill, dogs barked. "Hurry," came Machar's muffled warning. "They're coming!"

Tristan's heart beat faster. He groped, his fingers sliding over rocks. The light was so dim, he felt, rather than saw, the Augury. Beside it lay the hiding stone, his dagger, and the sack of coins. Securing them all in his knapsack, he stood and made his way back to the others. The dogs were barking louder now.

"We must make for the river." Machar was already running. "The road beside it heads north."

The others followed. Tristan brought up the rear.

Just before they reached the bottom, Machar pulled them into a thicket on the side of the trail and bent over, breathing heavily, leaning on his hands on his knees. "We must . . . bypass the guardhouse."

"Are you all right, my lord?" asked Ewan.

Machar waved a hand in dismissal. "For months, I've done naught but walk my cell, small as it was. And the gruel wasn't all that nourishing. But I'll be all right."

The barking came ever closer. They forged into the brush, circumventing the guardhouse. For some time, they parted branches and tripped over rocky ground until they emerged from the thicket. Ahead were a line of huts, the road, and the river.

"With the way we smell, those dogs willna have any trouble finding us." Ewan sniffed his arm and puckered his face.

"Maybe we should cross the river?" Tristan suggested. "That would throw them off."

Machar leaned heavily against a trunk, breathing hard. "Good idea. First, let's get as far north of Lugdunum as we can."

The road was level, the moon and stars lent enough light to see by, and now they moved faster. Darkened thatch huts and one- and two-story wooden buildings clustered on both sides of the road. Beyond, moonlight glinted off the Saone's waters. They entered a section of town where wooden placards with painted images of bread, anvils, shoes, and pipes hung dimly over the cobbled street.

But the barking of dogs seemed closer, only around the last corner.

Finally, the city ended. Now, the river bordered the road on their right, with vineyards and orchards on their left.

The dogs stopped barking. They were off their leashes. Tristan could see the animals loping down the road, not a hundred feet away.

"Here's a boat." Machar rushed down the slope to a skiff pulled up on the bank.

Ewan and Machar began hacking at the rope tying the boat to a tree.

"The dogs—they're almost here," came Caitir's hoarse cry.

Tristan was last, and the animals were almost upon him. While the others tried to free the boat, he yanked his sword from its sheath and stood his ground. He backed down the bank.

Snarling and growling, the pack slowed, began inching down the slope with teeth bared.

Then he recognized the lead dog. The white-haired, shaggy wolf-hound he'd fed at the inn only days ago!

Intent on attacking, the dog seemed not to recognize him. The rest of the pack followed its lead. The white dog lowered its head, snarled, and lunged. Jaws snapped at Tristan's leg.

He backed up and struck out with his sword.

The animal jumped out of the way.

From behind came Caitir's shout, "The boat's in the water. Come on, Tristan."

But if he even turned his head, they'd be upon him. A second dog circled to his right. A third was trying to flank him on his left. Then the leader lunged, snapping and growling.

But it stopped. It sniffed once, twice. Then it froze.

Meanwhile, the dogs on both sides were closing in, muzzles lowered, snarling.

Suddenly, the white-haired leader turned, put its back to Tristan, and faced its brothers. With a menacing snarl, it drove back the first, then the second attacking canine. The pack stopped its advance. The dogs sat on their haunches.

From the road came a new voice, an unwelcome, familiar voice. Sitting atop his horse was Chlodric, the dog master, with his unkempt beard, scruffy hair, and dirty tunic. "Get 'im," he shouted. "Attack!"

But the dogs simply sat where they were.

Chlodric dismounted, withdrew a truncheon, and began wading into his animals. "You worthless curs—attack, I say." His bludgeon came down on the first dog. Whimpering in pain, the animal slunk away. Chlodric raised his club and hit a second dog, cursing it, ordering it to obey.

The lead dog whirled away from Tristan. In three leaps, it hit Chlodric on the chest and knocked him to the ground. Its jaws clamped on the arm holding the club. Its head shook from side to side, bit into flesh.

Chlodric screamed.

The other dogs now joined their leader. Their jaws ripped into the man, tearing flesh as they'd been taught, but now turning on the master who had mistreated them for so long.

Tristan spun and raced toward the boat. Machar's and Ewan's oars were holding it against the current about ten feet from the bank. He waded in, quickly finding himself in waist-deep water. He threw in his pack and sword, and the others helped him climb in without capsizing them all.

He shot a glance back to the bank where Chlodric's lifeless body lay under the now feral pack.

On the road, a dozen men on horses dismounted and raced to the dogs, beating them away from the corpse. A hundred feet downriver, at least fifty more soldiers were jogging toward the scene. Breathing heavily, Tristan wondered if they would bring archers.

Machar and Ewan rowed away from the bank.

"Look!" Caitir pointed toward shore.

The lead dog had left the others and jumped into the water. It was swimming toward them.

"It's coming to me," he whispered. "Slow up."

"What? Are you daft?" Machar's tone was incredulous, but he did as asked, rowing only enough to keep the boat from floating downstream.

The dog paddled furiously, but the current was pulling it away from them.

"Meet it, and let's bring it aboard." Tristan gripped the rail with both hands as the rowers let the skiff float downstream. When they were even with the dog, Tristan and Machar grabbed its flanks and heaved it into the boat. The dog shook, spraying them with water and rocking the boat. Then it sat in the middle, looking up at Tristan.

"What are you going to do with a dog?" Machar scowled. "A dog that killed its master, no less."

Then Tristan told him how Chlodric had been starving and beating his animals, how Tristan had fed them, and how they'd had a confrontation at the inn. He ended with, "I can't leave it."

Machar only shook his head while he and Ewan began rowing in earnest toward the far bank. They were fighting the current, but they did make progress. Soon, they entered calmer waters on the eastern bank.

"I'm guessing they'll go south to the bridge then march north from there." Machar nodded toward the city. "If we continue paddling along this bank, we can cross again to the west and outfox them."

"The first thing we must do"—Caitir sniffed her tunic—"is wash and bathe."

"Aye," added Ewan. "Otherwise, no matter which bank they're on, they'll be able to follow us by smell alone."

For the first time in days, they all laughed.

But moments later, as Tristan looked west, the shadows of riders followed there as well.

CHAPTER 32

A FRIEND, INDEED

For most of the night, they rowed north in calmer waters beside the eastern bank, out of the main current. On the opposite shore, a troop of riders shadowed their progress at a leisurely pace. Sometime around midnight, riders also appeared on the eastern road beside them, blocking any thought of landing. Once, the near riders even shot arrows, but they landed well short of the skiff.

On either side, green rolling hills punctuated by jagged cliffs filled the horizon. They passed occasional villages, but the pursuing riders seemed content to wait for their quarry to land. They would have to beach eventually, and Tristan wondered how their slow-moving craft, always fighting the current, could ever outpace the faster horses.

All night the dog had sat at his feet, occasionally looking up at him. Several times, he bent down to pet it.

"What are you going to call it?" asked Caitir.

"I don't know." He reached over and scratched it behind the ears. Its head leaned into his fingers, and it whined. "Fionn. Aye, Fionn will be his name."

"Because he's white?"

"Aye."

⬥·✦·⬥

NEAR MORNING, TRISTAN AND CAITIR were taking their turn at rowing when a large tributary branched to the east. "That should stop the riders beside us," said Tristan. "They'll have to travel far inland to find a ford or a ferry."

"Maybe now we can find a place to wash?" Caitir's voice was hopeful.

"Aye." Ewan wrinkled his nose. "I smell so bad, I do not even feel like eating."

Caitir turned around and shot him a smile.

A bit farther on, a second, smaller river also led east, and Tristan steered the boat up its narrow channel. Only about a hundred yards in, it opened onto a small lake. He ran the boat aground on the northern shore, out of sight of the main river, and they disembarked.

While Machar built a fire, Caitir picked up her belongings. "I'm going up the bank to wash myself and everything on me. You men find a different spot. I'll wrap myself in my sleeping fur and bring my wet things back to dry by the fire. No peeking, now. Hear?"

Tristan smiled, nodded, and he and Ewan found an isolated place on the shore where they could undress, bathe, and scrub their clothes. At least their sleeping furs were wrapped in leather and didn't need washing. Fionn followed and sat on the bank, watching. Machar soon joined them.

When they'd dried their things and eaten a meal, the sun was lightening the eastern sky. At Machar's suggestion, he and Tristan, with Fionn at his heels, hiked back and peered through the trees to the Saone's opposite bank.

"I see no sign of them," said Machar.

"Nor I. Perhaps they think we've left the boat and gone ahead on foot?"

"Aye. And they cannot leave the castle shorthanded for long. I'm guessing they've given up the chase. We should cross the river and make our way inland."

"Aye."

Following this plan, the group rowed the skiff back to the Saone. They passed through the main current and approached the western bank. When they pulled the boat on shore and stood on the river road, Tristan glanced north and south. "I see no sign of them."

On the road itself, the army's recent passing had left its mark. Deep ruts of many wheeled carts. Piles of horse dung. Giant mammoth prints with even larger piles of dung. Lost articles fallen from packs. A tin cup here. An old wineskin, cracked and useless, there. A shoe without laces. Discarded apple pits and chicken bones.

When Fionn sniffed the mammoth dung, he growled.

Machar stared at the evidence then pointed to the tree-covered slope rising in the west. "Let's climb that hill and get as far from the river as we can. That should foil any pursuers."

Away from the river, the hill rose quickly. Following a trickling stream, they struggled through dense undergrowth and brambles. With Fionn close at his heels, Tristan led as they scrambled around rock outcroppings and small waterfalls. At the summit, a footpath led north along the ridge. They walked this for about a league until they came to a break in the trees. Below, the river wound like a silvery snake through tree-lined hills.

"We've lost them," breathed Machar.

But in that voice, Tristan sensed weariness. Machar had been a prisoner for months. Sure, he'd rowed and hiked with the rest as they climbed to the ridge. But several times, the group waited as he stopped to rest. "How are you feeling, my lord?"

Machar found a stump and plopped down on it. "Sore knackered, I fear."

"Then let's stop for the day." Tristan pointed to a flat clearing a hundred feet beyond the western slope. Hidden from the road, there, they could make a fire. "Let's camp and go on tomorrow."

Machar nodded, and they headed for the site.

They built a fire, ate, and rested. But all day, a thought nagged at Tristan. When evening came, he and Ewan climbed back to the ridge. "The army is marching ever northward," he said. "Somehow, we need to get ahead of them."

"From what you've said"—Ewan pulled on his mustache—"they plan to stop and engage the Armoricans."

"Aye. While they're fighting may be our best chance to pass them."

All the next day, they traveled along a narrow trail that climbed hills, descended into valleys, and twisted through deep forest, only to climb again to a ridgetop. Machar seemed greatly improved from the day before.

Occasionally, they caught sight of the Saone below. Once, the ridge swerved almost to the brink of the river road. Then, below, Tristan glimpsed six turbaned, black-garbed men racing south on horses, their capes flying behind them in the wind. But their arms were too long for ordinary men, and at their hips, each carried two knife sheaths.

"What kind of men are those?" whispered Caitir, her face grimacing in fear.

"They're Gopalese assassins," answered Machar.

Then Tristan recalled for them what Faolukan had said about the assassin-trackers in his vision.

"We must make haste." Machar's glance shifted north. "For surely, they'll find where we crossed the road. And by tomorrow they'll be following us on this very ridge."

Thus did they renew their trek north on the hillcrest at an even faster pace.

By sunset, they were exhausted. They made camp in the shelter of a pine forest on a bed of pine needles. As Tristan lay on his furs, he wondered if the trackers had yet found their trail. Surely, they'd have to abandon the horses in the thick undergrowth and proceed on foot. Perhaps that would slow them.

Somehow, they had to avoid the assassins and get ahead of Gundovald's forces.

But their progress was slow, too slow.

THE NEXT DAY, THE RIDGE trail descended, and they followed the river through a rolling landscape. Far ahead loomed a new mountain range. But its peaks did not approach the grandeur and height of the great Blue Mountains separating Burgundia from the east.

Each day Machar continued to gain strength, and each day they trekked a bit faster.

They followed the army's track northwest on a dirt road now ground to powder from the tromping of soldiers' feet, animals, and carts laden with war supplies. As the mountains rose ever higher in the distance, they crossed a flat country of meadows, isolated farms, and small villages. Always did Tristan look behind for signs of the assassins. But he saw nothing.

On the third day out from the river, the army's trail led them up a wide valley rising into the mountains. That evening, close to the peak, they camped beside tall pines in a depression a hundred yards off the main trail. Though the sun still lit the western sky, the mountains had already cast cool shadows over the valley. A breeze sifted cold mountain air through the pines. A few needles fell onto Tristan's lap as he ate cheese and drank wine beside their fire. A full moon rose in the east.

Fionn sat beside him, patiently waiting for his next morsel. Tristan tossed him another hunk of cheese. Since joining them, the dog was gradually abandoning the feral ways Chlodric had taught him. Only once, when Ewan dropped a piece of sausage and when Fionn had it firmly in his jaws and when Ewan tried to take it back—only then did the dog growl and bare his teeth. When Tristan chastised him, Fionn simply sat on his haunches, looking quietly up at him. Unapologetically, the dog then swallowed the sausage in three quick bites.

Now Tristan leaned over and scratched him behind the ears. Fionn whined in appreciation.

"The army's taking the pass through the Central Massif," said Machar, munching on bread. These last few days, his face had lost its paleness, and he walked with greater vigor. "My guess is we're only a day behind."

"What about the Gopalese?" asked Ewan, taking a bite from one of Gundovald's apples.

Machar shrugged. "I've seen no sign of them."

"Maybe they never found our trail?" asked Caitir.

"Maybe." Machar finished his bread and lay back on his furs. "But not likely."

Tristan finished his meal and found his furs.

In the cold mountain air, Caitir snuggled up on one side of him. Fionn lay on the other. Then sleep called.

TRISTAN WOKE TO THE SOUND of low growling. He opened his eyes and sat. Fionn was standing a few feet from the fire, facing the shadows under the pines. "What is it, boy?" He squinted to try to make out what caused the dog's alarm.

The moon cast only dim light beyond the clearing, making it difficult to see.

Fionn growled louder, took two menacing steps toward something under the pines.

Tristan reached for his sword.

The moment he did, a dark form, cloaked in shadow, moved.

Fionn leaped into the air. A thud sounded, followed by more growling and a cry of pain. The dog dragged a black-turbaned figure into the light. He'd snapped the man's right arm, for it now hung at an odd angle.

On the ground, the assassin still held a knife in his left hand. He tried to stab the dog, but Tristan stepped forward and plunged his sword into the man's chest. Then, hearing movement and a scuffle, he whirled to the right.

Machar's sword was dropping a second Gopalese.

"From the trees!" came Ewan's shout.

Tristan whirled again. Four more black-clad Gopalese raced toward them, a knife in each hand.

Fionn was a white blur behind them.

The Gopalese spread out and rushed at the four, now standing with weapons ready. But Fionn flew in from the back, knocking down one of the assassins. His jaws broke another man's arm in two. Before the knife in the other hand could move, Fionn had the assassin's wrist in a death grip. The man screamed.

A fourth Gopalese fell to the ground, arrows sprouting from his chest.

Machar and Tristan met the last two assassins and dropped them with a few quick strokes of their swords.

Breathing hard, Tristan stood amidst the scene of carnage that had become their campsite. "It was Fionn who woke me."

When the dog padded up to him, panting, Tristan bent over and patted his head.

"I take back everything I said about him," said Machar. "If it hadn't been for the dog, we'd all be dead now."

Fionn looked up at Tristan with eager eyes, panting tongue. Tristan scratched behind the dog's ears then reached for his sack. "Good dog. You saved us." Then he threw Fionn a large hunk of sausage.

They cleaned their blades then finished the night at a new site a half-league upslope from the dead Gopalese.

CHAPTER 33

THE BATTLE OF
THE PLAINS

The next morning, the road topped the pass through the Central Massif and started down the other side. Signs of the army's passing were fresh, the horse and mammoth dung barely dried. Once, they even startled a wake of vultures feasting on a dead man by the wayside. About halfway down, the path rose to an overlook.

Below, the golden grain fields of Armorica stretched across a gentle, rolling landscape. Through the center of the plains cut a wide river with a road following the eastern bank.

But only about a league below them, a dark mass—seething with movement, glinting occasionally with steel—spread out on the eastern bank. It left in its trail a swath of trampled grain. Above, it threw a plume of dust carried east by the wind.

Within the mass, Tristan could make out tiny figures of horses, men, and mammoths—all moving toward some unseen foe. Borne up on the breeze came the din of clashing swords, neighing horses, trumpeting mammoths, and thousands of voices raised in battle.

The wind shifted, carrying away the sound.

"The army." A grim line tightened Machar's lips. "They're engaging the Armoricans now."

"We'll catch them well before sunset," added Tristan.

"Aye. They'll have to stop and regroup before moving on. Now would be our chance to pass them."

They descended the slope, keeping a watch for sentries. Beside the trail on their left, small streams and rivulets joined, quickly forming a roaring, rushing river. Machar called it the beginnings of the Seine, Armorica's largest river.

But their progress was slower than expected, and they didn't arrive on the plains until sunset. The sounds of battle had long since quieted, and at the last overlook, they saw no sign of the army. Machar suggested they leave the main road and travel through the fields. "Less chance of running into sentries." Then he added, "But it appears the army may have already moved on."

Even away from the road, the fields were trampled. About a half mile from the river, they found a footpath bounded by rock fences that marked the borders of some farmer's field. There, at the eastern edge of the army's crossing, they hurried along.

They passed a stone farmhouse, but when Tristan poked his head inside, it was ransacked and dark, without a hearth fire. They continued north.

In the northwest skies, hundreds of vultures and crows circled in the sun's dying light.

They climbed a small hillock overlooking a scene of carnage and mayhem. Lying in piles scattered over the half mile from the footpath to the river were thousands of corpses of both men and horses. The nearest bodies lay only a dozen yards away. Most wore the uniforms of Armorica. Abandoned lances, swords, helmets, shields, axes, and bows lay beside their dead owners.

Farther off, men in Burgundian uniforms held cloth to their noses as they trundled carts through the graveyard. Some had dismounted, bent to the debris, not to bear away the corpses, but to throw the best weapons and armor onto their wagons.

Were they just going to leave the bodies for the carrion birds?

The buzz of flies filled the air. Feral dogs and even a pack of wolves slunk through the dead.

218

"The Armoricans were annihilated," whispered Machar. "They didn't stand a chance."

"Aye," said Caitir. "I see few Drochtar or Burgundian among the dead."

A sudden breeze carried such a stench of death his way that Tristan gagged and brought a swatch of tunic over his nose.

"Look." Holding his nose, Ewan pointed north.

Far to the north, the smoke of many campfires rose into a darkening sky.

"The army's encamped there," said Tristan.

"Aye," said Machar. "And we can't go much farther this evening, or we'll run into them."

"Perhaps tomorrow," said Tristan, "we should cross the river to the western bank. That would keep us far from the army sentries."

Machar laid a hand on Tristan's shoulders. "A good plan, that. I suggest we backtrack to that abandoned farmhouse, spend the night, and cross the river tomorrow by daylight."

Tristan led them south, away from the smell of death, back the way they'd come.

Soon, a light rain began to fall, and by the time they reached the farmhouse, it was pouring. Ewan started a fire in the hearth, and Caitir made a stew of sausage, barley, and turnips.

After he'd eaten, Tristan banked the fire high then laid as close to its warmth as he could. Fionn curled up beside him, and Caitir nestled at his back.

As the rain lashed the door and shutters and the fire crackled, Tristan dreamed.

ABOVE, THE SAILS LUFFED AS the ship entered a harbor. He stood at the rail and peered across a glassy bay at a small village, no more than eight dozen mean huts clustered on a hillside. Tall cypress and

219

palms marched down the hillside to the shoreline. Was this Etrusca? Behind him, the early evening sun painted the western sea in reds and yellows.

The place was vaguely familiar. Once before, Tristan had been here, in a different vision.

Ahead, the birds he'd followed for nearly a month stopped above a single cowhide tent pitched at the edge of huts. The lowly tent was set apart, as if even these humble fishermen couldn't abide it among their dwellings.

Above the hillside hovered a brilliant cloud, and its light shot a beam of extravagant color that bathed a circle around the tent.

The birds had compelled him to leave his rule and his kingdom and to follow. Thousands upon thousands of them, brilliant-hued, with gentle beaks, they'd led him silently across the sea. No sound did they make, only the gentle flapping of their wings. By night, they glowed and hovered to the south. By day, they flew just ahead of his southerly course.

But what kingdom and what country he sailed from, he didn't know. Back in the ship's cabin, a gift of great value lay in a strongbox. All through the journey, the captain had assured him of its safety.

Sailors beside him gawked at the hillside scene. For up and down a celestial beam traveled dozens of siòg, each bathed in brilliant colors, all going in and out of the isolated tent. Even from across the bay, a heavenly chorus filled his ears with such sounds as no human had ever before heard, music of such joy, it brought tears to his eyes.

He was overwhelmed with such a sense of peace, wonder, and destiny as he'd never known. For here, in this place, something wonderful was happening, something that would change the world forever. And he was witness to it all.

It was a vision of things to come, of some great event happening many years from now.

But how many years? And was it he himself who watched? Or was he seeing this event through the eyes of another, just as he had on one other occasion?

He touched the sleeves of his tunic—robes of scarlet, embroidered with golden thread.

On his fingers—rings of gold, emeralds, and diamonds.

He lifted his tunic. His chest bore the insignia of a king, silver-threaded, embossed with gold, emeralds, and rubies.

Was it he who watched? Or another?

TRISTAN WOKE TO THE PATTER of rain from the hut's open door. Ewan came in from outside and shut the door. "Going to be a miserable day for a hike."

"Time to get up." Caitir shook him gently and offered a bowl of yesterday's stew.

He sat and ate.

"Why are you smiling?" she asked.

"A dream," he responded. "A wonderful dream of things yet to come."

"Does it involve me?"

But he wasn't ready to tell anyone about it. He didn't understand it. Did it have anything to do with them? So he smiled, looked at his spoon, and lied. "Aye."

She cocked her head and smiled back.

Tristan finished the last bite of stew, rolled up his furs, and joined the others as they stepped into a light drizzle under gray skies.

At the river, they took the road north along the eastern bank. But today, the path was mired in mud. They hadn't gone far when they again disturbed wakes of vultures feasting on yesterday's corpses. Fionn raced after a few of these, scattering them to flight. After a time, he tired of this game and just padded beside Tristan.

Everywhere lay bodies, some without arms, legs, or heads. Nearly all wore the uniforms of Armorica. Some had gone to the river to escape where, apparently, they'd been met with an ambush.

Finally, the group came upon a skiff nearly hidden by brush under an overhang. Dead Armoricans lay beside it, cut down in the attempt to flee by boat. They slid down the muddy bank, pulled the boat from its hiding spot, slipped it into the water, and carefully stepped in.

As Tristan rowed them out into the main current, Caitir stared at the surging waters. "The river's running fast today."

"Aye." Machar pulled his hood close about him. "Perhaps we should just float all the way to Bredehaven. The current would be with us."

"Bredehaven?" As the rain pounded, Caitir, too, huddled deeper under her cape.

"The port on the coast," said Tristan between strokes, "where Faolu-kan's fleet awaits his army."

Indeed, with a favorable current and Tristan's rowing, they were traveling faster than a horse could trot for any distance. Soon, they passed the battlefield on the right.

Straggling army units began appearing on the road beside them.

"Pull your capes over your heads," ordered Machar. "Do not let them see you."

As Machar manned the tiller, Tristan rowed them as far to the center of the river as the current allowed. Here, they were at least a hundred yards distant from the bank and the army. Raindrops spattered over the water.

After a time, Tristan gave up the oars to Machar. Through a mist raised by the drizzle, he glimpsed the army trudging along the river road beside them. The men's heads lowered against the rain. Few seemed inclined to notice their lone boat in the channel.

The soldiers struggled to make progress through the mud. As the boat continued downstream, the army column became stuck behind a line of carts. Men pushed and pulled on the wheels, struggling to get the carts through the muck.

When Tristan saw the mammoths, he gawked. Massive beasts so tall their trunks tore off the limbs of overhanging trees so they could pass. Their Gopalese masters, sitting in covered baskets atop the monsters, kept slowing their mounts so as not to crush the infantry ahead of them.

For miles, soldiers and their mounts stretched in what seemed a never-ending line.

"We'll be at the port long afore them." Ewan snugged his cape farther over his head.

"At least something's finally going our way," said Caitir.

As she spoke, they came even with the lead cohort, barely two hundred feet distant. Tristan could clearly make out the heavyset man in the lead, astride an enormous black stallion.

His black-tar beard, long, curling hair, and short neck announced him as Gundovald, the butcher of Burgundia. And at that moment, as if sensing he was being watched, Gundovald turned in the saddle. He stared out across the water, directly at the four.

Breathing faster, Tristan ripped his gaze away.

CHAPTER 34

BREDEHAVEN

Carried by steady rowing and a surging current, the skiff raced steadily downstream toward the sea, leaving the army behind.

Soon after, the rain stopped. Later that afternoon, they pulled their craft onto the wharf at Lutetia, the largest city on the River Seine. There, the populace was close to panic, with folks running hither and yon on desperate errands. Clearly, news had arrived of yesterday's battle and the approaching Butcher of Burgundia. The city occupied an island, but Tristan saw few, if any, defenses. Apparently, most of the army had been lost in what some passersby were now calling The Battle of the Plains.

Leaving Ewan and Caitir on the dock to guard the boat, Tristan and Machar began a frustrating search, ending only when they found a merchant who hadn't sold all his stock; people were buying everything in sight. With Zalán's coins, they hurriedly bought all the cheese, bread, dried beef, grapes, and wine the man had. "And now," he said as he closed and locked his shop doors, "me and my wife are leaving the city."

They returned to the boat and again rowed downstream.

For the next three days, they traveled ever north under sunny skies, sleeping in the boat. Throughout, Tristan kept to the thought that at last they were ahead of the enemy. Even though he no longer had the Scepter, they knew the enemy's plans. If they could arrive in Ériu in time to warn them of the coming danger, perhaps the Ériu could put up some kind of defense.

But he bemoaned the loss of the Scepter, devising, then discarding various plans to steal it back.

While the army was moving, he couldn't take it back. Neither could he steal it while it lay aboard a ship at sea. In both cases, Gundovald would have the device at all times in his possession. Better to wait until he landed on Ériu's shores and made camp. Then, if he ever left the Scepter in his tent and ventured out—that would be the time.

Tristan *must* steal it before it fell again into Faolukan's hands. The last thing Tristan wanted to do was face the arch druid while he controlled the device. With the Scepter in his possession, who knew what powers the druid could wield?

On the fourth evening after they left the battlefield, the river swept them into Bredehaven port where gulls cried, ships creaked at anchor, and waves lapped against the docks. They moored their craft and disembarked onto wet stone, for it had rained that afternoon.

Upon entering the harbor, they sighted the waiting enemy fleet. So many black-hulled, four-masted ships sat at anchor, they filled the bay. And so many conscripted and mercenary sailors staggered drunk or strutted sober about the docks, Tristan became alarmed.

Machar herded them into an alley. "This place is fraught with danger. We need to find a ship bound for Ériu or one we can hire and leave here—fast. Tristan, how much coin do we have?"

He counted out forty-three gold pieces.

"That should be enough." As one drunk sailor wove by, Machar closed his hand over Tristan's bag, and Fionn growled. He waited until the man had passed. "We're looking for a smaller one- or two-masted vessel. I'm guessing anything bigger will already have been conscripted."

They followed Machar from the alley then strolled beside the docks, stopping at every small ship still in port. Too many berths were empty.

"Appears to me"—Ewan pulled on his mustache—"that many captains have fled with their vessels."

"Aye," agreed Machar.

They walked the length of every jetty, stopping by each vessel at anchor, asking the captain or first mate if it was for hire. One after another declined, saying—often with a curse—that they were ordered not to leave port, or that they already had business ferrying goods and men to and from the Drochtar fleet.

Finally, at the end of the city dock, on the last berth on the last wharf sticking out into the harbor, they came to a single-masted ship looking badly in need of repairs.

A grizzled man of advanced years leaned against the railing.

"Good captain," said Machar, "is your ship for hire?"

Holes filled the man's leather apron, and he appeared to have only one good eye. He limped closer. "What? Hey? You want to hire me vessel?"

Immediately, Tristan recognized the accent. "From what country do you hail, good sir?"

He narrowed his good eye, while the other—perhaps glass—stared in a different direction. "From Ériu. What's it to ye?"

"Because that's where we want to go." Machar beamed. "And we've got the coin to pay."

The captain thumped on the wheelhouse, and out slunk a thin, emaciated youth—a younger version of the elder—who looked like he hadn't eaten or shaved in a month. The captain faced him. "These here want to take *The Happy Lass* to Ériu. What say you, Artair? They've got a dog with them."

The young man smiled and nodded. "If it means we eat, Da, then aye."

The captain again faced them. "We'd be more than willing to go. Me name's Tomey mac Friseal. And indeedy, I was planning on doing just that when circumstances allowed. To get out of the occupation that's coming. But we's got one big problem."

"What's that?" asked Tristan.

"Me and Artair here—and every other sailor in Bredehaven for that matter—has been ordered not to leave port. Has been killing me business, it has. About starved to death we are. But let me think. . . ." He scratched the stubble on his chin and strode to the rail overlooking the harbor.

He whirled back. "Methinks with this afternoon's rain, there might be a fog tonight. Just like yesterday eve. And being as *The Happy Lass* is docked here on the last wharf, a ship being rowed out—but quietly, mind ye, so as no one's to notice—such a ship might just not be seen, nor heard. 'Tis risky, that kind of business. They does patrol the harbor entrance. And if they catch us, we're as like to be fed to the ice giants they's got corralled onshore, waiting to board the ships. At night sometimes, I can hear them roar. Or they'll throw us overboard in deeper waters. Are ye still game?" He squinted his eye.

"We are," said Machar.

But Tristan wondered what kind of defense one puts up against a horde of ice giants. And how would they ever get them to sit still long enough for a long sea voyage?

They introduced themselves, and Machar bargained for a price.

"We's got one additional problem, though," said Tomey mac Friseal when negotiations had finished. "They's confiscated me rowboat, and now we's got no craft to row us into the channel."

"No problem, that." Caitir stepped forward. "We docked one not far from here."

Artair then tugged on Tomey's arm and whispered something in his ear. Tomey faced Machar again. "One more thing we need, Machar mac Maon, and right quick."

"What's that?"

"Vittles for the journey. And plenty of them."

Ewan beamed. "Leave that to me."

Thus did Tristan and Caitir leave the others. Together, they rowed the skiff back to Captain Tomey's wharf. By the time they rejoined the group, Ewan and Machar had bought supplies.

Then the group drank mugs of foaming ale and feasted on the fresh bread, cheese, salt pork, and apples that had been pouring into Bredehaven in anticipation of the army's arrival.

After the meal, Tristan wondered again how he would ever get back the Scepter.

CHAPTER 35

THE VOYAGE HOME

Night fell, and just as Tomey predicted, a heavy fog crept across the bay, obscuring even the nearest vessels and all but two lanterns at the dock's end. From across the harbor came the dull clanging of a bell being struck at regular intervals.

"To guide the boats bringing men and supplies 'tween shore and the fleet," Tomey explained. "But now's the time, lads." He and Artair untied the moorings and pushed the ship from the jetty. Then Tristan and Tomey climbed into the skiff. While Tristan dipped oars in the water and rowed, Tomey sat in the stern, one hand on the tiller, and peered ahead. The rope leading to the ship tightened with a snap. Tristan's oars dug deep, and he pulled hard, but the larger vessel seemed barely to move. Finally, it inched away from the dock.

"Tomey, why do you call your ship *The Happy Lass*?" Tristan strained at the oars.

The captain gave him a sly grin. "Named after me wife of thirty years. Back home in Leinster, she is. But when I'm there, she's anything but happy. They tell me 'tis only when I'm at sea that she's got a smile on her lips. So that there"—he pointed at the vessel behind him—"is me *Happy Lass*."

Tristan grunted as his oars churned the water.

Tomey looked beyond Tristan to the way ahead. "Hard to see anything in this soup."

As he rowed, they settled down to the steady scrape and clack of oars, the sound of water dripping off paddles. Once, unhappy with how much noise they were making, Tomey stopped him and tied rags around the oarlocks to muffle the sound.

Then came the clanging of a bell, close, not more than fifty yards ahead. Tomey held up his hand, and Tristan stopped. "Patrol ship," Tomey whispered.

Tristan turned in his seat and peered through the mist. Ahead to the right—a dim lantern on the prow of another boat where four men rowed, towing a much larger vessel. Tristan froze. The ship's bell sounded again. The patrol boat was crossing their path, heading into the harbor. If any of the men rowing or their tillerman or the man standing in the larger vessel's prow saw them now, there was no escape. The moments stretched endlessly as the ship inched past.

Then the fog swallowed the ship's stern. Its intermittent, clanging bell receded, slowly, into the night.

Tristan breathed deeply.

"No one expects a soul to be about now," whispered Tomey in his ear. "Let's wait a bit. Then we'll go on."

Tristan wiped mist from his forehead.

After a time, they began again. Tristan rowed until a wooden buoy rose from the dark on their left.

"Marks the main channel for the big ships." Tomey frowned. "We should have been here long ago. Making slow progress, we are."

"Time for someone else to row," said Tristan. His muscles aching, he was now drenched with sweat.

They returned to the ship, and Machar replaced him at the oars.

WHEN IT SEEMED HALF THE night had gone and everyone had taken a turn at the oars, they finally took the ship out of the fog into deeper waters and a light breeze. A half-moon lit the way as Tomey and Artair raised the ship's lone sail. The skiff trailed behind.

But when Tristan looked up at the small gray canvas, tattered at the edges, and when he saw how slow was their progress through the sea, he turned to Tomey standing at the tiller. "Captain, how long do you ken our voyage to Ériu will take?"

Tomey spat over the side and narrowed his one eye. "About two weeks, I reckon."

Behind him, Machar moaned and pulled Tristan aside. "Sure, and at this rate, the fleet will catch up to us."

"They might. But the troops at Bredehaven, their mammoths, and their ice giants still have to board."

"True. Still, I fear they'll pass us." Rubbing the back of his neck, Machar scowled at the unpainted planking beneath his feet. "Let's hope we don't run into bad weather. This scow is barely seaworthy."

Tristan agreed.

"Did I mention, lads, that she leaks a wee bit?" Tomey scratched his stubbled chin. "So, at all times, we all needs to take turns at the bilge pump. Artair, go below and show them how 'tis done."

As Artair led, Ewan rolled his eyeballs but stepped down the ladder behind him into the hold. Moments later, to the sounds of cranking, a stream of water gushed out of a wooden chute leading up through the deck and over the side.

THE NEXT MORNING, THE WIND picked up, and they made better progress. All day, Tristan watched the eastern horizon for signs of the fleet, but saw nothing.

When Tristan explained their predicament to Captain Tomey, the captain scratched the stubble on his face and stared at the deck. "What if I's to take a more southerly route then turn north when we sights Ériu's fair shores?"

"Aye, captain," said Machar. "Do it. It'll add time to our trip, but better that than be surrounded by a hundred enemy ships."

Tomey steered the vessel due south for half a day before again heading west.

On their second morning at sea, Caitir bailed, and Ewan slept on deck. Then Machar took Tristan to the bow where the sea sloshed noisily against the hull and the sun glinted off the whitecaps ahead. While the men faced the sea ahead, Fionn padded up behind Tristan and sat.

"I've been wanting some time alone with you, Tristan." The Capulum warrior sent him a scowl. "When we arrive back at court, I don't know what's to become of you. And I still don't know what to make of you. Your visions seem true enough, and you did get the Augury. But the Scepter lies still in enemy hands. And then there's this: you are not flaith. You did not meet the prophecy. So how can you really be the chosen one?" He closed his eyes and shook his head. "That's exactly what others will say about you. By law, you and Ewan could be executed for what you've done—concocting a plan to masquerade as royalty and mislead the Company."

Tristan lowered his head. He feared this day would come, the day when their deceptions would finally be revealed.

But then he remembered Elyon's words and his charge to Tristan. Where before he might have agreed with Machar, now the importance of his mission and Elyon's earlier commands filled him with resolve.

"I ken what you're saying, my lord. And at first, I, too, was uncomfortable with Ewan's plan. But then on the balcony in the palace at Ewhain Macha, Elyon himself spoke to me, saying I was to go after the Scepter. And I did retrieve it, did I not? And on the journey, he gave me visions that later came true. And in our hidden camp on Drochcarn's foul slopes, he wrote the words on the scroll I retrieved from Balor. In the sight of Ewan, Caitir, and Milosh, he said that *I* was the Toghaí, the chosen one. Then he told me I was also the Augury."

Machar's mouth opened, but he didn't speak.

"I did not ask for this charge. Nor did I want it. But there it is. It was Elyon's choice to give me this task, and I must take it up. We've lost the Scepter, aye, but somehow, I'll get it back. For Elyon has told me that no one but me can save Ériu or the world. So I cannot—nay, I will not—give up."

Machar stared at him, his forehead scrunched. Long moments passed. Then his shoulders loosened. "I believe you, lad. After hearing you tell it that way, I do." He glanced over the bow. "But how are we going to convince the high king or his druid? Or the kings of the provinces?"

Tristan followed Machar's gaze to the western sea. "How, indeed?"

Their crossing of the Sea of Albion was uneventful. They tacked against westerly winds, making steady progress. The bilge pump ran constantly, draining the water ever leaking into the hold.

Then, on the third night out from Bredehaven, Tristan had another vision.

HE WAS WALKING ALONE THROUGH a land denuded of green leaf and needle. To all sides of him, the forests contained only burnt trunks, charred limbs. Ahead rose the city of Ewhain Macha, but it was black and devastated, a hideous scar upon the land. The lower city had tumbled into ruins. Not a soul walked the rubble-filled streets. The skeletons of the fallen lay strewn, helter-skelter, across the roadway. Thorns and weeds poked through cracks in the cobbles.

What great disaster had befallen this place that no one and nothing had survived?

He climbed the path to the fort where the walls lay broken and scattered across the slopes. The drawbridge was down, scarred and half-burnt by fire, and the gatehouse—a pile of rubble. The portcullis was charred and smashed in. Within the fort itself, the palace was a mound of jumbled stone. White bones lay everywhere.

Breathing hard now and sweating, Tristan raced toward the tower.

But it was gone.

Where once the epic monument had climbed regally to the sky, now lay only scattered blocks of stone, charred wood, and a toppled ruin.

In sympathy, the skies above cloaked themselves in funerary black, and a cold rain began falling.

His feet slipped over the stones. He fell face forward and slid into a crack between blocks.

The open eye sockets of a skeleton stared up at him. White hair covered its head. Beneath white bones, a tunic much like his own lay ragged and rotting. And on its right arm—Caitir's armband!

He was staring at himself.

HE AWOKE WITH A START to the creaking of timbers and the swinging of his hammock in the hold where he slept. His heart was leaping against his rib cage. Outside, the hull groaned against a light sea. Forehead covered with sweat, he slipped out of the hammock and ran up on deck with Fionn padding behind.

A profusion of stars brightened the sky.

What was the dream trying to tell him?

Was that Ériu's future? Would the Deamhan Lord defeat the forces of good, swarm over the land, and lay waste to everyone and everything?

He shuddered. Fionn whined and licked his hand, and he reached down to pet the dog. Did the dog sense his discomfiture?

How could he reconcile this vision with the one in the Etruscan port, where the unknown king had felt such an overwhelming joy, hope, and peace?

What should he make of it? That ahead lay two divergent paths? That the future could fork in either direction?

He ran to the rail and grabbed it. Moonbeams and starlight glinted brightly off wave crests. Never had he seen such beauty upon a sea at night—so incongruous with his last vision.

Was tonight's vision the future if he failed to retrieve the Scepter?

He fingered Caitir's armband.

Filled with a sense of resolve to bring back that which was lost, to never let that future come to pass, he returned to his hammock and tried to sleep.

Thirteen days out from Bredehaven, land appeared on the horizon, and everyone rushed to the bow.

"If I reckon rightly, 'tis Leinster's southern coast," said Tomey, who then spat over the side. "And glad am I to finally be home again."

"Aye." Machar stood beside Tristan at the rail. "What a pretty sight she is."

Tristan stared at the low, green hills, at the land he sometimes feared he'd never see again. They'd finally made it home. But, for all his trouble, what did he bring back? Only the Augury. Machar was right to be concerned. They'd been gone over a year, and for all the trials and the deaths of companions, he was returning with little to show for it. And now that his ruse was unmasked, how would the nobility of Ewhain Macha receive him?

"Time to sail north for Áth Cliath," said Machar.

Tomey frowned. "I 'spect so. But let's hope we do not sight the fleet, hey?" Then he turned the ship to a beam reach and, still keeping well out to sea, headed north.

On the following morning, they passed the Wicklow Mountains to the west. By afternoon, the two points marking the harbor of Áth Cliath appeared on the western horizon. But as they neared the port, Gundovald's fleet already lay at anchor on the farthest end of the bay. Had they already taken the city? Or were they simply waiting for Faolukan to join them?

From the north, two schooners appeared, sailing toward them, coming on fast.

Tomey peered at the approaching threat. "What does we do now, lads? We can run for the coast. But them ships are faster. I fears they'll outrun us."

"We cannot let them capture us," said Tristan. "Make a run for it."

PART VIII

ÉRIU

CHAPTER 36

AN UNHAPPY LASS

As Artair pulled on the sheets to trim sail, Tomey turned the tiller, and the ship veered southwest, toward the coast.

"Why do they care about us?" Caitir stood beside Machar and Tristan. "Why not just let us on our way?"

"They're an occupying force, lass," said Machar. "They might just want to search us, make certain we're not a threat. But we can't let them do that."

"I fear me ship's at great risk," muttered Tomey. "And with it, me livelihood."

"If you get us close enough to shore," said Tristan, "we can take the skiff and go the rest of the way. Without us aboard, you're no threat to anyone."

"Appreciate that, I does," answered Tomey.

The Happy Lass struggled against the wind, and with each passing moment, it appeared the approaching schooners would soon overtake them. Though Tomey manned the tiller, his gaze was drawn increasingly aft.

By the time Áth Cliath had receded over the horizon, *The Happy Lass* was only a mile from the rolling hills and tree-lined shores of Leinster where Machar suggested they disembark. But now the first enemy schooner lay only fifty yards aft of starboard. The second was still a mile distant.

Tomey gave the tiller to his son and peered over the stern. "Oh nay, nay. I ken that fellow on the bow in the black cape."

"Who is he?" asked Ewan.

"One of them as patrolled the harbor at Bredehaven. We had words, we did. We're in a fine mess of trouble now, I fears."

As the first schooner neared, all but Artair now stood at the aft rail. The tall man in a black cape waved for them to come about.

But Tomey gave him his back, took the tiller from his son, and kept *The Happy Lass* heading straight for land.

The enemy ship closed the gap to thirty yards on the starboard side. The black-caped man shouted across, "Pull her about, or we'll sink you. I know your ship, captain. You left the harbor at Bredehaven without authority."

Tomey shot him a scowl and kept to his course. "He canna sink us, 'less he rams us, and he won't. I'm not going to stop till I slams her hull ashore. I fears me ship is lost, anyways."

The black-caped man made one more attempt to stop his quarry. But *The Happy Lass* was not responding. Then he motioned to a group of ten archers standing behind him. They stepped to the rail with bows in their hands. Someone else wheeled up a brazier filled with blazing logs. The tips of the archer's arrows were wrapped in cloth. They dipped them in the flames and shot.

Flaming arrows slammed onto the deck. Some caught in the sail. Two went beyond, dropping into the water with a hiss.

"Quick, Artair." Tomey pointed at the burning sail. "Put it out. Or we're finished."

As the flame began devouring the canvas, his son hastened to obey. He climbed a shroud and beat at the fire with a broom.

Another volley hit higher, with half of them catching in the sail, the other half dropping to the deck. Flames covered half the sail now, and Artair stopped his efforts. A burning rope snapped, brought with it a spar, knocked over a bucket of tar on the deck. Black, oily flames spread across the planks.

Just as Artair began to climb down, a third volley of arrows struck. Without flame, they were aimed at him.

Two missiles struck Artair in the back.

He fell to the deck with a crunch of bones.

Artair was dead.

Tomey abandoned the tiller, ran to his son, and knelt. "Oh nay. Not me only son." He stood and raised a fist at the black-caped man. "You bashtoons. May Manannán mac Lir himself rise up and sink the lot of you."

The black-caped man answered with new instructions. Another volley fell on the deck around Tomey. Three arrows hit him in the chest. He staggered forward, picked up a harpoon, and thrust it toward the schooner. But the strength had left his arm, and after only a few feet, the weapon plunged into the waves. Tomey took two more steps then dropped to the deck.

Caitir ran to him, lifted her gaze to the others, and shook her head.

Without sail, the ship was now dead in the water.

"Quick," Machar ordered, "pull in the skiff."

As Tristan and Ewan hauled frantically on the line, Tristan glanced amidships. The deck had become a crackling pyre. Flaming arrows hissed into the water around the skiff.

Finally, they hauled the craft against the stern. With packs in hands, they climbed into the rowboat. Tristan helped Fionn climb aboard. More fiery arrows fell in the water around them, one even landing in the skiff itself. But nothing was there to catch fire. Tristan threw overboard two flaming missiles.

"This boat willna outrun them." Ewan brought out the single set of oars.

"Pull around to the port side, out of sight." Tristan dug feverishly in his pack. "I've got an idea."

As Machar steered, Ewan pulled at the oars with all his might. Soon, the port side of *The Happy Lass*—and a towering wall of flames—hid them from the enemy vessel.

Tristan took out the hiding stone that the wizard Zalán had given him back in Glenmallen. To Caitir and Ewan, he asked, "Do you think it will work if we're moving?"

"I do not ken, my lord," said Ewan, docking the oars. "But try it."

"Do it!" said Caitir.

"What is it?" asked Machar.

Tristan held the stone and willed it to show only the sea around them. Suddenly, the air stilled.

"It worked!" said Ewan. "Now let's see if we can row, too."

On the ship beside them, a flaming spar crashed to the deck. But as Ewan's oars churned the water and the larger ship receded, the bubble of quiet air followed them.

"A hiding stone?" said Machar, his mouth agape.

"Aye. When we passed through Glenmallen, the eladrin were gone, and Zalán had set up another protective valley. Before we left, he gave this to me."

"Have you more wonders in you, lad?"

Tristan only smiled.

When Ewan had taken them a hundred yards from the burning ship, the enemy vessel circled what was left of its stern, rounded the port side, then crossed its bow.

"They're still searching. They canna see us." Caitir was beaming. "Thank you, Zalán."

As they gained even more distance, the fire soon burned down to the vessel's waterline. Then *The Happy Lass* broke up and sank.

The schooner continued to search the surrounding waters for survivors. Then it gave up and headed north.

As Ewan rowed them the mile to shore, Caitir's glance sought the bottom of the boat. "Tomey and his son died trying to save us."

"Aye." Ewan gazed back at the place where they'd gone down and shook his head.

"May Elyon bless them for helping us." Tristan's gaze followed Ewan's.

"They knew the risks." Machar frowned. "But you're right. Too many have died on this trek. And we've little to show for their deaths. All that we've brought home is ourselves, alive."

"We have the Augury, my lord," Ewan offered.

"Without the Scepter, I fear 'twill not be enough."

Tristan gripped the rail. Machar was right. They had failed their most important mission. But he wouldn't give up. "You're forgetting one thing, my lord."

Machar faced him. "What?"

"For the first time in millennia, the Scepter will soon be on our shores. And that gives us an opportunity to get it back. Somehow."

"I hope, lad, that you're right."

Ewan rowed in silence until he rammed the skiff onto the pebbled beach. He jumped out into knee-deep water. Tristan followed. The moment his foot left the boat, the protective bubble disappeared.

But the hiding stone had done its work. They were safely ashore. And home.

But without the Scepter. And with an army about to occupy Ériu's main port.

"Uh-oh." Ewan stood on shore with his hands atop his head. He pointed north, and the others turned to look.

From north to south, black-sailed ships filled the horizon.

Faolukan's fleet had arrived.

Chapter 37

CONSPIRACIES

Of the Company's original seven, only three remained—plus Caitir. These four now threaded their way north through winding forest trails toward Ulster's main port. As evening shadows stretched long across their path, they approached a small hut overlooking Áth Cliath.

With Fionn at his heel, Tristan knocked on the door.

Behind him, pigs grunted, and chickens clucked.

"Who are you?" came a child's voice from behind.

Tristan whirled.

Before them, a young girl of about seven stared at them, wide-eyed. "Are you from the ships in the harbor?"

"Nay, child." Ewan smiled. "We're from *a* ship, but not from the port."

"May I pet your dog?" Grinning, she stepped forward and, with no hesitation, slid a hand over Fionn's head, then slipped her fingers under his ears and scratched.

Fionn tilted his head into her hand, half-closed his eyes, and whined.

"I think he likes you, child," said Tristan.

"Name's Teàrlag."

"He likes you, Teàrlag."

At that moment, a blond-haired man wearing a worn leather tunic stepped out, followed by his red-haired wife. The room beyond was a tiny, one-room affair. No shelter would be had there tonight.

"What can I do for ye, my lord?" The man glanced at his daughter, petting Fionn, and scowled.

"We've only just arrived home after a long journey. Over a year abroad. Can we take shelter in your mow?"

"That you can, my lord." He bowed. "And me wife will bring you each a bowl of mutton stew."

"Thank you. We'd also appreciate a bit of news. What's the state of affairs in Ulster?"

The man's eyes widened. "Sure, and a long time away you must have been. Bad times has come upon us, my lord. The worst of times, I'd say."

Then he confirmed that, aye, the kings of Leinster, Connacht, Meath, and Munster had broken from the Alliance of Kingdoms and were marching toward Ulster. For the last month, their army encamped only five leagues from Ewhain Macha. Connell mac Conn, the Ard Righ and High King of the land, had sequestered himself in his palace with the druid Corc. Connell's one act of defiance against Corc had been to appoint Eacharn, the former captain of the guards, as general of the army. Eacharn, and what was left of the King's Riders—those who hadn't yet deserted—were holed up in an abandoned fort, surrounded. Other than a few skirmishes, no one had engaged in battle. But rumor had it that such a battle would come soon.

"What about that fleet down in the harbor?" asked Machar. "Have their soldiers come ashore yet?"

"Nay," answered the man. "None as yet. They's sent raiding parties to steal supplies from folks in town, but no invasion. And they's left us a warning, they have. Anyone who resists when they do land willna live to see the morrow."

"What about a defense of the port?" Machar frowned.

"Defense, my lord?" He laughed. "Half the town has fled. The king kens our situation but hasna sent a single soldier to help. Most of me neighbors downslope have fled. Many has gone to the southern hills. Defense, my lord? There is none."

Machar gave the man a gold coin. Tristan also thanked him.

242

But as they were walking to the open-sided mow, Teàrlag skipped behind Fionn. "Can your dog sleep with me, tonight, stranger?"

Tristan eyed Fionn, then the girl, and smiled. "Of course. If it's all right with your da."

She whirled and ran back to the hut.

As they were plopping down in the fragrant hay, darkness descended. The farmer's wife returned with their supper and a candle. Teàrlag followed, her eyes downcast.

"Me daughter's asking if your dog can sleep in the house tonight. I'm terribly sorry she's troubled you in this way. I——"

Tristan raised a hand. "His name's Fionn, and he seems to have taken a liking to her. If he'll allow it, then let her sleep with him."

Teàrlag jumped, clapped her hands, and ran to Fionn, who accepted her hugs. When she pulled on his mane, Fionn looked once toward Tristan.

Tristan waved him off and said, "Go, boy."

The dog let himself be led off with the girl.

After they'd eaten, Machar sat back with a sigh against one of the timbers supporting the roof. He lit his pipe from pipeweed he'd gathered earlier beside the trail and puffed. "Tomorrow, we should head directly for Ewhain Macha. They need to know the state of affairs regarding the Scepter. And someone needs to intervene between the rebellion and the king's men."

Tristan shifted uncomfortably on the hay. "I can't go with you, Machar. I have business here."

Machar scowled and blew a smoke ring. "How do you think you're going to get the Scepter now?"

"I–I don't know. I only know I must try."

"Gundovald will give it straight away to Faolukan. Then you'll have to take it from the arch druid himself. How are you going to do that?" Machar's gaze was like Uncle Cowan's before he administered a tongue-lashing.

Tristan brought both hands to his face then dropped them to his lap. "I don't know."

"What's your plan?" asked Ewan, sitting to Tristan's right.

"I–I don't know."

Caitir scooted across the hay and leaned close to Tristan. "Whatever he plans to do, I'm going with him."

His face pensive, Ewan examined the candle a moment. "Sorry, my lord Machar, but I'm pledged to follow Tristan. As are you, if you remember. Back when you learned that he and Caitir had stolen the Scepter from Schwarzburg Castle."

Machar pursed his lips. "Aye, I did say that, did I not? But much has changed since then. We've learned of your and this lad's deception. And—"

"And Tristan is the Toghaí, my lord!" Ewan's voice rose. "How many times must he prove it? He'll get the Scepter again, of that I'm certain. Or . . . or . . ."

"Or we're all doomed." Machar closed his eyes, leaned against the timber, and brought the pipe to his lips. "All right, Tristan. I'll wait until I hear some kind of plan from you. Some way to take back Elyon's greatest gift to mankind. Then I'll decide what to do. I'll give you . . . three days. After that, I must leave for Ewhain Macha."

Tristan breathed out. "Three days then."

"He'll think of something," said Caitir.

But Tristan wasn't so sure. Because, as of that moment, he had no idea how he was going to get the Scepter. No idea at all.

No SOONER HAD THEY BLOWN out the candle and laid down to sleep, and before Tristan could even close his eyes, another vision came upon him.

He sat straight up and stared into the dark. . . .

Replacing the shadows of trees, a ship's cabin appeared before him—a captain's stateroom. Dark paneling covered walls punctuated with brackets holding candles in glass chimneys. Then Tristan's gaze fell on a short, squat man.

244

The massive bulk rising from the chair was Gundovald's. His black beard curled. His yellow eyes with their jet-black pupils focused on someone entering the room—Faolukan himself.

Gundovald bowed as the arch druid crossed the distance to him. As before, Tristan shuddered at the sight of him. Darkness clung to the man, dimming even the candles in their sconces. An ancient white scar slashed the druid's right cheek and ran down under a thin gray beard that snaked to his chest.

"We meet again, my friend." Faolukan gave a slight nod—not a bow, barely even an acknowledgment. "Glad am I to confide in you. There is simply no one else."

"Proud am I to be your confidante." Gundovald puffed out his chest. Then he smashed a fist against his breast in salute.

Faolukan returned the gesture with far less force. Tonight, his entire demeanor appeared subdued.

Gundovald motioned toward a table holding a single candle, and they sat. The Burgundian filled two silver goblets with wine from a decanter, setting one before his guest.

"Have you taken the port yet?" Faolukan sipped his wine.

"Nay. We only arrived two days ago. I was waiting for your arrival."

"No matter. We shall take it tomorrow. There'll be no resistance, I'm certain." Faolukan drank then closed his eyes and rubbed his temples.

"Is something wrong, my lord? You look troubled."

"Aye." Faolukan raised unfocused, empty eyes. "'Tis Crom Mord."

"You spoke of such concerns before. Has it gotten worse?"

"It has. I fear . . . he's gone insane."

"What?" Gundovald's eyebrows rose.

"Aye. He rages almost constantly now. Some kind of black mist now fills his cabin—perhaps a physical manifestation of his mood. The few who dare enter return stricken with such fear, half have refused to go back. At the halfway mark of our voyage, we sacrificed the last of the slaves brought for that purpose. Then he called me into his presence and clamored for more victims. When I explained we could not kill the very men needed to man the ship, he flew into a rage that continues even now. 'Twas then I learned that he has feasted on sacrifices so long, he now depends on them just to survive. On the journey, his power has waned."

"This is bad. Very bad."

"Aye."

"Once we land, will you begin the sacrifices again?"

Glass half raised, Faolukan looked up from his wine. "What are you suggesting?"

"That we starve him."

Faolukan lifted his gaze, his face twitching, his eyes narrowing. "Are you serious?"

Ever so slowly, Gundovald nodded. "If we let this continue and if we subdue all the lands of Erde and if he remains in this state, will he let us rule? You hinted before he was of a mind only to destroy. If so, will anything be left for us?"

"I fear not. He seems bent on complete and total destruction of all we touch."

Gundovald shook his head. "We cannot let that happen."

"Nay, we cannot."

"And the cause of this malady?"

"'Tis what I said before. When the prince of Ulster threw that ring into his mouth, something happened to him, something profound. I fear the device carried within it something of Elyon. Now Crom Mord dwells constantly on that event, thinking of naught but revenge and destruction. And of feeding on souls I cannot give him."

Gundovald stared at the lone candle flickering between them.

From across the harbor, a chorus of ship's bells sounded, marking the start of the next watch. Water slapped against the hull outside the window.

The Butcher of Burgundia dropped both palms on the table. "Then our course is clear. We must put an end to him."

Faolukan cocked his head and narrowed his eyes. "By starving him?"

"Yes. But far more will be needed. When he is weak enough, you must use the Scepter against him."

The arch druid's face was impassive, unreadable. Slowly, he pushed back from the table and stood. He walked to the window and looked across the dark harbor waters where over a thousand ships rocked at anchor. "You realize, do you not, that we cannot kill a spirit such as him? The best we can do is drive him down to the Underworld."

"Then that's what we must do. And you know the only device that can do that."

"Still, I greatly fear to pick up the Scepter for any purpose."

"But I've felt its power, my lord. 'Tis incredible. Surely it will drive him out of the idol and down into the depths if you so command. I trust that, afterward, you will heal. After I picked it up, I did."

"You may be right. It has been so long since I touched the thing . . . perhaps my fear of it has grown out of proportion to reality. Your plan may just work." Faolukan whirled toward Gundovald. "I'll do it."

"When?"

"Samhain would be the time. That's when the window into the Otherworld is widest. That's when the spirits can move back and forth most easily."

"Less than two weeks away. Two more weeks for him to starve and grow weaker."

A rare smile played briefly over Faolukan's lips. "We shall do it. I will empty the ship where he sits and quarantine the vessel. Then I'll move my flag to another. With each day that passes, he will weaken. On Samhain eve, I—nay, we—will use the power of Elyon's foul device to drive him into the depths."

"In the meanwhile, shall we continue the conquest of Ériu?"

"Nay. After we take the port, we will wait. Without the port bringing goods in and out of Ewhain Macha, our opposition will also lose heart. And with the Scepter in our hands, when we do march, nothing they do will be able to stop us. Samhain eve will be the end of Crom Mord. The next day, on Samhain proper—a good omen, that—that's when we'll march on Ewhain Macha. Only twelve days from now."

"This is good, very good." Gundovald rubbed his hands together. "Just think, between us, we'll soon rule all of Erde. Every city, town, and village will be under our thumbs. All will bow down before me—and you, of course. In the lands you've given me, my statue will rise from every square. They'll send me their sons and daughters for my slaves, my armies, and my pleasure. I will take their wheat, their livestock, and their gold. I will put my men in every village to watch over them, and whoever objects to my rule—even a whisper raised in complaint—that person will be tied, hands and feet, and drawn by oxen until they are rent asunder.

"As a reward for my men, I will demand the right of first-night from every comely bride, even before her husband has slept with her. Indeed, my men and I will have the right to sleep with whomever we choose, whenever we choose, and my wealth will increase to a level never before seen on Erde."

"Your ambition is great, my friend." For the first time, Faolukan bowed. "Let what you have said come to pass. For your goals are also my goals." He raised his goblet high. "To the conquest of Ériu."

Gundovald hoisted his own goblet. "To the conquest of Ériu, then of all Erde."

Even as the two men drank, the vision vanished, and the dark forest appeared again before him.

Should he wake the others and tell them what he'd seen?

Nay. The day had been long, all were exhausted, and everyone needed sleep. But now his plans must change. If Faolukan planned to drive the Deamhan Lord back to the Underworld, then why not wait and let him do it? Especially if the attempt to use the Scepter might harm the arch druid in some way. Aye, now it made sense to go first with Machar to Ewhain Macha. Now Machar's plans to stop the kingdom from tearing itself apart should be paramount.

He laid down on the hay and tried to sleep. But slumber came late.

CHAPTER 38

EWHAIN MACHA

The next morning, as they ate bowls of barley pottage provided by the farmer's wife, Tristan told his companions about the vision.

"If our enemies now war against themselves"—Machar set down his bowl—"this is indeed welcome news."

"Aye," said Tristan. "So I've decided 'tis best to wait. Let Faolukan use the Scepter against the Deamhan Lord. I will go with you to Ewhain Macha."

"Good." Machar beamed. "If, at this crucial time, we can do anything to stop a foolish war between our peoples, we must at least try."

They'd barely finished eating when the farmer ran in from the yard, his eyes wide. Teàrlag followed with Fionn padding behind her. "Troops are landing on the wharf. They's invading, my lords."

Machar looked to Tristan with wonder in his eyes. "Your visions, lad—they are indeed true."

They grabbed their gear and, with the child and Fionn padding behind her, walked to the overlook. Boats from every ship were hauling men to the port's two jetties sticking into the harbor. A steady stream of soldiers swarmed the dock, spilling into the town. On the trail leading up from town, dozens of folk were fleeing on foot, many burdened with heavy packs or leading horses laden with household goods.

Machar turned to the farmer standing beside them. "What route do you suggest to get to Ewhain Macha that bypasses the town?"

"Go back the way you came for about a mile. You'll see a large oak on the right. Take the trail there. Leads to the Ewhain Macha highway."

Machar thanked him again.

"I'm taking me family south to me wife's cousin's. It'll be safer there."

"And . . . and . . . and," sputtered Teàrlag.

"Out with it child," said her father. He faced Tristan and opened his hands as if to say, "What can I do with her?"

"And can Fionn . . . can he come with me?" she asked.

Tristan looked at her, at the dog, and at the farmer. He'd grown fond of the dog. But Fionn would be good protection for the farmer's family on their journey. And where he was going, a dog would be nothing but a liability. He walked over, knelt, and hugged him. "You've been a good dog, Fionn," he whispered. "A good companion. But now you need to go with her." He raised his eyes to the child. "Do you promise to take good care of him?"

She nodded her head half a dozen times. "I will. I will."

"Then I give him to you." He stepped away.

"Thank you, kind sir." Teàrlag ran to Fionn, hugged him, and led him off.

As Tristan and Company walked south, Tristan gave a last glance back at Fionn. Then they hurried down the trail, ahead of the approaching refugees. A few leagues along the way, they bought a horse from a farmer. After another league, they bought three more.

ON HORSEBACK, THE TREK TO Ewhain Macha took two days over a trail, rutted and in ill repair. But they traveled well ahead of the refugees.

When they reached the River Blackwater, it was low enough to ford on horseback. Then they crossed onto the plain where The Battle of Two Rivers had once been fought.

As before, a shudder rippled over Tristan's shoulders. It was as if the ghosts of the soldiers of Ériu—those who had been slain here so long ago—called out to him, still bemoaning their defeat.

Beyond the field, they arrived at a junction of trails, and as Machar forged ahead, both Tristan and Caitir stopped and stared at the left fork, for that trail led to the home they'd left so long ago.

Ewan rode up behind him and said, softly, "It leads to Hidden Pines, does it not?"

Tristan shifted on his steed and faced Caitir beside him. "You can go home now, if you want. No need for you to endanger yourself any longer."

She stared at the path then lifted her gaze to him. "Nay, I'm going with you. We'll see this through together."

Looking into her eyes, he smiled. "I knew you'd say that."

Once more, they both glanced down the left fork.

"Do you ken?" she asked. "Will it be the same for us when we return?"

"I don't know." How long ago was it now? Well over a year? Would Aunt Brigid and Uncle Cowan be in good health? Would they still be living?

He had a sudden urge to take the fork, to see his life as it once was—his uncle's hut, the smithy where he'd spent so many long hours, and the village square. His world had been turned upside down, and at the end of that path was something he feared was now gone forever.

"What's holding you folks up?" came Machar's voice from fifty yards ahead. His horse was turning in circles. "We've still a day's ride ahead."

Tristan shook his head. He lashed his mount, and they caught up with Machar.

Sometime later, Machar tried to convince Tristan to resume his ruse as Prince Neil, but Tristan declined. "Elyon himself has told me I must now be myself."

Machar only scowled and muttered his fears about what the flaith might do when they found out.

Tristan feared the same. But his course was set. If Elyon said he must now be Tristan mac Torn, then that's how it must be. The time for deception had passed.

They rode on through forests of deep pines and oaks, following the River Liffey's western bank through hamlets and villages. They topped Artair's Ridge and descended again into thick forest.

By late afternoon, they passed through a wide field. The trail bent around a corner, topped a hill, and the city lay below them. But at the trailside ahead stood a sculpture that sent Tristan's heart jumping and the blood rushing to his head.

A rusting iron post bore a massive, iron quarter-moon—the mark of Faolukan's domain.

"Corc!" Machar spat to the side. "This is his doing."

Tristan stared at the abomination. Was Connell's druid so firmly in control that the Ard Righ didn't even know what went on in his own kingdom? "'Tis worse than we feared."

"Aye." Ewan stopped beside him. "No wonder the kings of the other provinces rebelled."

"This bodes ill for talking with anyone in the palace."

Moments later, they entered the outskirts of the once great capital of Ulster, the seat of the Ard Righ of Ériu. But the squalor of the populace seemed far worse than when he'd left. Roundhouses that should have been full of children's laughter, women's cooking, and men coming in from the fields lay abandoned and collapsed. Smoke trailed from only a few. Outside the occupied huts, men and women sat with sullen, downcast faces. A crowd of begging orphans followed the Company.

Scantily clad women lounged in doorways and called out to the three men to partake of what they offered. Tristan winced, imagining that his mother might once have stood among them. Still, he'd never seen anywhere in Ériu such a wanton display from harlots on a main thoroughfare. Usually, such women hid in the back alleys.

"This is not good." Ewan waved his hands as they passed an elderly couple begging for coins, their faces thin, their clothing ragged.

"Aye," said Machar. "The state of the kingdom has indeed worsened."

Ahead was the slope leading up to the drawbridge and the fortress of Ewhain Macha itself. Machar dismounted. "Before we go up, we need news of the state of affairs."

"I've some friends who've worked in the palace all their lives." Ewan dismounted, followed by the others. "Maybe I can coax someone to come down and talk with us. We can take rooms and supper over there." He pointed to an inn about twenty yards away, its painted, off-kilter sign depicting a faded pipe and mug. "While I send one of these waifs to get him."

They agreed, and Ewan approached one of the tow-haired urchins behind them. He spoke at length with the boy, offering him a silver piece with the promise of another when his task was done. Beaming, the boy fairly ran up the slope to the fort.

Ewan led them to a nearby stable where they paid the stablemaster and left their horses for the night.

Back at the inn's entrance, Ewan faced them. "This is one of the poorer establishments, serving the common folk. I've only been here once."

Inside, the floor was tracked with dried mud. The reek of spilt ale and vomit permeated the air. A few patrons huddled by a back table. The Company sat close to the door, pulled the hoods of their capes over their foreheads, and waited.

A thin, elderly man rose from a barrel, strolled over, and peered at them suspiciously.

Machar asked for a room and paid for it.

Then Ewan ordered ale for each, and the man returned with a tray and mugs.

Warily eyeing the group, the innkeeper collected his due and returned to his seat.

Tristan sipped his ale. Watered-down and without flavor. He pushed it away.

"I hope this doesn't take long," said Machar, glancing occasionally toward the group in the corner. "I don't want to attract any attention."

Before long, the boy brought back a portly man about Ewan's age, wearing a blacksmith's burn-scarred tunic. Ewan paid the waif, who beamed and ran out the door.

When the blacksmith saw Ewan, a smile broadened his face, and he rushed forward.

Ewan stood, and they hugged, beating each other on the back. "Sit, Kessan, for we're starved for news."

"Ewan!" the man nearly shouted. But then he shot a quick glance around the room and sat. "The king and Corc called you—all of you—traitors, swore to hang you if you ever showed your faces here again." Now he was whispering. "But you were gone so long, word on the streets is you were all killed on the journey." He glanced at Tristan then stared. "My lord . . . Prince Neil? Is that you?"

Tristan shook his head.

"Your secret's safe with me."

Ewan put a hand on Kessan's. "What news of affairs in the palace, my friend?"

The blacksmith brushed coal dust from his tunic. "The king hasna ventured out of the fort since you left. He's brought us all to ruin, he has. He and his druid. The king's body lives, but I'd say there's nobody home upstairs. I've seen him wandering the palace grounds, and when I look into his eyes, they're . . . vacant. Just fondles the jewelry around his neck. 'Tis Corc's doing, that piece. I fashioned the silver. But 'twas Corc who ensorcelled it."

Kessan spat onto the floor in the innkeeper's direction. Still sitting on his barrel, the innkeeper waved his finger and scowled. Kessan turned his face back to the group. "Corc about runs everything now. And Maeve! What a tragedy!"

"What of Maeve?" asked Tristan, his voice rising. "What's happened to her?"

"Over a year ago, Corc accused her of treason, and he convinced the king to sign an edict. On penalty of death, says the thing, she canna leave the city. And then Corc added this: 'Anyone caught feeding or sheltering the woman called Maeve nic Connell, formerly Princess Maeve, will face the hangman's noose.' That's what it says. The king's mind was so addled, he was convinced she was a traitor, and he signed the blasted thing. Them words are nailed up on a post in every square, so I've got them memorized. It stripped her of her title. Can you imagine? Now, the poor lass sleeps in the alleys, eats from garbage piles, wanders around like a waif. Sometimes, folks leave a hunk of bread or a slice of cheese on a doorstep at night, hoping she'll find it before the rats do. And since you've gone, the vermin have become quite healthy, too."

"Vermin of every kind," said Caitir.

"Outrageous!" Machar slammed a fist into a palm.

Tristan put his hands on top of his head and shook it. "Nay, nay. Where might I find her?"

"This time of day—probably sleeping in an alley somewhere. Or wandering near a baker's or butcher's shop. Anywhere there's food."

"What else can you tell us?" asked Machar.

"The king's spies—Corc's spies, really—they're everywhere, listening to conversations and reporting back to Corc's personal guard. We need to watch that group in the corner, by the way. I donna trust anyone anymore."

"The druid has a personal guard?" asked Caitir.

"Aye. Calls them the Black Cloaks, he does. And they comes in the dead of night and slits the throats of any who dares criticize the king's reign. We've reports of entire families found dead on the morrow."

Ewan whistled.

"How many of these Black Cloaks are there?" asked Machar.

"Maybe only a dozen. But everyone's afeared of them."

Machar turned to Tristan. "With a few more men, we could put a stop to that."

"Glad am I that someone's come to save us from what's happened," said Kessan. "'Cause bravery in the land of Ulster is now in short supply."

"And the king's army?" asked Machar. "Eacharn leads it?"

"Aye. He's holed up in a fort northwest of Ewhain Macha. They say Eacharn had orders to attack, but his force was so outnumbered, he took refuge in the old, abandoned Dún Monaghan. His army is trapped inside. The rebellion now lays siege to it."

"And the rebellion itself? Who leads it?"

"Lords Cé of Munster and Angus of Leinster. I hear Cairbre the Wise has also joined them. Folks also say he's learned the art of white magic and has become a wizard, though I do not ken if this is true."

"A white wizard?"

"Aye. They say he dabbled in such long ago, but now resumes the practice."

Machar gave them a sly grin. "As I've known all along."

"You've come from the coast, have you?" Kessan asked Ewan.

Ewan nodded, and they told him how the enemy was taking Áth Cliath.

"We knew it was coming. That fleet's been sitting out there for days." The blacksmith pursued his lips to spit again on the floor, saw the inn-keeper's scowl, and swallowed instead. "Well, I've got to get back to me forge 'fore someone gets suspicious."

"Thank you, Kessan." Machar pushed away his half-finished ale.

After Kessan left, Tristan faced the others. "We have to find Maeve. We cannot leave her like this."

Machar raised an eyebrow. "She's not your real sister, lad. Yet you talk like you have feelings for her."

Caitir frowned.

"In my brief time with her, I came to know her—as a sister. I cannot explain it. Regardless, she's been ill-used by her father and Corc."

"Aye, we must search for her." Machar's brows furrowed, and he stared into the mug he'd hardly touched. "With Connell in the state he's in, she's now the rightful heir to the throne. If we can restore her, every-one will surely rally around her. She'll give the people hope."

They spread out and searched separately, planning to meet later back at the inn.

On his own now, Tristan passed run-down stone huts, waifs, beggars, and rats skittering into cracks under doors. An air of defeat and melan-choly seemed to hover everywhere in Ewhain Macha.

He searched until dusk darkened the alleys and stripped the main streets of most passersby.

Ready to give up the search, he left an alley and turned right onto a main thoroughfare. There, a ragged figure of a woman raced for a cat drinking from a saucer on a doorstep.

Saddened nearly to tears, Tristan slowed, tried to get a better glimpse.

Surely, this was a beggar, not the former princess of the realm?

CHAPTER 39

MAEVE

With a vaguely familiar voice, now hoarse, the woman shooed away the feline, lifted the clay bowl, and drank. Mewing in outrage, the cat slunk toward the shadows.

Tristan had been looking for a woman with lush, black hair; long, black eyelashes; and eyes that were at once deep, black, and inviting, but also bored with the world. He remembered how, in her palace quarters, Maeve had dangled her shapely legs over the bed and glanced up at him with a quick, flashing smile that nearly bewitched him. Back then, he had a hard time remembering she was supposed to be his sister.

For a moment, he wondered if the woman drinking the cat's milk was really the same person. Wild hair straggled nearly a yard to her chest. Dirt colored it a dingy gray. Rips and mud marred a too-short leather tunic, ragged at the edges, stopping above her knees. Mud and scratches covered her bare legs. A cape of rags hung on her back.

As he approached, his feet echoed on the cobbles.

She dropped the bowl, clinking, beside the stoop. When she saw him, she backed away. Her hand shot to the hilt of a dagger at her belt.

How many men had tried to attack her in her wanderings?

"Maeve?" His voice was barely a whisper. "Is that you?"

She flashed him a wary look as if she was about to bolt.

"Don't you know me?" Tristan took a step closer.

Her eyes narrowed. Her mouth opened, closed. But her hand slipped off the dagger. "Neil? Is that you? But your hair—'tis white."

"Aye."

Then she ran into his arms, and they hugged. She needed a bath.

"B–but you were supposed to be dead. That's what Corc said."

"I know. Yet here I am. But I'm not your brother." Before this went further, he had to end the deception he'd left her with.

She pulled away from him. A smile briefly lit her eyes and lips. "But of course, you are."

"I'm not, but the story can wait. Maeve, you need food, clean clothes, and a bath. We need to get you away from here."

"Leave the city? But I canna leave. Or I'll die."

"Corc's edict? Forget him. Machar and Ewan are with me. We'll protect you."

"Nay, you don't understand. He gave me a poison. Several times a day, I have to take the antidote. Or I'll die."

"Antidote? Poison? What are you saying?"

"Corc gave me a long-lasting poison he concocted—in my food. He said this particular poison will live in me forever. Just to stay alive, I must chew the leaves of the antidote at least three times a day for the rest of my life. I can tell when the poison starts to work because then I begin to feel . . . sick. Every four or five days, I get more of the leaves from Corc. So leaving the city is not . . . possible."

"Show me these leaves."

She rummaged in the pack atop her ragged cape, opened a leather pouch, and brought out a wad of dark-green, desiccated leaf.

Bringing it to his nose, Tristan smelled a sharp, but pleasant odor. "I've never heard of a poison that can stay in a person's body forever."

"But he's a druid, nay? He must have ensorcelled it."

"Perhaps. Or maybe he's just tricked you?"

"And if he hasn't?"

"Aye." He frowned. "Maybe Machar knows something about this. Or Cairbre. Aye, we've learned he's now a white wizard, and he's in the rebel's camp. Cairbre would have knowledge of such things. If Machar doesn't know, we'll take you to Cairbre when Machar goes to talk with the leaders of the rebellion. But we can't leave you here like this."

She hugged him again. "Don't tell me you're not my brother. You care about me. No one else in this world does."

He took her to the doorstep where they both sat. There, he told her the whole story, beginning with how the real Prince Neil died in his uncle's hut and how Ewan convinced him to take the prince's place. Then he related how they stole the Scepter and the Augury, but lost the Scepter.

When he'd finished, she stared at the cobbled street. "Neil's dead? And you're really only a blacksmith's nephew?"

"Aye, Maeve. But Elyon says I'm the Toghaí, the one chosen to save this land, though I haven't done a very good job of that so far."

She cleared her throat, waiting until he met her gaze. "I do not care what you say. To me, you're still my brother. You look and act and talk so much like him—you canna be anything but kin. I feel it. I know it. And right now, you're the only one who cares about me. Neil or Tristan or whoever you are—you're the only family I've got."

A smile tugged at his lips. "Thank you, Maeve." He patted her knee. "Can I ask you: Do you still have that pendant you were wearing?"

"Nay. One day before going down for supper, I left it in my room. When I returned, I searched everywhere, but couldn't find it. I was frantic. And then I became ill—really sick. Three days later, I found the pendant lying under my pillow, even though I'd looked there a hundred times before. But when I picked it up again, it had not the same effect on me as before. It was just a piece of jewelry. Gradually, I got better."

"Someone recast it. Recasting it removes the spell from the thing."

"Corc's spell?"

"Aye. He ensorcelled you, just as he did your father."

"Father." She shook her head. "I fear he's lost his mind, and he'll never be the man he once was. He mumbles incoherently. He canna put two sentences together so anyone can understand him. Corc now runs everything."

"If Connell doesn't recover"—Tristan slammed a fist into a palm—"I vow right here and now to do all I can to put you on the throne."

She smiled, leaned over, and kissed him on the cheek.

The sound of clinking drew Tristan's gaze to the cobbles beside him. The cat was licking the empty bowl with a vengeance, rocking it back and forth. He faced Maeve again. "What happened to make Corc banish you to the streets?"

"After the pendant lost its effect on me, I became increasingly concerned by how he was running the kingdom. I began arguing my case before Father and Corc. But Corc wouldna hear it. He warned me again and again to stop. Then I wrote a note to Captain Neas of the King's Riders, under Eacharn's command. I'd heard rumors he secretly favored the rebellion that was forming against the palace. I planned to join him, Neil—I mean, Tristan. Join him and overthrow Corc and my father." One hand grabbed his shoulder and squeezed. "But 'tis really Corc who's in control now. Anyway, someone intercepted it and gave it to the druid. That's when Corc convinced Father I was a traitor. That's when they banished me to the streets. He was afraid to kill me outright."

Tristan nodded.

"I later learned that Neas died by poison. So maybe I'm safer out here anyway."

"Nay, Maeve. We're going to get you out of the city. Come." He stood and gave her his hand. "'Tis late, and we need to join the others."

"Your betrothed and Ewan and Machar?"

"Aye. Let's go."

As he led her back to the inn, the moonlit streets were deserted. The others were already sitting at a table.

The moment Tristan brought Maeve inside, the innkeeper leaped to his feet and ran over. "You canna bring that wench in here. It'll be my neck in the noose. Get her out!"

"This wench, as you call her"—Machar stood to his full height and put a hand on his sword hilt—"will soon become the queen of Ulster. So take care whom you turn away, innkeeper."

The thin man glanced frantically about the room at the dozen patrons staring at the scene unfolding before them. He opened his hands, his eyes tearing up. "Please . . . you ask me to risk my life."

Machar pulled Maeve, the Company, and the innkeeper out into the street. He lowered his voice. "Innkeeper, do you have rooms in back, with an entrance to the alley?"

"Aye?" But the man's tone rose as if suspicious at the question.

"Can we hide the princess in a room back there? One room for the women. Another for the men? We'll pay you well for the trouble. And if we defeat the forces lined against us, if we succeed in restoring this kingdom to its rightful state and Maeve sits as queen on the throne, it will save your head."

The man shifted his feet, squeezed his hands together, and grimaced. "If this is the way it is, then, I guess"—he wrung his hands—"it must be so."

"We also require a bath," said Maeve, her tone returning to the habit of command. "And the best meal your poor kitchen can offer. And your best wine, if you have it. Also, if you can manage it—some better clothes for me."

The innkeeper opened his hands, his forehead scrunching as if she'd just asked him to gather a handful of stars and stuff them into a basket.

She waved a hand at Machar. "You have the coin to pay him for this?"

When he'd confirmed he did, she turned back to the innkeeper. "Do all that, good sir, and I'll spare your life."

Chastened, sweating, and still wringing his hands, the man slumped forward, his chin dipping slowly in agreement. Then he gave instructions for how the women should find the room that he would hasten even now to unlock.

As Caitir and Maeve left for a nearby alley, Machar, Ewan, and Tristan reentered the inn and took the best table by the firepit. During the wait, Tristan told them about the poison Corc had given Maeve and how she feared to leave the city without the antidote.

"I've never heard of such a poison," said Machar when he was done. "But Cairbre will know."

Soon the ale arrived, and its quality was vastly improved. Some-time later, when the meal was finally brought, it came not from the innkeeper's mean pot over the fire, but from an establishment on the hill, carried down by the innkeeper's daughter, rousted from her room for that purpose. With the meal came a large decanter of excellent, imported wine.

It was the best meal they'd eaten in weeks.

The innkeeper assured them that the women were receiving the same food and that his daughter was even now heating water in their room for a bath.

WHEN THEY HAD EATEN AND drunk their fill, the men found their room. Soon, a knock came on the door, and Caitir entered, smiling. "Come with me, you men."

They crossed the hall, and Caitir opened the door to the women's quarters. Maeve was facing the wall. When Caitir shut the door behind them, she spun toward them.

Standing before them now was no street waif, but the princess of Ulster, the heir to the throne of Ériu. And she was radiant.

Black, shining hair, newly cut, ended at her shoulders. Smooth cheeks, marred by only a few scratches, glowed in the light. A new garment of coarse blue cloth draped her slim form. She flashed her black, shining eyes at Tristan, and he saw there much of the woman he'd left behind.

"Welcome back, princess," he said. Then he bowed.

As did the others.

When Tristan stood from his bow, Maeve's gaze fell upon each of them in turn. But as she turned her head, Tristan saw tears welling up in her eyes. "Thank you," came a whisper. "All of you. Thank you."

With two steps, she crossed the distance to Tristan, threw her arms around him, and they hugged. "Especially you . . . brother."

Machar cleared his throat, Maeve wiped her eyes, and Caitir led Maeve to the bed on the floor. "Time now for you men to go. She needs sleep."

"Do you ken how long it's been since I've slept in a bed?" Maeve stared at it as if seeing such a thing for the first time. She grabbed a pinch of the weed from her pouch and chewed. Then her eyes wandered lazily over the group, and she yawned.

"Tomorrow"—Machar headed for the door—"I will buy another horse. We must leave for Dún Monaghan at once. And stop this foolish war."

CHAPTER 40

THE WAR COUNCIL

Before they left the next morning, Tristan convinced a reluctant Maeve to leave the city and her supplier of the antidote. "Cairbre will be there, and he'll know what to do. And if he doesn't, we can return here tomorrow."

The ride to Dún Monaghan took all morning. When they burst out of a deep forest of oak, ash, and alder, the hillfort rose in the distance. Surrounding it were encamped the armies of the rebellion with pennants from four kingdoms. Campfire smoke snaked from between the tents. At the base of the hill, soldiers stood ready with pikes and spears, while archers lounged farther in the rear.

Machar led them toward a Leinster banner at the center of the nearest encampment. "That'll be Angus's. I'm guessing he'll be the leader."

They dismounted and walked to a large canvas pavilion. Machar pushed aside the flap, and they entered. In a far corner, a group of high flaith huddled on cushions at a low table where they sat with horns of ale. By their expressions of concern, they were in serious discussion.

A portly, middle-aged man with flowing brown hair saw the newcomers, opened his mouth in surprise, then stood from the group. He rushed toward them.

"My lords!" he shouted to the men behind, "'tis Machar, returned from the dead." He saw Machar's companions and added, "And Squire Ewan. And . . . my lord Neil?" When he saw Tristan, his eyebrows arched.

"Aye, Angus." Machar beamed. "We've returned."

The men left the table and rushed forward with their drinking horns. Tristan recognized only Cé of Munster, a wee man whose flaming red hair and severe look went well with the chain mail beneath a black tunic.

"And is this . . . Princess Maeve?" Cé took a step back then bowed.

"Aye, my lords." Maeve stood up straight.

"You escaped Corc's edict?" asked the portly Angus.

"Not quite. But if someone can put it to rest, I'll stand with you against my father and Corc."

The men exchanged glances then erupted in shouts of approval, more deep bows, and calls for ale for the newcomers.

But Maeve tempered their enthusiasm by explaining what Corc had done to her.

When she'd finished, Angus waved to a lanky youth standing in the corner. "Get Cairbre. Bring him here at once."

The young man nodded and raced away.

The other two leaders were introduced as Blàthan mac Naoise from Meath and Gabhran mac Onchu from Connacht.

Then Maeve introduced Caitir as Prince Neil's betrothed and a commoner from a village in Ulster. This brought surprised exclamations, a few jests, but no outright objections. Apparently, the events of the day far outweighed the desire of a known womanizer for one of his beautiful conquests, no matter how lowly her station.

"But all of you, sit and join our war council." Angus waved them to the table where other youth were already bringing cushions and drinking horns.

When all were seated around the board, Angus spoke first. "What of the Scepter? Did you get it?"

A shudder raced down Tristan's back. He'd feared moments like this ever since they started this quest. But he could no longer continue the subterfuge that he was Prince Neil.

"He did get it," interrupted Caitir. "And I helped him. But we lost it."

"Lost it?" Angus scowled. "Where is it now? And what happened to Dermid and Camran? And Finnean and Luag? Why are they not with you?"

"Dead." Machar took a deep breath and let it out slowly. "All of them."

"As well as others who joined our quest on the way," said Tristan. Then he said what he had long feared to say. "But before we go on, I must tell you all something of great importance."

Machar scowled and fixed his gaze on the tabletop.

"I–I am not Prince Neil."

Blank looks. Puzzled expressions.

"I'm only a blacksmith from Hidden Pines. Prince Neil was killed coming to my village, and he died in my uncle's hut. Ewan, here, saw that I was the prince's exact double and convinced me to take his place."

Like a blanket falling over a corpse, silence encompassed the tent.

His face pale, Angus turned to Ewan. "Is this true, squire?"

Ewan closed his eyes and nodded his head. "'Twas the only thing that could save the kingdom."

"B–but . . . that's a treasonable offense." Cé's face was reddening. "For both of you."

"Aye," said Angus.

"Nay, my lords." Machar held up a hand. "Ewan, you started to explain your part in this. Do go on."

"Aye, Machar." Ewan faced the others. "What you do not ken is that Elyon himself has affirmed that this lad, here, is the Toghaí. We went into the heart of Drochtar, my lords. Into the dread city of Cathair Duvh. And whilst I and Caitir and another of our companions—now dead in Burgundia—were bespelled, he also took Elyon's second gift from the deamhan Balor. That we do have with us."

The silence in the room was now that of the crypt. One after another of the men looked at their brothers then at Tristan.

"But"—the muscles on Cé's face bulged—"but you pretended to be flaith. And you were not flaith. Such an offense—'tis punishable by death."

"Not if I have anything to say about it." Maeve slammed a fist on the table, startling everyone. "Regardless of what he says, I ken this man is somehow kin. I do not know how, or why, but 'tis a feeling in my gut."

Angus bowed to her. "But, my lady, this is serious. To have fooled us all, to have broken such a sacred law as—"

She pounded the table again. "Nay. No action will be taken against this man. Somehow, we will unravel this mystery. He has done incredible things that only the Toghaí should have been able to do. Tristan, tell them the tale."

Then he told them everything from the moment the Company arrived at the inn in Áth Cliath where Faolukan met them, to the invasion of the port a few days ago, and their ride here that morning. He even told them about the visions and how Gundovald and Faolukan were planning to overthrow Crom Mord using the Scepter. He ended with this: "And, my lords, when Samhain comes, I must return to their camp. I must take the Scepter back from them. Elyon has given me this mission. And somehow, I must finish it."

Silence stilled the room. But unknown to them, another figure had entered at the far end, standing in the shadows. Now he stepped forward.

An old man dressed in a white robe, gray beard trailing to his chest, walked to the table and lowered himself beside Tristan.

Cairbre!

"I heard it all." He laid a hand on Tristan's shoulder and stared into his eyes. "The signs pointed to you, young man. I was sure of it. The fact that you are not flaith is puzzling, to be sure. But after hearing your tale, I believe we must overlook that particular sign." He glanced around the table at the high nobles. "My lords, witnesses have seen Elyon's confirmation of this man's identity." He faced Tristan. "You say the Augury is Elyon's second gift, and you have it with you?"

"Aye."

His eyes narrowed. "An Augury . . . how interesting. That makes perfect sense. It fits the missing sections where it was scratched out inside of the tower." He touched Tristan's shoulder. "Bring it out. Let the Augury decide what you are."

Tristan swallowed. He dug in his pack and brought out the round leather case. When he pulled out the golden scroll and set it on the table, it began to glow.

Everyone stared at it with awe.

Cairbre brought shaking hands toward it, tried to open it. The scroll wouldn't budge. He set it down and sent a questioning glance to Tristan.

Tristan grasped it and, as if it were only parchment, quickly unrolled the metal. It lay like a shining mirror of crystal gold before them.

Each man turned toward their brothers, their faces alight with wonder and awe, their mouths open, but apparently unable to speak.

"Scroll," came Cairbre's whisper. "Confirm or deny that this lad is the Toghaí."

The scroll's light increased to blinding intensity then dimmed. Brilliant, glowing letters began writing themselves across its surface.

Tristan mac Torn . . .

The men stared and leaned closer.

is the Toghaí . . .

Cé's jaw dropped open.

my chosen instrument . . .

A smile broadened Angus's mouth.

to fight the Deamhan Lord.

The writing stopped, and the letters began to fade.

Cairbre's gaze was still fixed on it when he whispered, "Are you . . . are you really Elyon?"

The light increased a thousandfold, shining into every corner of the room with a thousand brilliant colors. It burned into their eyes, washed their skin. Shooting through Tristan came the essence of something pure, holy, and powerful.

Then the tent began to shake. Logs in the brazier fell in upon themselves and showered sparks. The tent poles wobbled. The ground beneath them heaved and dropped.

New letters—bold, blazing, searing letters—filled the surface of the scroll.

I Am.

Who I Am.

Then the light dimmed, the ground stopped shaking, and the letters faded.

His face pale, Cairbre bowed to Tristan. "You *are* the Toghaí. I do not understand how, but 'tis clear." His gaze swept the others. "We must accept this. You will not take any action against him for misrepresenting himself as flaith."

The shock on their faces was so great and the silence so long, Tristan wondered if they'd all been struck dumb.

Finally, Angus slammed one fist on the table. "I raise my horn to the Toghaí. I give him whatever support I can. Let's hope he can get the Scepter back from the enemy before 'tis too late."

Cé, too, raised his horn. "Who can argue with what we just saw? I, too, pledge my troth."

Blàthan and Gabhran added their support to the others.

Angus raised a hand for silence. "Good! We are united. Now let us continue this war council with Machar and the Toghaí."

"First," said Machar, "let me tell you what I have in mind. My hope in coming here was to convince Eacharn to give up this fight and join us. And with Maeve on our side, he might just do that."

Cairbre stepped toward Maeve and rested a quavering hand on her elbow. "They called me here because they said you were poisoned?"

Maeve nodded and explained what Corc had done to her.

"Let me see this antidote."

She passed him a wad of green, odiferous leaf.

Cairbre sniffed it, took a small bite, then spit it out. He frowned. "I ken this plant, and 'tis no antidote. 'Tis a drug used to relieve pain. But it addicts the patient with a sense of well-being and euphoria. When it wears off, it demands to be taken again. And eventually, if taken long enough, it sickens the patient when denied."

A growing anger marred her face. "He deceived me."

"Aye, he did. Give me all you have left."

"What?"

"All of it. You must rid yourself of this anvil he's tied you to. At once."

Maeve pulled out the leather bag and held it. She began to pull out a pinch, but Cairbre's hand grasped hers.

"You must take no more of it. Starting now."

She swallowed and gave him the bag.

"For the next three days, you will experience great discomfort. You may even feel like you are going to die. But afterward, you will be free of what Corc's done to you." To Machar and Angus, he said, "She will not be able to go anywhere until this passes."

"Very well," said Machar. "We'll wait until the third day. On the fourth, she will accompany us, and we will take our proposal to Eacharn."

"Let us pray to Elyon he listens to reason," added Cairbre. "Let us pray we can unite the forces of Ériu before the greatest foe we have ever faced. For if what Tristan says comes to pass, when Samhain comes, the enemy will march in overwhelming numbers."

CHAPTER **41**

THE PARLAY AT ÓÚN MONAGHAN

For the next three days, Tristan listened to the scraping of stones on blades, the neighing of horses, and the clinking of dice from bored soldiers. He wandered in and out of the tent Maeve was assigned. And there, he watched Cairbre minister to an ailing princess.

For two days, she thrashed. She sweated. And she moaned. Outside the tent, Cairbre posted a guard, day and night, to ensure she did not, in her raving, try to escape. On the third day, she improved greatly, but still suffered.

By the morning of the fourth day, as Cairbre predicted, she was cured of the drug's effects. Looking a bit bedraggled, she emerged from the tent, sober and businesslike, conversed with Machar, and went back inside. Caitir came and went with food and water for washing. A soldier deposited items wrapped in burlap, and Caitir took them inside.

Meanwhile, outside the tent, Machar gathered the delegation he would take up the hill to the fort. Angus, Cé, and Tristan readied themselves in full battle gear. Tristan wore a borrowed bronze breastplate and a bronze helmet with wings. Caitir told him he looked like a champion.

When Maeve emerged from the tent, the men outside stared at the transformation in awe. She stood erect before them, a vision from another age. A coat of mail shone bright in the sun atop a leather vest. A bronze helmet with nosepiece topped her head. Shining mail covered leather stockings up to her thighs. A baldric carried a long sword that she now drew and raised high. "For Ériu," she shouted.

From all around her, the shouts echoed back, "For Ériu." Men drew their own blades and raised them high.

Machar smiled and bowed. "Truly, Princess, you are now a warrior-queen, ready to lead us into battle against our foe. And to show Eacharn whose side you're on, I brought this." He held up a flag with the seal of Ulster.

She nodded then said, "Lead us to Dún Monaghan, Machar mac Maon. Let us hope that after today, the Ériu will fight as one."

Bearing a white flag, Angus led them up the hill. Maeve rode behind with the Ulster banner. Six infantrymen ran behind and tried to keep up.

Above them loomed the hillfort. Once, its stone walls were twenty feet high and circled, unbroken, around two acres of hilltop. Now, sloping dirtworks topped with wooden spikes filled several wide gaps amidst tumbled ruins. At a narrow gate of iron, barely wide enough for a man and horse, they halted.

From the battlements, a familiar voice called down. "What business have you with us, Angus? And why do you fly the Ulster pennant?"

"Have you no eyes in your head, Eacharn?" asked Angus. "Look who carries it."

"Princess Maeve?" came Eacharn's astonished reply. "Is that really you?"

"Aye, Eacharn. 'Tis me. And I've come in peace to parlay with you and end this division between kingdoms. The enemy from Drochtar is on our shores. They've taken Áth Cliath."

At once, Eacharn's form disappeared from the ramparts. They waited in silence until the iron door creaked open.

"Leave your horses and your foot soldiers and enter." Angus identified the new voice as Osgar mac Oisean, Eacharn's second-in-command, assigned by Corc himself.

A tall stern man with dark features, Osgar led them in single file through a stonework tunnel into a ring of spears. Once inside, he ordered, "Drop your weapons."

"No need for this, Eacharn." Machar waved at the spearmen. "We're not here to cause trouble."

"Machar mac Maon?" Eacharn rushed forward. Eacharn's chest nearly burst his chain mail, his brown mustache drooped to his chin, and his bushy eyebrows rose to his forehead. "Then you've returned, alive? We were told otherwise."

"Breathing and walking before you."

"And is that . . . Prince Neil?"

"It is. And it isn't. But let us sit and talk, for we've much to discuss."

Eacharn dismissed the guards. The group, including stern-faced Osgar, walked to a tent at the far corner of the bailey. Inside, logs burned in a brazier. Two boys brought a board, laid it atop stones, and created a table. The group sat on grass around the board, while the youths hurried to bring them drinking horns brimming with ale.

"Here's to peace between us, Eacharn." Machar raised his horn high. "For we're facing a far greater enemy than Ériu has ever faced."

"I'll drink to peace." Eacharn looked to his second-in-command. "But we'll only have it under agreeable terms."

"Fair enough." Machar drained his horn, as did the others.

"And where's the rest of the Company?" asked Eacharn. "Finnean, Dermid, Camran, and Luag?"

Something darkened Machar's features. "All dead. As well as others who joined us along the way."

Groans filled the room. Heads shook. Faces grimaced.

"And the Scepter?"

"We had it. But Faolukan's ally, Gundovald of Burgundia, took it from us."

Eacharn frowned. "You said the enemy is here on our shores?"

"Aye, Eacharn. A fleet of over fifteen hundred ships now occupies the harbor of Áth Cliath. We're guessing they've landed nigh onto sixty-five thousand men."

"With cthyllin ice giants," added Tristan. "And mammoths."

The men with Eacharn glanced from one to the other, plainly surprised and chagrined.

Eacharn's jaw dropped open while beside him Osgar noticeably paled. "We've heard none of this."

"No hint this was coming?" Angus frowned. "Nothing from Corc?"

"Nary a word."

"He's turned the king to the enemy, Eacharn." Cé shook a fist in the air. "You canna trust either of them now."

Eacharn lifted a hand as though to touch Maeve's arm then lowered it, his voice coming softly. "How are you, Princess? I thought Corc had put some kind of spell on you, preventing you from leaving the city."

"'Twas a trick. He forced me to take a drug that I needed more of every day—to live he said. That's how he kept me there. But I shook it off."

"I was against what they did to you." Eacharn flattened one hand on the table, staring at it while his face creased and his voice rumbled lower. "I even spoke up. But there's no speaking against Corc on anything nowadays."

"I thank you for that, Eacharn." She nodded. "But I'm here to ask only one thing. To give your allegiance to me, not to Corc or my father. The king is . . . ensorcelled. Not right in the head. We must save this land. And my father has . . . relinquished his right to lead."

"But how can I do that? Whilst the king rules, my duty is to stand with him. Just as 'tis your duty and the prince's."

"Eacharn," said Machar, "this lad is not the prince."

The commander of the king's army raised his eyebrows. "I do not understand."

Then Tristan told him the story of how Ewan convinced him to lead the expedition, summarizing how he and Caitir took the Scepter from Faolukan, found the Augury, and returned to Ériu. He ended by telling them, once again, that he was the Toghaí.

"Only a few days ago, with the Augury before us," continued Machar, "Cairbre asked the golden scroll if this lad was, indeed, the Toghaí. The answer we received was"—Machar shuddered—"simply breathtaking. Without a doubt, he is, indeed, Elyon's chosen one."

Osgar frowned and, almost imperceptibly, shook his head.

A shiver coursing through him, Tristan shifted his position and rubbed feeling back into the hand he had been leaning on. The smell of crushed grass mixed with ale and old leather.

"Given that," concluded Machar, "Princess Maeve must now lead us."

"Whilst the king lives," said Osgar, "I canna agree."

"Think, man!" Machar slammed his fists down beside his empty horn, rattling the board. "When a king becomes addled and witless or when he's being led by enemies of the realm, the Great Charter demands that the succession fall to the next in line. Ever since we abandoned the election of flaith to the highest office, we've relied on the royal family to lead us. The Cairt Mhór Charter provides for exactly this eventuality. Maeve is next in line. Given the circumstances, the leadership must fall now to her."

Eacharn's ponderous brows dipped and nearly touched. "I ken what you say is . . . true." He stared off into a corner of the tent. "What will happen to the king?"

"Nothing," said Maeve. "I will insist that his life be spared."

But a dark look passed from Cé to Angus, after which Angus shook his head at Cé.

"We will ensure that Connell lives," said Machar. "But Corc—'tis a different matter."

"How can we trust that my lord Connell willna be killed?" Eacharn looked from Angus to Cé, his forehead darkening. "Most of you have been calling loudly for his head."

"Though I've longed to do just that," said the portly Angus, "I give you my word, I will not kill him."

"And you, Cé?" Eacharn faced the wee lord. "Will you also give me your word? That Connell will live?"

Cé's face hardened. He stared through red locks at the horn between his palms.

"Lord Cé?" Stern-faced, Angus shifted in his seat and planted two fists on the table. "Will you let King Connell live? You must agree."

Cé raised his glance. "Aye. I willna kill him, even though 'tis death he deserves."

For a time, Eacharn watched their faces then nodded. "Give me a moment." He waved to Osgar, and the two of them strode out of the tent. From the yard, Tristan heard sounds of an argument, but so low he couldn't make out anything that was said.

Much later, Eacharn returned, alone. "I agree. With the Deamhan Lord's troops on our shores, we must unite against our common foe. Machar has invoked, and I am now reminded of the charter of Cairt Mhór. Thus, I hereby relinquish command of Ulster's forces to Princess Maeve." He bowed low.

"And Osgar mac Oisean?" asked Machar.

"He will come around. The men have been in the king's service so long, 'twill be hard for some of them to adjust. I'll gather them this very afternoon and bring them 'round. For that, I would like the princess to stand with me. The men will surely rally to her. Until I've got them all convinced, the rest of you should return to your camp."

"Agreed." Machar stood. "When will your troops be ready to march to Ewhain Macha?"

"Tomorrow."

"Then let us seal a pact between us." Machar offered his hand.

Eacharn took it then shook hands with the rest of the delegation.

"My lords, one more thing . . ." Eacharn frowned at the floor. "Two months ago, we heard a report of a ship landing on Munster's southern shores. Odd folk disembarked, at least two hundred of them—men, women, and children. But then, as the villagers tried to approach the strangers, the entire bunch—just disappeared."

"What do you mean—'just disappeared'?" asked Machar.

"The report was that one instant these folk stood on the road facing the crowd of villagers. And the next—poof! They were gone. Do you ken anything about this? Could it be some trick of Faolukan's? Some kind of advance unit of druids sent to stir up trouble in our midst?"

Head cocked to one side, Machar folded his arms across his chest. "I ken naught of this. What did these folk look like?"

"The villagers were so rattled, we received no consistent description. Some said they were lehbrágans. Others, that they were ghosts. Still others reported that black masks covered all their eyes, and that—"

"Black masks?" Tristan interrupted. "That's what they said?"

"Aye. Does that mean something to you?"

"Possibly. But . . . nay. It couldn't be."

Raising a brow, Machar met Tristan's gaze. "Do you think they escaped Glenmallen, crossed the mountains to Burgundia, and fled across the sea?"

"I don't know. Seems unlikely, but—"

"What are you talking about, my lords?" asked Eacharn.

"A people called the eladrin." A smile widened Tristan's mouth. "We thought Faolukan's forces wiped them out. If some have arrived in Ériu— they might be able to help us."

"Well . . ." Eacharn narrowed his brows. "They've disappeared."

"Perhaps," said Machar, "they just want to be left alone."

"Not much help in that, is there?" Eacharn waved a hand in dismissal.

"Nay." Tristan shrugged. "Not much help at all."

They left Maeve with Eacharn. But as Tristan crossed the yard with the others, he passed Osgar.

Tristan only caught a few muttered words—*Traitors . . . betrayed us*— before the man saw him and became silent.

Then the glance Osgar shot Tristan was as sour as vinegar at the bottom of a barrel.

CHAPTER 42

ΡΛΝΙϹ ΙΝ ΤΗΕ ϹΙΤΥ

Later that afternoon, Maeve rode back from Dún Monaghan. She reported that Eacharn had convinced most of the King's Riders that Ulster must rejoin the Alliance of Kingdoms under her leadership. Only a handful, led by Osgar mac Oisean, did not agree.

The next morning, Eacharn rode down from the fort, alone. From atop his horse, he glanced at Machar, Angus, and the others. "I regret to inform you, my lords, that during the night, Osgar left with his malcontents. They must have ridden toward the city."

"Nothing we can do about that now," said Machar. "Bring your men down to join us as soon as you're ready."

While the besieging armies broke camp, Eacharn led Ulster's force from the hillfort to the cheers of the men below. A smiling Princess Maeve rode at the front of the Ulster crowd. United at last, the armies of the five kingdoms began the long march toward Ewhain Macha.

By afternoon, the slow-moving army still had two leagues to reach the city. There, they decided to make camp. But Machar, Eacharn, Angus, Tristan, Cé, and Maeve rode on ahead.

"Before the army enters the city," said Machar to Maeve, "you must talk with your father. We must counteract any rumors or falsehoods these malcontents might be spreading about our purpose." Then he leaned over in the saddle and spoke so only Tristan and Maeve could hear. "We must reach your father first to protect him in case he becomes intransigent. Angus and Cé have sworn to spare his life, but . . . I do not ken. Earlier, they also swore to slay him. So this trip is as much to save his life as for anything else."

Her eyes shining, Maeve firmed her grip on the saddle's pommel and nodded in appreciation.

Only a league before the city itself, as darkness descended, the six began passing groups of townsfolk pushing carts laden with household goods, some with children in tow. Others led goats or horses. Lighting their way, lanterns swung from poles atop their wagons.

"Why are you leaving the city?" asked Machar of one couple leaning on a cart piled high with leather goods and tools.

"The Deamhan Lord's army is at the gates." Fear etched the woman's face. "The whole of Ewhain Macha is in a panic."

"With nary a soldier of the realm in sight," added her husband. "Our coward, the king, and his druid have barricaded themselves inside the fort. And they willna let any of us lower city folk inside." Then the two hurried up the trail.

Twisting in his saddle, Machar turned to Tristan. Worry tightened his features. "They weren't supposed to attack yet. I don't understand how they could get here so quickly."

"Aye." Angus glanced ahead at more groups of panicked townspeople crowding the trail. "The road ahead may soon be impassable with refugees. What should we do?"

Machar's frown deepened. "Someone needs to go back and get the army moving again. Let's hope 'tis not too late."

Angus rose in his saddle before settling back. "That task must fall to me."

"Aye," said Machar. "But when you return, stop just short of the city. One of us will meet you on the trail and let you know the situation."

"Agreed," said Angus, "we mustna fall into a trap."

Thus did they part, with Angus lashing his mount back the way they'd come and the others hurrying the last three miles to Ewhain Macha.

The group entered the city's outskirts at sunset. The whole town seemed alive, in a state of unrest, with shop owners nailing boards over doors, and the streets thick with fleeing men, women, and children. Horses neighed uneasily, and the barking of dogs rose into the night.

But of enemy troops, there was no sign. Machar stopped one man walking briskly north wearing a backpack and leading a young child by a rope around his middle. "Where is the enemy? Why is everyone fleeing?"

"They're almost here." The man's wild eyes darted south. "No time to talk." Then he half-jogged, half-walked to the north.

"I see no troops." Cé looked south.

"Yet everyone's in a panic," said Machar. "We must do our business in the fort quickly."

They galloped the last hundred yards to the slope beneath the fortress. Dismounting, they led their horses up the path. At the top, the drawbridge was up.

"Ho, there," called Eacharn to the guard on the battlements. "Let us in."

"I canna," came the weak reply from a young soldier. "Osgar's orders. He says you've gone to the other side."

"You ken who I am, Bràn—the commander of the army of Ulster. You will let down that bridge this instance, or tonight, you'll be making your bed in the dungeon."

Silence was followed by another weak reply. "They's got a delegation from Faolukan in here. Just arrived, they did. If I's to let you in, it'd be my head. And if I's to lower the bridge, the townsfolk might come in."

"Fools," Eacharn whispered under his breath. He spat to the side then shouted up. "Do you not ken, lad, we're at war with Faolukan and his brood. And I'm giving you two breaths and a sneeze to lower that bridge, or you'll wish you were never born."

The youth disappeared from the wall. Long moments they waited until, finally, chains clattered against wheels and wood creaked. When the log bridge thudded onto the ground at their feet, Eacharn hurried across, followed by the others. As soon as they entered the fortress, the bridge rose again.

Jaw muscles tensing, Eacharn stood before the lanky youth now holding a torch. "What in the name of Lugh's wings goes on here? Who let Faolukan's brood inside the fort? And how many of them are there?"

"Three men and a druid. 'Twas Corc's orders, my lord. And Osgar's. Osgar says they's making arrangements to surrender and save the city."

"Nay, nay," came Maeve's harsh whisper.

"Why did Faolukán change his plans?" Machar turned to Tristan.

"I don't know. Maybe he heard the armies were locked in a siege at Dún Monaghan?"

Machar faced Eacharn. "The moment that army arrives, it will immediately begin plundering and ravaging the city. No one will be safe from rapine and murder. Surrendering the fort will only make their work easier."

Bràn swallowed.

Eacharn stretched a hand toward the young soldier. "Do not tell anyone you let us in. Give me your torch."

"Aye, general." Bràn passed him the torch. "I'm glad you're here. I was not in favor of surrendering."

Eacharn cast him a look of disbelief. Then they hurried past the better shops and houses on the hill and headed for the palace. But when Maeve saw the black-caped soldiers standing at the palace entrance, she led the group off the square into an alley. "Those are the Black Cloaks, Corc's private guard."

Machar slammed a fist into a palm.

Eacharn shook his head. "I should have stopped that sort of thing long ago."

"They'll never let us pass," continued Maeve. "But I ken a secret way into the palace. Follow me." Taking the torch, she led them, twisting and turning through lanes to the back of the king's blacksmith shop. She looked up and down the alley to ensure they were alone then pulled a key from under a brick in the shop wall. After another ten paces, she unlocked the door of a wooden shed and ushered them all inside.

A second door, locked, led into the blacksmith's shop. Ignoring that, she passed the torch to Machar then dropped to her hands and knees. As she began scraping away the straw covering the floor, Tristan knelt and helped her expose a slatted wooden opening in the floor.

"A secret way in?" asked Eacharn, his voice rising.

"Aye. And until now, only the blacksmith, the blacksmith's son, the king's cupbearer, and the royal family kenned it was here." Maeve lifted the door to reveal glistening stone steps leading down into darkness. "Follow me. And shut the door behind you."

Thus did they descend twenty feet down damp stone steps. They ended at a tunnel where one passage led east, the other west. At the bottom, a key hung from a hook.

Maeve began heading west.

"Where does the other tunnel go?" asked Tristan.

Her brows furrowing, Maeve stopped. "The blacksmith's son has his own shop just outside the city ramparts, with another shed similar to the one above. 'Tis a means of escape for the royal family—a last resort."

For at least two hundred feet, she led them down a wet, stone-lined passage. Water dripped on Tristan's neck. Rats scurried ahead. Finally, the way opened with a shower of hay into the darkest corner of a wine cellar.

"Upon pain of death, all who ken of this passage are charged with keeping its secret." Maeve shut the door and scattered hay over it. "I assume none of you four will ever leak word of it?"

When they all nodded, she led them up steps into a hallway outside the kitchen. From beyond the nearest door came the sounds of pots banging, knives chopping, and women chatting. Maeve led them briskly through a series of dark hallways lit by occasional torches until they stopped outside a ponderous oak door. She dropped the torch into an empty sconce a few yards away and returned.

"This leads to the throne room and reception hall," she whispered. "If Father and Corc are talking with a delegation, they'll be here. Follow me."

She eased open the door and led them into the darkest recesses of a grand hall. They found themselves in shadows at the room's center, behind a line of granite pillars marching down both sides of the room. Courtiers crowded the room's far end before a dais. Still in shadows, they moved slowly to a closer vantage point. Now Tristan could clearly see the king on his throne, his eyes vacant, his mouth hanging open, his staff leaning dangerously askew.

Beside him sat Corc in white robes.

In the front row of courtiers stood dark-faced Osgar mac Oisean, Eacharn's traitorous former second-in-command. Beside him were a Burgundian druid and two soldiers. Against the far wall, to the king's right and left, two pikemen stood at attention. Beyond the farthest pikemen waited two Black Cloaks.

But were the pikemen sneering at the Black Cloaks? And was Corc's private guard fidgeting uneasily beside the king's men?

The king's herald faced the court. "My lord Connell mac Conn," he shouted, "King of Ulster and Ard Righ of all Ériu. And my lord Corc, regent to the High King of Ulster. May I present the honorable Lord Bertold, chamberlain to King Gundovald of Burgundia and duly appointed emissary for High Lord Faolukan, the arch druid and regent for the Deamhan Lord, supreme ruler of Drochtar and all the eastern lands."

The uniformed Bertold strode forward, his black mustache neatly trimmed, his steps abrupt. He bowed slightly then stood erect.

Corc stepped forward and offered his hand. "In the name of the king, I welcome you to Ewhain Macha. Long have we waited with eager anticipation for your arrival, my lord Bertold." Corc bowed low. "We are at your service."

"This is traitorous," whispered Machar, "and it needs to stop."

"Aye." Slowly, silently, Cé drew his sword from its sheath. His eyes were ablaze as he looked to Machar. "And it will stop now."

Chapter 43

BLOOD ON THE THRONE

Machar laid a hand on Cé's sword arm. "Not yet. Let us first hear what the emissary has to say."

Maeve shot a look of concern at both of them. "Remember," she whispered, "my father must live."

"Aye, my lords," agreed Eacharn. "I hold you to your promises."

Machar nodded, but Cé merely glowered at the men on the platform and gripped his weapon all the tighter.

Corc motioned, and a page positioned a chair for Bertold on the dais beside the king. Now all three men sat in a semicircle facing the court.

Maeve and Eacharn gasped. Machar frowned. Even Tristan knew such a breach of protocol was unheard of. A chair for a Burgundian on the dais? An ally of the Deamhan Lord?

"We received news that the entire army is at the gates," said Corc. "Is this true?"

"Nay," said Bertold. "Just twelve centuria, camped south of the city. They've orders to wait until tomorrow, after the results of this council. Then they'll move. The main force is still encamped at the port."

Twelve hundred men instead of sixty thousand. Both Machar and Maeve breathed out their relief.

"W–who are you?" Connell spoke for the first time, his voice thick, his eyes glazed.

"The emissary from Faolukan, my lord." Corc waved a hand in dismissal. "'Tis of little import."

"Ah, so." Connell slumped back in his chair, absently fingering the quarter-moon pendant hanging from his neck.

Bertold smiled as one might at an idiot then faced Corc. "I'm here to ask for the city's surrender. I understand the Ulster force and the armies of the rebellion are locked in siege to the north?"

Corc looked to Osgar, who spoke from his front-row seat. "That was the case, my lord, but no longer. I wish it were not so, but the armies joined yesterday. They'll probably arrive here on the morrow."

Bertold scowled and whipped his head toward Corc. "Then 'tis paramount you give up the fortress and tower tonight. Twelve hundred men should be able to hold the fort for the next three days."

"At once, my lord." Corc bowed. "But what happens in three days?"

"The main force will arrive."

Was Samhain already that close? Tristan would need to leave soon for Áth Cliath. Still, he had yet no plan to retrieve the Scepter.

"My lord Bertold, we must first get the king's permission." Corc inclined his head toward Connell. "My lord?"

Spittle dribbled from Connell's slackened jaw as he turned a lazy glance toward the druid. "Aye?"

"My lord, will you give your permission for Faolukan's advance units to occupy the fort?"

"Occupy?"

"Aye, my lord. We're giving them control of the city."

"'Tis dark in here."

"Of course. 'Tis dark. But 'twill save lives. If we do not acquiesce, there will be bloodshed."

"What . . . do you suggest?"

"Say aye."

"Aye." Connell's smile was that of an idiot.

Corc smiled and faced Bertold again. "You have permission to—"

"Over me bloody corpse." Cé's feet pounded on stone, sending sharp echoes across the hall. "Traitor of a king, you willna surrender to this pack of wolves." He emerged from the pillars and turned left toward the crowd near the throne.

"For Ériu!" Machar yanked his sword from its sheath and raised it high. "Against Drochtar!" Machar raced behind Cé.

Maeve drew her sword and followed Machar.

Eacharn took a different path leading down the center aisle. Tristan followed him.

The pikemen on either side of the king began running to intercept the intruders when Eacharn called out, "Hold, guardsmen! As commander of Ulster's armies, I call upon you to stand aside."

Three of the pikemen halted in midstride. The fourth slowed, appeared confused. Then he, too, stopped.

With all the fury of a madman, Cé fell upon the Burgundian emissary, Bertold, on the dais, who'd barely had time to draw his sword. With only the second blow, Cé's blade cut deep into Bertold's arm, and the chamberlain backed away. Cé struck right and left with such surprising force, each blow drove the man back. Cé pressed the attack, found an opening, and sliced his blade into the man's neck. Bertold dropped to the dais, his head hanging askew.

Barely had Cé stepped over the slain Bertold than the wee, red-haired man whirled against Corc.

"Nay, my lord." The druid backed up against the throne, his face twisted in fear, his hands fumbling with a dagger at his belt. "You do not ken what—"

Cé's blade plunged deep through the tunic covering the druid's chest, twisted viciously, and came back dripping. Corc's body slumped to the carpet at Connell's feet.

Meanwhile, Osgar and the two Burgundian soldiers looked to either side as Machar, Maeve, Eacharn, and Tristan circled in.

The Burgundian druid yanked a dagger from the folds of his robe and lunged at Maeve. But with two quick strokes, she dispatched him.

While Maeve fought the druid, Machar engaged Osgar, who tried to flee down the center. Their swords struck once, twice, but Machar dropped the traitor before the battle had barely begun.

Eacharn rushed the first Burgundian soldier. They engaged in a quick series of blows. Then that soldier, too, fell dead.

As the battle raged, the crowd of overdressed courtiers either scattered or cowered against the hall's far end. A few women screamed and raced for the door.

Tristan engaged the second Burgundian soldier, whose desperate sword struck at him again and again. The clanging of steel on steel rang through the hall. But the man was no match for Tristan's skill, and he, too, sank bleeding to the floor.

Upon the dais, Cé stepped over Corc's body. Even as the pikemen began running toward him, he advanced on the king.

"What?" Connell rose unsteadily from his seat, his eyes wide as saucers, his hand gripping the sides of the throne. "What?"

Cé's eyes were on fire as he drew back his blade.

The pikemen were nearly upon him.

"Nay!" came Maeve's cry from the side.

Cé plunged his steel straight into the king's chest below the rib cage. He twisted the sword, yanked it out.

Connell mac Conn, Ard Righ of all Ériu, was slain.

The king's corpse slumped off the throne. His arms flung themselves over Corc's lifeless body. In death, as in life, he grasped his counselor for support.

The two nearest pikemen pressed in from either side of the dais. As Cé lifted a startled gaze from his day's work, two long, curved spearheads pierced him through—one from the right, another from the left.

His sword slipping from his hands, Cé opened his mouth and collapsed.

Four men now lay dead upon the dais. Another four were splayed before it.

"Nay, nay!" Maeve ran to her father.

"Enough killing!" shouted Eacharn. "'Tis over."

Maeve stepped over the corpses of Cé and Corc and cradled her father's head in her arms. "Nay, Father." She moaned. "You didna ken what you were doing."

Tristan came up beside her. "I–I'm sorry."

Tears wet her face as she rocked back and forth, nestling Connell's head in her lap.

"Arrest them!" Eacharn pointed to the two Black Cloaks now slinking quietly toward a side door.

All four pikemen raced after them. Despite Eacharn's command that the killing cease, the Black Cloaks whirled with swords drawn. Another short battle ensued, ending with the Black Cloaks also lying dead on the floor.

Eacharn came up beside Tristan and Maeve. "I'm sorry, my princess. I should have stopped him."

"Nay, 'twas my fault." Machar cleaned his sword on a dead Burgundian's tunic. "I saw the vengeance in Cé's eyes. I should have restrained him."

"Nay." Maeve wiped her tears, gently laid her father's head on the bloodied carpet, and stood. She sheathed her sword and faced the men. "'Twas no one's fault but Corc's. And my father's. Sure, he was addled. But he let himself become so." As if stifling a sob, she breathed in suddenly. "I canna blame you, Machar. Or you, Eacharn."

Both men bowed.

"'Tis well of you to say so, my lady," said Machar. "For you will now become queen."

She looked at him with widened eyes as if the realization just hit her.

"Our army . . ." Maeve turned a tear-filled gaze toward Eacharn. "The enemy to the south . . ."

"Aye, my lady." Eacharn straightened. "And I'm thinking that after we properly man the fort, we should split the force and send men 'round and trap them in a pincer movement between us."

"Can you move the men yet tonight?" asked Machar.

"Aye. And if the enemy has encamped, I'm thinking they'll not be wanting to move again till dawn. That's when we'll strike."

"Then let it be so," whispered Maeve as again she knelt, red-eyed, to her father's corpse.

Eacharn bowed and left the room with two of the pikemen.

What had happened here tonight had changed Ériu for the better. With Connell's rule ended, Maeve's would now begin. But as Machar ordered servants to begin removing the bodies, Tristan's thoughts drifted once again to the Scepter.

In the end, everything depended on him.

But he had no idea how to bring back what was, once again, lost.

PART IX

THE TWO RIVERS

CHAPTER 44

THE ROUT

Tristan helped Machar take the princess to the king's private dining room so servants could remove the bodies and clean up the mess in the throne room. Maids then brought them a late supper of bread, cheese, beef, and mead.

Tristan and Machar ate, but Maeve only picked at her food. When she finally pushed her bread trencher away, her face was red and puffy. "I need to lie down." Then she headed for the stairs to the upper chambers.

Tristan and Machar fell into chairs draped with bear fur near the wall. He didn't know how long he'd slept when the echoes of footsteps woke him.

"Cairbre, my lord." Machar was already standing. "Welcome."

Behind Cairbre entered Angus, Caitir, Ewan, Blàthan, lord of Meath, and Gabhran, lord of Connacht.

"We saw the scene in the throne room." Cairbre shook his head. "And we heard briefly from the servants what happened. A nasty business, tonight, Machar. But long overdue. Aye . . . long overdue. Regrettable what Cé did—killing Connell . . ." He frowned. "How is the princess?"

"She's sleeping." Tristan rubbed his eyes and stood as Caitir approached and took his hand.

Machar then described in detail the evening's events.

"Terrible as it is, what happened tonight changes everything for the better." His expression solemn, Cairbre pulled on his beard. "Tomorrow, we must crown Maeve as queen of Ériu. The Great Charter demands it."

His glance sought the kings of the various provinces in the room. "Will all of you agree to that?"

When they nodded, Machar looked to Angus. "Who, in Munster, will take over for King Cé?"

"His brother, Iùrnan mac Colla is the logical choice. I'll tell him what happened."

"Is he a hothead like his brother?"

"Nay," said Angus. "He'll agree to crown the princess. I'll get his approval tonight."

Cairbre faced Tristan. "You and I now have a task to undertake in the Tower."

Machar gave a solemn nod. "The Augury?"

"Aye, the Augury." Cairbre took a torch from the wall and walked toward the door. "Tristan, follow me."

THE TOWER OF DÓCHAS ROSE before them like something out of legend, an epic monument climbing majestically to the sky. Cairbre pushed on the banded oak door and led Tristan inside. Cairbre's torch illuminated spiral stone steps climbing the near wall. They circled up inside tower and disappeared into darkness.

"The Augury, like the Scepter, has its own receptacle." The Capulum scholar dropped his torch into a wall sconce and pointed to a stone column about four feet high rising from the floor's center. From the top surface, his hand scraped away loose stones and debris. "We kenned this was here, but until I saw the Augury, I wasn't totally sure of its purpose. May I have your knife for a moment?"

Tristan passed him his dagger.

Cairbre dug in the pillar's center, removed dust and pebbles, and revealed a three-pronged metal holder. He pulled on it. Nothing happened.

"Age has stolen my strength." He motioned to Tristan.

Tristan yanked, and the prongs rose to a height of six inches.

"Now place the Augury inside."

Tristan removed his backpack and then the scroll from its leather container. When he touched the faded brass exterior, it revealed itself as the golden scroll it had always been. He brought it near the holder.

The Augury began glowing, brightly illuminating every corner of the Tower, its rays even shooting up the long central shaft.

He set it inside the three prongs. Slowly, they began closing then snapped shut.

The ground beneath them shook. The light increased a hundredfold. Tristan shielded his eyes.

Then the light dimmed. But the Augury's splendor remained. No longer did it appear as a roll of tarnished bronze. Now, clearly, it revealed itself as something otherworldly, an artifact belonging to Elyon, the Creator.

"Wonderful." Beaming, Cairbre took a step back, his glance fixed on the Augury. "Never would I have imagined such a day would come." He placed a hand on Tristan's shoulder and bowed. "The Capulum is in your eternal debt. Now you, Tristan, must press on to the end and bring back the Scepter. . . ." He removed his hand, lowered his head, and shuffled out the door.

Tristan stood looking at the scroll. Somehow, the Augury and the Scepter were connected. Somehow, both were necessary for Elyon's purposes. And both were needed to return Elyon's full power and protection to Erde.

He left the Tower and followed Cairbre across the yard to the palace.

MUCH LATER, AROUND MIDNIGHT, EACHARN returned. Only Machar and Tristan now remained in the dining room.

"What news, Eacharn?" Machar rose from his slumber in the chair.

"I've brought four hundred charioteers and as many swordsmen to defend the fort. They're already billeted in the barracks."

"When will the rest arrive?"

"They're setting up camp now at the edge of the lower city. I've ordered them to keep out of sight until morning. I've also sent three hundred archers and as many swordsmen to the edge of the field where the enemy's encamped. And more mounted soldiers—nearly five hundred strong—are now riding a little-known trail that parallels the main road. Well before dawn, they'll emerge south of the enemy. Everyone has orders to strike at dawn—archers first." Eacharn slammed one fist into another. "The Blackwater lies to their east, so they willna escape. Aye, tomorrow we'll teach them a lesson they'll not forget. And I've learned one more thing to our benefit."

"What?"

"Some days ago, I sent a scout to Áth Cliath. He's returned. The enemy has few horses, so we'll not be facing much in the way of cavalry. I suppose they had to make room on the ships for their other cargo."

"Ice giants and mammoths?" added Tristan.

"Unfortunately, aye."

With nothing happening until morning, Tristan and Machar went upstairs to rooms the servants had prepared and tried to sleep.

WELL BEFORE DAYBREAK, TRISTAN ATE a quick breakfast with those who'd stayed the night in the palace. When Maeve came down, she appeared much rested and recovered from the ordeal of her father's death. After everything that had happened, he marveled at her inner strength.

Then Cairbre, Machar, Angus, and the kings of the provinces met in the throne room where servants had spent all night cleaning. The group included a short, fat, dour-faced Iùrnan mac Colla, acting now as the king of Munster in place of his brother Cé.

Up on the recently cleaned dais where Connell only yesterday lost his life, Machar officiated over a hastily planned, but profound ceremony.

In his hands, he lifted a slender torc of gold, festooned with emeralds and rubies.

"Many centuries ago, that crown was only used for a few years by Queen Deirdre," Ewan whispered in Tristan's ear. "She only lived a few, short years."

Machar glanced around the room at the courtiers, the provincial kings, a handful of city leaders who hadn't fled. Before him stood Princess Maeve. A gown of blue silk covered the leather leggings and vest she wore beneath; after the ceremony, she'd be ready to ride.

Machar drew himself to his full height. "By command of the kings of the four nations and by right of the Great Charter, the flaith of this land have given me the privilege of bestowing on you the torc of the realm. Kneel, Princess Maeve nic Connell."

Maeve knelt before him and bowed her head.

"I hereby crown you queen of Ulster and of all Ériu. I crown you Ard Banríon, the leader of the five kingdoms." Gently, he opened the torc, slid it around her neck, and let it shut. "Arise, Queen Maeve."

To clapping, the stomping of feet, cheers, and shouts of "long live Queen Maeve", she rose.

"Now that that's done," she said with a smile. "'Tis time for war." She threw off the silk gown. Maids ran to catch it.

To more shouts and cheers, everyone followed her as she strode from the hall.

They met again in the torch-lit courtyard where Maeve disappeared into the stable. Moments later, dressed in chain mail over leather, she drove a chariot across the cobbled bailey. Standing high on the platform, with a brass helm atop her head and a longsword held aloft, she drew cheers from every soldier in the yard.

"Now there's a queen to lead us," whispered a nearby servant. "Not like King Connell at all."

Tristan watched with Caitir at his side.

Then Caitir mounted a white gelding. From the palace armory, she'd taken a heavy leather vest, a shield, and brass helmet. A quiver and bow hung over her back.

Tristan mounted a spotted gray stallion that Ewan held for him.

"I'm still your squire, my lord." Ewan winked. "The Toghaí, especially, needs a squire, nay?"

"Aye." Tristan smiled. "I think he does, Ewan."

With dawn nearly upon them, they joined four hundred chariots already waiting in the yard. Following torchbearers, they crossed the drawbridge and descended the slope into town where the bulk of the army even now stood ready to march. The line of soldiers stretched back through the streets as far as Tristan could see.

Maeve rode to the front of the charioteers and cavalry. Tristan followed her. Archers, including Caitir, trailed them on foot, then the swordsmen, axmen, and pikemen.

When the new queen of Ériu raised her sword, a great cheer rose from the army, rippling back all the way to the forest.

The enemy was camped in a field, two miles over the next rise.

Onward they marched.

DARKNESS STILL CLUNG TO THE trees around them as Tristan sat his horse with the cavalry and chariots. The archers had moved to the front. As Caitir passed him, he waved to her.

He wished she'd stayed behind, but she wouldn't hear of it. "I can shoot as well as any of them," she insisted. "What good will hiding safely in the palace do me if we lose this fight?"

He couldn't argue with that. But as she passed, marching with the other soldiers, he swallowed a lump in his throat.

Elyon, please keep her safe, he prayed silently. *Don't let anything happen to her.*

As they waited, all that broke the stillness was the occasional neighing of a horse, the coughing of a man, the clinking of armor, and the rustling of leather.

A light fog hovered over the trail and the field ahead, barely covering their ankles.

When dawn brightened the treetops, the archers inched into the field, the mounted troops close at their heels. From the fog rose the tops of the Drochtar tents and a black banner holding a yellow quarter-moon scimitar. Men were just now moving about, leaving their tents, starting morning campfires.

Then came warning shouts from the camp.

The approaching army had been discovered.

From somewhere in their midst, a horn blew, then another.

Soldiers poured out of tents, wearing a helmet here, a shirt of mail there, but none were fully dressed for battle. Soon, a ragged line formed outside the clustered tents.

The first volley of arrows rained down on them. Gaps appeared in the line of soldiers as men fell, arrows sprouting from their chests. More men ran up as the camp emptied.

Too late, shields rose above the men's heads. A second shower of arrows dropped more of them.

Eacharn lifted a horn to his lips and blew three short blasts, and the archers withdrew.

As Caitir ran to the rear with the others, Tristan whispered a prayer of thanksgiving to Elyon.

Eacharn blew three more blasts, and the chariots and cavalry charged.

Tristan followed Maeve as she lifted her sword high and led the charge. The enemy soldiers tried to put up a defense, but with terrible speed, the chariots and mounted warriors bore down upon them from the north, cavalry from the south. Then in marched three hundred swordsmen from the west. Behind the chariots came the rest of the army, nearly eight thousand five hundred strong.

The battle was short, intense, and decisive. The clash of metal on metal, axes on shields, pikes on armor, the deep-throated cries of battle, the screaming of horses and men—all filled the air.

Tristan felled two of the enemy.

Once, he looked up as Maeve struck down a púca climbing aboard her chariot. In death, the thing's wolf-head shrank back into that of a bony-faced, forty-year-old man while its furred hindquarters and forepaws morphed into human legs, naked and bleeding.

When it was over, the dead and dying littered the field. Few of the Ériu had lost their lives.

"Victory is ours," came the cry of a young soldier. "Hail to Queen Maeve!"

"Hail, Queen Maeve!" came the echoing shouts.

Still atop her horse, she raised her sword to the men's cheers.

Wiping his sword on the grass, Eacharn glanced at Tristan and grunted. "Compared with what lies ahead, 'tis but a minor skirmish."

"Aye, my lord." Machar sat his horse, raised himself in the saddle, and plopped back. "With sixty thousand soldiers matched against our ten thousand, we're in sore need of a miracle."

A rider galloped across the field, stopped before Eacharn, and dismounted. "My lord!" He tried to catch his breath. "Three enemy riders broke through our lines to the south. We sent a dozen men after them, but their horses were swift. They escaped."

Eacharn nodded. "It matters little. We kenned they would move against us soon. Our only hope is to stop them . . . at the two rivers."

"The two . . . rivers . . . my lord?" Machar's gaze drifted south over the field. "Of course."

"Aye. 'Tis the only place we can mount a proper defense."

Tristan also gazed south, remembering the tale of the great battle, long, long ago—the Battle of Two Rivers.

The battle where the Deamhan Lord once defeated the army of Ériu.

Where evil prevailed over good.

Where the darkness began.

Now in the same spot, there would be a reprise, a second battle, a second chance.

But they'd be facing overwhelming numbers. And without the Scepter.

CHAPTER 45

THE EVENTS OF SAMHAIN EVE

L ate in the day, as Tristan followed Maeve's chariot, the army arrived on the field. Where the road left the forest, they spread out and made camp. To the left, the River Liffey, too deep to ford, rolled downstream to the south. The field itself was four hundred yards of open marsh grass, now dry. Beyond, the sun gleamed off the Blackwater where it joined the Liffey, which ran all the way to Áth Cliath. Below the junction of rivers, the Liffey was impassable to all but an occasional ferry.

The same feeling Tristan had every other time he crossed this field came upon him now—as if an invisible aura hovered about the ancient battlefield. Were the ghosts of dead soldiers still haunting the place? He shuddered and went to help raise the tents.

The next morning, Eacharn put the army to work digging an eight-foot-deep ditch about a hundred yards from camp. They used chariots to haul away the dirt. Other men cut trees in the forest to make spikes to line the bottom.

All day, as Tristan dug with the other soldiers, the approach of Samhain weighed heavily upon him. Tonight was Samhain eve, when the Otherworld spirits would come closest to this world—the night when Faolukan and Gundovald would carry out their plans to overthrow the Deamhan Lord. He hoped it would work. Were not two mortals a better enemy than a spirit lord?

By evening, with nine thousand men digging, chopping, and working furiously, the trench was finished and lined with wicked, six-foot spikes. But Tristan was exhausted.

That night, Machar joined him, and the two sat alone by the fire. "You ken what tonight is, lad?"

"Samhain eve."

"Aye. No one's paying much attention to it now, what with everyone working so hard all day. And that's good. Too many still cling to the old beliefs. But tomorrow, if your vision holds true, Faolukan and Gundovald will march. And still, we do not have the Scepter. Have you—?"

"Nay. No more visions." Tristan winced. He couldn't control when Elyon opened a window into the enemy's affairs.

"I understand." Machar laid a comforting hand on his shoulder. "But the day after tomorrow, when the enemy comes charging across that river—we'll need all the help we can get."

"I wish I could help. But not right now."

Machar nodded. Then he rose and went to the tent he shared with Eacharn.

For some time, Tristan stared at the fire, wondering what would happen if the Scepter remained in the enemy's hands, and if—

THE FIRE RECEDED, REPLACED BY the image of a rowboat being pulled over dark waters. In the stern, a lantern swung from a pole. Two men plunged their oars into the sea. The oarlocks creaked. Water slurped on the backstroke, dripping as the oars came forward again.

Within the boat sat Faolukan, Gundovald, two rowers, and a third soldier. Gundovald wore a backpack. All peered ahead into the night.

The stern of a larger ship rose out of the dark. Emblazoned on its hull, in gold letters, were the words *Scáth An Bháis*.

Shadow of Death.

The men pulled the smaller craft to the port side, where the third man grabbed a rope net hanging over the side to steady the boat against the gentle swells.

Taking the lantern in one hand, Faolukan grasped the rope ladder and clambered up to the deck, followed by Gundovald. The lantern hit the hull every time Faolukan's hand also hooked a ladder rung.

In the vision, Tristan floated beside the two, shadowing them, able to move wherever he wanted.

All three soldiers remained in the rowboat. Faolukan now glared down at them. "Two of you—come up!"

Looks of fear passed between them, but no one moved.

"You two in the center—climb! *Now.*"

The two soldiers left the boat and began climbing.

But as Tristan climbed onto the deck after the men, no lanterns hung from poles. No one ran to greet them. For no watch had been set. He looked fore and aft. The ship was deserted.

Shadows clung to the vessel's every surface, even to the ropes. And with the shadows came a gut-wrenching fear. For here, twelve days ago, was where Faolukan and Gundovald had abandoned Crom Mord.

"Follow me," said the arch druid. Holding his lantern, he stalked across the planks aft to a set of louvered doors and yanked them open. Down a short flight of steps, he strode, then through a hallway to a cabin door. There, he stopped.

"Bring it out," Faolukan ordered Gundovald.

Gundovald slipped the knapsack from his back and removed a leather-wrapped object. He unrolled the package, revealing the Scepter. Being careful not to touch its surface, he grasped one end using the leather.

Faolukan eyed the two soldiers. "You will enter the cabin and remain with us. You will not leave until ordered. Is that clear?"

The first, a dark-haired, pock-faced youth of no more than eighteen, shot nervous glances at the door, at Faolukan, and at Gundovald. But his head bobbed up and down in agreement.

The second, a white-haired Ferachtir man of middle age, looked at Faolukan with a face drained of blood, raised a shaking hand to wipe the sweat from his forehead. But he, too, nodded.

"Good." Faolukan faced Gundovald. "Once inside, when I stand before Crom Mord, hand me the device."

"Aye, my lord. Let's do this. Let's get it over with."

Faolukan raised the handle, paused, and then pushed the door open.

They stepped into a cabin filled with shadows.

Crom Mord occupied the room's center. And even though Tristan's vision of the idol came from leagues away, still his heart pounded, his temples burst with sweat, and his fingers dug into his palms.

Fear—like a thick, dank fog drifting over a moonless night—penetrated every corner of the room.

The pock-faced youth bolted toward the door, but Gundovald's hand snatched his shoulder and rammed the youth against the wall. Gundovald shook his head, and the youth slumped, shaking, to the floor.

Atop the idol sat a lizard head. Razor-teeth filled its mouth, within which waved a forked, red tongue. Surrounding the head was a lion's mane. But where fur should have been wriggled a mane of vipers. Snake tongues lapped in and out. Massive, clawed feet seemed to dig into the floor planks.

So, Faolukan, you've come back, came words that screamed inside Tristan's head. *Are you ready to resume your service to me? Have you brought me sacrifices?*

Tristan knew it was only a work of stone, but the eyes seemed to bulge, to follow the men in the room. The snakes seemed to wriggle. And the tongue to writhe. But it was only an illusion. Wasn't it?

Then its eyes found the Scepter.

What are you doing? Fools! Do you think to overthrow me?

"G–give it to me." Faolukan extended an open palm toward Gundovald.

Still holding the Scepter by the leather, the Burgundian handed over the device.

The moment Faolukan's left hand grasped the Scepter, flame engulfed his fingers. The smell of burnt flesh stung Tristan's nostrils. A trail of smoke rose from Faolukan's arm. Then a dark light, filled with every shade of gray and black and red, burst out from the Scepter—nearly the opposite of what Tristan experienced when he had held it. The dark wave rocked Gundovald back against the wall, knocked the youth to the floor, and sent the older soldier crashing to his knees.

Nay! You cannot do this. Stop at once! The screams that etched themselves inside Tristan's head were strident, urgent. *Stop, fools!*

Faolukan grimaced and, his hand shaking violently, stepped toward the idol. "I call upon you, Faolan the Traitor, to leave this idol of stone. By the power of this Scepter, I command you to leave the idol Crom Mord and return to your spirit state. Then, I order you to return to the depths of the Underworld, there to remain forever."

Instantly, a gray light gathered around the Scepter, forming a black mass. The black shadow rushed toward the idol and surrounded it. Black vapor completely engulfed the idol.

Fire licked and writhed around Faolukan's hand where he held the Scepter. Pain twisted his forehead. Strings of flesh hung now from his palm. His arm shook so violently, the Scepter waved back and forth.

Then he dropped it.

The Scepter clattered to the floor.

And the black vapor left the idol. The cloud drifted to the right, darkened, and formed the shape of a man.

Tristan stared at the idol of black stone. All of the former movement—the writhing tongue, the wriggling snakes, the moving red eyes—all were gone!

It was only a statue. And an ugly one at that.

Yet the fear that had permeated every corner of the room remained, coming now from the dark mist forming in the shape of a man.

Fools! came words that screeched inside Tristan's head. *You thought to banish me to the Underworld. But only Elyon's device could undo the curse Elyon placed upon me. And that is what you have done. Now, I am free.*

Faolukan's normally impassive face now registered shock, fear, disbelief. He staggered back. "Nay. 'Tis impossible. Nay."

The youth bolted out the door and ran down the hall.

The cloud figure sped toward the arch druid, engulfed him, spread over every part of him.

The arch druid screamed. Then he fell to the floor, unconscious.

Gundovald tried to open the door, but the druid's body, encased in black vapor, lay against it. The Burgundian's eyes wild with fear, his glance raced around the room, found no escape, and landed again on the door. He yanked, moved the body a few inches, yanked again. The old soldier came to his aid.

Then Faolukan opened his eyes and sat up.

The two men backed up, rammed against the idol, then the wall.

The arch druid rose to his feet. It was Faolukan's body. But it wasn't him.

The same fear that Tristan had felt upon entering the room, that had issued from the Crom Mord idol, now issued from Faolukan.

Gundovald put a hand to his mouth, fumbled for the sword at his belt. He yanked the blade from its sheath, held it out. But it wavered and shook.

The soldier slumped to the floor.

"That's right, Gundovald," came words from Faolukan's mouth. "You and the druid have freed me."

"B–but how . . ."

"Only Elyon's device could break Elyon's spell. So now, I possess the traitor's body. And now, after millennia imprisoned in an idol of stone, I am free again to walk Erde, to take my revenge on all that Elyon has created. Every living creature in Elyon's domain will now feel my wrath." He paused, raising his right hand to his forehead. "How long it's been since I could feel like this.

"But I possess his body, do I not? So why not also keep his name? The name of Faolukan. Then all who obeyed him will obey me. But I am weak, Burgundian, and I need a life spirit to restore my strength."

The Deamhan Lord in Faolukan's body walked toward Gundovald.

The Burgundian raised a shaking blade and tried to strike.

But Faolukan's sword was already out. And with two quick strokes, he dropped Gundovald, bleeding, to the floor.

As the Burgundian left this world, a wisp of vapor rose from his body, swirled toward Faolukan, and entered.

The Deamhan Lord breathed a sigh of pleasure and faced the soldier. "Get up off the floor, you sniveling coward. If you obey me, I will not kill you."

Shivering all over, the soldier rose.

"Use the leather and pick up that befouled device. Then follow me."

Trembling, the man grabbed the Scepter with the leather and followed Faolukan out the door, down the hall, and up onto the deck.

Faolukan led him to the aft rail. He pointed toward the dark waters below.

"Throw it—there."

The soldier pitched the Scepter as far as he could. It splashed into the sea, sank from view.

"I feel better already." Faolukan stared at his left hand, black with strips of burnt, shredded flesh. "Except for this wound."

He whirled toward the soldier. "Now let us go into the port and begin collecting the life spirits of every man, woman, and child who remains. Before morning, I want them all."

The soldier raised a pale, stricken face to the Deamhan Lord, who now walked and talked in Faolukan's body. But when the man tried to respond, only a guttural noise issued forth. He nodded.

TRISTAN WOKE FROM THE VISION, trembling and sweating, his fingers digging so deep into his palms, they bled. He hugged himself and rocked back and forth.

As the Deamhan Lord's foul presence dissipated, he wondered how he was ever going to get the Scepter now? No one could ever swim to a depth of twelve fathoms and live. For surely, the harbor was at least that deep.

And now, they faced a far worse enemy than before. The thing he feared most in all the world was to stand face-to-face with the Deamhan Lord.

He rose and began running through the camp.

He must find Machar. And Cairbre. And Eacharn.

CHAPTER 46

PREPARATIONS

After Tristan told the group gathered around the fire about his vision, their faces became pale, startled, unsettled.

"This is worse than we could ever have imagined." Machar closed his eyes and dropped his head into his hands. "The Deamhan Lord . . . free to move about as a man. Who can stop him now?"

"Aye." Cairbre stared out into the night. "More than ever, we need the Scepter. But now it lies at the bottom of the harbor." He glanced around the fire. "How deep is the bay? Does anyone ken?"

"Twelve . . . fifteen fathoms," said Ewan. "Well over a hundred feet."

"No one has ever dived to that depth and lived." Eacharn shook his head. "No one can hold their breath that long. The dive would kill them."

"What, then, can be done?" Tristan looked at the solemn faces, grimacing foreheads, downcast eyes.

Machar faced Cairbre. "'Tis said you have dabbled lately in white wizardry. Is that true?"

"Aye. 'Twas a passion of my youth that I eventually abandoned. Given the nature of our enemy, I've recently been relearning the craft, rereading my old books, now thick with dust."

Maeve leaned forward, the fire casting shadows over her face. "Can you do something, anything, to let a man dive so deep and live?"

Cairbre frowned. "You must understand, this ventures into the realm of water wizardry. 'Tis not my area of expertise. I've only one book that even addresses the subject."

"But can you come up with something?" asked Machar.

"I don't know. I brought most of my old scrolls. If you will excuse me, I will retire to my tent and begin a search."

"Capulum Righ"—Machar lowered his voice toward the white-haired old man—"may Elyon guide you in your study. For only by his hands will we defeat the evil now arrayed against us."

Cairbre bowed his head, stood unsteadily from the fire circle, and ambled off into the night.

"I suggest we all get some sleep." Machar's eyes swept the circle of dejected leaders.

"Aye," added Eacharn. "For tomorrow, we must finish the trench. Then we must let the men rest."

"Aye, Eacharn." Machar stood. "For the coming battle will decide whether Ériu will live in the light. Or in the dark."

Tristan rose and walked slowly to his tent. But halfway there, he stopped, stretched, and stared at the moon. How peaceful it appeared, compared with the tumult swirling around him now.

Was it true, he wondered, that Erde shared this white, glowing ball with another world, a place called Earth? And was Erde really just an echo of that Earth as legend had it? Was Erde only a reflection of the original, like looking into a pool of water and seeing yourself, only rippled, changed, different from the original?

And if this were so, were people on that other world looking up, right now, at that very same moon? And were those people, like Erde's, also looking to Elyon in their struggle with evil?

He shook his head. Who knew the answers to such questions?

He shuffled across the grass toward his tent and sleep.

THE NEXT DAY, THE ARMY laid a grillwork of thin saplings across the trench and covered it with leaves and grass. From a distance, it appeared like a break in the field where someone had trampled a path. Perhaps good enough to fool a charging cavalryman or foot soldier.

Every fifty feet, a bridge of logs attached to ropes allowed them to cross to the south. The plan was to pull the bridges out of sight at the last instant.

Late in the day, when the work neared final readiness, a young messenger found Tristan as he heaved bundles of grass onto the sticks.

"My lord," said a breathless lad of perhaps fourteen, "your presence is required at once before General Eacharn."

Tristan left his work and strode to a tent where Eacharn, Machar, Queen Maeve, and the kings of the other four provinces stood in a cluster.

Eacharn frowned at Tristan. "We've received a strange delegation, Tristan."

"At first, we thought to imprison them," said Maeve. "With their golden skin and dark eyes, who has ever seen the like of such folk? But then they began asking for you by name. Or rather by the name of Prince Neil."

"And then I saw them." Grinning, Machar stepped out of the way, revealing two eladrin standing in back.

A woman with black eye sockets and lids, hair as white as a cloud, skin as golden as a sunset, but as old as Erde, approached. His chest warming, his eyes tearing, Tristan raised his forearm. She met his with hers in the typical eladrin greeting. He bowed. "My lady Keenala, High Reginalia of Glenmallen, welcome."

To her side stood a younger man with dark hair, half-a-head taller than she. Tristan raised his forearm and greeted him in like manner. "And Thallinor né Thalidreel, chief of scouts, how glad am I to see both of you."

"He's been promoted to general of the army," corrected the queen of Glenmallen.

"A general unworthy of the name, my lady." Thallinor bowed. "For the army is no more."

"You did your best." Keenala glanced at the taller, bulkier men, her gaze stopping again on Tristan. "When the enemy broke our defenses and destroyed our valley, we had little choice but to flee, what few of us remained. And then I remembered what you said, Neil mac Connell—that some of the men of your country worshiped Elyon." She nodded her head, briefly closing her eyes. "So we have come here to help in any way we can. For you were right. In the face of great evil, one cannot stand aside and do nothing as our ancient customs demanded. Sometimes, one must act. And sometimes, one must fight. So your enemy is now our enemy."

Eacharn stepped forward. Awkwardly, he held his forearm out in greeting. First Keenala, then Thallinor, met his welcoming arm. "Glad we are for the offer, but"—Eacharn appeared to inspect their height, their slight physique, and frowned—"but what can wee folk such as yourselves do against Cthyllin ice giants, mammoths, and fierce Drochtar warriors riding warhorses at full gallop?" He stood with folded arms, awaiting an answer.

"My lord Eacharn," said Tristan, "these folk are masters of illusion. They possess skills of magic like none we have ever seen."

"Hey?" Eacharn arched one eyebrow. "Is this true?"

Keenala bowed. "It is true, my lord. But Prince Neil exaggerates."

"'Tis now Tristan mac Torn, my lady," said Tristan.

"Ah. So your ruse was discovered?"

"You knew?" Machar's jaw dropped.

"Aye," she said. "Elyon himself spoke to me in a vision, telling me who he really was."

"Well, if 'tis magic you can bring against the enemy"—Eacharn swept a hand to the south—"we welcome any help you can give us. How many did you bring to the field?"

"Eleven. The other nine are mages."

"Good. We will provide you a tent, and—"

"Thank you for the offer, but we've brought our own shelter."

"I expect we'll see action tomorrow at the earliest." Eacharn pulled on his considerable mustache. "What kind of magic are you prepared to conjure up?"

Keenala and Thallinor exchanged glances. "We will wait to see what the battle brings and step in where we think we can do the most good."

"Fair enough."

All in the room thanked them then the two left.

Eacharn faced Tristan. "They wouldna speak to anyone but you, lad." He caught Machar's gaze. "Do you have any other secret allies you havena mentioned?"

Smiling, Machar shook his head.

"Well then, this council is adjourned."

They filed out of the tent.

Tristan started back toward the trench when a soldier approached him from behind and touched his shoulder. He spun to face a tall, lean man with a familiar scowl etched permanently across his lips. His face and forearms were covered with burn marks from many years at the forge.

"Uncle C–Cowan?"

"Aye, lad." A smile briefly broke his scowl. "When they came through the village asking for volunteers, I joined them."

Cautiously, his uncle opened his arms. Tristan stepped forward, and, awkwardly, they hugged. Then they separated.

"I heard tell about you from the others. You've made quite a name for yourself here, you have."

Wary at the compliment, Tristan gave his uncle a slight nod.

"I . . . I forgive you for running off. We thought you dead. Your aunt and your cousin—both are in good health. But how they've grieved over you, boy."

"I'm sorry. It was unavoidable. The prince who died in your hut—he looked exactly like me. His squire convinced me to take the man's place."

"Not a very honorable thing to do, was it?"

Tristan squirmed. "There's a lot more to the story."

"I'm sure there is." His uncle's frown returned. "I was made to understand you were part of that ill-fated venture that failed to bring back some grand artifact that might help us?"

"Aye. But 'tis not over." Why was it that everything Cowan said made him feel small?

"Well, now that you're tight with the higher ranks, I suppose you'll have little use for a man like me and his forge back home?"

Tristan said nothing. How quickly Cowan turned everything back to his forge and his profits.

Cowan jerked his head toward the far end of camp. "I brought me bellows, me tongs, and me tools. Some have helped to fashion a brick furnace. For I'm to make shoes for horses and fix swords, lance heads, and arrow points."

"All will be sore needed before we're done."

Cowan's gaze sought the ground. "Well, 'twas good to see you, lad. I suppose, when this is ended, you willna be coming back to the forge?"

"I–I don't know. I thought perhaps I'd open my own works . . . somewhere. But whether this will soon be over, and how it will end . . ."

Cowan's eyes narrowed. "Aye. 'Tis a nasty business we're involved in. And if it does end well—and there's plenty grumbling it won't—you'll be wanting, I suppose, to be free of your lowly uncle, will you not?"

"'Tis not that, Uncle. Caitir and I are to be wed. We thought to open a shop in another village—someplace where my father's name and my mother's . . . indiscretions . . . are unknown. We'd like to start life anew."

Cowan raised his eyebrows. "Ah, marriage it's to be? Well, I should congratulate you, I guess. I can tell you I've grown used to not having you around to help in the shop. I can do without you, I can. And I understand why you'd want to rid yourself of the reputation of that worthless brother of mine and, of course, of meself." He half-turned to leave then slowly turned back. "Good luck to you, Tristan."

"And may Elyon go with you, Uncle."

He cocked his head. "There's a name not often heard." He began shuffling away. "Aye, not often heard . . ."

Tristan stared at Cowan's back. His uncle's words had left him in turmoil. All the dishonor he'd once felt living in Hidden Pines came roaring back. How quickly his uncle had stripped him of whatever confidence he'd gained! How small he suddenly felt!

He shook his head. More important matters weighed upon him now. Tomorrow, the battle for the survival of Ériu would begin.

CHAPTER 47

THE SECOND BATTLE OF TWO RIVERS

The day broke bright and clear without a cloud in sight. First thing in the morning, Eacharn had the men take down the tents and move the supply wagons up the road toward Ewhain Macha. Ten thousand men now spread out in a line nearly two hundred yards wide.

As Tristan glanced up and down the ranks, he swelled with pride. These were the five kingdoms of the Ériu, now come together as one to defend their homeland. Farmers; masons; leather workers; bakers; silk, wine, and spice merchants; herdsmen; hunters; flaith and commoner; soldiers and peasants. All had joined together to fight the enemy.

When Maeve saw her people gathered with swords, shields, axes, spears, pikes, and even sickles, she called for her chariot and a driver. Jumping aboard, she raced down the line, holding her sword high. The cheers and stomping of feet that went up from the line were enough to shake the ground and burst the ears. They lifted Tristan's spirits. He could almost believe that, aye, today, they might just defeat the combined armies of Drochtar, Ferachtir, and Sarkenos. And the Deamhan Lord himself.

As Maeve rode past, Tristan caught sight of Keenala conferring with her mages. They'd brought with them three globes of hazy, white glass. With three mages to a globe, they spaced themselves equidistant from each other along the front.

Eacharn then gave orders for the archers and the chariots to cross the trench and take up advance positions on the western bank of the Blackwater. He asked for anyone who could shoot a bow to join them, and also for swordsmen and pikemen to protect the archers—in case some made it across too soon. Tristan added his sword, jumping onto the platform of a chariot as the driver clattered his cart over a makeshift log bridge and bumped over the field. Along the way, he waved to Caitir marching on foot with the other archers. Eacharn himself led the group with his own chariot and driver.

Only four hundred yards separated the bulk of the army from the river, and when the chariots arrived on the western bank, an air of electric excitement ran through the group. They'd managed to field two thousand archers, with half that many chariots, chariot drivers, and swordsmen to protect the lot.

But the enemy had not yet arrived, and the excitement soon quelled. Men lounged at their posts, sat on the ground smoking pipes, or talked with their brothers in arms.

At midmorning, a party of enemy scouts appeared on the river's far side before turning back. Afterward, the river's opposite shore was quiet.

At noon, they ate bread and cheese provided by women from the main body and drank water from the river. Back at the line, it was said, the soldiers ate a stew of barley, beef, and onions from great kettles that had simmered all morning.

In early afternoon, the enemy's advance units appeared, five abreast, on the opposite bank. Flying the flag of Drochtar, they wore the blue-and black-swirled uniforms he'd come to despise.

"Steady, men," came Eacharn's shout. "Hold your fire till they begin to mass."

Within the Drochtar contingent were archers, swordsmen, and pikemen. Behind them came armored cavalry, but few of these. They spread out in a line on the far shore.

Following these came the black- and yellow-striped uniforms of the Ferachtir, and then the brown robes, turbans, and black face scarves of Sarkenos. The eastern shore quickly swarmed with troops.

"Now!" came Eacharn's hoarse cry. "Fire!"

The archers raised their bows, aimed, and let loose the first volley.

A few of the enemy raised their shields, but not enough. Scores of men fell.

The Ériu archers then began shooting at will, and hundreds of the enemy dropped where they stood.

Tristan heard the shouts to raise shields. A ceiling of wood, leather, and brass rose over the heads of the gathering enemy throng.

Now the opposite shore seethed with an ever-growing mass of troops. There seemed no end to them.

The cavalry, what few there were, rode first into the river, and the archers concentrated all their fire on these. Horses reared, fell with arrows sprouting from their necks. Men rode with projectiles sticking out of their legs and arms until they, too, fell into the slow-moving current, their bodies carried downstream.

Foot soldiers entered the stream, more than the archers could aim at. Some were able to climb the western bank, and this is where the Ériu pikemen and swordsmen ran to meet them.

Now Eacharn called for the chariots to take the archers from the field. As the bowmen retreated, the swordsmen and lancers stepped to the fore, meeting an increasing number of foot soldiers, and some cavalry, swarming across the Blackwater.

Tristan engaged soldier after soldier, dropping as many as ten men.

With perhaps a thousand men defending the retreat, the men of Ériu fought, gave up ground, and fought again. Tristan and his fellow frontline soldiers retreated perhaps seventy yards before the chariots returned.

Then Eacharn gave the word for them to abandon the field.

Tristan jumped aboard the first chariot that stopped beside him. His driver whisked him away from the gathering mass of enemy troops, across the field, and back to the main line of defense.

"Well done," said Eacharn to the men returning from the front. "We lost only a few dozen and felled hundreds, if not thousands, of the enemy."

As the last chariot rumbled across the logs, men raced forward to haul the bridges out of sight.

The enemy army kept coming. A hundred yards away, they massed. Tristan thought their numbers would never stop growing. Moment by moment, more troops came up from behind. The body of soldiers stretched two hundred yards wide and nearly as many deep. Where before Tristan had been buoyed by the army of Ériu, now he trembled at the sight of so many Drochtar, Ferachtir, and Sarkenian troops.

Then the center parted, and a pathway opened. At least twenty war mammoths tromped forward.

All along the line of the Ériu, Tristan heard gasps and cries. For who among his people had ever seen the like?—these monsters from the mountains of Gopal. Atop each beast sat a white-turbaned Gopalese driver in a carriage. At least twenty feet tall, the behemoths shook the ground as they spread out in front of the army. Their fifteen-foot trunks, tipped with iron points, swayed as they walked. Who could stand against these creatures? How could one fight them, except with arrows? Yet heavy leather draped their sides, and brass plates covered their foreheads and legs. So even arrows would have a difficult time finding purchase. Their feet alone could crush a man to pulp.

When all twenty animals were positioned, some invisible signal prompted them to move forward.

Beside Tristan, men began backing away from the line until the shouts of leaders ordered them to stand firm and take heart.

The beasts strode ponderously across the distance, the ground rumbling with their approach. Eacharn gave the order for the archers to open fire. Arrows rained down on the beasts, but few hit their marks. Even when they did, the missiles seemed to have little effect. Pinpricks on a behemoth. Nothing, it appeared, could stop them.

Until they reached the trench.

The first animal fell in, sending its rider sprawling ahead. The creatures' cries of pain were earsplitting. All along the line, the mammoths dropped into the spike-lined trench, their enormous weight ensuring they became firmly skewered on the stakes. Their screams were unbearable.

Only one animal somehow stepped over the six-foot-wide ditch. Its rider drove it into the line of defenders like a boulder through a wheat field, its tusks throwing men aside like shocks of grain. But arrows soon found the driver. And men attacked the beast with spears and swords from the sides and from behind. Then it fell.

Men cheered the victorious result.

But no sooner had they celebrated this victory than another threat appeared—

Cthyllin ice giants.

At least two dozen of the monstrous figures now stepped through a path opening in the Deamhan Lord's army. They spread out, taking positions the mammoths had recently occupied. Each stood twenty-five to thirty feet tall. Shaggy brown hair covered their heads, chests, and legs. Each wore a loincloth of ragged fur. Their sallow faces held small eyes, dull and empty, that stared across the field. Each carried a club as long as a ship's mast with a head like a barrel, clustered with spikes.

Once again, the men of Ériu quaked at the sight of monsters never before seen in their land. A few of the merchants and farmers, their sons and daughters, tried to bolt. Once again, Eacharn and his captains ordered them to hold fast.

Then the cthyllin charged. As one, they strode across the field, each step eating up a dozen feet of ground. When they came to the trench, they merely stepped over it and continued on.

Tristan stood beside Eacharn, whose mouth now hung open. To Machar, he whispered, "What can we do against such as these? They'll break the line for certain."

Machar only shook his head, fear etched on his face.

Keenala and Thallinor held a brief conference, spoke to the three mages a few feet away. Faster than Tristan thought possible, Keenala raced left while Thallinor ran to the right. Moments later, they returned.

"My lady," said Machar, "what do you have in mind?"

"What is the one thing cthyllin ice giants fear above all else—even above water?"

"I know not, my lady."

Keenala faced the oncoming giants, now only a hundred feet from their lines, and smiled. "Mice."

At that moment, a swarm of mice seemed to burst from the ground ahead of the line. A black cloud seething with vermin, raced for the cthyllin.

The giants stopped, stared at the approaching threat, and whirled. They began running back the way they'd come.

But when they came to the trench, something had happened to it. Wherever the mammoths did not lie dying, an unbroken stretch of grass had appeared.

No longer seeing the ditch, at least half the giants stepped into it, skewering themselves on the spikes. The rest ran pell-mell toward the Deamhan Lord's troops.

The mice blackened the ground—hundreds of thousands of them racing for their quarry. Now even the men of Faolukan's army left their posts and fled before the oncoming swarm. But none ran faster than the ice giants. They overtook the fleeing soldiers, even using their clubs to sweep a path of escape. Behind them, the giants left a path of the dead and injured.

The mice chased them east, driving them toward the Liffey. And the cthyllin, though fearful of water and unable to swim, plunged into the river up to their knees. The rodents swarmed the bank, covered every plant, rock, and bush. Then the swarm entered the river, chasing the cthyllin even there. In full panic, the giants strode out until the Liffey's strong current swept them off their feet, sucking them out into deeper waters. One after another went under, bobbed to the surface, and went down for the last time.

The mice swarmed back toward the enemy soldiers. But when they were almost upon the frightened men, the entire lot simply disappeared. One moment there were thousands of swarming rodents—the next, nothing.

Tristan knew what happened. Someone, perhaps a druid, realized it was an illusion. And when that person no longer believed and began passing the news along, the vision collapsed.

Once again, the men of Ériu were saved, and a great roar of victory went up.

Tristan waited for the enemy army to make its next move. Instead, they withdrew to the middle of the field.

"What are they doing?" he asked Machar.

"If I were them, I'd build bridges to cross the trench. To do that, they'll have to drag logs across the Blackwater. That may take them the rest of the day."

"Aye, my lord," added Eacharn. "And by tomorrow, we'll be facing the main body of their force. Then, I fear, we'll be out of tricks."

CHAPTER **48**

Ðisaster

As the afternoon wore on, the enemy tried a different avenue of attack. The defenders' trench stretched between the two rivers, all the way from the Liffey in the east to the Blackwater in the south. To the west beyond the field, the Blackwater emerged from a canyon with sides too steep to climb. To the north, deep forest also made it difficult for any large force to navigate.

But just above where the Blackwater left the canyon and entered the field and where the trench ended was a fifty-foot stretch of open, sloping ground. Here, the Deamhan Lord sent a force of swordsmen to punch its way through.

Eacharn had anticipated this and stationed five hundred soldiers at the gap, protected by archers.

From a vantage point above, Tristan, Eacharn, and Machar watched as the armies struggled for control of the gap.

Wading into the shallower Blackwater, the Deamhan Lord's forces were met with a volley of arrows. Many fell, but too many made it across. Then the soldiers of Ériu met them in a pitched struggle with swords, axes, and spears. The area of struggle was only fifty feet wide, so the forces were evenly matched. Here, the enemy's superior numbers could not overwhelm.

And here, fierce fighting went on all afternoon until, by evening, the dead of both sides were piled so high, the gap narrowed to only a few yards and became useless as a conduit for invasion.

Finally, as dusk approached, the Deamhan Lord's forces withdrew across the Blackwater. At Eacharn's command, men set fire to the bodies, and the entire area of the gap now burned with the stench of burning flesh.

For the moment, at least, both sides encamped where they were to await the dawn.

Tristan joined Machar, Maeve, and Eacharn at their fire where they ate a supper of mutton stew provided by the camp maidens.

"I've made a rough count," said Eacharn, "and we've lost nearly a third of our number."

"We haven't even met the main force yet," added Machar.

"Aye." Eacharn nodded. The lines in his face testified to his concern. "Tomorrow will decide the outcome."

Cairbre ambled in out of the night.

"My lords"—as he spoke, his hair was askew, his face pale and wan— "I've found something in one of my books."

"Capulum Righ!" Machar sprang to his feet. "You look terrible. Have you slept recently?"

"Nay. I've been poring over my texts by candlelight in a tent up the road. No time for sleep. I found a description of a device that may allow Tristan to bring the Scepter up from the deep. Part of the text was damaged, but in another book, I found how to resurrect what was lost. But naught is for certain. Nothing can I guarantee. To proceed further, I need an expert goldsmith. And several ounces of gold."

"We've a blacksmith at the edge of camp." Eacharn waved north. "I hear he's skilled."

"For your task, you may have this." Maeve pulled a torc from around her neck.

"Nay, my lady." Cairbre's eyes widened. "Not the torc of the realm, the one with which you were crowned?"

"'Tis not that. 'Tis one of my personal torcs. If it will help bring back the Scepter, then I willingly sacrifice it."

Cairbre bowed, took it, and shuffled off to find Tristan's uncle Cowan, one of the army's blacksmiths.

MORNING SHADOWS HAD BARELY LEFT the field when the armies of Drochtar, Ferachtir, and Sarkenos began to move. They left their positions of the night before and swarmed toward the front line of the Ériu. When they came to the trench, men rushed forward and dropped hundreds of bridges over the gap. Then the army poured across the trench, massing only a hundred feet from Ériu's defensive line.

The enemy was now within bowshot, so Eacharn ordered the archers to fire. In that instant, the enemy's archers also shot, and the sky blackened with missiles flying in both directions.

Tristan and everyone around him hunkered down and raised their shields.

Arrows clattered onto armor, plunked on shields, and fell into the dirt. Too many sank into flesh. Men fell, groaning and screaming, beside him.

A great roar issued from the enemy lines. Men beat swords on shields and shouted a blood-chilling cry. "For Drochtar! For the Deamhan Lord!"

Then the enemy charged. They ran toward the defenders with swords, axes, and spears held high. Among them, Tristan now saw hundreds of púcas, men who'd been bespelled by Faolukan, who now spent part of their lives as half-man, half-wolf, bear, or lion.

"Raise pikes! Lock shields!" Eacharn roared, and men in the front lines lifted their shields to form an unbroken wall. From several places, those soldiers who carried the ten-foot pikes raised them at the last instant.

The enemy troops smashed into the defensive wall with all the power of a battering ram. Tristan was in the second row, standing beside Eacharn, Machar, and Maeve as the frontline soldiers staggered under the blow. To his right, some of the enemy were pressed from behind by their own men and driven into the long, serrated pike heads. When an opening briefly appeared in the shield wall, Tristan plunged his sword into a raving, clawing, lion-faced púca. The creature dropped dead and began morphing back into man, naked and bleeding.

A few of the enemy were able to rip the shields from the defenders' grasp. These were met with slashing swords, crashing axes.

Three quick bursts Eacharn blew on his battle horn—the signal to advance. Those beside Tristan pushed on the man carrying the shield in front. Tristan shoved against the muscled youth standing before him.

The front line of the enemy staggered. Some tripped and fell.

Then, as one, the front men dipped their shields aside, and the first and second lines swung with swords, hewed with axes, and jabbed with pikes. Temporarily stunned by the maneuver, the opposing troops tried to fight back. Many fell.

Then all order seemed to break down as man fought man, man fought púca, and both armies mingled in hand-to-hand combat.

The din was thunderous. Swords clanged against armor and metal. Axes crashed through helmets. Blade struck blade. Men shouted battle cries, grunted with exertion, or screamed from wounds.

Dust from the struggling feet of thousands mingled with the smell of sweat, leather, and horse, mixing with the metallic taste of blood and the foul odor of spilt bowel—all rising like some funerary perfume over the field.

Tristan engaged one after another of the enemy. Men's weapons seemed to swing at him from all directions and at his fellows. He fought not only the enemy, but even for space enough to fight.

The siòg's skills served him well. No one could stand against him. Around him, the dead began to pile up.

But no man could fight the tide of battle, and it carried him where it would. The overwhelming numbers of the enemy began taking their toll. Gradually, though the men of Ériu fought well, they steadily lost ground.

Yard after yard, they were pushed back.

Time after time, Tristan found himself alone, fighting the enemy by himself, surrounded by bodies he himself had dropped. Then he would glance behind, see how far ahead he was, and retreat.

Finally, Eacharn's battle horn sounded three long blasts. "Retreat and stand," said the signal.

So he and all those around him whirled, ran back ten paces, and reformed another line.

The enemy charged again.

Beside him now was Maeve, dressed in mail, swinging her sword. He was amazed that she would fight so close to the front. But she was a spunky lass, filled with resolve to uphold her realm. And she felled her share of púcas, soldiers, and men twice her size.

The battle wore on. The Ériu held their own, killing many more of the enemy, man-for-man, woman-for-woman, than they themselves lost.

Once more, they retreated. Tristan worried for their decreasing numbers. He estimated they'd lost at least half the men they started with. Possibly more.

Again and again, Eacharn called for quick retreats, a reforming of the lines, and another stand. And each time, they left more dead and dying behind. There was no going back for the wounded. The enemy's swords made a quick end of all who could not follow.

After the latest retreat, the enemy's horns blew some kind of signal, and the opposing line halted its advance. Like autumn leaves before a storm, the frontline troops fled to the side, making a wide path.

A figure dressed in a black helmet, black armor, and carrying a spike-filled mace, stepped forward. From him came wave after wave of shadows. The space around him became dark as night, black as a cave. Even the troops he fought for backed away, cringing in terror. With the shadows came an aura of gut-wrenching fear. For this was no mortal man.

Here came the Deamhan Lord in the body of Faolukan. His left hand he held close and immobile at his side. Only his right hand grasped the mace, a spike-studded metal ball attached by a chain to a leather-covered handle.

The ball burst into black flames. Then the Deamhan Lord swung the mace in a circle. With the ball came the sound of angry bees, a trail of acrid, oily smoke.

The Deamhan Lord strode toward the Ériu. His mace circled.

Then it struck.

It smashed shields to pieces, swept aside swords as if they were kindling, and broke lances with a single touch. He waded into the defenders' line, dropping men as if he were shearing wheat. Man after man attacked him, only to see their swords shattered and the whirling ball of fire and spikes plunge into their skulls or their sides, take off a leg or an arm, smash holes through armor, and cut through flesh and bone.

Then the front line of the Ériu broke.

The Deamhan Lord turned left, toward where Tristan, Machar, and Eacharn stood. He slew the warriors standing before him, making his way toward the leaders.

Eacharn blew five quick blasts, paused, and repeated the signal. "Retreat from the field," it said.

Tristan turned and withdrew ten paces before he whirled.

The Deamhan Lord was closing in on Queen Maeve. Unaware of the approaching menace, she was locked in combat with a Drochtar soldier. She felled her opponent. Only then did she see what approached.

Nay, nay. Tristan's heart, already thumping too fast, skipped beats.

It was too late. The Deamhan Lord blocked her retreat.

She lifted her sword, swung it in circles around her head, and plunged straight for his midsection.

His mace hit the blade and shattered it.

She staggered back, lifted her shield.

The metal ball swung in its next arc, shattered the wood, and smashed into her right arm. It plunged deep through mail and leather then into bone. She screamed.

Maeve slumped to her knees, her arm hanging broken by her side.

The mace swung around again, hit her helmet, and smashed through it.

Maeve, the new queen of Ériu, lay dead on the field.

All along the front now came the cry. "The queen has fallen. Queen Maeve is dead."

Around him now, his fellow defenders were in full retreat, fleeing for their lives. Queen Maeve's death had taken the last of their will to fight.

Tristan had no choice but to join them. Everyone raced for the end of the field and the trail leading to Ewhain Macha.

Ahead, Eacharn formed a line of archers to protect the retreating soldiers. Tristan ran through them, glanced quickly back, and saw their arrows striking home. The charging enemy troops, taken by surprise, had no time to raise shields, and many fell.

But the Deamhan Lord strode steadily onward, swinging his mace, bringing his cloud of shadows. The sight brought sweat to Tristan's brows and speed to his feet.

Everyone around him was in full panic now. Fear, confusion, and terror etched the faces of the Ériu soldiers. For who could fight the Deamhan Lord himself? How could farmers, tradesmen, butchers, and herders win against such overwhelming numbers with such a fearsome champion opposing them?

Where the field ended and funneled into the trail, Eacharn and Machar formed another line of archers. Most of the army had now fled far up the road.

Panting and sweating, Tristan stopped before Machar. "Have you seen Caitir?"

"She went on ahead, lad. As should you. You're the Toghaí. Your task lies not here, but elsewhere."

"We'll see how the Deamhan Lord fends off a barrage of arrows." Eacharn waved a hand at him. "Leave the field, lad."

Tristan began running up the road with the other fleeing soldiers. But he stopped to look back.

The enemy surged after the retreating defenders, toward Eacharn's line of defense. Eacharn gave the signal, and the archers loosed volley after volley, dropping many of the oncoming enemy.

But once again, the Deamhan Lord strode forward.

Eacharn signaled again, and every arrow shot toward him.

But at a wave of his hand, the missiles veered left and right, sinking into his own soldiers standing beside him. Then the Deamhan Lord began walking straight for Eacharn and his archers.

The general of the Ériu army whirled and fled.

Barely had the noonday sun risen, and the rout of the Ériu was complete.

The Second Battle of Two Rivers was lost.

PART X

THE RETURN TO
THE TOWER

CHAPTER 49

CAIRBRE'S DEVICE

Chariots arrived to pick up Tristan and the archers who'd made the army's last stand. As he was driven up the road, he glanced back at the receding enemy. They were reforming, preparing a pursuit.

Machar rode in the chariot racing behind him. "Right before the battle," he cried, "Cairbre was looking for you. And rather desperate, I'd say. But then the fight began." Machar grabbed the rail as the cart bumped over a rut. "I told him to leave the field. He's probably up ahead."

Tristan ordered his driver to pass the men and women fleeing before them. They surged in front of soldier after soldier but soon stuck behind a slow-moving wagon. Eacharn caught up to it, gathered some men, and, much to the owner's displeasure, pushed the cart off the road, tipped onto its side.

"We need speed today, not supplies," Eacharn muttered. "There's food aplenty stored in Ewhain Macha. If we ever get there."

As the man's team was freed from its harness, Eacharn commandeered one of the horses for Tristan. With a mount, he could more easily navigate his way past the straggling line of dejected soldiers. Far up the line, he added a saddle from a horse that had died from its wounds. In this struggle, neither man nor beast was spared.

He passed soldiers wearing on their faces, hands, and arms the cuts and gouges of battle. Makeshift bandages, red with blood, covered more serious injuries on men barely able to stagger along. Some would never make it to Ewhain Macha. Still others, it was obvious, bore wounds of the spirit—the aura of defeat and the knowledge that, if the Ériu could not stop the oncoming force, no one was likely to survive. He saw it in their eyes—the look of the vanquished, a fear of coming doom.

Farther up the column, Tristan caught up to Cairbre. Sitting a horse led by a young soldier, Cairbre was hunched over his saddle.

As their mounts came side by side, he cried out. "Tristan!" Then he called to the youth ahead of him. "Stop a moment. This is important."

When they both dismounted and pulled their steeds into the trees beside the road and out of the way, Cairbre removed his pack from his horse, rummaged within, and produced a tightly wrapped leather parcel. "I've fashioned a device for you, Tristan, and wrapped a spell around it. It should allow you to swim down and retrieve the Scepter."

"Swim down?" He pursed his lips. He'd hoped Cairbre's magic would raise the Scepter while he sat in a boat. Did the old man expect him to swim down over a hundred or more feet to look for it?

"Aye." Cairbre unwrapped leather to reveal an open metal jaw fashioned of pure gold and attached to a leather band. "'Tis a fish's mouth, and when you strap it over your own mouth, you should be able to breathe underwater."

Wide-eyed, Tristan stared at the thing.

"The spell comes from water wizardry, and I admit I'm no expert in the subject. I tried all manner of combinations to get it right. Once you strap it on and begin to breathe underwater, you cannot break the surface. That will end the spell. I'm fairly sure it will work, but—"

"But what?"

"I'm not entirely sure how long the spell will last. I had to recreate that part from other texts."

"So if it fails when I'm twelve fathoms down?"

Cairbre opened his hands in a question. "I do not ken, lad. Let's hope that doesna happen."

Tristan took the golden artifact, turned it over several times. Cowan had done an expert job, as usual. It even carried a set of tiny, metal teeth.

"How will you find the Scepter at the bottom of the harbor?" asked Cairbre.

"I was hoping you could help me there?"

Cairbre only shook his head.

"Right." Tristan wrapped it up and laid it in his pack. "So now everything depends on this. And on me." He lifted a pleading gaze to the old man. But Cairbre had already done everything he could. No one could take this task from him.

"'Twill be all right, lad." Cairbre smiled. "Elyon will watch over you."

Tristan swallowed. "Then I must leave for Áth Cliath at once." He looked toward the ragged line of fleeing soldiers. "Will you tell Eacharn, Machar, Caitir, and the others where I've gone?"

"Aye, lad." Cairbre laid a hand on his shoulder and squeezed. "All the hopes of Ériu—indeed, all of Erde—go with you now. May Elyon speed you on your way. Now you must press on to the end."

Those words, coming from Cairbre, affected him deeply. How many people—even Elyon—had spoken those very words to him?

He said goodbye and mounted. Then he rode as fast as he dared up the road until he found the first trail heading west. He knew these roads, and this path crossed a deer trail that would take him south and parallel the main road. If he could find that trail, he could slip past the advancing enemy troops unseen.

As he left, he shot a last glance at the main column of retreating soldiers, chariots, wounded, and horses. He took a deep breath.

The army would garrison itself in the fort at Ewhain Macha. From there, they'd mount a last desperate defense. The Deamhan Lord's forces would then lay siege.

They were following the same pattern as after the first Battle of Two Rivers so long ago—

Defeat on the plains.

Retreat to the fort.

A three-day siege.

And then—disaster.

Only one thing could save them now—

The Scepter.

THE DEER PATH WAS NARROW, slow, and winding through brambles, scrub, and close-grown pine. He cursed his sluggish pace. Several times, he lashed his mount to greater speed. But branches slapped him in the face, his horse stumbled on fallen limbs, and once, he even lost the trail and had to backtrack.

The path veered close to the main road. On the other side of yew branches, enemy troops marched north. Quickly, he slid from the saddle, hid behind a stand of low pine, and peered through the boughs.

Seemingly without end, the line of púcas and foreign troops trudged on. Even from this distance, Tristan could see the hate, greed, lust, malice, and anger etched on the faces of the Ferachtir, Sarkenian, and Drochtar soldiers. The Deamhan Lord had bewitched them and made his desires, their desires. Conquest was no longer their goal. Now they wanted only rapine, pillage, and desolation—complete and utter ruin of everything crossing their path. Not a soul left alive. All this he saw in the soldiers' ensorcelled eyes.

He shuddered. How could they win against madness such as this?

Then the fearsome visage of the Deamhan Lord himself, walking in Faolukan's body, passed by. Behind him trailed shadows that darkened the trunks along the way and clung to the men around him.

Tristan shivered and averted his eyes. Holding the reins, he slumped to a seat on the pine needles, listened to the tromping of thousands of feet on the road, heard the occasional roar or growl of the púcas.

When silence replaced the sounds of war, he stood and peered out.

The enemy had passed.

Pulling out the Ferachtir uniform he'd retrieved at Lugdunum Castle, he put it on. Then he led his horse through the trees back to the main road. He mounted and rode south. This wasn't his original plan, but the new route would take far less time than winding through thickets and brambles. He feared to arrive at the Tower before the Deamhan Lord's soldiers destroyed it.

Twice, he passed straggling units heading north. When an officer questioned him, he said he bore a message for the harbormaster, and the man let him go.

He pushed his horse as fast as he dared. Soon, he arrived at the edge of the battlefield. Already vultures and crows feasted on the slain. Just as at the Battle of the Plains back in Armorica, the enemy left not a single unit to take care of the fallen.

The smell of death wafted over the field, a sickening fume as thick as smoke from a funeral pyre. His horse whinnied in protest. He wrapped a cloth around his nose and, kicking the mount's sides, urged it forward.

Twenty yards ahead stood Cowan's battered tent and makeshift forge where he'd served the army of Ériu. Bodies lay everywhere, but not far away, one in particular caught his attention.

Slowly, not wanting to look, but knowing he must, Tristan slipped from the saddle and knelt. Shaking hands pulled the corpse onto its back.

He gasped.

Cowan's thin, burn-scarred face, ashen in death, stared up at him. He closed his uncle's eyes and sucked in breath. Selfish and mean-spirited in life, Cowan had died a hero's death—giving his life in service to Ériu's cause. Tristan wiped a tear from his cheek and stood. His aunt Brigid and cousin Searlie would need a protector now—that is, if anyone survived the coming struggle.

He glanced across the field of the slain. Tears filled his eyes. Not just for Cowan, but for all the sons and daughters of Ériu who'd fallen today. And for all the pawns of the eastern lands, bespelled and misused by Faolukan and the Deamhan Lord. Evil had surely run amok in the land.

And then he remembered the vision of the Etruscan port village—the sense of hope, joy, and destiny he'd beheld through the eyes of some unknown king. Something would happen in that poor hut, nestled on that remote hillside, something that would change history for the better.

It had been a vision of the future, but which future?

But with the memory of the first vision came the second where he walked through the devastated landscape of Ewhain Macha. The field before him now and the army marching toward Ewhain Macha and the Tower—surely, this pointed to the second vision, not the first.

He wiped moisture from his eyes.

Did everything depend now on him and him, alone?

He shuddered and mounted his horse. Thrashing its flanks, he prodded it to a gallop until the battlefield and the stench of death lay far behind.

Chapter 50

The Harbor

When he emerged from the trees south of the port, Tristan guessed it was after midnight. He took the main road north and, at the same farmer's hut they'd visited where they'd first landed, he stopped. By torchlight, he examined the hut and stable—both burned to embers. Like so many others in the path of the invaders, the farmer and his family would have little to return to. He was glad the man had taken his wife, daughter—and Fionn—and fled.

After leading his mount into the forest, he tied it to a tree. He hoped there were no wolves about. But this close to the village, they might not show themselves. He undressed to his loincloth, folded his tunic and leather buskins, and hid them with his pack. The night air cooled his skin; the pebbles and sticks of the path struck sharp under his bare feet.

He walked the distance to the overlook.

Below and far to the left, torches lit the wharf and a few buildings where the jetty began. Moonlight revealed that disaster had befallen the town. The familiar shapes of buildings were replaced by collapsed ruins, a few standing timbers, and rubble. If the Deamhan Lord had carried out his plans, not a soul down there would remain. Fortunately, most of the townsfolk had fled long before the lord of darkness began his sacrifices.

He shifted his glance east, to the harbor. Lanterns hung from the sterns and bows of well over a thousand ships, winking through a light fog. Somewhere out there was the *Scáth An Bháis*, the Deamhan Lord's vessel. The only way he knew how to find it was to steal a boat, row out in the dark, and examine the stern of every ship.

But how was he ever going to find it among all those vessels?

He descended the brush-covered slope, stubbing his feet on rocks, scraping his skin on branches, to a point south of the port. As he walked the beach toward the wharf, his bare feet sank into cool sand. Crickets chirped in the salt grass.

Up under the trees and away from the rocky beach, he spied a dark shape. He climbed.

Aye, a boat, secured under canvas, covered with pine branches!

Someone had hidden their craft from the invaders. He removed the tarp, righted the craft, and slid it over the rocks into the shallows. He went back for the oars and then pushed the boat out.

Tonight, the sea was calm, lit by starlight and moonlight, easy for rowing. But still difficult for diving into dark depths.

The nearest ship was three hundred yards away. He rowed, the oar-locks creaking, the oars slurping, the water dripping. Farther out, a ship's bell clanged, followed by another, then another. Changing of the watch. He was far enough away that they probably couldn't see him yet, but as he neared, anyone looking down would certainly notice him.

Nearby, a fish jumped, startling him with its splash. He rowed on.

As he approached the first ship, he followed the port side and rounded the stern. Looking up, he found the name—*The Hope of Havby*. How many ships had the enemy conscripted from ports near and far? Havby was far to the north of Nordmark, just to the south of Noregr.

He left that vessel and headed to the next. But that was *The Angry Boar*.

Out here in the bay, a light mist hovered over the waters.

Across the harbor, a forest of naked masts rose from dark hulls like ghost ships in the fog. How many lay at anchor out here? It would take all night to find the one ship he sought.

He rowed to the next one. Somewhere, someone played a slow mournful tune on a flute, lonely and haunting in the dark. A dirge for Áth Cliath?

After examining the aft plate of the tenth vessel—*The Raging Storm*—he turned and headed for the next ship.

Then someone called down from the deck above. "Ho, there, sailor! What are you doing?"

He didn't answer, just kept rowing toward the next lighted ship.

"By what authority are you out tonight?" came the voice again. "Answer me."

He rowed faster.

Moments passed. Then up on the deck of *The Raging Storm*, men began shouting. Soon, he heard the creaking of a winch and a longboat splashing into the sea. At least four rowers were now headed his way. Lanterns in the bow and stern lit the sea around.

As Tristan neared the next vessel, that one, too, was not what he sought. But much farther out, by itself, lay a ship without lights. All the other vessels carried lanterns on their bow and aft decks. But this one, a hundred yards distant from any other, was dark. With all his strength, he pulled toward it.

The four men rowing in *The Raging Storm*'s longboat were rapidly gaining on him.

When his target was a hundred feet distant, his pursuers were the same distance behind. Again, someone called out to stop and return, and he ignored them. Behind him, oars clacked in oarlocks, and a man cursed in his direction.

When he was fifty feet from his goal, they were only forty behind. Almost upon him.

Finally, he dew aft of the black ship, silent and dark in the harbor. By moonlight, he could barely make out the words—*Scáth An Bháis*.

The Shadow of Death.

A length of rope was already secured to his waist. He brought out Cairbre's talisman, its strap tied around his neck.

"Stop, you, and come about!" His pursuers would be upon him in moments.

He freed the device, looked at it, and shivered. Would it work? And even if it did, how was he going to find the Scepter in the dark?

No time to think now.

He secured the golden jaw over his mouth, feeling the ridges Cowan had made. It fit perfectly over his lips. He was breathing air through it now, but how would he breathe air underwater?

The enemy rowboat was only a dozen paces away.

"Here, now," came the man's voice. "You can't escape, lad."

He tied the strap behind his head. The fish's jaw fit snugly over his mouth.

Staring down into the dark waters, he took five deep breaths. Then he dove into the depths.

The water was cold, but strangely, he didn't shiver. He kicked his legs, and oddly, he glided effortlessly through the water. Down he swam, straight toward the bottom. Still, he held his breath. How long could he swim before he was forced to breathe through Cairbre's contraption? He kicked and swam with all his might. Maybe he could go all the way without it?

He'd often swum to the bottom of lakes—perhaps fifteen feet deep at most—and he knew he should have begun feeling the pressure on his ears by now. Yet surprisingly, he didn't.

Another odd thing—no water came through the open fish's mouth strapped to his lips. As if some invisible barrier kept it from flooding into his mouth.

The waters were dark. No light whatsoever. He should be blind—it was pitch black down here—but his eyes adjusted. Far, far below, he could even make out the bottom. How was this possible?

But he saw no Scepter.

He'd descended maybe halfway down when spots began bursting in front of his eyes. He had to take a breath. But he dared not trust Cairbre's spell. How *could* it work? Stopping, he turned around and looked up. His lungs were about to burst. He was going back.

No longer could he hold his breath. He exhaled, feeling like he would pass out. Bubbles rose before his face. His legs kicking frantically, he began swimming up.

Involuntarily, his lungs sucked in.

But he didn't drown. Instead, cold, clear air—tasting of salt—filled his lungs.

Cairbre's spell worked!

He flipped upside down and began swimming again toward the bottom. Now he knew why the pressure didn't bother him. And why he could see when he should have been blind. And why he glided so easily through the water.

Cairbre's spell let him see and swim and breathe like a fish.

Moments later, he reached the bottom. Sand, rocks, and gravel littered the area. He looked around in all directions. Shadows wavered beside the rocks. Nothing.

Above him, his pursuers' lanterns were two bright lights on either side of a dark hull. They were moving away. And now he saw they towed his rowboat behind them. He'd have to swim all the way back to shore.

He saw, too, the shadow of the Deamhan Lord's ship.

In the vision, the Deamhan Lord had directed the sailor to throw the Scepter off the stern. So he swam in that direction.

Long moments later, he spied something glowing behind boulders. With all his might, he kicked toward it.

There, between two rocks—the Scepter!

He picked it up and felt, once again, its power flow through him.

Thank you, Elyon.

Quickly, he tied the rope from his waist around one end, and with the Scepter secured, he began swimming toward shore.

He estimated he was at least a mile from the beach, a long way to swim underwater in the dark. But Cairbre's device allowed him to kick and paddle like a fish. With every stroke, he covered more distance than was possible.

But hadn't Cairbre warned the spell could end at any time? Just in case, he began rising toward the surface. He was only ten feet away when he took a breath, and—

Water poured into his mouth.

He jerked the device from his lips and closed his mouth. Suddenly, swimming became more difficult, the water made him shiver, and the light faded. Kicking furiously, he broke the surface, paddled to keep his head up. He coughed and choked, gagging on saltwater.

When he was breathing normally again, he looked around.

His pursuers were nowhere in sight. They must have returned to their ship.

In the other direction, the shore was about half a mile distant, with the wharf lights to his right.

The spell had departed, and now he must swim under his own power. But his arms and legs, unaccustomed to swimming, burned with his recent exertions. For a time, he floated on his back to rest.

Then, stroke after stroke, he made his way to the beach, strode out of the water, and collapsed on a rock, breathing heavily.

But as he lay exhausted on the shore, he glanced down, smiling, at the object of his quest now back in his possession, the one thing Elyon had promised would save the world from disaster—

The Scepter.

CHAPTER 51

THE LOWER CITY

That night, Tristan took the back trail, avoiding the port itself, riding until he and his horse could go no farther. When he stopped in a clearing well off the path, he built a fire to stop his shivering and dry his still-wet clothes. But the Scepter lay firmly inside his pack, and with that knowledge, he slept soundly.

Dawn's light came quickly, and, after changing into the enemy's uniform, he rode the next day on the trail in the wake of the two armies. Several times, he met riders bearing messages for the port, but his Ferachtir uniform and his white hair worked to avoid suspicion. He passed again through the battlefield, hiding the second night far off the road on a deer path. Though he wanted to go on, his horse needed rest.

Morning broke on the third day since leaving the army. He rode hard through one burnt-out village after another. He climbed Artair's Ridge, descended into deep forest beside the Liffey, then crossed the field where they'd defeated the twelve centuria. The rotting bodies of the slain still lay open to vultures, crows, and now, even wolves.

In early afternoon, Tristan climbed the ridge where the iron quarter-moon announced Corc's and Connell's capitulation to the enemy. But when Tristan finally looked down on Ewhain Macha, he gasped.

All the lower city was now a smoldering ash heap. Black, smoking timbers rose from mounds of charcoal. Stone buildings lay in tumbled ruins. Everywhere lay bricks, stones, and the timbers of fallen and burnt storefronts. The bodies of horses, men, women, and children filled the streets. Carrion birds circled and feasted on the dead.

He feared he was too late. Had the second vision, the future of a desolated, ruined world already come to pass?

But nay, the enemy army was still laying siege to the fort on the hill. Thousands upon thousands of troops were encamped, waiting to take the upper city. The Tower still rose above the city walls. Though damaged, the ramparts were intact.

But in the few days Tristan had been gone, the enemy had built three trebuchets. These now hurled stones from the ruined town up against the walls. Already, they'd smashed huge sections of the wall into rubble. A twenty-foot-high barrier was, in places, now only ten. One tower of the gatehouse had become nothing but a mound of bricks. Half the draw-bridge had broken in; he could see through the upper boards into the fort.

Even as he watched, a triple volley of rocks hurled toward the wooden bridge. The noise of stone breaking wood was deafening. One boulder punched through and left another enormous hole.

At the bottom of the hill on the road leading to the fort, the enemy had built a siege engine. A massive tower on huge wooden wheels, its chains held a ramp that could lead troops onto even the highest rubble pile.

It began moving up the road, its wheels grinding and squeaking.

From somewhere under the siege engine's base came the bellowing of oxen, the lashing of whips, the rhythmic chanting of hidden slaves as they pulled.

Slowly, the war machine inched up the hill. Behind it followed a seemingly endless column of soldiers. But the Deamhan Lord had so many troops, he wouldn't need half what he'd brought to take the upper city.

By the speed with which the trebuchets were breaking down the wall and the siege engine was climbing, Tristan guessed they'd be inside the fort before sunset.

He'd arrived only in time to see the fall of Ewhain Macha.

Once the Deamhan Lord entered the fort, he'd go straight for the Tower. His goal would be to destroy it. Indeed, more than one centuria marched behind the siege engine with nothing but sledgehammers, iron prybars, and chains. Entire units whose sole purpose was the Tower's destruction.

Once the Tower lay in ruins, even with the Scepter, how could Tristan ever stop the Deamhan Lord?

He must place the Scepter within its cradle on top. Only then, he'd been told, would it release its full power. Now the Deamhan Lord had grown so strong, all of Elyon's devices and plans would be needed to defeat him—

The Scepter, the Augury, and the Tower, all in combination.

He must enter the Tower before it fell.

After riding down the slope, he entered the outskirts of the ruined lower city. Everywhere throughout the rubble, the enemy had set up tents. Now he realized much of the smoke still rising from the lower town came from the campfires. Men gathered in full armor and stood around the fires waiting for the siege engine to do its work.

Another round of stones crashed into the upper walls. Debris clattered down the slopes.

Even wearing his Ferachtir uniform, he couldn't follow behind the enemy. The Deamhan Lord would still get there before him and block entry into the Tower.

Above all else, he feared to face the Deamhan Lord. He could never win such a fight. Who on Erde could?

Then he remembered the secret tunnel Maeve had shown them. But among all this debris, could he still find it? Few, if any, buildings stood intact.

Skirting far around the enemy tents, he headed for the part of town where he guessed it should be. Maeve had said it was a blacksmith's shop, but not where it was.

When he found the city quarter opposite the palace, he began a lane-by-lane search. But nothing was recognizable. Debris cluttered every street. Sometimes, he couldn't even find the streets, so clogged with rubble were they.

There—a wooden sign lying half-hidden under bricks, bearing a hammer. Kneeling, he kicked rubble and dirt aside and revealed, in fading paint, an anvil, hammer, and bellows. Once, this had been a smithy. But was it the right smithy?

He climbed over the rubble pile toward what must have been an alley. Burnt timbers testified that, here, a shed had once stood. He scraped away ashes and found the edge of an iron door. Lifting a blackened timber to the side, he freed the opening. His hands scraped away more ashes. Aye, this was the door he sought.

He lifted it high, its hinges squeaking and complaining.

"Ho, there!" came a voice from behind. "What have you found?"

He whirled. Fifty feet away, a Ferachtir patrol—five men armed with swords—was heading his way. He glanced down at steps descending into darkness then back at the approaching soldiers. Should he fight them here, or try to escape in the tunnel? But he mustn't show the enemy a secret way into the palace. He let the metal doors slam shut.

"I say, what have you discovered, soldier?" asked a fat, white-haired captain.

"Naught of interest. Probably a wine cellar."

"Naught of interest?" The captain poked a lanky youth in the side. "A private stash of wine, and you say 'tis of no interest?"

Tristan shrugged. He let his hand slip to his sword hilt.

Grinning and jesting, the five soldiers gathered beside him and looked down at the iron door.

"And who are you and what unit do you hail from, that you take so little interest in such booty?" The portly captain put hands on hips and regarded him warily.

"Nicu Tăranu, fifteenth centuria, ninth legion, southern army." He beat his fist against his chest in salute. For now, he'd continue his former ruse.

The captain returned a bored salute then knelt to the iron doors. "Must be some great treasure below to have it locked behind these, hey?" He shot a smile at his companions.

A middle-aged man in a tattered tunic knelt, helped the captain squeak open the doors, and peered down. "After you," said the soldier to his captain.

The captain nodded and lowered his considerable bulk onto the first step. The others followed. Tristan brought up the rear, descending into a cold, dank cellar.

At the bottom, someone found torches and lit two.

The tunnel led west, of course, and the group followed. But it quickly ended in stacks of barrels forming a narrow aisle.

"Ah, this is it," said the captain. With an ear close to the oak, he rolled one barrel on its side. The sloshing of liquid within brought a smile to his lips.

Tristan had guessed well that the blacksmith might also have stored wine here. The captain pulled out a cork near the bottom, and a stream of wine poured out. Lifting the barrel on top of another, he lowered his head under the stream. When he emerged from a long swill, he said, "Good stuff, this."

Tristan lifted his gaze to the dark recesses beyond. The aisle between barrels turned a corner. Did the passage continue from there? If so, he mustn't let these men find it.

Then the others began pushing and shoving their captain aside as they, too, fought for the stream. Someone broke into another barrel, and they began drinking from it.

The passage shuddered as yet another round of stones smashed into the city walls above. One of the top barrels fell, revealing the passage beyond.

"What have we here?" asked one of the soldiers. "The way goes on."

Tristan backed up. His blade left its sheath, echoing in the tunnel.

"What are you doing, soldier?" The captain stood, staring at him, his face wet with wine.

"Defending my country."

The soldiers stopped drinking from the barrels and stared at him. Untended, wine splashed onto the floor.

"He's a spy!" yelled the captain. "Get him!"

Blades left their sheaths.

The man in the ripped tunic struck his short sword toward Tristan's midsection.

Tristan knocked the blade aside, exchanged several blows with him, and left him dead on the stone.

Two others, including the lanky youth, now rushed him, swiping recklessly. He easily parried, blocked, and returned quick strokes that soon took both their lives.

Cursing, the captain drew his sword to strike a blow, but his weapon hit the rock ceiling. Tristan stabbed him in the abdomen, and he, too, fell.

The last man, a hulking soldier with a scarred face, drove his blade toward Tristan's ribs. Tristan knocked it aside. But no sooner had he counterattacked than the man expertly blocked blow after blow. This soldier was good, far better than any opponent he'd recently fought.

Tristan exchanged strike after strike, their blades ringing loudly in the passage. Finally, he saw an opening and knocked the weapon from the soldier's hands. But before Tristan could strike, the man whirled and ran back toward the opening.

He'd soon bring others.

The ground shook again as stone projectiles brought down more of the city wall. A few chinks of stone dropped from the ceiling.

Behind the stack, the tunnel led away into darkness. But barring the way was a locked iron gate.

Taking his picks from his knapsack, he positioned them within the mechanism until he heard the clicks announcing he'd opened it.

He pushed through, clanged the door shut, and entered the tunnel.

His torch flickered, his feet echoed, and water dripped from above. Rats scurried ahead as he began an upward climb under the fortress walls.

A shower of pebbles fell, and the passage rumbled as yet another round of boulders slammed into the upper city walls.

His feet sloshed through a low spot. Then a long set of stone steps climbed upward. The torch briefly burned away cobwebs.

The regular rhythm of the trebuchets' missiles slamming into the walls stopped. From above now came only silence. Had the siege engine reached the walls?

At the top of the stairs, he followed a straight tunnel until, once again, he found himself at another set of steps. Here, the ring of keys still hung on its hook at the bottom of the stairs leading up to the king's black-smith shop. But before he emerged on friendly ground, he undressed and discarded the Ferachtir garb. After donning his own clothes, he began to climb.

The stone steps ended at wooden doors. Pushing these aside, he emerged in the smithy's shed. From the lane beyond came desperate shouting, the clashing of swords, the echoing of feet on stone.

He raced out of the alley onto a main street—and into total chaos.

Enemy soldiers were pouring through the lanes, engaging the Ériu in hand-to-hand combat.

The walls had been breached.

CHAPTER 52

THE TOWER

Racing as fast as his feet would carry him, Tristan dodged enemy troops fighting Ériu's farmers, merchants, herdsmen, and its few professional soldiers. He spun around a corner onto a main street leading past the palace. Ahead, behind a row of buildings, stood the Tower.

Flanked by dozens of warriors with pikes, swords, and axes, the Deamhan Lord strode down the center of the main thoroughfare. Following him were the first of many centuria bearing instruments of demolition.

Around the Deamhan Lord swirled a cloud of darkness. From him issued invisible tendrils of fear, crossing the distance, worming their way into Tristan's chest. Like a caged, frightened animal, his heart thumped wildly against his ribs.

He drew his sword and raced along the street's perimeter. A Drochtar axman swung at his head, and he ducked. An enemy pikeman thrust a long serrated blade at him, but his sword knocked it aside.

He kept running.

Stop, came a voice thick with a druid's word spell.

It had seen him.

You want to come back. Stop! Not only did he hear the voice—the Deamhan Lord's voice—but it echoed inside his head. Icy shivers ran along his shoulders, down his arms, and settled in the muscles of his legs. Somewhere deep within him, he wanted to obey, to stop running.

But nay, he must shake it off, keep on running. All of Erde depended on him.

The Tower was a hundred feet away. In the middle of the street now, Tristan looked back. The Deamhan Lord was close, but seemed unable to match his pace. Steadily, relentlessly, the lord of evil trotted behind.

Do not let him pass! the voice now focused on the men around it. Its timbre and the echo in Tristan's mind reverberated with dark energy. Bespelled, it carried an invisible power meant to override the will. Soldiers all over the street now began chasing after him.

Then a tall man wearing chain mail was running at his side—Machar!

"Did you get it?" He shot a glance at Tristan.

"Aye," Tristan managed between breaths.

Machar smiled and swung his sword at a soldier running in from the side. Their blades clashed once. But Machar didn't stop to finish the fight, and they ran on.

Only fifty feet ahead, the ancient Tower filled the sky. Already, two soldiers were attacking the base, swinging their hammers, chipping away at stones that had stood for millennia.

Two Sarkenian swordsmen already guarded the door.

Machar and Tristan fell upon them with all the fury of men trying to save their lives, their country, and their world.

But these turbaned warriors possessed far greater skill than any Tristan had yet encountered.

During his battle with the first soldier, Tristan found himself facing downhill. He caught a glimpse of the Deamhan Lord striding toward him. But the moment his eyes left his opponent, the Sarkenian's sword bit into his left arm.

Pulling back, he blocked the next thrust and plunged his blade into the Sarkenian's chest up to the hilt.

He sheathed his sword. His free arm went to the wound drenching his left arm with red.

Machar fought with abandon until a powerful stroke knocked his opponent's weapon across the cobbles. He, too, finished off his foe.

The Deamhan Lord was fifty feet away and closing.

Stop! *Step away from the Tower.* The words came with even more power than before, worming their way into his thoughts, echoing back and forth, tugging at his will.

Gripping the handle, Tristan yanked the door open. He entered the Tower of Dóchas.

Machar followed then dropped the bar over the door and stepped back.

Tristan ripped the knapsack from his back. He pulled out the Scepter, grasped it in his right hand.

Brilliant light flooded the floor, the steps, and shot up the tower. It pulsed with a thousand rainbow colors and filled him with hope that he would prevail.

Sitting on its pedestal, the Augury responded with its own throbbing glow. A beam of light shone between the two.

Tristan headed for the steps.

Pieces of the door exploded inward and flew across the floor. He caught a glimpse of the Deamhan Lord's spike-filled mace before it drew back outside.

"Run!" came Machar's hoarse shout. "I'll hold him off." He slipped to a position beside the door with his sword ready to strike.

Tristan's feet slapped on stone, hitting the first of the spiral steps.

Then the wooden door burst inward, sending a hundred splinters across the floor. Tristan looked down. Surrounded by an aura of darkness, the Deamhan Lord stepped through the gap.

Machar swung his blade in from the side, striking for the head.

Barely in time, the mace's chain blocked the stroke. But the sword nicked flesh, and a thin swath of red appeared on Faolukan's left cheek.

The Deamhan Lord brought his injured left hand up to the wound, touched it gingerly, and drew back fingers red with blood. He stared at them in disbelief.

Blood. The dark spirit had taken Faolukan's body. So, aye, it could bleed. Which meant it could die.

Then the Deamhan Lord saw the Augury glowing from its pedestal and the beam of light between the Augury and the Scepter, and he backed up a step. Pain wrinkled his brows.

Tristan climbed farther, his feet echoing on stone. When he heard the mace dragging across the floor, he glanced down again.

The Deamhan Lord swung his weapon.

Machar tried to block it with his sword, but the mace shattered the blade. He threw his broken weapon aside and backed up.

The mace swung again.

He tried to duck, but the spikes caught him on the shoulder. The blow sent him flying against the wall. Machar slumped, motionless, onto the floor.

The Deamhan Lord looked up, saw Tristan, and began climbing.

Breathing hard, Tristan raced up the steps. His wounded left arm now throbbed with pain, wetting his tunic. His heart struck his ribs as though it wanted to escape.

Stop! came the word spell again. *You do not want to go up there*! The words bounced around inside his head, brought confusion and doubt. He found himself wanting to go down. But he knew it was only a spell, and, knowing, he could resist it. He kept climbing.

On the lower part of the Tower, he was able to keep a twenty-foot distance from his pursuer. But on the final section, as the spiral stairs narrowed, he was breathing harder, his legs were poured with hot metal, and his arm was on fire. He imagined the Deamhan Lord's breath upon his neck, and he shot a glance behind. Nay, it was only his fear.

But with every yard he climbed, his adversary was gaining.

You are weak, came the voice. And he felt weak.

When Tristan finally burst from the Tower's staircase onto the top landing, the Deamhan Lord was right behind him. Tristan slammed the door and ran for the center. Fortunately, someone had already removed the round center stone and cleared away the gravel from the Scepter's receptacle—Cairbre's instructions?

The tip of a metal rod lay exposed. He grabbed it and pulled. It rose to a height of five feet. Tristan gripped it and twisted. It locked in position.

The Deamhan Lord burst onto the platform, swinging the mace in an arc.

Slowly, seven metal leaves descended from the rod.

Tristan ducked as the mace hurled toward his head. The spiked ball hit the metal rod and bounced off.

You must stop what you are doing, came the voice again, and it filled Tristan with dread, doubt, and fear. *Stop!* But did it now contain a hint of desperation?

Tristan's hands were wet with sweat, sticky with blood. He lifted the Scepter high. As a wind blows away fog, its light stripped away the darkness surrounding the Deamhan Lord. He faced the body of Faolukan, now the lord of the deamhans. "I am the Toghaí, chosen by Elyon, and named by him."

You are nothing. But when the Scepter's shining, golden light washed over him, his face scrunched in horror. The hand holding the mace lifted the weapon, but now, it trembled.

"In the name of all that is good and right and just, I banish you to the Underworld." Tristan jammed the Scepter into the holder and pushed down.

No, stop! came the words, echoing as if from a man at the bottom of a deep shaft.

The seven metal leaves snapped shut with a loud click.

From the base of the Tower—from the Augury?—a shaft of light shot through the floor stones, engulfed the Scepter, and blasted even to the cloud ceiling above. High in the clouds, it illuminated a golden circle—momentarily as bright as the sun—that expanded in all directions. Soon, it covered the entire sky.

What Tristan had experienced before when he'd held the Scepter now paled in comparison with what happened next.

A burst of light alive with colors beyond counting issued from the Scepter. Its brilliance spread out in ever-expanding, ever-pulsing rays, shooting to the horizon in all directions. With the light came a feeling of peace, joy, and a radiant hope that lifted weights from his feet, tingled with energy along his arms, warmed his legs, and settled deep into his chest. He wanted to sing, to shout for joy, to clap his hands. It was as if his entire body were smiling, laughing, rejoicing.

Like shadows before the sun, the darkness and evil that earlier pressed down upon his mind fled.

The Deamhan Lord gasped, clutched his breast, and staggered against the far railing. His face contorted in agony. He dropped the mace. It clattered over the stones.

For one moment, the Scepter's light narrowed to a single blinding ray. It focused in a circle encompassing the Deamhan Lord's chest.

And in that instant, like a puppet whose strings had been cut, Faolukan's body collapsed to the floor. Even as Tristan watched, the face that had cheated death for millennia cracked and dried up. The time Faolukan had stolen from the ages returned for its revenge to reclaim the theft. His skin shrank, shriveled, and dissolved into dust. His armor collapsed onto white bones, and even the bones crumbled to fine powder.

From the pile of clothing and armor rose a black cloud. Barely holding the shape of a man, it wavered. The vague outlines of its vaporous face writhed, twisted, and contorted with pain.

A long, drawn-out moan pierced the air. The man's shape elongated into a black gaseous stream. Then it flew over the edge of the Tower, out of sight.

Tristan ran to the railing.

The twisting black shadow dove straight for the bowels of Erde. It touched the cobbles, flew straight through, and was gone.

The Deamhan Lord had been banished to the Underworld.

From Tristan's high perch, he looked down upon soldiers, who, only moments before, had been locked in combat.

The púcas were morphing back into men. Their naked bodies lay curled up and twitching on the ground, their hands clutching their knees.

The Ferachtir, Drochtar, and Sarkenian soldiers, who had only recently fought with ensorcelled fierceness, stood motionless, the fight gone from them. Some looked at their weapons and threw them aside. Others stared up at the sun as if seeing it for the first time. He imagined they were waking from a dream, not knowing where they were, why they were there, or what they were to do next.

From all over the fortress, Ériu's soldiers sent up a great cry of victory. Men shouted and hugged their brothers in arms. Some even began to sing.

A bell tolled from the palace belfry.

The Scepter had returned to the Tower.

The Deamhan Lord was defeated.

A new age had begun.

CHAPTER 53

TRISTAN

Tristan's wound was bandaged, and a few days later, he and Caitir said their goodbyes to Ewan, Cairbre, Angus, and Machar. The Capulum warrior was nursing a broken arm and shoulder, but he, too, was recovering. Then the couple left for Hidden Pines.

When he rode into his village atop a warhorse, as Caitir followed on a speckled mare, he didn't know what to expect. He barely dismounted when villagers gathered around. "Welcome back, Tristan," they shouted. Garlands of flowers and baskets of sweet pastries they brought him. Everyone, it seemed, knew of his exploits, how Elyon had named him the Toghaí, and how the flaith of all the land now favored him.

Where before the villagers threw at him scorn and ridicule, they now showered him with praise and honor. He accepted their kind words as best he could, but he couldn't help wondering about their change of attitude. How sincere were these accolades? Did they only desire his favor because of the sudden influence he'd now acquired?

When he stepped through the door of the hut where he grew up, Aunt Brigid and Cousin Searlie hugged him with tears of happiness. And when he told them of his coming marriage to Caitir, their joy knew no bounds. He promised to start up the forge again, to be their protector and make his home here—his and Caitir's.

Because of the grand welcome he received, he realized he could now remain in Hidden Pines. No need now to travel to some remote village to escape the dishonor of his parents. All that was forgotten.

It was a new era—not only for Ériu, but for Tristan.

A month later, on a warm autumn day as golden leaves shimmered in the trees, he and Caitir were wed. It was the grandest affair Hidden Pines had ever seen, more like a holiday festival than a wedding, with folks arriving from leagues around dressed in their best.

Wearing a bandage around his shoulder and arm, Machar arrived on a white stallion.

But the news Machar brought was troubling.

"They've named Torradan mac Rodachan as regent," he confided in Tristan with a frown. "Tristan, we're in a crisis of succession. Connell had no heirs but Maeve. Torradan has a good heart. But the man's so old, he sometimes forgets even who I am. So I must help him rule until the council figures out what to do."

Tristan nodded and helped him down from his mount.

Machar had brought with him servants and a wagon loaded with mead, ale, honey, and wheat flour. Trailing the wagon were two dozen cattle for the feast. Women took the flour and began baking pastries. They roasted beef in great underground ovens, covered with leaves and then dirt. When they finally pulled the meat from the ground, it was the most succulent Tristan had ever tasted.

Soon after Machar arrived, Ewan, Cairbre, Angus, Keenala, and Thallinor rode in. No wedding in Hidden Pines had ever seen such a gathering of high flaith and foreign dignitaries.

Cairbre performed the ceremony.

Tristan stood with his bride before a crowd said to have numbered over two thousand.

"You are blood of my blood, bone of my bone," Tristan said to Caitir. "I give you my body, that we two might be one. I give you my spirit, till our life shall be done. By the power of Elyon from heaven, may you love me. As the sun follows its course, may you follow me. As light to the eye, as bread to the hungry, as joy to the heart, may your presence be with me. Oh, one that I love, till death parts us asunder."

When Caitir, with tears in her eyes, repeated the vows, he thought his heart would burst with joy. And when they kissed and stood before the assembled throng, such a shout went up, it was said folks heard it three villages away, though surely they must have exaggerated.

The flutes, harps, and bodhráns played long into the evening. Folks danced with abandon, stomping their feet in time to the music, kicking their legs high. Tristan and Caitir danced until their buskins nearly wore out.

For five days did the celebration go on.

And when the last guest left, the villagers cleaned up the aftermath.

He and Caitir built a new home beside Cowan's old hut and moved in. Tristan reopened the smithy, and business was good. Everyone for miles around wanted their horses shod, their plows repaired, their knives made by the savior of Ériu.

And from far beyond Hidden Pines, news filtered back that the world itself had changed for the better.

Old grudges were being dropped. Folks everywhere seemed happier, more content with their lot. The profits of merchants throughout Ulster increased. The harvest that fall was the best in years. And the pall of doom that hovered over the land lifted.

But life back in the village was not what he imagined it would be. The journey had changed him. And as fall shivered into winter, he began to wonder if this was what Elyon had in store for the rest of his life. When everyone around him seemed to find new reasons each day to rejoice, Tristan became unsettled, restless, discontent.

Something was missing. He had something yet to do. But he knew not what.

Caitir, too, felt the unease. And often they'd look at each other, and one would ask the other, "Is this really what we were meant to do?"

SPRING CAME. AND ONE BRIGHT morning, as flowers poked through the ground, the chaffinches sang, and new leaf burst from the trees, Tristan was working in his forge. He hammered on a red-hot sword, dunked the blade into the trough, and let it hiss.

But as he pulled it out, dripping and steaming, Ewan appeared under the far awning.

Tristan dropped his work, wiped his hands on his leather apron, and ran to his friend. They hugged and beat each other on the back.

"My lord," said Ewan, "glad I am to see you again. Glad, indeed."

"And I, you. But what are you doing here? I thought you now served my lord Machar?"

"I do, and that is why I'm here." Ewan grinned. "I've orders to bring you with me at once to Ewhain Macha, you and Caitir and your family."

"What's this about?"

"I'm pledged not to say."

Frowning, Tristan did as requested. He, Caitir, Aunt Brigid, and Searlie gathered clothes and food for travel. He retrieved their two horses from the village pen, and they followed Ewan.

Even though the trip was urgent, the former squire took the longer route, passing by the plain where the great battle had been fought. By now, all the dead had been buried.

The trail led them beside the River Liffey and through the forest. Along the way, new villages were being rebuilt where the old ones had burned down.

On the ride, Ewan kept silent about the purpose of his mission, only insisting it was important, if not urgent, that Tristan arrive before week's end.

The mystery surrounding his request only deepened.

As they topped the ridge overlooking the city, much of the rubble and burnt timbers had been removed. Every day, new houses of stone were rising from the ashes.

The sun was already setting as they rode into the lower city, climbed the slope, and crossed a new drawbridge into the fort. Ewan led them straight to the palace where a young page wearing a bright-striped tunic ran to greet them.

"I regret to inform your lords," said the youth, "that all is not yet in readiness. Tonight, we have no rooms in the palace, only in Lord Cormag's guesthouse on the other side of the fort."

"What!" Ewan's voice rose. "This is not the welcome we'd planned."

"I . . . I'm terribly sorry. Under the circumstances, Lord Machar is doing his best. Tomorrow, the situation will certainly change for the better. 'Tis what I'm told."

"Can I speak to Lord Machar?" asked Ewan.

"At the moment, he's extremely busy. Tomorrow would be better."

Ewan faced his charges, opened his hands in apology, and shook his head. "Appears we must wait till the morrow."

"Can you tell me why we're here?" asked Tristan. He wondered now if they were to be witnesses to some grand event and his presence here was but an afterthought. Was that why all the guest rooms in the palace were full? All thirty of them?

Ewan shrugged and led them to the small stone house Lord Cormag had built. Legend had it that King Cormag, now long dead, had built it for visiting lords of Connacht with whom he did not get along, whose presence he wanted to keep as far from the palace as possible.

At the far end of the upper fortress, they found rooms, were given supper by maids-in-waiting, and slept.

The next morning, Ewan ushered only Tristan and Caitir back to the palace. The squire led them through the front door, straight to the throne room. When he pushed open the high, rounded doors, Tristan gasped at the august group of men and women assembled around a long table. He recognized Lords Angus of Leinster, Iùrnan of Munster, Blàthan from Meath, and Gabhran from Connacht. The elderly man nodding in his chair must be Torradan mac Rodachan, the current regent whom Machar was helping to rule. All the kings of the provinces were here. Also at the table was Cairbre, smiling in Tristan's direction.

Keenala, High Reginalia of Glenmallen, sat off to the side.

Sitting against the far wall, alone in the shadows, was an old woman, her skin wrinkled, her hair white with age. She bent over her chair, and when she lifted a hand to scratch her face, it shook. Out of everyone present, she seemed woefully out of place. Was she a servant of some sort? Then why wasn't she standing, waiting for orders?

"Welcome, Tristan mac Torn." Machar stood and met him with an open hand. "I'm terribly sorry about the lack of accommodations yesterday. We've been preparing rooms for so many, last night we had no suitable rooms for you and your family."

Tristan nodded. "I've slept in worse places."

Machar smiled. Well did he know the places they'd slept on their journey together. "We've brought you here because of something that's recently come to light, something of great importance to the kingdom. Will you and Caitir please sit?"

When Machar motioned to chairs at the table's end, Tristan and Caitir sat.

Machar faced the old scholar. "Cairbre, I turn this over to you."

Cairbre cleared his throat. "Most of you present today know nothing of what I am about to reveal. Nor do the flaith of the five kingdoms now gathered at the palace. And when I tell you, I'm certain it will shock everyone."

The kings of the four provinces frowned, shifted in their seats, and narrowed their eyes. Lord Torradan of Ulster only yawned.

"At least for me, a haze of mystery has always surrounded the birth of Prince Neil and the death of Mordag, King Connell's sister. The story never quite made sense. And so, when we were faced with naming Lord Torradan as temporary regent, the Capulum devoted all its resources to searching for a proper heir."

Tristan glanced around the room at the puzzled faces. What could this possibly have to do with him?

"When Prince Neil was born," continued Cairbre, "his mother died in childbirth. But for some reason, Fionna, the midwife, abandoned the newborn prince on the queen's deathbed and vanished from sight, never to be seen again."

"Aye," said Angus, "we all ken that."

A few pounded their fists on the table in agreement.

Cairbre cleared his throat. "The story then circulated that Neil's aunt Mordag hid herself outside the birthing room. When the midwife left the room, Mordag saw the babe alone. Then she stole the child and took it into the forest. The servants saw her leave.

"But King Connell returned early from his hunting expedition. When the servants told him his sister had stolen the babe, he pursued her. He soon caught up with her, and they argued. She told him that her son, not his, deserved to be on the throne and that she'd planned to kill the child. Filled with anger, the king slew her there in the forest. And he returned his son, Neil, to the palace.

"And that's the story everyone believed—until now." Cairbre eyes found the far end of the room, and he raised his voice. "'Tis time, madam, for you to come and take a seat."

The old woman rose, walked unsteadily to the empty chair beside Cairbre, and sat.

The kings of the provinces exchanged puzzled glances, frowning at this woman of obviously low birth.

"Now tell us your name and who you are." Cairbre's expression was solemn.

"My name is Fionna." Her voice wavered. "And I was the midwife who helped birth the queen's two babes on that terrible night."

The men at the table gasped and stared at the woman. Iùrnan of Munster rose from his seat. "What babes?" he asked. "The queen had only one son."

"Nay." Cairbre waved him back into his chair. "The queen had two." He nodded to Fionna. "Tell your story."

"Me lords, the queen had twins. And when I returns to the birthing room from getting some clean rags, I hears Mordag leaning over the queen and talking to her. She smiles and says she's going to kill her children, both of them. Then Mordag takes a pillow, puts it over the queen's face, and suffocates her. And I's standing right behind her the whole time."

More startled expressions and murmuring from around the table. Cairbre held up a hand for quiet.

"But Mordag discovers I's been there whilst she did her murdering. So she threatens me. She warns me that, lest I does as told, I's to be blamed for everything. And if I's ever to speak a word of what *we's* about to do—*we*, she says!—her guards would make an end to me life, right quick. And no one would ever know or care." Frightened eyes scanned the others at the table, her face twisted with worry. "Me lords, I was only a young lass and scared out of me wits." She wrung her hands, shook her head. "What else could I do?"

"Do go on, Fionna," said Cairbre, his voice soft.

"So Mordag takes one child and was going to take the boy far into the woods and feed him to the wolves. I was to take the other child to a stream, drown it, and then bury it. She even gives me a handful of coins—a pittance for what she asked of me.

"But the moment I leaves the palace by the servant's door—no one looks twice at a servant carrying a bundle—I changes me mind. I fears to drown a babe, especially a prince, I does. But I also fears to cross Mordag.

"So I goes to me neighbor, a man by the name of Torn. A while back, he marries this harlot, you see, and he tries to make a decent woman of her. She gives up the streets, she does, and the two were trying to make a life together. But they couldna have children. So I goes to him and sells him the child for twenty crowns. 'Tis all he has in the world, he says, and he'll be going deep in debt to get back what he spent, but he and his harlot are desperate for a babe. So I tells him I stole the child, and he must keep the secret till his death. And so I sells him the babe. And ever since, I's been living in the hills of Connacht, scared someone will find out what I done."

"You forgot to mention their names," said Cairbre.

"Ah, that I did. When the two babes were birthed, the queen was as surprised as I that two comes out. If the babe was a boy, she and Connell planned to name the child Neil. But when she saw the second babe, she told me his name was to be Tristan. Aye, and that's what I told Torn. The babe's name was Tristan."

"Thank you, Fionna. You are dismissed."

She rose, bowed several times, and shuffled out the door.

The kings around the table were speechless. Their glances kept going to Tristan.

Tristan's heart raced, and he was breathing fast. How could this be true? How could he be king over all these high flaith?

"Thank you, Cairbre." Machar slapped both hands on the table. He looked at each of the rulers of the four provinces. "My lords, our search for an heir is complete. For the man sitting at the end of the table is not Tristan mac Torn. He is Tristan mac Connell, the rightful heir to the throne of Ériu."

Angus raised his arms to the ceiling. "Imagine it—a king who is also the Toghaí!"

"We couldna have a better choice," said Blàthan.

"I agree," added Gabhran.

And so they all stood and bowed before Tristan.

But he could only gape in wonder at what was happening. He could find no words to speak.

Caitir nudged him in the side. "What does that make me?" she whispered.

Machar grinned. "And, of course, this makes Caitir nic Cathal our queen."

"And a fine pair they make," said Cairbre.

A wide smile lifting his mustache, Angus turned to Machar and Cairbre. "So this is why you've gathered every high flaith from across the land? You've been planning a coronation all along?"

Machar nodded. "We knew it must come soon. But we needed your agreement before proceeding. Thus the secret meeting. And it appears your agreement is unanimous." He faced Tristan. "What say you, my lord Tristan. Will you accept the honor?"

Tristan rose from his seat and bowed before the lords. "Aye, my lords. I will accept. And I thank you for your trust in me." He raised his glance to the ceiling. "And I thank you, Lord Elyon, that your light shines once again over Ériu and the lands of Ereb. May you guide me well."

Cairbre closed his eyes and whispered, "We made the right choice."

THUS IT WAS THAT, THREE days after Tristan arrived in Ewhain Macha, yet another celebration began. In the open square before the palace, before a crowd numbering thousands, Machar lowered the golden torcs onto the necks of Tristan mac Connell and Caitir nic Cathal. There followed two weeks of feasting, games of skill, dancing, music, and revelry. It was the grandest affair anyone could remember.

The common folk of Ériu were more than pleased that one who had lived all his life as one of their own now ruled the land. And Caitir herself was not even flaith. The nobility were happy that the Toghaí, the one who really did fulfill all the prophecies, now sat on the throne.

King Tristan ruled with wisdom, mercy, compassion, and strength. Most important of all, he brought back the worship of Elyon, he who created the worlds.

With only Ewan to accompany him, King Tristan often rode out into the villages to see for himself how the people fared. And after he had melted down the gold throne that Connell made, he declared a tax holiday for an entire year.

Queen Caitir sat beside him, shared his bed, and, in time, bore him two sons and three daughters. And the sound of their running feet filled the palace.

Thus did the Scepter in the Tower of Dóchas spread peace, prosperity, and happiness throughout the land.

And it blessed not only Tristan's rule in Ewhain Macha. It blessed all of Erde.

EPILOGUE

The ship's hull scraped against the wharf's pilings. Above, seagulls cried and circled. But Tristan couldn't take his eyes off the many siòg traveling up and down the celestial beam of light on the hillside. In and out of a nomad's cowhide tent, they floated, accompanied by music of such beauty, he wanted to jump and sing and shout for joy. It was as if Neavh itself had come to Erde, here in this village of poor fishermen's huts on the coast.

Beside him, Queen Caitir's eyes widened with wonder. She glanced at him, held his hand, and stared again at the scene. Above, the cloud of heavenly birds that had led them for so long hovered with sparkling brilliance.

Ten years had passed since he'd been crowned Ard Righ, High King of Ériu, ten years since the visions had stopped. For ten years the Augury had lain secure in the Tower's base, with the Scepter shining out over the people of Erde. With peace and prosperity spreading like a sunrise across the world, there had been no need of visions.

But then, two months ago, the visions began again, visions that brought him here.

For the last five weeks, he and his entourage had followed the heavenly birds through a storm on the Sea of Albion and down the rugged coast of Armorica. Off Esperandula, they outran pirates, finally sailing the warm waters of the Golden Sea. Now their ship docked at this remote Etruscan port. Ahead flew the flock of birds with their delicate beaks, brilliant plumage, and elegant wings, showing the way. But never once on the journey did they sing.

With him, he brought the Scepter, the Augury, and a strongbox full of gold. His council strongly objected to removing the Scepter and

Augury, tried to prevent him from leaving with the objects, but Machar had overruled them. Machar insisted that, if Elyon's visions drew the king, then the council must acquiesce. No one was happy about what he did. But then they hadn't seen the visions he had.

Beside him stood Neil mac Tristan, their oldest. A lad of nine, with tawny hair, a slight physique, and an inquisitive mind, he begged relentlessly to be taken along. And his father could not say nay. "'Tis a wonder to behold, is it not, Father?" The lad's gaze was fixed on the slope.

"Aye, Neil. 'Tis that."

Sailors roped the ship to the dock, and they disembarked. The jetty's planks creaked as Tristan himself bore the Scepter and the Augury down their length. Behind him, Ewan carried the box of gold. Queen Caitir and young Prince Neil brought up the rear.

At wharf's end, they mounted stone steps cut into the hillside. In all directions, rows of green vineyards stretched across the slope. Seagulls circled the jetty. But as he climbed, the ethereal music from the siòg drowned out their cries. By the time he'd reached the middle of the slope, he was sweating, breathing heavily from the climb. But he barely noticed.

A woman dressed in a gown of royal purple stepped before him. He gasped and bowed.

"Uta, queen of the Pruss, ruler of Beilzig City—what a surprise!"

"We're all so grateful to you, Lord Tristan, for what you did." She, too, bowed. "There is peace once again across Ereb and between the Pruss and the Naz."

He smiled, took her hand, and kissed it.

As he rose, another woman appeared suddenly beside Uta—a slight woman with black eye sockets and golden skin, one bearing an ageless beauty. He raised his forearm in greeting, and Queen Keenala, High Reginalia of Glenmallen, returned the gesture. "How goes it in Glenmallen, my lady? I hear you've restored your valley to its former beauty."

"It goes well, Lord Tristan. We've much left to do, but in the last nine years, we've made good progress."

"Everyone seems to be here. Have you seen Zalán?"

A frown crossed her lips. "Ah, Zalán. To honor the child, he sent a messenger in his stead. But the man has come and gone. Did you know that, when we returned to Glenmallen, Zalán moved back to his old valley, but without the sleeping spell? He became mortal, Tristan. Sudden old age prevented him from attending."

Tristan nodded.

"But his messenger told me to greet you in the wizard's name."

"That was nice of him." Tristan smiled.

"Father." Young Neil tugged at his sleeve. He pointed ahead, toward the cloud shining brightly on the weatherworn tent.

Tristan, Neil, and Caitir crossed the last yards to a large canvas whose flaps were tied open. It was the tent of nomads, set up inside a corral, apparently the only open space given them. Nearby, a few goats and sheep chewed hay.

A young woman sat on a ragged carpet holding an emerald-bedecked jar of spice. Her long flaxen hair fell in curls over her shoulders. A tall, bearded man, handsome and young, knelt beside her, held her hand, and, whispering something in her ear, smiled.

Before them in the tent's center lay a babe whose face shone with an ethereal light. No sound from him came. It was to him that the siòg flew from above. One after another, they landed inside the tent before him, approached on bended knees, touched their foreheads to the ground, and departed.

A feeling came upon Tristan that this child would change the world. Upon this child lay the hope for all mankind, for all the races of Erde. But it would come only after agony, struggle, and rejection.

Feeling as if the gifts he bore were unworthy, he stepped forward.

But one of the siòg appeared suddenly before him, blocking the way.

Malavhìn!

"Greetings, Lord Tristan, Ard Righ of Ériu." He smelled sweet mountain snowbells and a wash of crisp, clear air. "I welcome you to the birth of Kyrios."

"Kyrios?"

"Aye, the one and only Son of Elyon come to Erde to live as a man. And he will take all the sins of Erde upon himself."

"I do not understand."

"Someday, you will." As her eyes focused on what he'd brought, they twinkled. "Your heart is good, Tristan mac Connell, but it is not yet time to give him the Scepter. Or the Augury. Someday, he will come for them. But not today."

He tightened his hold on his gifts, and disappointment must have crossed his face, for she smiled. "Your gift of gold is more than enough."

"Thank you, Malavhìn."

She nodded.

"But I have a question that's been bothering me for some time."

She raised her eyebrows.

"Why did Elyon not tell me I was born of Connell, and that all along, I was really the Toghaî?"

"Because, Tristan"—she began to rise into the air—"Elyon wanted you to believe in him, to trust only in him. He did not want you to put your trust only in prophecy."

She waved him toward the child. Then she flew toward the entrance and joined the rising column of light with the other siòg.

Tristan took the box of gold from Ewan, inched toward the child who would change the world, and knelt.

OTHER BOOKS
BY MARK E. FISHER

The Scepter and Tower High-Fantasy Trilogy from Extraordinary Tales Publishing:

- ❖ Book One: *Quest For the Scepter*
- ❖ Book Two: *Into The Druid's Lair*
- ❖ Book Three: *Return To The Tower*

Historical Fiction from Lighthouse Publishing of the Carolinas, Heritage Beacon Imprint:

- ❖ *The Bonfires Of Beltane*
- ❖ *The Medallion*

To learn more about Mark's books, please visit:
www.MarkFisherAuthor.com

PLACES AND THINGS

❖ Albion—The great island to the east of Ériu (Similar to Britain).

❖ Amridmor—The largest city and oasis in the desolate Ferachtir wastes.

❖ Ard Cúl Dín—[Ard Cool DEEN] The fortress town once hidden in the Blue Mountains west of the Waldreich. Faolukan's forces destroyed it when its magic veil was broken. It was once described as the last refuge of the Capulum.

❖ Argyn—A nomadic people of the Romely Plains, mortal enemies of the Deamhan Lord.

❖ Armorica—A country of northwestern Ereb (similar to northern France).

❖ Áth Cliath—[ATH Clee-ah] Main port town of Ériu.

❖ Battle of Two Rivers—An ancient battle at the intersection of two rivers in Ériu—the River Liffey and the Blackwater—in which the forces of Faolukan defeated the armies of Ériu and began Erde's long Dark Age.

❖ Beltane—A Celtic holiday celebrated on May 1, midway through the spring season, it marks the beginning of summer. Fires are lit on hilltops, and the spirits of the Otherworld come close to this world.

❖ Bothach—[BO-hak] The lowest group on the Celtic class system with no property rights: criminals, unskilled laborers, and indebted farmers.

❖ Bredehaven—A port on the coast where the River Seine dumps into the Sea of Albion.

❖ Burgundia—A country of southeastern Ereb (southern France).

❖ Cairt Mhór—The Great Charter, wherein the five realms of Ériu united as one under the Alliance of Kingdoms. The charter also changed the means of selecting their high king or queen. When the process of electing a high king from the realms' high flaith became so fraught with bribery, fraud, and abuse, they forever bequeathed the office to the Conn royal family of Ulster.

❖ Capulum—A secret organization of scholars, warriors, and priests, who for millennia had been dedicated to the preservation of ancient knowledge and the recovery of the lost gifts of Elyon.

❖ Cathair Duvh—[CA-hair Dove] The remote capital of Drochtar and the Deamhan Lord's base, lying in a mountain valley of Drochcarn, the mountain that never sleeps.

❖ Crimson Oil—A potion that heals nearly all injury and sickness, coming only from the siòg.

❖ Crom Mord—The dread idol inside which the Deamhan Lord now resides.

❖ Cthyllin Ice Giants—A race of giants living in the far northeast, who subsist on mammoths and aurochs.

❖ Curragh—[COOR-ah] An ancient Irish boat, constructed of a wooden rib frame covered with hides and tarred. From six to seventy feet long, with one to possibly three sails.

❖ Deamhan—When Elyon cursed the rebel siòg under Faolan the Traitor (now the Deamhan Lord) and banished them from Neavh, they became Deamhan, incorporeal demon spirits who inhabited stone or wooden idols, or possessed foul beasts.

❖ Drijvendby—[Dry-vend-by] The country and city of the "island" region of northern Ereb, protected by the Great Sea Wall.

❖ Drochtar—Far eastern land of barren, windswept, volcanic plains, now living under the cloud of the Deamhan Lord's rule.

❖ Drochcarn—The mountain of shadows in Drochtar, "the mountain that never sleeps", whose mountain valley holds Cathair Duvh.

- ❖ Eladrin—A race of small, human-like beings, marked by black eyelids and wide eyes who are masters of illusion. Now they exist only in the enclaves of Glenmallen and Glenriding.
- ❖ Elbakken—A race derived from the eladrin who once lived under the northern Sfarsit Mountains. Hunted nearly to extinction by Faolukan, only a remnant survives.
- ❖ Elyon—God.
- ❖ Ewhain Macha—[Ewan MA-ha] The largest town of Ulster and ancient capital of Ériu.
- ❖ Erde—The world containing the continent of Ereb and the mainland continent of Erde, with a vague resemblance to Europe.
- ❖ Ériu—[AYR-yoo] A Celtic country similar to ancient Ireland.
- ❖ Etrucsa—A country of south-central Ereb (similar to Italy).
- ❖ Fell Bogs—A stretch of swamp and mire that once held the great nation and city of Überhort. During the Great Upheaval, the land sank, and the rivers flowed in, creating the bogs.
- ❖ Feighn—(original Irish: fine) An extended Celtic family unit that all lives in a single roundhouse.
- ❖ Flaith—The highest Celtic social class; the nobility.
- ❖ Glenmallen—Hidden valley of the eladrin in the southern Blue Mountains.
- ❖ Glenriding—The eladrins' second enclave in the Nordmark Range, east of the Plains of Romely.
- ❖ Great Bridge, The—A massive stone bridge that's the only way to cross the impassable River Pruwyn into Conachtir. Heavily guarded by the Black Guard of Samotun.
- ❖ Gol Oras—The main town of the Romely plains.
- ❖ Great Lands, The—Another name for the continent of Ereb, vaguely similar to earth's Europe.
- ❖ Great Purge, The—The seventy-five-year period during which the Deamhan Lord's servant, Faolukan, sent his armies to ravage the world of Erde, pillaging, raping, and killing.
- ❖ Heyerrah Bosch—The Good Tower that Patrick built in Sarkenos to imprison the Deamhan Lord and Faolukan.

❖ Hidden Pines—Tristan's small village in Ulster northwest of Áth Cliath.

❖ Kobold—Short, blue-skinned, annoying, and insulting, this small creature lives alone, likes gold, silver, and gems, and spends its days mining underground or admiring its hoarded treasure.

❖ League—A distance of about three miles.

❖ Lehbrágan—(Orig. leipreachán, or leithbrágan) Sprites, leprechauns, or "the little people". In this story, the lehbrágan is a race that separated from the sióg and lost its spiritual gifts. Standing only four foot high, the men are bearded. They work as shoemakers, leatherworkers, or clothiers, and are reputedly hoarders of gold and silver. They wear red or green. Descended from the Tuatha Dé Danann, they once lived underground.

❖ Lost Era, The—The two-thousand-year period after the Scepter and Elyon's second gifts were stolen during which Erde entered a dark age and civilization declined.

❖ Lugdunum—Capital of Burgundia, seat of King Gundovald. (The ancient name for Lyon, France.)

❖ Malavhìn—The sióg whom the Roamers captured and the only source of the crimson oil.

❖ Manannán mac Lir—[ma-NA-nan mac lir] Celtic sea deity and also ruler of the Underworld.

❖ Mam Giorag—The heavily guarded pass in the southern Sfarsit Mountains, reputedly the only way to cross into Drochtar.

❖ Naz—The secretive forest people of the Waldreich.

❖ Neavh—Heaven.

❖ Otherworld—The realm of spirits and deamhans.

❖ Pneuma, The—The Spirit of God.

❖ Primejdie—A Ferachtir game of high stakes, played with knives or spears, where the players are blindfolded. After betting on their chosen square, they throw their weapon, and if they hit it, they win. But if they hit the square of jeopardy, they lose everything brought to the game. For the loser, the stakes sometimes ratchet up, becoming a matter of life or death.

- ❖ Pruss—A river and forest people who are archenemies of the Naz. Their capital and main city is Beilzig, an island in the River Grauwin directly above Golob's Maw, the great falls.
- ❖ Pruwyn—The raging, impassable river blocking the southern entrance to Conachtir from Romely, on whose banks the Black Guard of Samotun constantly patrols.
- ❖ Púca—A shapeshifter. In Irish mythology, a type of fairy that could change into terrifying shapes. In this story, they are tools of the Deamhan Lord and Faolukan.
- ❖ Roamers (also called the Seachranach [Shach-rah-nach])—A wandering tribe of gypsy-like refugees from Erdelstan who have settled in Ériu.
- ❖ Roundhouse—A communal structure, round and from twenty to forty feet in diameter, built of a wicker frame covered on the outside with thatch and on the inside with furs.
- ❖ Samhain—Ancestor of our modern Halloween, this is celebrated at the end of October. It marks the end of the harvest and the beginning of winter. Samhain and Beltane are the two times of the year when the spirits of the Otherworld come closest to this world.
- ❖ Saxia—The country that once occupied the Fell Bogs, before the Great Upheaval.
- ❖ Schwarzburg—A kingdom and castle hidden deep in the Waldreich where Tristan, masquerading as Prince Neil, stole the Scepter from Thrag, the barghest that Faolukan had imprisoned in an underground maze.
- ❖ Seachranach—see "Roamers".
- ❖ Sfarsit Mountains—The high mountain chain that blocks the way into Drochtar.
- ❖ Shuderrah Bosch—The Deamhan Lord's Dark Tower near Samotun where he ruled Sarkenos.
- ❖ Siòg—[Shee-og] Orig. Irish: Sìobhrag—A race of fairy creatures, similar to angels, who serve Elyon.
- ❖ Thrag—A barghest in Faolukan's service, in whose presence all light dims and blackens. Some say he's like a bear or dog walking

on hind legs, but no one has ever seen his true form. Faolukan imprisoned him in the maze beneath Schwarzburg Castle until Neil mortally wounded him when he stole back the Scepter.

❖ Toghaí, The—The one chosen by prophecy to find Elyon's missing gifts and end the darkness.

❖ Tollan Caillté—A northern passage under the Sfarsit Mountains, hidden by spells and cut through the mountains by the nearly extinct elbakken.

❖ Tower of Dochás—[Do-HASS] The ancient tower beside the palace of Ewhain Macha, rumored to have once held the Scepter. Also called the Tower of Hope.

❖ Tuath—[TU-ah; *pl.* tuatha] A Celtic clan composed of many feighns.

❖ Valley of Flowers—A valley guarding the Pass of Arr in the Nordmark Range, protected by the wizard Zalán and his ensorcelled flowers. One of only two passes into Ferachtir other than the Great Bridge over the River Pruwyn.

❖ Waldreich—[VALD-rike] A vast dark forest occupying the south-central region of Ereb. Home to the Naz, a secretive forest people, and to wolves and dark magic.